FEAR AND DESIRE

"I know you love this place, Branwen. You are sensitive to your Llanfaren. It speaks to you—and through you, it speaks to me. I want you to do something for me, just this one thing and then we will go."

She nodded gravely, focused on Harry, and felt the tension fade.

"Close your eyes," Harry said. She did. "Empty your mind. You are here in this place, there is nothing else, no one else. Just you, here by the abbey church. Open yourself, let Llanfaren speak to you, and tell me what you feel . . ."

EYES OF THE NIGHT

EYES
OF THE
NIGHT

DIANA
BANE

JOVE BOOKS, NEW YORK

Grateful acknowledgment is made for permission to reprint the following: 6 lines from "The Second Coming" by W.B. Yeats. Reprinted with permission of Macmillan Publishing Company from *The Poems of W.B. Yeats: A New Edition*, edited by Richard J. Finneran. Copyright 1924 by Macmillan Publishing Company, renewed 1952 by Bertha Georgie Yeats.

EYES OF THE NIGHT

A Jove Book / published by arrangement with
the author

PRINTING HISTORY
Jove edition / June 1992

ISBN: 0-515-10862-6

Jove Books are published by The Berkley Publishing Group,
200 Madison Avenue, New York, New York 10016.
The name "JOVE" and the "J" logo
are trademarks belonging to Jove Publications, Inc.

10 9 8 7 6 5 4 3 2 1

I wish to thank Scott Peck
for writing People of the Lie.

This novel is entirely fiction. The characters are all imaginary and do not represent any persons living or dead. Likewise, though many of the physical settings are recognizable places, Llanfaren exists only in my mind.

—Diana Bane

"Noncooperation with evil is a duty."
—Mahatma Gandhi

EYES
OF THE
NIGHT

PART ONE

———————

CHOICE
Wales,
1962–64

1

The wind blew cool and full of mist from across the Irish Sea. Dawn touched the ink-blue sky, turning low-spread savannas of cloud to rose and gold. Branwen stood upon the wall and lifted her hands to the sky, palms open, unconsciously echoing an ages-old gesture of entreaty to the gods. She closed her eyes, deep in concentration, oblivious to the sheer fall of rock below her feet—down the castle wall, down the vertical cliff face, thence into the sea.

Branwen Tennant had come to this high place to pray in the new morning of her seventeenth birthday, but she could not find the words for her prayer. She was hollow with loneliness for the mother and father, brothers and sisters, who had always been with her on this day. In fierce determination, she lifted her arms higher; still no words came. She willed her silence to be her prayer.

A great stillness grew in and around Branwen, wrapped her in quiet folds. Then suddenly, effortlessly, she slipped out of time. Her soul spun out on trails of light and her consciousness flew with it: 'round the castle on its rock, through the arch of the ruined abbey, over the copse of old oaks, across the roofs of weathered cottages in the little village on the eastern flat of Llanfaren Island. She felt a oneness with all she saw; she felt linked to Llanfaren. And she heard a voice that sounded like her own say, "You are not alone."

Gently, softly, Branwen expelled a long-held breath and

heard its sighing sound. She felt her feet planted firmly on the castle wall-walk, felt the moisture of the mist on her cheeks, saw through her closed eyelids a golden glow of light. Then she opened her eyes. The sun blazed forth, and Branwen blinked. The words lingered in her mind, and she spoke them aloud: "You are not alone." She crossed her arms as she shivered, whether from the cool wind or with the thrill of recognition she did not know. She recognized that the words told truth. A powerful experience, undeniable yet strange. Not religious, and yet it had seemed somehow . . . She hesitated because the word she instinctively chose was not in her usual vocabulary. It had seemed somehow *holy*.

Most incredible, the loneliness that had earlier tied her tongue, that had tormented her for months, had simply dissolved on the morning air. Branwen lifted her arms once more, and her voice rang out clear and strong: "Thank you!" No matter that she did not know whom she thanked.

Smiling now, Branwen turned and began the long walk down to the castle kitchens. She tossed her long black hair back over her shoulders with a movement of her head that was unconsciously regal, while her feet skipped lightly down steps worn into shallow curves by hundreds of years of passing feet.

"We'll never get electricity in this godforsaken place!" Lucy Kerr's voice sounded as brittle as her tightly waved red hair looked. "And by the time the Trust grants our request for a transfer we'll be either frozen or blind, or both!"

"Much of rural Wales has no electricity, my dear," said her husband. John and Lucy Kerr were administrators appointed by the National Trust to care for Llanfaren Castle. They lived in the castle as did Branwen, who was their assistant. To be the Kerrs' assistant was the same thing as being their servant—which, of course, was not what Branwen had expected. Probably not what the agent who had hired her and sent her to the Kerrs had expected either. Branwen was intelligent: she had finished her schooling just after she turned sixteen. Her teachers had encouraged her to apply for an academic scholarship to University College at Aberystwyth, but she hadn't. What was the point, when she knew that as the oldest of eight children she had to go to work and help support the family? The job with the Trust, which was itself more than Branwen had hoped for, should have given her an opportunity to use her fine mind, her knowledge of

Welsh history and culture. But John and Lucy Kerr cared only that she was young and strong and willing to do physical work, which they were not, and that she spoke Welsh, whereas they did not.

"Many of the great houses given to the Trust have no electricity, my dear. We are not the only ones with this small inconvenience, you know." John tossed the mail he'd brought from Almwych Port onto the kitchen trestle table where Lucy was reading the newspaper by lamplight. He began to sort the envelopes into neat piles. On the other side of the table and with less light than Lucy, Branwen sat peeling vegetables for their evening meal.

"This is no great house, that's for certain," carped Lucy, turning a page of the paper with a slap for emphasis. "Blasted castle, dark all the time, cold all the time. If it wasn't for you being of the blasted aristocracy, you might have a real profession like other men."

Branwen had heard all this before, and it was always the same. She hated to hear John Kerr blamed for his family when it was no more his fault to be noble but penniless than it was her fault that she came from a mixture of wild Welsh and Irish blood with neither money nor princes in her past. She didn't want to hear it all again, and so she interrupted.

"That isn't true, you know," she said in her clear voice, its Welsh lilt evident even in so few words.

Astonished by this interruption from one usually so quiet, Lucy snapped, "What's that, girl? What isn't true?"

"Llanfaren is not a godforsaken place," said Branwen. She looked up from her work, directly into the older woman's eyes. She was amazed, herself, that she dared speak up to Lucy. But there was that word again, small and insistent in her mind as it had been in the early morning. The sharp paring knife in Branwen's hand glinted with the lamp's reflected flame as she said, "Llanfaren is a holy place. An ancient holy place."

"Humph!" Lucy narrowed her eyes and broke the contact. "If it's so holy, why's the abbey gone to pieces? I'll tell you why, because the monks were dissolute, that's why. Just as I said, godforsaken!"

Branwen shook her head, forbore to say that the Dissolution had had nothing to do with the morals of the monks. It was a political decision of Henry the Eighth and anyway had not reached Llanfaren's remoteness until much later than Henry's time. She said, "The monks at Llanfaren came from Ireland very early, in the sixth century. St. Patrick himself may have come here. When they arrived to start their monastery, they found Druids—a whole school of Druids—already here. The two religions, the old and the new, coexisted on this island for a long time. Eventually, of course, the Druids died out. And after that was when the monks took over the top of this crag and built their monastery here, on the highest place."

"Legends," Lucy scoffed, "nothing but legends. St. Patrick, my eye! And anyway they didn't last, did they? This is a castle, miss, and has always been a castle. The abbey lies in ruins down the hill. Everybody knows that!"

John Kerr had sat down at the table, and now a rare smile curved his thin lips. "The bit about the Druids may be legend," he said, "but the other is probably true. An abbey is only a monastery with an abbot at its head, and monasteries were large establishments. Many buildings. The ruins down the hill were clearly once the abbey church. The castle may well have been built over, or onto, one or more other buildings. The chapter house, a library. Isn't that so, Branwen?"

"Just so," she agreed and said no more. Her newfound courage had deserted her. Branwen feared Lucy's anger, pure and simple; and Lucy's anger was never far from the surface. She lowered her eyes. Dark lashes cast shadows on her cheeks, and the paring knife flashed as she resumed her task of peeling carrots and potatoes.

"Who made *her* the authority, that's what I'd like to know!" Lucy grumbled under her breath and punctuated the remark with a rustle and slap of the paper.

Branwen remained quiet at her work. She felt no need to defend herself. But John uncharacteristically would not let the matter drop. He said, "Don't you remember, my dear? The Trust agent who sent Branwen to us said her knowledge of Welsh history, as well as her speaking of the language, should be useful to us."

"I'd forgot. But it doesn't matter, does it, as nobody cares. Nobody comes here anyway because Llanfaren is an isolated, godforsaken place!" *Slap. Rustle.*

Branwen smiled. Of course Lucy had gotten the last word. She always did.

A silence fell at the table while John Kerr decided to let his wife have her way—again. He reached down beside his chair and came up with a brown paper-wrapped package. "Branwen, this came in the mail for you." He pushed the package across the table.

"Oh!" For an instant she was all child again, a child who suddenly found that her birthday had not been forgotten, after all. A radiant smile lit her face as she seized the box. "It's from my parents! It's—" But she swallowed the next words she would have said: "for my birthday."

Branwen looked at the couple with whom she had lived for almost a year, and with whom she would live for an unknown number of years to come. It had never occurred to her to tell the Kerrs about her birthday because they never celebrated anything. They seemed cold, loveless people—Lucy with her artificially waved and probably artificially colored hair, and a face lined by bitterness; John with his pale blue eyes, thin nose and thinner mouth, and ears too large for a head that might otherwise have been elegant. They cast a pall on her joy. So she said merely, affecting a shrug, "It's just a package from home." She rose from the table, crossed the stone floor, and left her present to wait unopened on the sideboard.

Much later, when she had cooked the supper, served it, and cleaned up afterward, Branwen climbed the stairs on the long winding way to her room. She had a flashlight in one hand and her present from home in the other. She went quickly and eagerly, for the nights after her work was done were the most precious part of her day. Unerringly her feet chose the right turnings through the great dark maze of the place. She was comfortable here now, but it had not always been so. In her first weeks at the castle, Branwen had had to count steps and turnings to avoid getting lost. Llanfaren Castle clung to the top and sides of an upthrust crag of granite at the northern tip of wedge-shaped Llanfaren Island. Inside and out the building twisted and turned, convoluted by rooms and corridors that through the centuries had rambled over many levels until its original shape and purpose had long since been obscured. To the newcomer's eye, Llanfaren was a remote, forbidding, labyrinthine pile of stone. But Branwen's initial fear of its endless supply of hushed, empty spaces had soon turned to fascination. Gradually, so gradually she did not realize what she did, Branwen was making Llanfaren her own.

Her attention at the moment was focused on her secret, a

birthday gift she was giving herself that waited in the unlikely place of her bathroom. Like any castle Llanfaren had had its garderobes, but in the reconstructed section where John and Lucy lived on one floor and Branwen on the floor above, there were real bathrooms. She stopped in her own room long enough to put her package on her bed, then sped across the corridor. She hadn't been able to check for a long time—what if the fire had gone out?

As soon as she opened the bathroom door, warmth rushed out to embrace her, and the birthday package from home was forgotten. Branwen closed the door behind her so that the heat wouldn't escape. In a corner of the large room stood a high old copper tank with ornate fittings, its top like the onion-shaped dome of a Byzantine church, its feet curled and scrolled like a mythical beast both feathered and furred. Branwen had filled the tank with water, and all day had kept burning in its under-belly a fire made from coals she had saved out of her own fire-place supply. Because there was no electricity in the castle and the one propane gas tank supplied hot water only to the kitchen, they had no hot water in the bathrooms. The days when servants would have kept these great tanks heated were long past, and not even the Kerrs expected such of Branwen. Instead, they all took showers in a stall off the kitchen pantry. But Branwen had longed for a real bath, and now for her birthday she was giving one to herself.

She turned the taps. Hot water steamed and gurgled into the deep tub. She adjusted the flow of cold water to get the temperature she wanted, then plugged the drain. For a moment she panicked. What if the Kerrs heard the water and came to investigate? But they wouldn't, the walls were too thick. And even if they did, what harm had she done? None—the coal was hers, and she'd had a chilly room for many nights to save enough coal to heat this tank of water! Branwen laughed. Let them come! She spun in a circle, scattering her clothes as she turned, reaching for the rose-scented bath salts she had bought and saved for this purpose as she glided by the shelf over the sink. Never had she felt so free!

Branwen sprinkled the packet of bath salts into the tub, and bubbles mounted up, shimmering like clusters of opals. She stepped out of the last of her clothes and into the tub, gasping with a shock of pure pleasure as the heat of the water enveloped her body. She turned off the taps and leaned back, immersed in bubbles up to her chin. The long mantle of her hair spread around her, a dark fan on the foam. She sighed. This was bliss! Fragrant, silky, warm bliss.

How she loved water! To be in or near it was perhaps her greatest pleasure. That was why she liked to climb to the walk on top of the castle wall, for there, especially at high tide, she could see herself surrounded by the sea. Gray and misty, black and thunderous, wind-whipped, zephyr-rocked, or blue-dazzled with diamonds of sun—in all its moods, she loved the sea. And there was so much of it here, for Llanfaren was truly an island, connected only by a causeway to the Isle of Anglesey, and at high tide even the causeway flooded, making it impassable.

Perhaps it was in her genes, mused Branwen, this love of water. As much as she missed her large family, she had to admit that there were times when she stood upon the castle wall and looked out over the ocean and felt that she was where she belonged. Possibly it could be a race memory from those Irish ancestors who long ago had sailed across this same Irish Sea to plant their seed in the wombs of the women who dwelt along Caernarfon Bay. Branwen smiled, lulled by the silky warmth of her bath. Someday, like her namesake the Branwen of legend, she, too, would cross the sea. Though not, God forbid, with such disastrous results! Had that Branwen also loved the ocean? Or had she found it strange, and feared it when she sailed across to meet the Irish chieftain who would be her husband?

Branwen shuddered, recalling the rest of the story. The Celtic Princess Branwen had been the cause of a great battle between the Irish and the Welsh who inhabited Anglesey, which was called Mona then. The Irish chieftain's family had insulted the princess, and so her father and brothers came and slew them all and took their weeping sister back home, across the sea once more.

Branwen slipped lower in the water, seeking the last of its warmth. She remembered that for a time in her childhood she had been secretly ashamed of her name. She'd become convinced that the Princess Branwen had been simply homesick and spoiled by all the men in the family. Even so, even as a child, she'd deeply understood the power of the Celtic legends, their wedding of brutality to beauty. Given to Branwen as her unspoken heritage was a soul-deep knowledge of the thin line between good and evil.

The bath water was tepid now, and her fingertips looked like white raisins. There was no more time for reverie. She finished her bath and watched with regret as the last of the water, bubbles gone flat, swirled down the drain. Branwen dried herself and rubbed hard at the wet tails of her heavy hair. Then she covered her skin with a lotion for protection against wind and salt-sea air, a protection she had long ago learned was necessary. All this she did automatically, without thinking and without feeling the body she touched. Her body was unawakened; she had never been in love, never been alone with a boy, much less a man. In school her life had been all for study. For the mind. They had been so sure, her teachers, that Branwen Tennant would be the first young woman from their village to go to university. But that had come to nothing. In her family there were too many mouths to feed, and since Branwen was the oldest, obviously she had to help. Each month she sent home most of her pay from the assistant administrator's job; the rest she saved, but she didn't know for what. University seemed a world away, a dream. Like sailing across the sea.

Branwen was an innocent in a comparatively innocent time. She had no idea that she was already a beauty, with her black hair and fair skin and blue-green eyes. Her mother had told her that she owed her physical appearance more to the Irish in her lineage than to the predominant Welsh. She was tall for a woman in her family, five-eight, an inch taller than her stocky, dark-eyed father. And Branwen was as fine-boned as her tiny mother who came only to her shoulder. As a result, the naked body to which Branwen paid no heed was as slender and supple as a willow wand. The full skirts and shapeless sweaters she habitually wore hid her fragile slimness, and hid as well the high round breasts budded at their tips in palest pink like tiny roses tightly furled.

She pulled on her terry wrapper, which she kept on a peg behind the bathroom door, eager now to open the present that waited on her bed. Gathering up her discarded clothes, she sped across the cold corridor. Though her hair was wet, she didn't take the time to light a fire in her fireplace; she plopped down on the bed and tore the brown paper from the package, and the patterned paper and ribbon beneath. She opened the box. A camisole of finest, sheerest cotton lay nestled in white tissue. With trembling fingers Branwen lifted it up and found a matching half slip beneath. Both were of the highest quality and workmanship, and Branwen knew well whose hands had made these exquisite garments. She knew well the hours and hours invested in the tiny pleats, the delicately inset lace, the thin, shimmering ribbons.

"Oh, Mam," she whispered, "you should have sold these. Never, after all that work, give them to me!" Throughout her childhood she'd watched her mother make such things for the wealthy who could afford them, and the rule for her and the other children had been: look but do not touch! Now with a reverence born of long observance of that rule, Branwen held the garments, touched them to her cheek. They felt as light and soft as a wisp of baby's hair, as the brush of a chick's wing.

A card fell out of the box and fluttered to the floor. She put the lingerie aside and picked it up. On its face varicolored letters spelled out HAPPY BIRTHDAY! Inside her mother had written "We miss you." All had signed their names: Mam and Dad; her brothers Gwilym and Owen; her sisters Glynis, Elin, Rhonda, and Evelyn; even the baby Rhys had printed his name in shaky block capitals, very well done for a five-year-old.

Branwen felt the cold of the room. She left the bed and made the fire in the fireplace. She spread the camisole and half slip carefully on her chair where she could admire them, thinking that her mother's handwork was not sewing, but art. She folded back the comforter from her sheets neatly. Then she slipped an old flannel nightgown over her head, got in bed, and opened the book she was currently reading. She reached for the birthday card, thinking to use it as a bookmark.

That was when she lost her composure, when the tears came. Branwen cried for her family, not out of loneliness as she had often cried before in this room. This time she cried out of love.

2

"Stunning!" exclaimed Harry Ravenscroft.

"Quite, quite beautiful," agreed Jason Faraday with an unusual touch of reverence in his deep voice.

"And unspoiled! Completely unspoiled!" Harry, in near rapture, flung out his long, thin arms as if he would embrace the castle that loomed up into the summer sky.

"Yes, unspoiled. I certainly hope so," murmured Jason. But he was not looking at Llanfaren Castle. He was looking at the young woman who swept the steep ramp that was the castle's only approach. Back and forth went the broom in a fluid, continuous motion, while her slender body swayed with her task. A sudden gust of wind molded her dress to her breasts and waist and picked out her hipbones, and Jason released an unconscious grunt of appreciation.

Harry heard the sound and turned to his friend, catching the direction of his gaze. "Really, Jason, would you bring your lechery even into our scholarly search? I referred to the castle, not the woman! We haven't come all this way to supply you with fresh female flesh. Although," he said as he looked back thoughtfully, "she is lovely, even at this distance. That black hair, the white skin—she'll have light eyes, I'll bet on it. A pure Celtic type, wonderful! Come on, old son, let's get up there."

The sound of the men's voices, but not their words, reached Branwen and she paused in her sweeping. She shielded her eyes with her left hand and looked down. By their clothing she knew them for visitors, not local fishermen or tradesmen, and was surprised. As Lucy had said some two months earlier, tourists seldom came to Llanfaren, although the castle and the abbey ruins were listed in the *National Trust Handbook*. The men came on, the castle clearly their destination. The taller of the two, also the thinner, gestured expressively with arms and hands as he walked. The other, square of shoulder, large-headed, bore himself gravely with his hands in his pockets.

After a moment's hesitation during which Branwen wished that John and Lucy had not gone into Almwych that morning, she laid aside her broom. She wiped her hands, smoothing her skirts, and went down the ramp to meet the men. There was no reason, none at all, why she could not show these men the castle equally as well as John or Lucy could.

As they drew near, the shorter man lifted his great head, and Branwen felt for the first time the power of Jason Faraday. He caught her with his eyes, trapped her in the intensity of his gaze. She stopped in her tracks—still, alert, waiting, eyes wide. She had about her the air of a young animal, newly tamed to the touch of a human hand. But she found her voice.

"Welcome to Llanfaren Castle." Her voice was pure as silver. She extended her hand to the man with the hypnotic eyes, saw that those eyes were brown. "My name is Branwen Tennant, I'm the assistant administrator. I'll be glad to take you around the property and answer what questions you may have."

"Jason Faraday." The man was not tall, no taller than she, but he was massive. His hand swallowed hers. "And this is my friend and colleague, Harry Ravenscroft."

Harry, who topped Jason by a good six inches, bent over Branwen, extracted her hand from his friend, and in a gesture that did not seem out of character kissed her knuckles. "We are charmed, Branwen Tennant. By all means lead on, and we shall follow."

"You're Americans," said Branwen over her shoulder. It was obvious from their accent, though Harry was dressed as any Englishman would have dressed for a day in the country, and Jason wore a lightweight sweater that looked Irish-knit.

"Yes," acknowledged Jason. "We're professors, from Virginia. Harry is a medievalist."

"True, true," Harry agreed, "and this summer I've found that I've neglected Wales for far too long."

"It's easy to neglect Llanfaren," said Branwen. "There is little written about this place, but I've been piecing together a bit more than the bare bones of the facts given out by the Trust. Now," she said as she turned and gestured back down the long ramp they had climbed three quarters of the way, "this ramp is probably the original. The stones, as you see, are laid without mortar and have been worn smooth over time. This is the only way into or out of the castle—although it's a reasonable assumption that at one time there was a way in from the sea that has since been closed up. Or lost. Llanfaren was not a castle originally, it was a monastery. Monasteries too had to be defended and were walled. This wall"—she paused in the high rectangular opening where once a massive gate had stood—"is the curtain wall. As you can see, it's six feet thick. It has been rebuilt here on the land side—but the rebuilding is over three hundred years old. On the sea side, where we'll go later, the wall is constructed upon ramparts carved out of the granite cliff itself. It's almost certainly the original wall of the monastery—though of what part, no one knows."

They went through the gate opening, Branwen pointing out the thick grooves that had held two portcullises, and crossed the open bailey. Part was stone-paved, part hard-packed barren ground. Arriving at the main door under its rounded arch, Branwen paused with her hand on the iron latch. For the first time she faltered. "There is, ah, a charge for admission." She mumbled the price, as embarrassed as if she had asked payment for inviting guests into her house. But Jason had anticipated this and pressed the correct amount into her hand. She looked up at him through her lashes and saw that he was amused by her embarrassment. Resolutely she lifted her chin, thrust the coins and note into the pocket of her skirt, and opened the door.

"The great hall," Branwen announced.

"Great, indeed," said Harry into the shadowy vastness. Their steps rang out into emptiness. The rafters of the ceiling were barely visible in the dark of their vault.

"There has been little restoration, I'm afraid," said Branwen apologetically. She was beginning, in the role of tour guide, to see the castle through Lucy's eyes. She knew that Lucy always hurried the few tourists they did have through the empty hall and into the reconstructed section, and she said as Lucy would have said, "We're a poor property here. There's not much income to spend. . . ."

Jason smiled, and with a firm, warm touch of his hand on her shoulder he stayed her rush through the room. "There's no need to apologize. Harry and I are not looking for riches, fine furnishings, things like that. Are we, Harry?"

"No, indeed." Harry had wandered into the center of the hall, where he crouched down in the gloom and studied the floor. "In fact, this is wonderful! As I said earlier, Jason, untouched! See, here the floor is darkened where fires were laid in the middle of the room. Eleventh or twelfth century, I should guess—they hadn't invented fireplaces yet."

Branwen felt a rush of affection for Harry Ravenscroft. She felt suddenly that she had found a kindred spirit, one who could appreciate Llanfaren's convoluted turnings through space and history and time as much as she did herself. The last vestige of her young self-consciousness vanished, and she led Harry and Jason not only through the rooms reconstructed at the turn of the twentieth century, but deep, deep into mysterious reaches of passages where walls crumbled and tiny rooms opened on one another for no apparent reason; where steps ended at walled-up arches, where wind whistled through old towers now open to the sky. She lost all consciousness of time and was amazed, when the three of them came to stand upon the wall-walk at its highest point, to see by the position of the sun that they had wandered through the castle for hours.

Harry threw back his head in exhilaration—the wind off the sea blew his fine, silvered fair hair about his lean face. He was handsome, thought Branwen, in an ascetic way. He might have been a monk here in an earlier time.

Jason approached the narrow parapet that bounded the walk on top of the curtain wall on both sides. His hands were, as usual, thrust in his pockets. A powerful man, broad-shouldered, wide-chested, strong in the thighs. A considerable contrast to his elegantly thin, scholarly friend. He had the craggy, square-jawed face of a lion and a mane of red-brown hair to match. Branwen felt the pull of his physical presence. Jason very nearly overwhelmed her. She was too inexperienced to know that what she felt from Jason was the force of his sexuality. That, combined with a merciless intelligence, he used to dominate men and women alike. Jason wielded his personal power as easily as he breathed air.

"It's a fine view," he said. He did not look at the sea, he

looked at her, and the air between them thickened with his intention.

Branwen, suddenly alarmed, ran to the far side of the wall and looked out, landward. "Oh!" she cried, genuinely distressed. "I'm so sorry! I forgot the time—you can't go back now. You're cut off!"

Neither man reacted as she expected. Harry paid no attention at all, as he seemed lost in thought. Jason strolled toward her slowly, casually unconcerned.

"You don't understand," Branwen insisted, desperation invoking more of a Welsh lilt into her voice so that she fairly sang, "the tide is coming in. The causeway is already flooding over. It will be hours now before you can leave the island! I'm sorry, it's my fault, I've kept you too long. . . ."

During this impassioned speech, Jason had crossed to where she stood. The musical rise and fall of her voice enchanted him. Her wide eyes, the same blue-green as the sea so far below, drew him as no other eyes had ever done. He knew how trite the thought was, but still it came and held true: *I want to drown in those sea-blue eyes.* She was so very young—the smoothness of her skin, like pearl and as translucent, bespoke her youth—and yet he could not help himself. He came close, too close, and said in a voice languorous and rich as velvet, "I find it no hardship to be isolated on an island with you, Branwen."

She needed no great range of experience to interpret his meaning. Indeed, she could have understood even if he had not spoken. His desire reached across the inches that separated them and touched her like a living thing. Instinctively she stepped back. She saw an immediate flash of fear in his eyes as he seized her shoulders in his hands and pulled her to him.

"You might have fallen!" he said, breathing raggedly, one hand on her hair at the back of her neck, the other in the middle of her shoulder blades pressing her to his chest.

"No," said Branwen. But she stayed very still in this unexpected embrace. She was confused—she wouldn't have fallen, she wasn't near the edge and there was, after all, the parapet. But her head was swimming, her nostrils were filled with the scent of man, and her hands burned where the open palms pressed against the softness of his sweater. She wanted to say that she was all right, would have been all right, but she could not speak.

"Here now," said Harry, who had been startled out of his reverie, "what's happened? What did you say about falling?" He came in long strides to join them.

"I'm afraid I, uh, frightened her," said Jason with irony, and with unusual honesty. His advances toward women did not usually result in fright, as Harry well knew. "She stepped backward and she was so near the edge, I was afraid she'd fall."

"I see," said Harry, his mouth quirked to one side in amusement.

Branwen disentangled herself from Jason's arms and tossed her head in that unconsciously regal gesture. "It was nothing, really." She turned her black-fringed eyes on Harry, who did not miss the flush of pink in her cheeks. "I . . . I'm still concerned that you're cut off from the mainland now."

"For five hours." Harry, understanding more than he wished about what had happened there, took over the conversation. "We anticipated that, which is why we reserved a room over the pub in that little village. Loathe as I am to share a room with a man who would go around frightening young ladies, they only had one."

"Oh," said Branwen. She looked Jason square in the face and arched a black eyebrow. "Why didn't you just say so?"

So, Jason thought, *she backs away from me, but look how she blooms after my touch!* He felt an odd catch somewhere in the vicinity of his heart, something he had never felt before. She was so beautiful, this child-woman. And how badly he wanted to hold her again! He answered her question honestly. "Because I was bewitched by the sound of your voice, that musical lilt. I forgot everything else. And I *am* sorry. I certainly didn't mean to frighten you."

"Branwen! Branwen, are you up there?" The voice was harsh, thin, masculine.

"It's John Kerr, one of the administrators," she said quickly. "I must go." She started off guiltily, crying out, "Here I am, Mr. Kerr!"

The sudden change in Branwen, the set of subservience to her shoulders as she ran from them, did not sit well with Harry Ravenscroft. In the normal course of events when they traveled together, any hint of a problem he left to Jason. Not this time. His long legs caught him up swiftly with the young woman, and he was at her side when John emerged onto the wall.

"What are you thinking of, girl?" John's words preceded him. "You're needed to help carry—" He saw Harry next to

Branwen, Jason close behind, and stopped short in surprise. "Oh, I say. . . ."

"We're tourists, sir, and I fear we've taken a great deal of your assistant's time. Allow me to introduce myself. I'm Harry Ravenscroft, and this is my friend, Jason Faraday."

"How do you do," said Jason, grabbing the man's hand and intentionally crushing it.

John winced but managed to say, "John Kerr. Pleased, I'm sure."

Branwen said, "Dr. Ravenscroft and Dr. Faraday are professors from America."

John had recovered the good manners of his breeding. "And you've given them the tour of the castle, have you? Well, I suppose we have to be grateful for that, but Lucy needs you now. Lucy is my wife, we're co-administrators here," he added with a nod he divided between Harry and Jason.

"Oh, dear." Harry placed a proprietary hand on Branwen's shoulder. "Miss Tennant is so knowledgeable, we should hate to give her up at this point. You really must let us have her a little longer. We had planned to go to the abbey ruins next, and we need the benefit of her superior store of information. Isn't that so, Jason?"

"Yes, it is." Jason turned the full force of his personality on John Kerr. "How fortunate you and your wife are to have an assistant with Branwen's, ah, Miss Tennant's, expertise. I'm sure your wife can spare her for another hour or so. That's very good of you."

"I, well, yes. Very good," stammered John. But Jason had already taken Branwen by the hand and swept past him.

"Yes, good of you," repeated Harry, following on Branwen's heels.

John shrugged. There was nothing for it but that he must carry all the parcels up the long ramp himself, then. Lucy certainly wouldn't help.

Branwen was not so sure she liked what had just happened; she felt as if she had been taken over by one set of masters from another. So, when she passed the pile of parcels at the bottom of the ramp, with Harry on one side of her and Jason on the other, she made a quick decision. "Wait, please. I know why he was looking for me, and it won't take long. Really." Not waiting for their consent or comments, Branwen tucked two tied bundles under each arm and picked up shopping bags full of groceries by their handles in each hand.

Jason and Harry looked at each other. "Not me, old son," Harry said with a shrug. "I'll not help the man."

"Not him, her," said Jason, gathering his arms full. Still there was another load, and he looked again pointedly at his friend.

"You're nuts," said Harry inelegantly.

"Probably," muttered Jason, and went after Branwen up the ramp.

"Where are the servants?" asked Harry when they returned together. "You must have help in a place this size."

Branwen laughed. "I'm it. I *am* the help. Thanks for trying to keep me out of trouble, but I'm sure Lucy's already furious."

"Why? We took her packages up, or most of them, which is more than I think we should have done," said Jason.

"Oh," Branwen said, sighing, suddenly tired and discouraged, "never mind. If I'm to go with you to the abbey, we'd best go now. It's almost teatime, and I haven't even begun on our supper. Come, this way."

She led the way around the base of the granite crag over which the castle was both sprawled and balanced precariously. Halfway around, on the sheltered side, hummocks of grass grew up and the ground began to rise in a gentle swell until it reached half the height of the granite outcropping. There was a suggestion of a path, badly overgrown with weeds.

"It looks as if your ruins seldom have visitors," Jason commented.

"That's so," said Branwen shortly. She was disturbed, stirred up inside. She could not analyze her feelings. She could only go on, show them the ruins and answer their questions. Then they would leave, and her life would continue as before; but when they left, Branwen knew she would feel a loss all out of proportion. She didn't understand, and it upset her.

"Here," she said unnecessarily, for the one enormous pointed arch rose up out of the grass like what it was: a ghost of the past. Branwen began to recite by rote the facts she knew about the abbey. She tried to ignore the heat of Jason's gaze as he sat on a tumble of stone and watched her. Wanting to hurry, to have over the inevitable parting that she knew would somehow bring her pain, she told none of the legends that so fascinated her.

Harry moved abstractedly through the great arch, past a standing wall with a single window opening, among fallen seg-

ments of shaped stone that he guessed had formed other,
smaller arches. Perhaps to a cloister. Most of the fallen stone
had been hauled away; perhaps it had gone into yet another labyrinthine arm of the castle above. He cared not so much about
the architecture of the ruins. Rather, he sought the particular
feel of the place, its atmosphere, that which he had felt so
strongly inside the castle. Inside, the sense of other, older pres-
ences had been palpable. Here he sought in vain—something
blocked the way. Suddenly he knew: Branwen. Branwen was
the key. Surely she did not yet know it, but she could lock or un-
lock the secrets of Llanfaren. *Perhaps not for everyone,* thought
Harry, *but certainly for me.* And blast that man, that John Kerr.
With his arrival Branwen had closed herself off. Even her voice
was tight as she recited facts that were useless to him. He could
have gotten them from any history book. What she had given
them inside the castle had been more, so much more than dry
facts.

Harry shot Jason a heavy look of warning. The men knew
each other well; Jason would understand, and keep quiet. Harry
moved until he stood in front of Branwen, directly in her line of
vision. She turned her head; he moved with her. She stopped
speaking, looked down at the ground.

"Why, Branwen?" asked Harry softly.

She lifted her eyes to meet his and in them he saw bewilderment. She said, "I don't know." She answered the question he
had only partly asked. She had understood the question, as he'd
thought she would.

Harry was a learned man, wise in ways few would have
guessed, even Jason. Harry sensed in Branwen a tender new
awareness, not just of her own emerging womanhood and such
things of the physical world, but of the unseen world beyond
and around her. An ability to reach deep into what is hidden of
past, and present, and future. He recognized this in her because
he had the same ability himself, but in him it was hard-won and
required much practice.

This meeting between us was meant, Harry thought. *It is no
accident. If she is my key, I am her bridge—her bridge to a
larger world. We need each other. And she knows it, too, though
she doesn't yet understand.* He extended his long arm, opening
his right hand to her. "Come, Branwen. We'll talk."

As Branwen placed her hand in Harry's, she heard faintly her
own voice speaking within herself, affirming: *He is a kindred*

spirit. And she followed Harry through the great arch. On the other side, in the shadow of the standing wall, he halted. He spoke simply, but his insight astonished her.

"I know you love this place, Branwen. That was evident as you took us through the castle. You are sensitive to your Llanfaren. It speaks to you—and through you, it speaks to me. I don't know why you closed yourself off just now, though I suspect it has something to do with that man Kerr. No matter. I want you to do something for me, just this one thing, and then we will go."

Branwen blinked, and her throat tightened. The mention of Kerr brought Lucy to mind, and her fear of the woman's anger, her fear for her job. Harry's mention of their going, though she knew they must, disturbed her further. But she knew, too, that Harry was important to her, even if she did not know how or why. One thing, he had asked; and one thing was not too much. She nodded gravely, focused on Harry, and felt her tension fade.

"Close your eyes," said Harry. She did. "Empty your mind. You are here in this place, there is nothing else, no one else. Just you, here by the abbey church. Open yourself, let Llanfaren speak to you, and tell me what you feel."

Behind her closed eyes, silence. Darkness. And in the dark, points of light growing, tiny flames. "I feel," said Branwen, her mouth gone suddenly dry, moistening her lips with her tongue, "I feel some kind of presence. Sacred presence. It's very old. Ancient. It feels like—like energy. Like a great humming. Through the soles of my feet. Along my arms. In my fingers. It's dark, and there's chanting. . . ."

Eyes still closed, she spread her fingertips. Her breath came deeply, evenly through parted lips though she spoke no more. Harry touched her hands, fingertips to fingertips, and he felt a vibrant humming energy pass from her to him, traveling in reverse the path she had described until finally the soles of his feet throbbed with it.

"Aahhh." He groaned heavily, almost in pain, curling his fingers into fists.

Branwen opened her eyes. "You felt it, too? What does it mean?"

"I felt it." Harry nodded. His smile was beatific, the sharp planes of his face alight from within. "I expect it means, dear girl, just what you said. We are standing on sacred ground.

There is an energy here, and you vibrate to it. Do you know more about this place than the boring facts you were reciting a few moments ago?"

"Only legend." Branwen felt close to Harry and had no objection as he draped his arm about her shoulders and walked her back to where Jason sat waiting. "I think, though, there is truth to the legend."

"Which is—?"

"That there were Druids here long before the Christians came in the sixth century. Druids, seers, magicians, shape-changers. By whatever name you call them, I believe they were holy men. And women."

"Ah. And women?" inquired Harry with a quirk of his lip.

"And women," said Branwen firmly. "Yes."

Jason rose to his feet. They had not been gone long, but the ruined wall had hidden them from his sight, and they looked very chummy now. Jason felt an irrational prick of jealousy. Harry Ravenscroft was the nearest thing to an asexual human being Jason had ever known, but still he didn't like the closeness he sensed between him and Branwen. "Have an interesting talk?" He couldn't keep the acid out of his voice.

"Yes. Very," said Harry with a wink meant to ease his friend's mind.

"I really must go now. Lucy—Mrs. Kerr—will be so angry," said Branwen. Even with the knowledge of Lucy's anger dogging her, still it was hard to leave them. She drew away from Harry and looked wistfully from him to Jason.

"But why?" asked Jason. "We're tourists, you were showing us around. It's your job, for God's sake!"

"It's not the job she expects me to do. I don't have time to explain. I just have to go. I mustn't lose my job here, I must not!" She glanced nervously over her shoulder at the angle of the late-afternoon sun. "I have to hurry. I'm sure you can find your way. Good-bye!"

Branwen took three steps backward, then turned and ran, her long hair streaming behind her like a black banner.

Later that night Harry and Jason sat drinking in Llanfaren village's only pub, where their room waited upstairs.

"I'm going back there tomorrow," said Jason. His craggy face had gone haggard with drink and with the intensity of his feelings.

"You're drunk," drawled Harry. He looked comfortably disheveled, a lock of his fair hair trailing toward one eye.

"Maybe. A little. But I'm going back. My God, Harry, I can't just go off and leave her. Anyone can see she's afraid of those people, whatever their name is." Jason's eyes caught the light of the single candle on the table, and blazed. He looked dangerous, as Harry well knew he could be.

"Kerr. Their names are John and Lucy Kerr," said Harry. "Listen, old son. You may be the smartest S.O.B. in Washington when it comes to power politics and under-the-table diplomacy, but you have no sense when it comes to women. And over this one you're behaving like an idiot."

"I beg your pardon—"

"Beg it all you want, but you listen to me. You're sitting here talking about being in love. What a pile of crap! You wouldn't know love if you stepped in it. You've never been in love in your life, and you know it. You lust after women, you conquer them, but you don't know how to love."

"And you do, I suppose?"

"No, I don't, but at least I know I don't. There's no room in my life for a woman, never has been, not that way. But we're not talking about me, we're talking about you, and right now you're lusting after a girl. A *girl*, Jason! How old do you think she is? Maybe eighteen, at the most. And you're thirty-eight. My God, snap out of it!"

"I think I love her," said Jason morosely. "Anyway, I want her, and I'm going back."

Harry sighed. He got wearily up from the table, stretching his lanky limbs. He carried their glasses to the bar for a refill, though his own was still half-full. He had to get away from Jason for a bit. His friend's behavior was alarming in that it was very nearly out of control—and Jason Faraday was always, always in control.

Harry put the glasses on the bar. The little pub was full of men with weather-beaten faces, and smoke, and noise. The barkeep was busy, he'd have to wait to be served, and Harry was glad of the respite. He had truly never seen Jason like this before. Love at first sight? Hardly. Not love, thought Harry shrewdly, obsession. And the idea of Jason Faraday obsessed struck fear into his very soul. The barkeep took the glasses from in front of him, and Harry didn't even notice. He was as close to prayer as he had ever been in his life: *Protect Branwen. Help her. Help me to help her.*

The barkeep returned and brought Harry back to reality with his demand for payment. *I'm a hypocrite,* thought Harry as he wended his way carefully back to their table, full glasses held high to avoid the many elbows in the way. *I want Branwen, too, and I need her for my own purposes. She* is *remarkable, and I sure as hell can't let Jason mess her up!*

He sat, and pushed Jason's glass across the table. Jason accepted it with a grunt of thanks. "All right," Harry began cautiously, feeling his way with words, "Branwen is special. You think you're in love with her, whatever that means to you. I *know* I want her to work with me on my project. That's why we came here in the first place, remember? To check Llanfaren out for a possible site. But I've got some other places to check out, too, and we have an itinerary to follow."

"*You* have an itinerary, I'm just along for the ride. You can go on without me. I stay here and, ah, what do you call it? Court. Court the girl. The woman," said Jason stubbornly, drunkenly.

Oh, God, help! thought Harry. He pushed the falling hair out of his eyes and leaned over the table, calling up all of his flagging energy. "We'll come back here before summer's end. Llanfaren checks out. I know I'll be working here, and I promise you we'll come back. When we do, we'll have a plan."

Jason straightened and looked at him, listening now at last. But his eyes still glittered like a hellhound.

"We made an impression on Branwen today, Jason. I think, ah, maybe you came on a bit strong for her, but no matter. What does matter is how scared she was when she left us. You heard her talk about her job, how important it is to her. And somehow she seemed to feel that spending time with us might jeopardize her job. Surely you remember that?"

"Uh-huh."

Harry paused. He sensed that he must not tell Jason what he felt so strongly—that it was of great importance that Branwen remain where she was, living at Llanfaren. It was her proximity to the place, her affinity with it, that made her potentially so useful to Harry. He said to Jason, "We must move slowly, or both you and I will lose her."

Jason played with his glass, drawing stripes down the beaded moisture with his finger. He was not a patient man, but he was deliberate; and he didn't lose. Not ever.

Finally Jason said, "All right. I see the wisdom in what you say. We'll come back in a month with a plan."

3

Branwen stood on the castle wall-walk, gazing down at the sea, as usual finding solace here. Not for the first time she reflected on how her life had been altered by the arrival last summer of Harry Ravenscroft and Jason Faraday, and she remembered how unsettling it had been to realize how important those two men had become to her in a matter of hours. It was as if they had brought their world of ideas and information to her and left with a piece of Llanfaren for themselves.

They had returned after their month of traveling about Wales, visiting castles, ruins, and other places of strong interest to Harry, but apparently less so to Jason. She had believed she would never see these men again—Harry, whose keen perception of her connection to Llanfaren made him seem even then like an old, dear friend; and Jason, an intense, intelligent man who was both extremely desirable and fearful at the same time.

Her bond to these professors was strengthened considerably when she agreed to assist Harry with his research project: recently she had been visiting various sites from a list he'd given her, writing down her impressions and observations in reports she sent periodically. She had initially been skeptical of the value of her intuitions, but Harry had convinced her how vital her work would be, compared to secondhand research that might have been done in America. He had even given her the little blue Morris Minor car they left behind, and she was given a flat fee of five hundred pounds as payment for her work. She missed the men but still felt a connection with them.

Despite having to make most of the visits on her time off from Llanfaren and having to avoid telling the Kerrs about her second job, she had felt more at ease than she had in a very long time. She felt useful and certainly less like a servant. No one in the village who saw her felt the need to relay the evidence to John and Lucy. She was well liked, and no one envied her the time she spent at the castle with such taciturn people.

The places she visited and especially Llanfaren were rich in history, and her sense of seeing back into the past became more and more pronounced. Writing all of her sensations down in her journal and reports to Harry made them seem somewhat less jarring. How the thoughts, or visions, or whatever they were, had come into her mind Branwen did not know. But she often sensed something significant just beyond the turn of a stair, a word forgotten but almost on the tip of her tongue. Perhaps Harry would understand, even if she herself could not. The academic community was likely to dismiss the kind of "observations" she had made as fantasy, and any interpretations on the part of Professor Ravenscroft as pure speculation, but that was Harry's problem now.

The students at Redmund College in Redmund, Virginia, had a favorite hangout they called the Catacombs, a name appropriate to its basement location and shadowy recesses jammed with high-backed booths. Like many of the more popular faculty members, Jason Faraday preferred the noisy gloom of the Catacombs to the chilly Neo-Gothic splendor of Redmund's Faculty Club. His preference sprang not from any egalitarian notion of consorting with students on their own level, but rather from its opposite: He went to be adored by the students. They did adore him. He was not so much a great teacher as he was a gifted motivator and manipulator, but his students were too young to know the difference and year after year voted him Most Outstanding Professor. In his chosen field of political science, Jason's Machiavellian grasp of the world did him little harm and much good, but he was no scholar. Therefore he tended to avoid the company of his colleagues at the Faculty Club, and was on his way there now only because Harry Ravenscroft had chosen the meeting place. Jason passed by the basement entrance to the Catacombs with regret.

After a somberly paneled entry hall, the Faculty Club dining room opened up like a cathedral. Off to one side, like an attendant chapel, the lounge was smaller, darker, and blessed with a bar. There Harry Ravenscroft sat ensconced in a high-backed wooden booth that was ironically similar to those in the Catacombs. He raised a hand in greeting as Jason slid in opposite him. After dispensing with the usual banter that could easily have passed for a sparring match, they finally came to the subject that weighed heavily on their minds for vastly different reasons.

"Well, as to why I asked you to meet me this afternoon," Harry said, "I have had a letter from Branwen. I thought you'd like to read it."

Jason would find nothing of interest in the letter, for it was all a careful recounting of Branwen's experiences in the places she had so far visited for Harry. But Jason would devour it word by word simply because it was in her handwriting. The man was besotted. For a moment Harry felt sorry for him. His obsession with Branwen would come to no good, for any of them. Obsession was negative, could only produce ill, never good. Yet it was sad that Jason should have had so little love in his own life that he could mistake his crazed emotional attraction for something so fine as love, so deep, so full of paradox. Harry had loved once . . . but that was long, long ago.

The letter was many pages, in a clear legible hand. Jason strained his eyes in the dimly lit bar. The words themselves were meaningless to him, but he envisioned her hand, noted the choice of words, the strong vocabulary, the carefully constructed sentences. Knew the intelligence behind the words on the page.

"She writes well," said Jason at last. "Especially considering the material you have her writing about. She'll do well here at Redmund. What do you suppose she will choose for a major?"

"Aha!" exclaimed Harry. "*Now* I understand. I must admit, the answer has eluded me, but now it all comes clear—"

Jason shook his head, as if awakening from a nap. He had scarcely been aware that he spoke aloud, wrapped as he was in his private dreams of Branwen. "What are you crowing about, Harry?"

"Branwen, of course. Why you have this persistent, irrational attraction for her. Why you're so determined to have her, of all women, a girl less than half your age!"

"Be careful what you say! We've been over this before."

"Yes, yes. But before, I didn't understand. It's *because* she's so young, isn't it? You've never had a lasting relationship with a woman near your own age. But Branwen is young, and she's bright, and beautiful, and perhaps most important of all she's from far, far away from here. Branwen is all those female students you've been attracted to and couldn't have, all the girls you've wanted to sleep with and didn't dare for fear you'd get caught. After all, Redmund is a small place, you'd get caught, lose your job."

"Who made *you* Dr. Freud?" Jason's voice was raspy, menacing.

"Doesn't matter. I'm right, admit it."

"Maybe you are. Maybe her age is part of it. I do get attracted to my students, and I can't do anything about it. It's torture. I don't expect you to understand." Jason sneered. He kept himself in tight control, but he was seething with anger. "Look here, Harry. I don't give a flying fuck about your project and I personally don't think you've got an ice cube's chance in hell of getting it funded, but I don't try to talk you out of going ahead with it. I don't belittle it, do I? Your crazy project is your business. How I feel about Branwen is *not* crazy, but even if it were, it's my business. You stay out of my business, Dr. Ravenscroft, and I'll stay out of yours!"

Harry bent his head under the gale force of Jason's anger. He hadn't wanted to make him angry, had wanted to make him see the truth and give it up. Harry looked up at the sound of Jason's heavy breathing, and the fury on his face made Harry instinctively pull back from the table. He tasted fear, a dull tinny acid on the back of his tongue. Not fear for himself only, but for the three of them.

"Sorry, Jason," Harry croaked. "I meant no harm. I was just trying to keep you from making a mistake. I don't want you to get hurt. Or me. Or Branwen."

Jason shoved the pages of Branwen's letter across the table. Perhaps he had overreacted. Usually he was able to confine his bad temper to times and places outside of Redmund's small, gossipy community, but tonight he had almost lost control. His jaw ticked with a jerk that made him blink. Not trusting himself further, he moved out of the booth.

"Wait," urged Harry. "Finish your drink. Accept my apology, and I'll buy you dinner."

Jason turned his large head and looked at the only male friend he'd had in his adult life. "I accept your apology, but I'm leaving now. Enough is enough, Harry." He went home and wrote a letter to Branwen, his second. She still hadn't answered the first.

Branwen had given much thought to Jason's letter and his lengthy descriptions of the academic opportunities at Redmund College—he said he could easily imagine her among the students—and the cultural opportunities of nearby Washington. He had written that he would enjoy introducing her to the sights of the capital, which he described in detail. Just as the force of his presence had had considerable persuasive power over her emotions, his words held out a dream, skillfully and subtly enticing her.

And Branwen was disturbed. She had the odd feeling that she would probably never live with her family again. She often longed to be with them but also felt strangely removed from them now. While her life with John and Lucy Kerr had been less than ideal, she had been learning and growing, had opened herself up to new experiences. But could she possibly go away to America as Jason implored her to do? Her inner Voice cried out to her, but she could not be sure what message she should get from it. So she burned Jason's letter, replied with a polite note on the bottom of a Christmas card, and decided to go on with her work as best she could.

By the time Harry and Jason returned for their second summer visit, Branwen had not only spent considerable time on work for Harry, but also on a cleanup project for John and Lucy. They—maybe it was more Lucy—had decided the Long Gallery needed to be rid of debris and grime, and Branwen had the chapped, work-worn hands to prove it.

Only her journal would ever know how Branwen had struggled through those months. At first it had been sheer stubbornness that kept her working when clammy mist, sometimes mixed with snow or rain, fell through the broken windows of the Long Gallery day after day. Gradually, as she became more accustomed to the demands on her body, that stubbornness transmuted into an indomitable will. Branwen did not toil to satisfy her employers, but to push against her own limits, to strengthen herself. She kept her own counsel, handled her own resentments, found her own satisfactions. And the longer and harder she worked, the less she feared Lucy Kerr. She would never defy her because realistically Lucy and John did have the power to take away her job. Branwen did not want to lose it, did not want to leave Llanfaren. By the coming of spring she had learned that it was possible to quietly and calmly go her own way when she chose. She could, and did, say no, not aloud but through her actions.

Thus, once her initial physical exhaustion had passed, Branwen had been able to continue on Harry's project. She had thoroughly explored the castle on his behalf. Finally in May, around the time of her eighteenth birthday, she had been confident enough to drive the car again without caring whether John and Lucy saw her or not. She had completed Harry's list by going to Puffin Island not once, but twice; and she'd gone on to visit places not on his list but of interest to herself.

Now Branwen had to face the continued kinship with Harry and her even stronger attraction to Jason, who had somehow charmed Lucy into allowing them to visit one of the oldest parts of the castle known as the Fifth Tower, as well as the rooms and corridors between it and the North Tower. Once there, even Jason had felt a strange presence and had been shaken by a vision of Harry and Branwen surrounded by a shaft of light, as if they had captured it, causing the rest of the room to grow darker. They had appeared to be at least seven feet tall, which had to be a trick of the light. Harry had glared intensely at Jason to stop his movement into the light and had pointed to a sign in the center of the floor. It was a circular slab of rock laid flush into the earthen floor, carved with a strange design, in the center of which was a cross. In the Fifth Tower there had been a strong impression of violence. Murder. The darkness, Harry had explained, was the representation of the evil and violence that must have taken place there in the past. Branwen and Harry had been deeply moved by the experience there as well, feeling the weight of the past like a heavy mantle.

Harry had explained his and Branwen's powerful psychic ability—the power to "read" what took place in the past during religious rituals, times of great passion or violence. Branwen's vision had revealed a shaft carved into the rock way below the tower. At the very bottom was a tunnel that led out to the sea. She had seen bones down there in the shaft, remains belonging to men known then as Wise Ones who had been thrown into the shaft to starve to death or die of their broken bones. She had actually heard the cries of the dead people, as if they could warn her that evil still lurked in these rooms that had once been part of a monastery.

But she had had enough of her disturbing observations and told Harry so. Where could all this digging into the past take them? She had been visibly shaken by the things she'd "seen" in the Fifth Tower and warned Harry that what they saw and the people they learned about—Druids, monks, and others—were not to be messed with. She agreed with Jason that they could easily be putting themselves in danger and that maybe the continuation of Harry's work on pre-Christian folklore should not include her.

Branwen discovered she was no longer uncomfortable with Jason. He was strong, knew himself and what he wanted. He found ways to make her feel wanted, desired. When Harry became insistent, Jason told her, "You don't have to do anything you don't want to do—not for Harry, not for those people the Kerrs, not for anyone." She looked up at him, seeing something she liked in those intense brown eyes that continually kept a hold on her.

Jason knew he could have kissed her then. Her need for support was great at that moment, and if he had kissed her she would not have resisted. But he didn't. His own words to her echoed in his head—Branwen didn't have to do anything she didn't want to do. She had agreed with him, though, when he told Harry to give up this quest, and her agreement made Jason incredibly pleased with himself. He intended to make sure that soon, very soon, she would want his kiss. And more.

4

Harry did continue his writing and his folklore studies throughout the summer and now often left Jason and Branwen on their own.

"Go, go. I don't want to go for a walk with you. Can't you see I'm busy?" Harry didn't even look up from his notes, pages and pages covered with his own spidery handwriting. They went.

The tide was out. The broad, wet stretch of sand between Llanfaren Island and Anglesey shone in the moonlight like a rippled sheet of silver. Branwen and Jason walked barefoot, carrying their shoes in their hands, making footprints that disappeared a minute later as if only fairies had passed. The air was fruity with the breath of late summer. A sudden ripe gush of wind lifted Branwen's loose hair and wrapped it about her face. She laughed, and with her free hand tried to disentangle herself.

Jason dropped his shoes, laughing with her. "Allow me to help," he said. Her long hair pleased him, not least because she wore it loose on his account, because he'd said he preferred it that way. It was darker, blacker than the late-evening sky, and like the sky it held a blue sheen. Her hair felt like smoothest, heaviest silk as he unwrapped it from her neck, smoothed it down her back with his fingers. The last inch-wide strand he brought forward, stroked it down along her cheek, along her neck where he felt her pulse beat; then slowly, slowly he caressed the long silky band over the hardness of collarbone and

33

down, until he felt a soft swell of breast begin beneath the thin
sweater she wore.

His eyes held hers. Branwen did not move. Her breath caught
in her throat. Jason's touch sent small, hot darts of pleasure
dancing across her skin. The whole long summer he had teased
and tantalized with lips and fingers, luring her to an exquisite
pitch of anticipation only to withdraw. He had held her close,
and she had felt his hardness rise against her, yet he did not go
on. Where once she had been wary of Jason, a little in awe, now
she longed for the release of a tension she barely understood.
Her pulse quickened. Never before had he touched her quite
like this, slowly, sensually, deliberately prolonging arousal. His
fingers moved on, down the swell of her breast to the nipple that
no man had ever touched. It bloomed, swelled, became incredibly sensitive. Branwen bit her lower lip to stifle a cry. She
closed her eyes, feeling a sticky wetness between her legs.

Jason murmured her name. He cupped the sensitive breast in
his hand, rubbed the nipple with his thumb, and placed his lips
in the curve of her neck. She drew her breath in sharply and
shuddered a little, but she did not pull away. Nor did she touch
him—she still held her shoes in one hand. His lips hot with a
passion he could barely contain, Jason plied the soft skin of her
neck, nipped with his teeth, then let loose his tongue as in one
motion he pulled her into his arms. She dropped her shoes. Her
arms went around him.

She is ready, Jason thought. *At last!* He opened her mouth
with a lover's kiss and lost all track of time and space; he nearly
drowned in her sweetness before one last shred of sense struggled to the surface. *Slowly!* it warned. *Remember, she is a virgin!*

Branwen's heart pounded. She felt bruised by that long,
consuming kiss, and yet she wanted more. She wanted to do as
he had done, to explore his mouth with her tongue as deeply as
he had probed within hers. When he moved away, she let him
go reluctantly.

"The abbey ruins will be beautiful in this moonlight," said
Jason. His voice was rich as velvet, mellow with seduction.
"Come with me."

They put on their shoes at the edge of the sand. Jason
wrapped his arm around her waist and fitted her against him.
Hip to hip, thigh to thigh, they walked through the whispering

grass, up the rise of the hill and into the hollow where the abbey ruins stood like sentinels.

This was either madness, or destiny, or both, thought Branwen. She looked up at the full moon, looked over at the great sprawl that was Llanfaren Castle, turned and looked at Jason's face. Naked hunger lit him from within like a flame. She touched his thick hair, which even in the moonlight had a reddish cast. She knew. She knew what he would do, and that she wanted him to do it. Her body burned for him, burned for the one who had awakened it. Love, all the conventional ideas about marriage, never even entered her mind.

"I want you, Branwen," said Jason.

"I know," she said in a clear voice, "I understand." And she reached for him. She kissed him as he had kissed her, as deeply and as long.

Jason's body was all broad, flat planes and hard muscle, thickly furred of chest and groin. His erect penis was a marvel to her—she touched him in amazement, almost with reverence. He groaned, and she felt a rush of heady pleasure. Felt the sweet, strong sense of a woman's power.

They lay on her skirt and his shirt, hidden from sight of the castle by the standing wall. Moonlight poured through the high, open arch of its one window. Branwen's white skin glowed, like nacre, like pearl. Her breasts were fuller than Jason had imagined, her hips more rounded; but her waist was so slim, her rib cage so fragile that he feared he might crush her.

"You're beautiful," he whispered, running his tongue in a hard edge between her breasts to her navel, and below. She arched her back, and he slipped a hand beneath her. "You have no idea how beautiful you are." He covered her damp inner thighs with swift, fluttering kisses, and as she opened her legs, she buried her hands in his hair.

Jason was amazed, and grateful, at how fast she learned, how naturally she responded. He had not made love to a virgin since his youth, when he too had scarcely known what he was doing. Now he knew, and he did it well. By her responses he knew that she felt pleasure, probably greater than his own because he controlled himself so tightly.

On his knees, he moved between her legs and looked down at her. Her eyes were closed, her hair spread out around her head like a dark fan. His heart lurched in his chest and he thought, *I love her. No woman has ever made me feel this way. I really do*

love her! He stroked her dark triangle of pubic hair, felt her wetness, moved his fingers into her soft, slippery folds, and was
caught by the mystery of her difference. One finger he gently
worked inside, then two, and her knees came up and fell open
for him. With her eyes still closed she smiled, a small, curving
smile of expectation.

When Jason entered her, Branwen felt a sharp twinge of pain,
immediately lost in a pleasure more incredible than anything
she had ever imagined. She was so surprised that her eyes flew
open. Jason's great head blotted out the moon, the sky. For the
moment he was her world. He filled her utterly. He stroked inside her with long, smooth strokes.

"Oh!" she cried, and "oh!" She grasped his shoulders, caught
his rhythm. His mouth came down on hers, his tongue thrust
into her mouth as he thrust deeper, harder into her body, and
they were one, one, one. . . . One! One thundering explosion of
exquisitely shattered senses. His cry and hers rang together
through the ruins.

In the silence that followed, Branwen could hear both their
hearts beating. Jason's head was on her shoulder, the weight of
his lower body was on hers, but he still supported his massive
chest on his arms.

He raised his head. Shaggy from exertion, he looked more li-
onlike than ever. It was hard to see his features, but his eyes
held a dark light of triumph. "I love you, Branwen," he said.

From far away, or else from deep inside, Branwen heard a
solid metallic thunk! The sound of a gate being closed, or a link
in a chain being forged. She looked up at Jason, a crease of
worry between her brows. "You don't have to say that just because of what we did."

"I know I don't, but I mean it." He rolled off to lie beside her,
grasped her hand, kissed it. "I do love you."

Awash in a myriad of feelings, emotional and physical, intense and totally new, Branwen did not know what to say. So
she said nothing. In the afterglow of lovemaking she sought Jason's warmth and the feel of his skin. She put her head on his
chest, and her hair spread over them both like a veil. He stroked
her hair, and she sensed that though she had not replied, he was
satisfied. She let out a long sigh. Relaxed completely, she felt at
peace.

Her inner Voice said, *You don't love this man.*

Oh, no, thought Branwen. *This time, Voice, you could be wrong.*

And the Voice fell silent.

Branwen did not tell Harry, nor did Jason, but he knew. Well, he thought, it was inevitable. Privately he still felt that Jason was not in love but obsessed, but it was impossible to feel sorry for Branwen. She glowed with satisfaction. She was luminous, incandescent. She looked and behaved like what she was, a woman in the first bloom of love. Harry wanted to caution her, to tell her that the feeling of being in love is a wonderful but fleeting thing. That real love comes later, if ever, to those who think themselves in love. He wanted to tell her that Jason could be ruthless and cruel, that Jason lacked her devotion to truth; that Jason was, in fact, in all respects unworthy of her. But instead, because Harry found to his own surprise that he himself loved Branwen in the indulgent way a father loves a child, he held his tongue. He endured her rushing away from him to be with her lover, he endured the small signs of physical possessiveness between the two although they cut him to the heart, and he endured the light that came into Branwen's eyes whenever she said Jason's name.

Harry could bide his time, for soon he and Jason would be leaving. Branwen would not be coming with them. She had already refused Jason's offer to find her a job and help her to get a scholarship to Redmund. Knowing Branwen as he had come to know her that summer, Harry was sure she would not leave Wales with Jason—or with any man—unless he married her. And Jason Faraday was not the marrying kind. Perhaps, now that he'd made the conquest, Jason would return home and forget her. They would write a few letters back and forth, and that would be an end to it.

Harry's own greatest concern now was for the future of his project and how he would keep his own relationship with Branwen alive. He thought of himself as her teacher, perhaps someday her mentor. Sometimes, when he was being excessively honest with himself, he admitted that he wanted to develop Branwen's psychic talent to match and augment his own. But if his project was not funded, he couldn't return to Wales. He had financed this entire summer and the one before out of his own pocket, and his financial resources were not limitless.

So much hinged on whether or not he got the grant! He

needed more time with Branwen, for she had steadfastly refused to use her special ability after the experience in the Fifth
Tower. As she had promised, she would do it no more. She had
helped him in other ways, sharing her knowledge of the history
and of the people, using it to help him evaluate and classify the
oral histories he'd collected over the summer months. Jason had
been a help, too, Harry had to admit. Jason was very good at
getting people to talk, and unobtrusive in his use of a tape recorder.

The week of their departure came. Harry dispatched Jason in
the car on errands so that he could have time alone with
Branwen. In the three weeks that she and Jason had been lovers,
such time had become rare.

She looked lovely. Her hair was loose, the way Jason liked it,
and she wore around her neck, in the open collar of a blue
chambray work shirt, a silk scarf Jason had given her because
its swirling blue and green pattern emphasized the color of her
eyes. She smiled at him, and Harry wondered if Jason saw more
in those eyes than their splendid color. Did he see the intelligence? At times the steely determination? Had he noticed, as
Harry did, that when she was uncomfortable in a situation she
would simply withdraw behind those eyes, using their long
black lashes as a shield? And how did her eyes look, Harry
wondered, what was their expression, when she was in the
throes of exquisite sexual pleasure?

"Harry? Why are you looking at me like that?" Her voice was
amused, musical.

"Oh, I was memorizing your face." He shifted in his chair,
noting with interest a warm tingling in his groin. Most unfa-
therly, his feeling at that moment. "It may be a long time before
I see you again."

"You will probably see me again tomorrow and several times
before you leave, and anyway, you'll be back next summer."
Branwen laughed and put her long, cool fingers over his hand
on the desk between them. They sat in the living room of the
cottage they had rented, which he had turned into a study.
"Aren't you being a little dramatic, Harry? Even for you?"

"No, Branwen. I'm serious." He pushed back the lock of hair
that always fell into his eyes—he was badly in need of a haircut.
"I probably won't see you alone like this again before we leave,
and there's something I want to give you."

"A present? But, Harry, you shouldn't. You've given me so much already."

Harry opened the desk drawer and brought out a pouch of soft leather, once light brown but now gray with age, drawn closed with a blackened leather thong. "For you, Branwen."

The pouch fit in the palm of her hand. It was soft and surprisingly heavy.

"Open it."

"It seems very old." She spread the pouch's neck and peered inside.

"Go ahead." Harry grinned. "Dump it out. It is indeed very, very old and there is nothing breakable, I assure you."

Branwen spilled the contents of the pouch onto the surface of the desk. The stones looked at first like a child's rock collection. They were more or less uniform in size, about as large as the end of a finger, wedge-shaped, a deep blue-gray color. Branwen picked one up between her thumb and first finger. "Why, it's bluestone! These are all made of bluestone!"

"Yes." Harry nodded. She was excited by the discovery, but still she touched the stones with reverence. Good, he thought, good.

"And there are markings on them." She turned the small stones over, one at a time, until the markings were faceup. She counted them, then looked up at him, puzzled. "There are only twenty."

"How many should there be?" asked Harry with mock ignorance.

"More than twenty. These are runes, aren't they? So the number would depend on which century was used for the source of the runic alphabet . . . but anyway, there should be at least twenty-eight. What is this, Harry? A child's toy? An old teaching game?"

Harry was disappointed. She was using her intelligence, when he had wanted something else, something more. He said, "I guess you could call it a game. A very ancient game. But not for children."

The bluestones seemed to pull at her fingers. Branwen spread her right hand, fingers wide, and held it over the stones. Her cool fingers grew warm. Irresistibly drawn, she picked up one stone, then another, and another, seemingly at random. Yet when she closed her hand over the stones she had picked, she suddenly saw Jason's face. Jason was not here, he was miles away, and yet she saw his face. He wore a severe, unpleasant expression. She opened her hand and looked at the stones in her palm. Very carefully she put them back on the desk.

"I don't think it's a game," she said, "and I don't think I should have these. I have no right!"

"What do you mean?" asked Harry laconically. "I give you a gift, and you say you have no right? Branwen, these runic stones are mine to give, and I give them to you."

"But bluestone is sacred," she said. She looked at him, then at the stones. Her hand went out—she pulled it back. Harry waited. His ploy was working after all. The stones exerted their power. Branwen was torn between two worlds, and he had placed her there deliberately. For her own good, he hoped. He waited to see what she would do.

The stones won out. As she looked at them, stared at them, glimpses of other places, other people, hovered at the edges of her vision. Unclear, but there, as if veiled in smoke. She forgot Harry. Slowly, reverently, Branwen arranged the small stones in a circle. In her mind they were small no longer, but higher than her head. A circle of Standing Stones, and she stood among them. She was one of many, as many as there were stones in the circle. The drumming began. She felt it in her feet, her legs, in the pit of her stomach. *Boom, boom, boom, boom,* calling the power out of the earth. Calling the power into the stones, into the circle. The power grew. She raised her arms, she spoke the words—and then the mist came, covering everything. She lost the Stones. She fought against the mist, she sent it away again and again. Finally through the mist she saw a face, wise yet impish, with high brow, long sharply arched nose, wide mouth quirked in a one-sided smile. She knew this man, but did not know where to place him. It seemed that he, like herself, was lost in the mist; that he belonged among the Standing Stones. He spoke, he called her "Branwen," and she tumbled through the ages, but the face and the man were still with her.

"Harry Ravenscroft!" she cried aloud.

"The one and only." He winked at her.

"You were there . . . but you're here." She put her fingertips to her temples, rubbed hard, and closed her eyes for a moment. When she opened them, she said, "Somehow I get the feeling that you tricked me into seeing—what I saw. Bluestone has power, Harry. It was, is—I don't know, I get lost sometimes between was and is—anyway, it has great power. Even such tiny pieces as these. But why am I telling you? You know all this. And so *why*? Why give these things to me?"

"I did it to remind you that you have the Sight."

"Oh, Harry, please. You sound like my grandmam. And besides, I don't see the future, only the past, and I wasn't going to do it for you anymore. You know that."

"Tell me about your grandmother. Does she also have the Sight? Does it run in your family?"

"No, she doesn't, but her sister did. And she used to say I did when I was little." Branwen laughed, remembering. "My mother told her no daughter of hers in this modern day and age was going to get caught up in any old superstitions! Not everyone in Wales encourages these things, you know. Certainly not my mam!"

"What do you remember of the things that caused your grandmother to say you have the Sight?" Harry persisted.

"I honestly don't remember anything. What I remember is seeing things, or having dreams, and having to keep them to myself. I guess that's why I'm so quiet. It became my nature."

"Do you still have the dreams? Clairvoyant dreams?"

Branwen hesitated. She had begun to have them again after coming to Llanfaren, but years of reticence were hard to break. She said, "Over the years I forgot all about them. But after I came to Llanfaren . . . this is so difficult, Harry. Why do you want to know these things?"

He reached across the desk and grasped one of her hands. "Because you *do* have the Sight! You see, I call your ability by its old name, its true name. Don't deny the Sight. You must learn to *use* it!"

Branwen tossed her head. "I don't deny it, Harry. I just haven't been applying that particular word to the things that have happened to me lately. But at the same time, I'm not so sure that I want to 'use' it, either. And I do know that I still prefer not to talk about this sort of thing."

"Why, Branwen? And why did you refuse to go back to the sacred sites with me? What made you say you had had enough of your observations? I've never understood."

Branwen reclaimed her hand and began to gather up the bluestones. One by one she dropped them into the pouch. "Because the things I've seen *are* real. I know it, even if I can't explain it. And because I sense that you're getting involved in something that's too much for me. I don't understand this ability I have, and I don't *want* to understand it. Nor do I want to use it. I suppose if I ever *needed* to use the Sight, I'd want to know how, but right now . . . No, thanks. Not me." She placed the last bluestone in the pouch and drew it closed. "Now I'll return the bluestones to you. Perhaps you have the right to sacred stones, but I do not."

For one of the very few times in his life, Harry Ravenscroft felt humble. To have such a gift as she had, yet to hold it so lightly! She extended the pouch to him but he shook his head. "Please don't argue with me, Branwen. The runic stones have been mine for a long time, a very long time. Now they are yours. You have as much right to their power as I do, maybe more. They are an aid to the Sight, that's all. The runes can be cast to spell out words, but without the ability to See, and to interpret what is Seen, the markings themselves mean nothing. That's why it doesn't matter that eight have been lost. Keep the stones. Practice with them. Who knows—someday you may want and need your own power."

Branwen's inner Voice said, *Keep them, he is right. Someday you will need the runic stones.* So Branwen bowed her head in acquiescence. "Thank you." She looked at Harry searchingly. What an enigma this man was! "Tell me, Harry, what is it that you want? What's really behind this research project? You call it folklore, but you and I know it's more than that. What are you after?"

Harry drummed his fingers on the table and narrowed his eyes. "If I tell you, you must keep the information to yourself."

"You mean you don't want me to tell Jason."

He nodded; his fair hair fell over his eyes, and he pushed it back.

"All right, I won't tell him."

"I want to find again the power we once had and lost. The power of the ones the Romans called the Druids. The power to make and to change, to summon and to bind!" His pale eyes glowed as he spoke, they glistened like silver.

Branwen shivered; her spine turned to ice. "Don't you wonder," she whispered, "if we, if *you* had such power once, why you lost it?"

Branwen kissed Jason good-bye; she hugged Harry. She laid her palm flat against the hood of the blue Morris Minor and said good-bye to the car, too. They would sell it where they had bought it, in Liverpool. They had not rented the cottage again. Harry had explained that he could return only if he got a grant to continue his research and finish his book. He could not afford to keep the car, or to rent the cottage again, without the grant money.

Jason drove. He backed the car out onto the road, turned it around, and headed for the causeway. Branwen stood in the road in front of the cottage, waving after them. Jason was angry with her, she knew, because she had stuck to her decision not to go to the United States with him. He could not understand what was so simple to her: Even if she could support herself and go to Redmund College on a scholarship, there would be no money left over to send to her parents. She had grown up knowing and accepting her obligation, as the oldest, to help support the rest. She would not let Jason belittle that, and he had been angry. With a chill Branwen had seen that the face of his anger was the face she'd seen while holding the stones.

Branwen sighed. She would miss Jason. Already her body ached for him. Perhaps it had been wrong, but she would never regret the sweet sexual lessons she'd learned from Jason at the end of this summer. He'd said he would return the next summer, whether Harry did or not. He said he loved her and would not leave her for long.

Branwen tossed her head and began the walk back to the castle. She did not really think Jason would return. She did not really think he loved her. And reluctant as she was to admit it, she knew that her Voice was right—she didn't love Jason. Not really. But he was exciting, and being loved by him was a powerful experience. Certainly better than being alone with John and Lucy!

She stopped at the bottom of the ramp and looked up. The gate to the castle seemed impossibly far away, the climb incredibly long. Her feet felt like lead. *Perhaps,* thought Branwen, *I have made a terrible mistake. Perhaps I should have gone to America with Jason, and Harry.*

As time passed after Harry and Jason's departure, Branwen knew she had to take some kind of action. She was now feeling extremely uncomfortable with Lucy and John. Lucy had such a menacing look in her eyes lately—probably because John had become somewhat obsessed with Branwen. It was as if he had recently begun to notice this young woman under his roof and

had been complimenting her and leering at her too often for
Branwen's and Lucy's comfort.

Llanfaren was quite stifling and threatening, and Branwen
had the idea that instead of losing her job completely she could
request a transfer to another post. She did not tell John or Lucy,
although to follow proper procedure she should have done. She
hid her letter, and on a Monday when Llanfaren was closed to
visitors, she walked the three miles to Almwych Port to mail it
herself. A transfer was Branwen's last hope, as no help could be
had from Harry now. She did not allow herself to think of Jason.

But she couldn't stop the dreams. She dreamed of Jason,
though she always banished the dreams upon waking. She
could banish them from her mind, but her body carried into
the days the traces of an erotic longing. Often she fingered the
pouch of bluestones, which she had taken to keeping under her
pillow. She slept with the bluestones in their pouch beneath her
head, knowing it was silly, bordering on superstition, but she
did it nonetheless. Branwen felt herself becoming desperate,
wanting to cast the stones, to use the Sight—anything to find a
glimmer of hope for the future. Days passed, nothing changed,
and somehow she resisted. She did not use the Sight. She did
not cast the stones. She seldom wrote in her journal because
when she did, she produced only morbid ramblings. The journal
brought no comfort. And her inner Voice hadn't spoken for so
long that she forgot about it.

Late in the month of April, as John sorted the mail, he handed
Branwen a letter from the National Trust. He raised an eyebrow,
but she merely said thank you and thrust the letter into her
pocket. Later she read it in the privacy of her room. Her request
for transfer was refused, but in the most complimentary terms.
She was too valuable an asset for the Llanfaren property. Rather
than a transfer, they granted her a raise in pay. A small raise, but
even a large one would not have been enough. Branwen was bereft.

The long letter from Jason arrived, just as he had calculated,
on Branwen's nineteenth birthday. He began by saying that he
regretted his long silence and hoped the present communication
would make up for it. He had been, he said, engaged in sensitive
government work that made writing to her, or to anyone, unwise. Now the work was successfully concluded, and he could
write what was in his heart.

Jason wrote to Branwen a love letter. The letter was perfect, a work of art, as arrogant in its praise and as compelling in its imagery as the man himself. Jason's words fell on Branwen's parched soul like rain. She clothed herself in his promises like armor. He said he would come in early June, and he did. He fulfilled all his promises, and more. Branwen cast the bluestones, and they warned her. Her long-silent Voice spoke and warned her. She put the stones away; she denied her Voice. Branwen married Jason.

PART TWO

EMERGENCE
Virginia and Washington, D.C.,
1965–67

1

"Hello, Harry." The door closed. "It's been a long time."

Harry knew her voice; even in so few words, the Welsh lilt was there. Stubbornly he refused to turn from his office window. He'd had a lot of practice at being stubborn in the six months since Jason had brought Branwen, now Mrs. Jason Faraday, to Redmund College and the small surrounding community of the same name. Furious with Jason, disappointed in Branwen, Harry had refused their invitations and absented himself from occasions where the Faradays appeared as a couple. He was not surprised that Jason did nothing to repair the rift in their supposed friendship, but he had expected Branwen to seek him out. When week after week had passed and she did not, Harry's disappointment had grown until it became disillusion: she was not the person he had thought her to be. She had allowed Faraday to swallow her up; she was Jason's creature now. So Branwen spoke, and Harry did not turn from the window.

"Um," Branwen said and cleared her throat, "I didn't call for an appointment because I was afraid you'd refuse to see me."

She paused. In his mind's eye Harry saw her straighten her shoulders and make the little queenly toss of her head that sent her long hair back over her shoulders—which, in fact, was exactly what Branwen did. She continued more strongly, "You may as well turn around and talk to me because I'm not leaving until you do, Harry Ravenscroft!"

Harry allowed a reluctant smile to tug up one side of his

mouth. He turned in place, leaning against the windowsill, and drawled, "Good afternoon, *Mrs. Faraday.*"

Branwen's chin came up, her blue-green eyes snapping with the spirit he remembered. Indomitable spirit, Harry thought against his will. With narrowed eyes he surveyed her. Since she stood on the other side of his desk, he could not see her legs and feet, but what he saw was at odds with the spirit in those dark-fringed eyes. Jason's creature, Jason's wife, her clothes proclaimed: black cloth coat, superbly cut, with a ranch mink collar; beneath the unbuttoned coat, a matching skirt and sweater the color of pale amethyst. Harry moved around the desk to see the rest of her—high-heeled black leather boots to the knee. Exactly what the well-dressed faculty wife was wearing this winter of 1965. ·

"Well," Harry said, "as long as you're here, we may as well sit." He gestured toward a pair of leather chairs, plump and shabby, separated by a low round table piled with books and papers. He didn't offer to take her coat and watched as she shrugged out of it, then settled back with her booted legs and feet tucked to one side. For a moment she seemed a stranger, just one of many women—students or colleagues—who had sat in that same chair. But she smiled and moved her head, and her long black hair spilled over one shoulder, and she was the young woman he remembered. Harry returned her smile, rubbing his hands together. "I feel like a drink! Sherry, my dear? It's all I keep in the office."

"Sherry is fine." Branwen, in her turn, observed Harry Ravenscroft against the background of his office on the top floor of one of Redmund's pseudo-Gothic towers. The room suited him: a gentleman scholar's habitat, all books and dark woods and the faded elegance of an oriental rug worn thin, its colors muted.

As Harry crossed the rug toward her, a small glass of sherry in each hand, a shaft of late-afternoon sun slanted through the window with merciless winter clarity. Harry's pale hair caught the light. Branwen, looking up, saw his head ringed in an aureole of cold fire; the same light turned the glasses of amber liquid in his hands to flames. She caught her breath, blinked, turned her head . . . and forced away the vision she had almost seen. Like an ancient memory, it was, and in her mind the echo of an old, old question: Who is this man, this enigma? Is he good or evil?

"Branwen?" Harry bent to her.

She took the offered glass, murmured thanks. The sherry was dry, nutty and sharp; it restored her. She saw Harry now in a familiar pose, long limbs casually draped about the chair opposite. "For just a minute there," she confessed, "I felt as if we were back at Llanfaren. You know what I mean?"

Harry shrugged, not answering. He sipped his sherry. Branwen, once again made nervous by his silence, crossed her legs and gazed at the light falling through the window. *How quickly the sun goes down in winter,* she thought, *in Virginia no less than in Wales. Soon it will be twilight, and I'll have to leave. I can't just sit here, drinking and feeling as if nothing has changed. There are questions. . . .*

Harry interrupted her thoughts. "Do you still have the stones?"

"The runic bluestones? Of course I do."

"I don't suppose," Harry drawled in an elaborately offhand manner, "that you might have, ah, consulted the stones about the matter of your marriage. Either before or after."

"Yes, I did." Relieved that Harry had broached the subject of her marriage, she went on. "Before, not since."

"And . . . ?"

"And," she said as she tossed her head, "what I saw is my business. I've put all that behind me, Harry. Those things belong to Wales, to Llanfaren. This is a new country, I have a new life. And there is so much to learn!"

"Your skills, your gift, will work here no less well than in Wales, you know." Branwen said nothing. When it was clear she would not respond, Harry said, "You have a new life, yes. You are enrolled in the English Department, I believe." As a professor of Medieval Studies, Harry divided his time among history, archaeology, and English. He had made it his business to look up her records; he knew not only where she was enrolled, but what courses she took; and when they were posted, he would know what grades she made.

"Yes, I'm in English. But that's not what I meant about having too much to learn. If I were just a student, it would be so much easier. It's all the other things. . . ."

"Harry, I thought that when I came here I'd have at least one friend. Besides Jason, I mean. *You.* What happened? Why do you go out of your way to avoid us? I've seen you do it, seen you look across the room at those awful faculty parties and spot

me and Jason, and then you're gone. Not to mention the fact
that you didn't come to our house either time you were invited.
You didn't even acknowledge the invitations! I *know* something
is wrong. There must be a reason!"

"Oh yes, there's a reason." Harry nodded. Her distress was
evident, and he was glad to see the passionately honest woman
underneath the new veneer of poise. He'd been amused and
heartened by her unconscious choice of words: "those awful
faculty parties." And other small things he observed, sitting at
closer range. Her clothes were in perfect fashion, but her face
was not—she wore no makeup at all. Though he was not an expert on such things, he doubted that she was even wearing lipstick. Her skin had the translucent quality he remembered, but
she was too pale, as if she had been under a strain for a long
time. Her hair was just as he recalled, long and straight from a
center part, not teased to impossible heights as was the fashion
nowadays. Her hands were well tended, but her nails were short
and unpolished, and there was no diamond on her left hand.
Only a plain, narrow gold band. That surprised him. He was
sure that Jason would want his wife to display a diamond of significant proportions. Perhaps, Harry mused, she was not entirely Jason's creature after all.

Abruptly Harry asked, "Does Jason buy your clothes? I don't
mean does he pay for them, I mean does he select them himself?
Tell you what to wear?"

"Yes." The question came at her out of nowhere and puzzled
her.

"Did he give you a diamond, an engagement ring?"

"He tried to, but—Harry, I don't see what that has to do with
anything!"

"Just humor me, I have my reasons. Jason tried to give you a
diamond, *but* . . . what?"

"But I wouldn't take it. I did something shameful, and I'm
not sorry. I made Jason sell the ring and put the money into a
settlement for my parents. I made him understand that if I married him and stopped working, I'd be taking away from my
family a source of income they really need."

"And of course Jason wouldn't want his wife to work."

"That's what he says."

"So he settled some money on your parents." Harry allowed
a silence to stretch in the room. He knew Branwen was uncom-

fortable; he wanted her to be. Finally he said, his voice hard:
"You realize that in a way Jason *bought* you."

"In a way, I suppose he did." Branwen's chin came up, defi-
ant, but there were shadows behind her eyes. "What of it?"

"I'm interested, that's all." Harry had made his decision—he
was going to be honest with Branwen. He didn't know yet exactly why she'd married Jason, but he had at least learned that
she hadn't completely capitulated to the man he now thought of
as his enemy. Harry would tell her the truth, hard as it might be
for her to take.

"So," he began, "you want to know why I didn't greet you
and your husband with open arms when you came here after
your honeymoon? I won't say I was glad to get the letter you
wrote from London telling me you'd married him, but it was
good of you to keep me informed. I'll tell you everything, but
first I'd like to know what Jason has said about this. You have, I
presume, asked him about this, ah, estrangement?"

"Yes. He said you've been acting peculiar ever since you
didn't get your grant for our project. That you're still bitter, and
seeing me would only remind you of your failure."

"My failure." Harry pulled a wintry smile. "An ingenious answer and, in one respect, true. I went off my head for a while
when the grant was denied. I have a hard time forgiving myself
for that. If I hadn't gone into one of my dark periods—I do have
them, you'll find, when you know me better—perhaps none of
the rest of this would have happened. Branwen, if I continue, I
must ask that you never reveal to Jason anything that I tell you.
Do you promise?"

There was a long pause while she decided. "Yes. I promise."

"Very well. To begin with, Jason and I were never friends in
the real sense of the word. I doubt very much that the man is capable of friendship. Therefore, I have serious doubts that he is
capable of marriage, either, and you must allow me that. When
Jason came here four or five years ago, we were thrown together through the simple fact that we're near enough in age, although I'm older, and we were both bachelors in a community
where social obligations are de rigueur, and almost everyone is
married. It was convenient for us to do things together—it
saved both of us from being paired off with uninteresting
women by hostesses who can't bear to have an odd number at
the dinner table."

"Since these social things are something I'm struggling to learn, I can understand that," agreed Branwen.

"Right. It took me some time, a year or so, to realize that Jason Faraday doesn't make friends. Rather, he cultivates people who can be of some use to him. I was useful because I opened the doors of a certain class of society to him. Your husband is a brilliant and charismatic man, but he came to Redmund with a lot of rough edges. I think from the first time I invited him into my home he wanted to emulate my way of life, and I was willing to take him around with me, let him learn. I didn't feel used because I found him interesting. Jason's sort of power, that ability to manipulate people at will, can be fascinating. Then there is the fact that I dislike traveling alone. Jason was an agreeable travel companion. I think he traveled with me because he'd never before had much opportunity to get around out of the country, but you saw for yourself that he was often very helpful. He pulled his own weight on our travels."

Branwen nodded.

"So we went along well enough until we had our first disagreement. About you, Branwen. I underestimated him. He was determined to have you, you see, but I thought after—" Harry hesitated, seeking the delicate word.

Branwen knew what he meant, and helped. "After we became lovers you thought he would lose interest in me. So did I."

"Did you?" Harry smiled. "Obviously we were both wrong. But, to the point: Jason deceived and betrayed me. All last year, when I thought he had done with you, he was plotting. He was so set on having you, he wanted to possess you, and he knew I would try to prevent that. So he arranged to be in Wales this past summer, and he also arranged things so that *I* would *not* be there. Oh, yes, I'm sure he knew that I would have done everything in my power to prevent you marrying him!"

Branwen was troubled, and her eyes grew dark. But she said nothing.

"I venture to say that you don't know very much about the man you've married. You couldn't—he gives very little of himself away, while at the same time he will drain another dry, if the other person doesn't stop him. You must never allow him to do that to you!"

She slowly shook her head, wordlessly, dark eyes enormous.

"I myself," Harry continued, "knew him less than I thought I did. Your letter this summer, saying that you'd married him, shocked me out of the apathy that characterizes my periods of darkness. I was astounded that he'd gone to Wales alone. I'd scarcely seen Jason the previous year—he spent much more time in Washington than he had before—so I'd no idea what he might have been up to. I'd had some vague thoughts about asking you to come over here and work with me on reconceptualizing that grant proposal, but I hadn't thought it through, I believed there was time. And then, wham! The news of your marriage hit me like the proverbial ton of bricks!"

"Oh, Harry!"

"It shocked me into action, I can tell you that. I have my own friends in Washington, a different crowd from Jason's but influential in their own way. I began to make inquiries. You see, Branwen, the grant I'd applied for was a government grant, and government is Jason's sphere of influence. Suddenly it seemed all too possible that Jason had used his influence against me, had arranged for my grant to be denied. In order to be sure, of course, that I would not be in Wales in the summer."

"Oh, no!" she cried, genuinely distressed. "Not after he helped you for two summers, surely not just so that he could come to Llanfaren without you!"

"Oh, yes. Tell me honestly. I am assuming you married Jason because he made it financially possible for you to get out of Wales and come to this country. But he would do it only on condition that you be with him, and you wouldn't be with him, to be blunt, live with him, unless you were married. If I had been there, Branwen, if I had been able to arrange for you to come to the United States on some other basis, would you still have married Jason Faraday?"

Branwen drew a long breath. "It wasn't quite like that . . . But there's no point in looking back. To answer your question honestly: No." Branwen hung her head, made miserable by the admission, which she was making as much to herself as to Harry. "No, if I'd been able to see any other way out, if you had come, I wouldn't have married Jason."

"Damn!" Agitated, furious with Jason as he had been for months, Harry leapt from his chair and paced the room.

Branwen sought to calm him. "Now that I am married, I really think it will work. I think I'll like living here once I get used to it. I'm grateful to Jason for helping my family, and I have opportunities I never would have had if I'd stayed anywhere in

England. It's up to me to make a go of it. Jason is good to me, really, and he does love me. . . ."

Harry stopped his pacing, angrily swept a pile of books off the round table, and sat on it in front of her. He took both her hands in his. There were tears, of anger or sorrow or both, in his eyes. "Branwen, dear heart, go carefully about this marriage. When I made my inquiries about Jason, what I learned was far more disturbing than the mere information that if he had wanted to stop my grant—and I believe he did want to—he could have done so. You see, Branwen, what I discovered is that no one knows exactly what it is that Jason does in the capital. They only have suspicions whom he does it for. Or if there are those who know what he does, they are afraid to say. He is neither liked nor respected, but he is *feared*. Jason Faraday is a man who moves secretly in very high places. That's dangerous, Branwen. And he is a deceiver. Never, ever forget, my dear, that your husband is a Master of Lies!"

Branwen shuddered. She snatched her hands from Harry and wrapped her arms about herself. Against her will she remembered what Harry had asked her earlier, about consulting the rune stones before her marriage. Yes, she had done it, but reluctantly, and then had thrust away from understanding the blurred, violent visions. The truth was that she did not want to See; her need to escape had been too great. Her Voice, as if coaxing, had been less frightening. *Wait,* the Voice had said, *there will in time be another way.* But Jason was so persuasive. How often in her knowing of him had the power of his attraction overridden the Voice? Often—so often that she never heard it anymore. And besides, she'd been too desperate to wait.

Harry thrust Branwen's half-full glass of sherry under her nose. "Drink the rest of this. You'll feel better."

She did. She noted that the room was now full of shadows, the sky outside the window had turned cobalt-blue. "I must go home," she said, pulling on her coat. "I came here today hoping there was some way you and Jason might reconcile, but I see there isn't. I wanted the three of us to do things together, as we did on Llanfaren, but that isn't going to happen. I'm sorry."

"You're right, it isn't going to happen." Harry reached out a staying hand. "I'm glad you came to see me, Branwen. Will you come again? I wasn't there in the summer, when you needed me, but I'm here for you now. As Jason's wife, you may need me more than ever. Let me be your friend."

Branwen stood, buttoning her coat with one hand. She laid the palm of her other hand on Harry's cheek. "You've given me a lot to think about. I have to be fair to Jason. I made a choice when I married him, and I have to honor it."

Harry grumbled, "You don't have to honor a commitment to a man who doesn't know the meaning of the word!"

"Which word," Branwen teased, "honor or commitment?"

"Honor!" Harry got up from his seat on the low table and followed her to his office door. He reached around her to open it and stopped with his hand on the knob, blocking her way. His reluctance to let her leave weighed on him like an omen.

"Do you forgive me for my bad manners these past six months?" he whispered. It was not at all what he wanted to say, but it would do.

"Yes. Don't be silly!" Branwen searched Harry's face. At this moment he was less an enigma, more of a man, and all full of tender concern. She felt deep caring radiate from Harry, she could feel it like a glow passing through her skin. This was a far gentler feeling than the heat of Jason's passion, to which she had become so accustomed that she craved it, almost like an addiction. Branwen reached upward and pulled Harry's face down to kiss his cheek. "Thank you for caring," she said.

Harry watched her leave and waited in the doorway until he could no longer hear her steps on the stone stairs. He was both glad and sorry that he'd been so wrong—Branwen might have given her body to Jason, but her soul was untouched. Branwen, whether her last name be Tennant or Faraday, was nobody's creature but her own.

He went back through his office and looked out of his window at the top of the tower, down to the courtyard below. She came striding across the paving stones like a tall black shadow. Harry reflected that she had not said she would come back to see him again.

Branwen's car was a refuge from more than the January wind. It was a place where she could be alone with her own thoughts, and on leaving Harry Ravenscroft this refuge was sorely needed. The car was a Mustang, black with a tan leather interior, a Christmas present from Jason. When he gave her the keys and the title in her own name, he had emphasized that the Mustang was something new from the Ford Motor Company, and she was one of the first people in the country to own one.

Branwen turned the key in the ignition, breathed in the wonderful new-car smell, and felt gratitude to the husband who had given her such a gift.

Harry's voice came into her head, saying, "Jason *bought* you."

I'm confused, thought Branwen. *I can't go home feeling this way. Jason will see that I'm disturbed and want to know why, and I can't tell him I've been with Harry.* She glanced at her watch, one of the few possessions she'd brought with her into the marriage, and saw that it was almost six P.M. Late. Jason would soon be home, if he wasn't there already. Next time, thought Branwen as she headed her Mustang away from the college, away from her house, she would go to see Harry on a day when Jason was in Washington. She was halfway to the highway when she realized that one decision had made itself: She would be seeing Harry again.

Branwen drove to a shopping center on the outskirts of Culpeper. She would pick up some of the deli food Jason liked and say she'd been shopping and forgot the time. In other words, she would lie to Jason. She'd never done that before. She didn't like to do it now. Was friendship with Harry worth such a price? Her mind whirled with the consequences of the decision that had made itself. In Redmund's closed academic community, it was not acceptable for wives to have male friends who were not also friends of their husbands. Branwen already felt like an anomaly because she was both wife and student. She didn't feel at home in either role. She was trying to find a new identity, and the narrow confines of academic society stifled her. That was why she had at last sought out Harry Ravenscroft. He already knew who she was, and she had briefly felt like herself again when she was with him. So, *yes*, friendship with Harry was worth the price. It *must* be because she knew without doubt that she needed him.

On her way back from the shopping center, the fragrances of pastrami and sauerkraut leaked out of their containers and canceled the new-car smell. The makings of Reuben sandwiches, to which she had been introduced by Jason. So many things to which she had been introduced by Jason! At last Branwen made herself think about her husband. Regardless of what Harry had said, she felt she knew enough about the man she'd married. She knew he was originally from a small town in southern Ohio, near the West Virginia border; his parents had moved to

Houston, Texas, and had both died there while Jason was attending Harvard on a scholarship. He had no brothers or sisters, he'd told Branwen's mam and dad. He was an only child born unexpectedly to his parents late in their lives. He had always been interested in politics, had majored in political science, gone on for a master's degree, and had supported himself all along by researching issues and writing speeches for various political candidates. This work had eventually brought him to Washington, and from there to teach at Redmund College while he continued in Washington as a consultant.

Consultant about what? And to whom? Harry had made it sound so, so sinister. Branwen had never wondered about Jason's consulting, had never really cared. The only thing that remotely bothered her was Jason's attitude toward his teaching. It had taken less than a week for Branwen, on campus as a student herself, to discover that Jason had a cultlike following among her fellow students. It got in her way when she tried to make friends, as soon as they found out who she was. In public Jason accepted, even encouraged, the adulation. But alone at home with her one night, he had sneered at "the gullibility of the mass mind," and called his students a prime example. He'd boasted that if he wanted to, he could turn these sons and daughters of the privileged few—who were on the whole polite, rather stuffy, and untouched by the social activism on the rise at other campuses—into a screaming fascist mob. She'd been shocked and had attributed his remarks to the fact that they'd stayed late that night at a party and he'd had more to drink than usual.

Now as she turned from the highway onto the tree-lined avenue that linked Redmund's residential streets to the campus, Branwen recalled that Jason had again in private shown contempt for his academic colleagues as well. Jason had no Ph.D., a fact that had surprised her when she'd found out. He had no plans to earn the advanced degree because, he said, if he hadn't needed it to get his job, he certainly didn't need one in order to keep it. Nor was he interested in furthering his reputation by publishing articles, as other professors did. "I can't be bothered with all that," he'd said, "not for the great honor of teaching one or two courses a semester!"

"My God! How could I be so stupid?" Branwen exclaimed aloud. Their house, red brick with white trim picked out by the street lamp, was visible half a block away, and she slowed the car to a crawl. She had just realized that ever since their first

meeting, she had thought of Jason Faraday as a college professor. But there was no way in the world they could live the way
they did on what Jason earned teaching one or two courses at a
time! She'd heard the term "private income" thrown about
among the wives at parties, and had learned it meant money inherited from one's family—most of Redmund's faculty, apparently, had private income. But not Jason. He hadn't come from
that kind of background. So most of Jason's money must come
from the work he did in Washington! Harry's words about
Jason's status in the capital suddenly jumped into a new perspective.

Now she was confused again. She had been inclined to dismiss all that Harry had claimed to have found out about Jason
from his Washington friends. She knew Harry could be
overdramatic; he got carried away by his ideas. She'd seen it
happen more than once at Llanfaren. It would be much easier to
believe that Harry had simply gone off the deep end into fanta-
sies over a grant that he'd lost for perfectly legitimate reasons
than to believe that Jason had schemed and plotted and done all
the things Harry said. But what if Harry was right, what if his
ideas were not speculation but truth?

Jason was at home. He'd left the garage door open for her.
She pulled her Mustang carefully alongside her husband's gray
Cadillac and sat for a moment, getting both her smile and her
story ready. Try as she would, she couldn't clear her mind.
What if Harry was right? she asked herself again. She believed
with all her heart that she would learn to love her husband.
What if she learned to fear him instead?

Jason Faraday was angry. Anger was his own personal bête
noire. He knew that if he ever lost control and let his temper explode at the wrong time in the wrong place, he could damage
himself in the eyes of others, so he monitored his anger. Right
now he was angry with Branwen. His feelings simmered along
at about a four on a scale of one to ten. Not too bad. But if she
didn't get home soon . . .

He rolled up the *Time* magazine he'd been trying to read and
whacked it on the coffee table, hard. Again, *whack!* Where the
hell was she? *Whack!* Harder this time. The sharp sound was
satisfyingly loud to his ears; his hand and forearm tingled plea-
surably with the force of the blow. Even as a child Jason had
found that the torment inside himself could be eased by tor-

menting other living things more helpless than himself. For a long time, secretly, he had teased and tortured and finally killed small animals—frogs, turtles, dogs, cats. Especially cats: at age seven he had killed a cat; after that he did it again and again until it became too easy and no longer satisfied the rage in his breast. Then had come some rough years when as much as he found release from his own pent-up anger from hurting other, smaller children, his intelligence warned him that this was not acceptable because it could get him into trouble. He had hit on what was, for him, a happy compromise when in adolescence his inner rage became linked to his sexuality, and he made the marvelous discovery that there were females who would let him hurt them during sex. Best of all, even the ones who didn't like being hurt would never, ever tell. By adulthood Jason had learned to control his innate anger and cruelty by being a skilled sexual sadist—in secret, of course, with partners he chose carefully and paid well. He had thought that marriage to Branwen might change him, since he was convinced he truly loved her. But now . . .

Whack! The magazine cover split, the ashtray and the crystal cigarette box on the coffee table jumped and clattered, and the bourbon in his short glass sloshed dangerously near the rim. The four had escalated to around seven. Jason smiled, a grim, dark smile Branwen had never seen—yet. His breath came heavily, and he felt the thing in his chest, the beast, the bête noire, begin to pound, wanting out.

"E-e-eh!" The sound came from deep in Jason's throat, harsh and ugly. He threw the rolled-up magazine across the room, threw it with such force that the pages hadn't time to unfurl and it hit the wall opposite with a thump and left a smudge of red ink on the white paint before dropping, battered, to the floor.

Breathing heavily, Jason grabbed his big head in his hands, pressing hard with the heels of his palms against his temples. He squeezed his eyes shut and saw explosions of red and yellow and orange; he waited until the angry fireworks faded into black. Then he opened his eyes, picked up the glass of bourbon, and drank steadily until it was dry. Outwardly calm now, he went to the dining room to refill his glass from the decanter on the sideboard, stopping on the way to retrieve the ruined magazine and drop it into a wastebasket.

"Bitch!" he muttered, and drank again. The beast in his chest had subsided, but Jason felt his blood surging through his veins.

A dark pulse, dangerous. *I've left it too long,* he thought, *been too long without an outlet.* Marriage, loving Branwen, hadn't taken away the need. . . .

Jason felt a degree of masochistic satisfaction in the realization that marriage hadn't changed him as much as he'd thought it might. He still needed an outlet for his darker passions, a way to vent the rage that had lived in him ever since he could remember. There were places he could go, things he could do. He went back to the couch, ripped off his already loosened tie, and began making arrangements in his head. He ignored the erection that rose while his mind raced with dark plans. He did not know that his eyes gleamed and his face was flushed, nor did he hear Branwen's car when she pulled into the garage.

The metallic sound of the storm door opening snapped him out of it. Branwen's voice, clear, a little breathless, called above her footsteps in the foyer. "Jason? Jason, I'm sorry! I went shopping over at Culpeper and I didn't realize how late it was."

Jason looked over the back of the couch at his wife, who stood framed in the arched entryway to the living room.

"I never meant for you to come home to an empty house," she said.

He smiled a feral smile. The heat already between his legs increased as he let his eyes devour Branwen's heart-shaped face, so pale above the fur collar of her coat. "Black, black, black is the color of my true love's hair," he said. He realized he was a little drunk. He didn't give a damn.

"What?" Branwen clutched the deli bag to her chest and smiled uncertainly.

"It's an American folk song." Jason came around the couch. Where only minutes before he had been angry with his wife, now he burned with desire for her. He used his beautiful voice, not singing but speaking, playing it like an instrument. "A folk song that might have been written for you: 'Black, black, black is the color of my true love's hair. Her lips are something wondrous fair. . . .' " He kissed her, tasting, biting, pulling at her lips. "Wondrous fair," he repeated gutturally.

"Jason!" His voice was mesmerizing. His hands moved over her. The bag disappeared, her coat parted, his lips were hot on her neck. "I thought you'd be upset with me for being late," she managed to say, and then could say no more.

Jason, hands and lips more insistent now, went on: "The purest eyes . . . and the bravest hands . . . How brave are your hands, Branwen?" He peeled the gloves from her fingers, unzipped his fly, and guided both her hands inside while once again he claimed her mouth with hungry insistence.

"Oh—my—God!" Branwen gasped as she surrendered, catching fire from her husband's heat. He felt huge, already slippery in her hands; and she was boneless, will-less, helpless, not knowing or caring how or where he took her, as long as he took her—*soon*!

Power! Control! Control, control, Jason repeated to himself over and over. He had great control, he was proud of that. He could sustain his erections for a long, long time, make women beg. *Now!* they would cry. *Oh, please now!* Even Branwen, innocent Branwen, he'd taught her everything she knew . . . but he hadn't had to teach her to beg. Only the word, he'd had to teach her the word: Come!

Branwen gasped. Control, Jason thought, and with a last nip forced his teeth to leave her turgid nipple. He'd never hurt her, he wouldn't hurt *her*, not his wife. Never. Control!

Jason heard himself groan. He'd taught Branwen everything she knew, yes, and she'd been a wonderful pupil—wonderful! Her strong, slender fingers worked at the base of his spine, fluttered like moths through the cleft between his buttocks. He groaned again and spread his legs as she reached lower. Control! *Control, control,* thought Jason as Branwen, searching with her tongue, found and stabbed his navel while her hands continued to inflame him. The fires of her passion might burn more cleanly, but they burned with a heat equal to his own.

He couldn't wait much longer. The foyer floor was littered with their clothes. Hands locked on Branwen's fragile rib cage, mouth locked on hers, their tongues entwined, he backed her up against the wall at the foot of the stairs. Her bones were delicate, but she was almost as tall as he—a perfect fit. And she knew what he wanted. She lifted her left leg high, wrapped it behind his waist. She was open, she was ready for him.

Branwen was lost in a world where nothing mattered, nothing except the exquisite moment of waiting for Jason to thrust into her. She panted, she dripped; she moaned his name; she dug with her heel at his waist, urging him closer.

He teased. With the engorged head of his shaft he touched,

withdrew. "Do you want me?" His voice was thick with blood and heat.

She, breathless, answered, "Yes, oh, yes!"

He slid into her briefly and once again withdrew. Branwen stopped breathing—she felt her entire existence poised on the tip of Jason's phallus. Again he entered, and again withdrew. Finally, "Hah!" he cried, exulting, and plunged deep.

She was alive again, drawing ragged breaths, her nails like claws fastened to Jason's shoulders as his thrusting skewered her to the wall. On and on, deeper and deeper, every thrust delivered pleasure so intense it was almost pain.

Jason felt both ecstasy and anguish. His control was gone. This time he wouldn't be able to keep Branwen hovering on the point of orgasm, wouldn't be able to watch that incomparable expression of yearning play across her passion-suffused face. Instinct overwhelmed him, and he drove toward his own climax, thrusting and grunting.

Branwen came before Jason. She nearly always did, and she had no way of knowing it was by his design—his ability to control the degree of pleasure she felt seemed to him proof of his power over her. She knew only the piercing relief of climax, spreading out and out from her center in cooling, concentric silver circles. Branwen released a long sigh and opened her eyes.

Tonight Jason was different. He hadn't paused in his pleasure to watch her, as he always did; he continued to pound away. He grunted like an animal. Branwen clung to his shoulders and waited for her husband to explode inside her. Her mind became too sharp, too clear. There was something . . . not quite right about this, she thought. But then she felt disloyal. She closed her eyes, leaned into Jason, and tightened her vaginal muscles to give him more pleasure.

"Are you sure you went shopping?" Jason asked.

"I'm sorry." Branwen looked up. She was alone in their king-sized bed, reading a thick anthology text propped on her knees. "What did you say?"

Jason leaned against the door frame of the master bath. His dark auburn hair was almost black with damp, and beads of moisture glistened on his hairy body. He was naked except for a towel wrapped around his loins. "I said, are you sure you went shopping? You were gone a long time, considering that you didn't have anything to show for it except the makings of a skimpy supper."

"I told you, Jason, I lost track of the time. I'm sorry, I won't let it happen again." While she spoke, Jason snapped the towel from around his waist and began to dry his hair with it. Branwen suppressed a shiver and carefully focused her attention back on her book. Why was it, she wondered, that Jason seemed so animallike tonight? He'd always had a leonine look, and she'd liked it. Not so tonight. The lion is king of the beasts, thought Branwen, and there was nothing kingly about him this evening; he was more . . . more brutish. Yet when he gave one last fierce rub at his head and sat on the edge of the bed, dangling the damp towel from his hands, his shaggy reddish hair stood out around his craggy face, and the leonine look was back. Glancing up at Jason through her lashes, Branwen, thought, *I really must stop being so critical.* She caught his eye and smiled.

"All right," Jason said, "everyone's entitled to one mistake. What were you shopping so hard for that you forgot the time? Obviously you didn't find it, did you?"

"A dress," said Branwen, looking at her book once more and turning a page. She hated being critical, and she hated to lie. Nevertheless, she went on with it. "And you're right. I couldn't find what I wanted."

"You went to Culpeper to look for a dress? I bought you clothes from the best stores in Washington! Those aren't good enough for you?"

"The clothes you bought me are fine. You're very good to me, Jason," Branwen placated. "And if you don't put on a robe and your pajama bottoms, you're going to catch a cold."

With the uncanny sense of one who is himself an expert liar, Jason suspected his wife was not telling him the truth. The earlier anger, assuaged by their violent lovemaking, threatened to return. It rumbled through him at level two. He glared at her. She looked so innocent in her white nightgown with its ruffled high neck, her hair in a braid hanging over her shoulder. She was back in her book, paying no further attention to him.

"Huh!" he snorted, a sound meant to express disgust. He stomped back to the bathroom and put on his robe and pajama bottoms, not for the reason she'd said but to give himself time to think.

Did he want to pick a fight with Branwen? Yes, by God, he did. If his anger level got too high, so what—she was his wife, and this was his house. Maybe she really had been shopping; he could still lean on her, push her, see if she still told the same story. Anyway, he was sick of her being so quiet, so even-tempered all the time. Except when he touched her, of course. Touch her and she was gone, and as good at sex as any high-priced whore he'd ever had. What if another man touched her that way? Or worse, a boy, a student near her own age? Boys that age were so horny all the time they could fuck mud. Would she respond to another the same way she did to him?

The thought struck Jason so violently that he gagged. He bent over the sink, his shoulders heaving, and was glad when nothing came up. Instantly he knew he'd had the briefest glimpse of how he would feel if he ever lost Branwen to another man. It was horrible: overwhelming anger followed, in a rush, by desolation. He'd never be able to stand it.

No! he raged silently. *It's not that I can't stand it, I won't stand for it!* He raised his head and saw himself in the mirror. His hair was wild, and so were his eyes. *No, by God, I won't stand for it!* he swore at his image. He combed his hair and brushed his teeth and went back into the bedroom. He climbed into his side of the bed, punched up the pillows, and settled himself against them. Branwen kept on reading, oblivious to him. Well, he'd soon change that!

Jason growled, "What kind of a dress?"

Branwen sighed. She looked sideways at him. "Is it really so important? It's late and I'm tired, and I have to finish this assignment before class tomorrow. This eighteenth-century prose isn't the easiest thing I've ever had to read, either!"

"Yes, it's important! Don't you forget if it weren't for me, you wouldn't have any damn class to go to, or any clothes to wear, or any car to go driving around the Virginia countryside after dark! When I ask you a question, I expect an answer!"

Branwen flinched before the verbal assault as if he'd struck her. Her throat closed up. When she was attacked, her tendency was always to withdraw, as she had done from Lucy Kerr. She began to do that, to surround herself with a thick layer of silence through which Jason's anger could not penetrate. She closed her textbook. She would go study and sleep in the guest room, with the door shut. Yet she hesitated. Marriage was a different situation altogether. Marriage should be a kind of partnership—she wasn't Jason's slave. She knew that silence would accomplish nothing.

Branwen put the book aside, sat up very straight, and faced her husband. "There is no need for you to speak to me like that. I'm not your body slave, to be talked to and treated however you please. I'm a woman, your wife, and I'm in a new country in a culture that's very different from what I've known before. I'm doing the best I can, and I really don't think you have any cause for complaint. Certainly you have no reason to attack me! You knew when you asked me to marry you that I came to you with nothing."

"That's beside the point!"

"No, it isn't." She was shaking inside but she lifted her chin higher. "If you're going to hold those things over me every time you're upset with me about something, then our marriage isn't going to work. I came to you with nothing. I'll be perfectly glad to leave with nothing, if that's what you want."

"Damn you!" Jason glowered—this was getting out of hand. "I don't want you to leave. I just want to know what was so important that you stayed out late, and I had to come home to an empty house."

"I want to buy a few clothes for myself. The things you gave me are right for when I'm with the other wives, or when we go out at night, but I want something more casual for wearing to class." That much was true, not a direct lie. She'd been thinking about this for weeks, working up her courage to use the credit card he'd given her. "And I only have one pair of jeans. I need more. Shopping takes time since I like to look before I buy anything. Now do you understand?"

Grudgingly Jason let his anger fade. It was enough for their first real fight. Shook her out of her even-temperedness, at least. Put the color into her cheeks and a snap in her eyes. She was lovely, really. Slowly, thinking that his anger had devastated many a female years older and more experienced than Branwen, he allowed himself to smile. "Yes. I understand. Buy all the clothes you want. But there are better places to shop than where you were today. I'll tell you where, give you directions."

"All right. I'd like that." Greatly relieved, Branwen returned his smile. "Now I'll go finish this assignment in the living room. I'm afraid it may take me half the night."

A few minutes later Branwen was settled on the couch, wrapped in a wool afghan and plowing through a tedious essay on Neo-classicism. Jason came in and sat down beside her.

"There's something I forgot to tell you," he said.

"Oh?"

"I have to go to Washington for a few days. I'll be very busy, working late, so I'm going to stay in the apartment."

"I didn't know you had an apartment in Washington." The things Harry had said came to mind, along with her realization that Jason's government work was more significant than he'd let her believe.

"Didn't I tell you? No, I guess I didn't. Probably I didn't because until now I've been able to get back here at night." He smiled his most persuasive smile, the one that bound people to him. "I didn't want to be away from your bed, you see. I don't want to now, but I'm afraid it can't be avoided."

"I don't mind. I'll be fine alone. When are you leaving?"

"Possibly tomorrow—I have to make some arrangements. If not tomorrow, then certainly the day after. If I'm not coming home tomorrow night, I'll call you." He moved to get up, but Branwen stopped him by putting her hand on his knee.

"Jason," she asked, "it's your Washington work that earns most of your income, isn't it?"

His jaw clenched. He was instinctively wary. "What of it?"

"It's just that all the time I've known you I've thought of you as a professor. Now I realize you're so much more than that. And I don't even know what it is that you do in Washing-- ton."

Her choice of words, her acknowledgment that he was more than a mere professor, pleased him. "I'm a consultant. You don't know anything about our governmental process, so you wouldn't understand." He kissed the tip of her nose.

"I could learn. I'd like to learn. Sometimes Redmund seems to me so, ah, stifling. I'd like to know what you do in the capital, I'd like to . . . help you."

"You come from an island off the coast of Wales, and you find Redmund stifling? But I do see your point." Jason chuckled. "My dear, the only way you could possibly help me would be as an ornament, a beautiful woman on my arm." He fell silent, studying her. "Now that's an idea. Somehow I never thought of you in that part of my life. Only here, at Redmund. You *are* beautiful—in the right sort of formal gown, you'd attract a lot of attention."

Clothes, again, Branwen thought, but she smiled. "I have a brain, too, you know."

Jason's eyes narrowed. "Harry was always saying that, how intelligent you are." Branwen determinedly kept her smile, though she hadn't realized until this moment how completely Jason discounted all but her face, her body, and her youth. He looked at her now speculatively, reassessing. "You have a retentive mind, don't you? You never seem to forget anything. You're good at remembering what you hear? Lectures, conversations?"

"Yes, I'm very good at that. I always remember everything I hear—sometimes I wish I didn't, but I do."

"Well, then." Jason sounded decisive. "You don't need to know anything about government or politics to look beautiful and remember what people say. I'll start taking you with me to parties."

"Jason, I don't want to go to parties. I want to help in some meaningful way!"

Now he laughed outright. "Parties in Washington are never for fun! Believe me, you will be helping—you'll learn that soon enough. I can't take you with me this time, but soon. Would you like that?"

"Yes. I would. I'd like that very much."

"Fine. We'll do it." Jason frowned at her textbook. "Aren't you through with that yet?"

Branwen smiled. She was pleased and excited. "You've hardly given me the chance."

"But I want you to come to bed with me."

"Sorry." She shook her head. "I can't, I really do have to read this stuff. You go on and get some sleep."

When Jason was in the archway, she stopped him. "Jason, you still didn't tell me what it is that you do in Washington."

"No, I didn't." He looked back over his shoulder, one eyebrow raised, his expression sardonic. "And I never will."

Branwen blinked and stared at Jason's departing back, too astonished to protest his flat refusal. Even spies could tell their wives that they were spies—couldn't they? What could be so important that Jason could not tell her, his wife? So important . . . or so terrible. After all, Harry had said that Jason was feared in Washington.

2

Branwen met Will at the first Washington party she attended with Jason.

It was a reception at the Brazilian Embassy, scores of people in formal dress, champagne and music and Latin tongues all flowing. She was surprised when, after half an hour, Jason left her alone with instructions he whispered in her ear: "Mingle, and keep your ears open. I'm going to disappear for a while but I'll be back."

Suddenly self-conscious, Branwen ignored his order to mingle and instead retreated to the shelter of the potted palm against the wall. There she sipped at her champagne and watched the crowd, wondering if she really wanted to be here after all.

"Hola, señorita!" He came up beside her as she gazed in the opposite direction. "Or is it *señora? Hasta la vista,* or whatever. Actually, I don't speak Spanish. Portuguese, either."

Branwen turned, attracted by the warmth and humor in the man's voice. She smiled. "Actually, neither do I."

"Aw, shucks!" He grinned, leaning one shoulder against the wall. "Looks like I lost my bet."

"Your . . . bet?" Branwen couldn't stop smiling. Something about this young man made her feel warm all over, relaxed and easy, though he was a total stranger. He was very tall, several inches over six feet, and had a spare, loose-limbed, broad-shouldered body. His dinner jacket hung open and his bow tie was slightly askew, and from his comfortable slouch it was obvious he didn't care. Neither handsome nor homely, he had the kind of face that would grow distinguished with age—bony cheeks, straight nose, generous and mobile mouth, and a noble forehead. His hair was light brown streaked with blond, straight, already receding from that high brow although he was certainly the youngest man she'd seen this evening.

"I bet my buddy over there," he said, turning, "—say, where'd he go? Well, anyway, I bet him that you were Argentinian. The women in Argentina can have that white skin, like yours, and that black, black hair the way you're wearing it, and the elegant dress . . . I thought I was making a pretty intelligent guess."

"Sorry," said Branwen, still smiling. "Wrong country. Wrong hemisphere, in fact." She enjoyed the compliments, though they made her more self-conscious. That afternoon she had gone to a hairdresser for the first time in her life, and he had sleeked her hair back and wound it into a figure-eight chignon low on the nape of her neck. The "elegant dress" was a simple, ankle-length column of sapphire-blue satin, its narrow shoulder straps sewn with tiny rhinestones. The man could be forgiven for thinking she might come from a far place—in the mirror she'd looked exotic, even to herself.

"Wrong hemisphere, hm? Okay." He squinted and walked slowly around her as if he studied a piece of sculpture, his attitude mock-serious. "Guess number two, based on the fact that I detect a wee bit o' an accent in your voice. Ireland? What the . . . I say, unhand me, villain!'

Branwen laughed. He'd been so intent on studying her that he'd walked right into the palm tree and was tangled head and shoulders in its fronds. "You should say *unfrond* me, I think!" she quipped in a musical cascade of giggles, stepping back, taking his hand, pulling him clear of the tree. He laughed, too, at her remark.

Suddenly they both stopped laughing. They became aware of their touching hands and looked into each other's eyes. Branwen saw that his were hazel, warm and light, like his voice and his manner. As she watched, the spark of mischief in them faded, the pupils widened. She drew in her breath sharply, and they both snatched their hands away as if any further contact might burn them.

"So-o-o," he said on a long breath, "am I right? Are you Irish?"

"That's very good, a very good guess. I'm Welsh, but with lots of Irish mixed in. My name's Branwen, Branwen Tennant. I mean—" She blushed, and her tongue tripped along in a furious lilt as she realized her mistake and hastened to correct it. "I mean, Tennant *was* my name, my family name, my Welsh name. I don't live in Wales anymore, I live in Redmund, Virginia, and my name is really Faraday. Branwen Faraday."

"Not Argentinian. Not a señorita." His voice was flat, and all the humor had gone out of him. The guessing game was over. "Faraday, from Redmund. You must be Jason Faraday's wife."

"Yes, I am. Who are you?"

"Me? Oh, yeah, I'm sorry." He stood up straighter and shrugged one shoulder at a time to adjust the hang of his dinner jacket. "I'm Will Tracy. Wilbur F. Tracy, Jr., but I prefer Will. I live here in Washington, but like you, I'm originally from a foreign country. It's called Kentucky. Ever hear of it?"

Branwen laughed again, softly, and nodded.

"My father, Wilbur F. Tracy, Sr. is the King of Kentucky. Or at least he thinks he is. He was also a senator, *the* senator from the Bluegrass state according to him, for umpty-ump years, but he's retired now. Gone back to the old home state to be king full-time. Uh, I hate to change the subject, but where's your husband?"

"He said he had to disappear for a while, but he'll be back. Do you know Jason?"

"Only by reputation. I heard through the grapevine that he got married. Mrs. Faraday—"

"Branwen."

"Branwen, I feel obliged to inform you that that thing you're holding in your hand is dead. . . ." She looked at her hand, incredulous, and he reached over and took the champagne glass from her. She'd forgotten she had it. He peered into the glass, a mournful expression on his face. "See, it's dead. It isn't breathing. No bubbles."

He looked so sincerely puzzled and sad that Branwen wanted to collapse with laughter more than she dared in this sort of a gathering. "I thought," she gulped, getting herself under control, "that everyone here was a diplomat or a politician. But you, Will Tracy, have got to be a *clown*! Are you always this funny?"

"No. Only about ninety-five percent of the time. It's an act, to cover up what a serious, responsible, and slightly dull person I am underneath."

"I can't believe you'd ever be dull. If you aren't a clown, what do you do here in Washington?"

"I think." His smile was both mischievous and sweet.

"You . . . *think*."

"Yeah. I work for the Parnassus Foundation, a think tank. Actually, I don't come to these shindigs very often. I just came tonight to keep my friend company—he's a junior in the State Department—because he asked me and I didn't have anything better to do." Will's voice softened, and he took a step closer to Branwen. "I'm awfully glad I did. Uh, Branwen, could I interest you in another glass of this bubbly stuff and a quiet corner where we might sit and talk for a while?"

"I—I . . ." Branwen stalled. "I'm supposed to be mingling. Besides, I don't think there *is* a quiet corner in this place."

"Please, I promise you, I have the very best nose for finding quiet corners."

"But . . ."

"And I'll tell you some of the same gossip you'd get if you'd been mingling, which is the only reason anyone mingles anyway. What do you say?"

"In that case," Branwen said, taking a deep breath, "I say yes. I'd love to get out of this noise for a few minutes."

Will took her by the hand and pulled her along at a purposeful pace until he'd found the place he looked for—a conservatory, attached to the far end of the dining room like a Victorian glass bubble. He drew Branwen into the doorway and then stood back for her to precede him. He quipped, "I'd make a tacky joke about the Brazilians having brought part of their jungle with them, except this has been here since I was a kid, and the place wasn't an embassy then. It was just somebody's house."

Branwen looked around, delighted. "This is incredible. Oh, look! Aren't those tiny orchids? And it smells so good, like a real forest!"

Will hung back for the pleasure of watching this woman move. She was as graceful and delicate as the ferns that brushed her skirt as she passed. The white curve of her neck sent shivers along his spine. *I'm nuts,* he thought. *The woman is married to Jason Frigging Faraday! She can't be as uncomplicated and naive as she seems.*

"It *is* quiet in here," Branwen said. "Shall we sit here?"

"Looks like a perfect place," Will responded. She had chosen a pair of wrought-iron chairs under an arch created by the spreading branches of fig and myrtle trees. Her dress repeated the deep blue of the sky through the glass roof above, and the tiny jewels on the straps of her gown sparkled like its stars. He caught his breath and suddenly felt as bashful as if he were back in prep school. "I forgot the champagne. You stay right there, don't move, I'll be right back!"

Will fled, his head swimming with the possible consequences of what he was doing. He and Branwen were alone in the conservatory. Of course other people would probably wander in, but what if they didn't? What if the only one to wander in was Jason Faraday, to find Will Tracy in a secluded bower with his very new, very young, very beautiful wife? *And yet,* Will thought, *it isn't so much that she's beautiful . . .*

With the advantage of his height Will scanned the room, his gaze skimming across heads that bobbed like so many corks upon the surface of a choppy sea. He sought one of the waiters who circulated with trays of champagne, and as his eyes worked, so also did his researcher's brain. He might be casual in his dress and speech, but there was nothing sloppy about his mind; it presented him with all that he knew about Jason Faraday on command, as efficiently as the new mainframe computer at the Foundation. Faraday had come to Washington in the fifties as somebody's Bright Boy—Will didn't know whose, he'd still been in college then. Jason had always been a staffer, never a politician himself, and the man had a killer reputation—mind like a steel trap, implacable will, that sort of thing. He wasn't attached to the present administration, and he certainly hadn't been part of JFK's Camelot crew. It was widely assumed that Jason Faraday was high up—very high up—in some aspect of covert operations. FBI, CIA, NSC, take your pick. Whatever he was, he very definitely wasn't Will Tracy's kind of guy. *So what the hell,* he thought, *am I doing in the conservatory with his wife?*

Will spotted a waiter and edged his way close enough to snag two full glasses. Smiling and mumbling, "Sorry, in a hurry, see you later," to colleagues and acquaintances in his path, he returned to the conservatory. He went the long way around the room and was relieved to find two other couples among the greenery. Branwen sat where he'd left her. She seemed to radiate a little pool of calm around her spot under the arching branches. His witty tongue and joking manner, which were really armor for a sensitivity so acute it was embarrassing, deserted him.

She hadn't seen him yet. He hung back in green shadows, filling his lungs with moist, damp, earthy smells and his eyes with her. It wasn't just that she was beautiful—not the right word for her—his brain presented him with one he liked better: lovely. Not just that she was lovely, but that she was different. Indefinably, unutterably different. Will felt a need to know her, a need more urgent than any he'd felt in all his twenty-seven years.

"I hope I wasn't gone too long," he said. He sat next to her. He hadn't spilled a drop before, but now his hand shook as she reached for the glass he offered.

"Not at all." Branwen's hand was steady, and so were her eyes on his face. "I was enjoying just . . . just being in this place."

The urgency of his need made Will tongue-tied. He could only search her face and note with wonder that she searched him, too, honestly, openly. She didn't chatter, nor did she turn away.

Finally he spoke, raising his glass in a toast. "To friendship?" His voice lifted in a question, his lips lifted at the corners in a hopeful smile.

"To friendship," Branwen said, but she did not smile. She said the words like a pledge, seriously, as if she already knew what lay ahead for both of them.

Jason's breathing slowed and tapered into an even rhythm; with a grunt he turned onto his side away from her, an infallible sign that he was now asleep. Branwen slid carefully out of their bed and slipped soundlessly downstairs in the dark, picking up her robe and slippers on the way. She prayed he wouldn't waken—he didn't like to wake and find her gone. Jason was a light sleeper, even when he seemed exhausted by their lovemaking, even when he'd been drinking. He was habitually restless in sleep, tormented by his dreams, and sometimes he would reach for Branwen and clutch her to him as if she were a talisman against nightmares. These moments in the night were the only times Jason seemed vulnerable, and his brief powerlessness both touched and frightened her.

Not tonight, she prayed, at least not for the next hour or so.

Her mind was overfull; she needed time alone to think, to sort things through. She went into the kitchen and by the light of the open refrigerator door poured a glass of orange juice. She drank a sip and kept the rest—if Jason came looking for her, she could say she'd just come downstairs because she was thirsty. She drifted without thinking toward the breakfast room, a small room between the kitchen and the dining room that had once been a butler's pantry. Jason didn't like the little room with its trestle table and high-backed benches tucked under a window on one side, and built-in drawers and glass-enclosed cabinets on the other side. He said it was cramped, but Branwen thought it cozy. Since they never used it for meals, she kept her typewriter out on the table, along with spiral binders full of class notes and manila folders of term paper materials. Her books were gradually filling the counter space opposite, and one of the drawers held pens and pencils and paper clips and miscellaneous supplies. Unintentionally Branwen had made the breakfast room her own space in what she still thought of as Jason's house. She had no interest in "decorating," as the other wives called it. Jason's house had more than enough of everything, and it never would have occurred to her to replace perfectly good things with others just because she would have preferred a different pattern or color or texture. Still, she gravitated when she was alone to her own space in the breakfast room, and she went there now in the small dark hours after midnight.

Branwen put her glass of orange juice on the trestle table and turned on the hanging lamp overhead. She wedged herself into the corner of the high-backed bench with her feet up under her and her knees pulled to her chest. For the first time in months she wished she had her mother here to talk to. Not that Mam would be any real help—she would nod and smile and listen and never say much; that was Mam's way. Branwen rested her cheek on her knee and smiled. They were far away, her family, but they loved her, and that was a help in itself.

Her smile faded. *I* need *help,* Branwen thought. *I'm in such a muddle I don't know if I can ever sort myself out!* She closed her eyes and concentrated, hugging her knees tight, tighter, going down and down into that place inside herself where all was quiet, all was still.

In the stillness her inner Voice, so long silent, said: *The help you need is here, inside yourself. All you have to do is be still and listen.*

"No!" Branwen whispered, and opened her eyes. She thought she had put the Voice away, along with Harry's rune stones and all the other things her mother would have called "a bit fey." "Don't pay any attention to your gran," Mam used to say. "She's a bit fey." And her mam had also said, "You don't want to be like your gran, Branwen, all full of superstitions and old nonsense. This is the twentieth century!"

But I am like Gran, Branwen thought. *Or at least I'm more like her than I ever was like my own mam. Gran always said I was most like her sister, the aunt I never knew. . . . And if my Voice is still here and speaks so clearly after all I've done to deny it, probably I should at least listen. I'm not likely to get any help outside of myself, anyway.*

She closed her eyes again and sank once more into her own quiet. Inside her closed eyelids she saw at first only a soft black, not the black of the Void or the Abyss that swallows up and destroys, but the black from which the spark is thrown to burst forth into Creation. As she watched, a glowing blue, deep yet bright, grew and spread and moved across the black field of her inner vision. Other colors came: pink and rose and lavender, and shafts of pure white light that pierced the colors and then were gone. Once a clear yellow bloomed like the opening of a great, shining lily. In time the blue returned and folded into itself, smaller and smaller and smaller, slipping away behind a black velvet curtain as if a play were ended.

With the colors there were no words. Random thoughts came into her mind, only to dissolve without a trace. That was all, the colors moving and filling her mind, yet when Branwen opened her eyes again, she felt quite different than she had before. Stable, secure. She didn't know how this process worked, this going within herself, nor did she know yet that there was a name for it: meditation. She only knew that it *had* worked, and for the first time in many months she was secure in the knowledge that she could and would find her own way. "Thank you, Voice, for coming back," she said softly. "I promise I won't deny you ever again."

Branwen breathed deeply, stretched, and finished her orange juice. Then she turned out the light and made her way silently through the house and back into bed. Jason grumbled and turned, but he slept on. She lay beside him and let her thoughts go free.

This marriage was her job now, she thought. She worked for

Jason in much the same way that she had worked for John and Lucy. But she didn't feel that she belonged in Redmund the way she had belonged to Llanfaren. *I should go to Washington on my own,* she thought sleepily. *I'll have my own friends. Will Tracy will be my friend* . . . She burrowed into her pillow, pulled the soft blanket up around her ears, and fell asleep with a smile on her face and Will's face in her mind.

"The place is called Raven Hill," said Harry, "and you mustn't think it will be anything like your English or your Welsh country houses, or else you'll be disappointed."

"Mmm," said Branwen. She was looking out of the car window and thinking that the Virginia countryside was as beautiful as any she'd seen, and as green. The colonists who'd settled here in the 1700s must have felt quite at home.

"It's small," Harry went on, "but I think the house compares well with Stratford Hall, or any of the plantations along the James River. Has Jason taken you to any of those places, Branwen?"

She gave Harry her attention. "He took me to Mount Vernon when we did a sort of whirlwind tour of Washington, soon after I came here. I don't remember much of that. Everything was so new to me then, and to see so much all at once, I was overwhelmed. In fact, I spent a lot of the first two or three months in this country feeling overwhelmed. I guess now that I think about it, Mount Vernon seemed rather small, too, but George Washington wouldn't have wanted it to be anything huge, like a palace. That was a part of the point, wasn't it, that he didn't *want* to be king?"

"Quite so—and actually Mount Vernon was his family home built long before he was President. Well, if you haven't been to any of the other old homes, I don't suppose you'll have much of a basis of comparison for Raven Hill."

"I, uh, did go to Monticello recently. Not with Jason. With a friend."

"Oh?" At this piece of information Harry raised not one but both eyebrows.

"Yes. I thought it was very interesting. My friend is a big fan of your Thomas Jefferson, so I learned a lot. I think what impressed me most was all Jefferson's little inventions around the place. That, and the fact that it seemed to me Monticello would be a comfortable house to live in, even now. Jefferson must

have been an exciting man to know. I was amazed to learn that
he gave his own personal library to the country to start up the
Library of Congress again after the first one burned in the War
of 1812. Can you imagine a man like that, with all the things he
had studied—and he seems to have been fascinated by
everything—giving up all his books? It's incredible! We went
into Charlottesville, too, to see how he'd designed the University of Virginia, and I thought it was lovely. Much nicer than
Redmund, much more real—Redmund seems somehow fake,
you know? But not even Charlottesville is as beautiful as Washington this time of year with all the cherry trees in bloom."

"My dear," said Harry, intrigued, "you are positively babbling! I don't believe I've heard you say so much all at once in
the whole time I've known you. You're usually such a quiet
girl." His eyes moved over her. "Excuse me, I should have said
woman. Can it be that you're quite taken with this country of
ours? Or is it simply that you're taken with your new friend?"

"I, ah, yes." Branwen felt her cheeks flush and went silent,
hoping Harry wouldn't pursue the subject. Inevitably, she
thought of Will. Will, who had introduced her to the Smithsonian and showed her how to find her way through the vast marble
halls of the Library of Congress. Will, with whom she had
walked the Mall under the cherry trees, pink blossoms falling
over them like a soft rain. Will: she had felt really alone with
him for the first time that day they drove in his car to
Charlottesville, and at Monticello she'd looked at the portrait of
Thomas Jefferson and thought Will looked like him and had
said so. Will had laughed, his eyes had danced, and he'd been
pleased. Will, who was opening a whole new world to her. . . .

Harry didn't miss Branwen's blush or the fact that she'd suddenly gone miles away from him. How very interesting! He'd
have to find out more about this, but at the moment his ancestral
home drew near.

"Pay attention, Branwen, you'll want to be able to find it by
yourself, you know." He cut his eyes to see that she came back
from wherever she had been. "We've come exactly seven and a
half miles west on the main road from Redmund, and now on
the left you see that very large oak tree and the unmarked one-
lane blacktop road beside it?"

She nodded as Harry turned his Mercedes sedan into the one-
lane road he'd pointed out.

"Well," he said, "this is not so much a proper road as it is my driveway."

"It's a very *long* driveway," Branwen remarked. Lush fields of new-green grass rolled gently away on either side, dotted here and there by more oak trees with their great spreading branches. There was not a fence in sight, nor any animals. "Do you keep cows, Harry? Or horses?"

"No, I don't. Though they do call this 'horse country.' I can't be bothered with animals and I don't want tenants on the place. Other than the Beechers, of course. Mrs. Beecher is housekeeper and cook. You'll meet her. Beecher, the husband, looks after the grounds. You'll see the house in just a moment, as soon as we top this rise. . . . Ah, there you are, my dear: Raven Hill."

Branwen was speechless. She had somehow expected something quite different from this four-square, two-story colonial house. It was built of brick, once painted white and now faded to pink with age. A white-pillared porch stretched across the front and wrapped around one side, stretching out over the drive to form a porte cochere. A gnarled and ancient wisteria vine climbed a trellis to hang its fragrant drooping chains of purple and white blooms all about the porte cochere, where Harry parked his car.

"Harry, I don't know what to say. It's so, so *pretty!*"

He chuckled. He could almost, but not quite, read her thoughts. "You sound surprised. You were expecting, perhaps, that with a name like Ravenscroft my family should have built something that would have appealed to another famous Virginian, Edgar Allan Poe? The House of Usher, for instance?"

"Well," Branwen said, grinning, "Maybe a dank tarn or two. For the ravens of Raven Hill, you know!"

"Alas, there are no ravens at Raven Hill. Except for myself." Harry leaned toward Branwen and captured her eyes. "Occasionally. When I feel so inclined."

Branwen looked into Harry's eyes. He was playing, joking with her, and she sensed it, yet there was in him an undercurrent of seriousness, too. He willed her to look, and she looked and saw in his eyes an image, tiny and black in the center of the gray irises where the pupil should have been. An image in profile, the nose a beak, a purpling sheen of feathers on its neck. Shapechanger! thought Branwen, as she dimly heard a rustle and whirr of wings. But aloud she said, laughing, "Nevermore!" and broke the spell.

Harry didn't laugh; for an instant he was filled with envy. How easily she Saw, and just as easily broke away! He forced a chuckle. "Come on, our lunch awaits."

"Let's go in the front so I can look at the view," Branwen suggested as she joined Harry outside the car. He nodded, and together they followed a curved brick path edged by tall azalea bushes heavy with fat buds. From the house on its hill the lawns sloped away on all sides to become gently rolling fields. "It's very beautiful, so peaceful. You and your family are fortunate to have such a home."

"Yes, it is lovely. Sometimes," Harry mused, draping his arm lightly around Branwen's shoulders, "I wonder how I happened to be born a Ravenscroft. The forces of darkness have never touched this place, and I intend that they never shall."

An odd thing to say, Branwen thought, but she made no comment. She asked if there was time before lunch for her to see the house, and Harry sent her off on her own while he went to confer with Mrs. Beecher.

Raven Hill was large in the proportions of its rooms, but the rooms themselves were few in number. She did not go upstairs, but if the second floor mirrored the first, there would be ten rooms in all. Off a central hall dominated by a curving staircase, two rooms opened to the left: a formal living room, which seemed to Branwen more like a music room because of its concert-sized grand piano, and a formal dining room. To the right of the hall was a library, a door that on inspection opened into a small powder room, and a smaller family dining room. A third room between the library and family dining room, which had obviously given up some of its space and its hallway door to become the powder room, was fitted up as an office. The furnishings throughout, though they might have been antiques, were both well cared for and much used.

When she went to join Harry who beckoned to her through double doors thrown open at the end of the hall, Branwen saw that a one-story wing had been added at the back of the house. Of course—she remembered that these old southern houses had had their kitchens in separate buildings originally because of the heat. The kitchen wing didn't quite match the rest of the house, and for Branwen that added to its charm; it proved that Raven Hill was a home and not a museum.

"I thought we'd eat out here on the terrace," said Harry, leading her to a glass-topped table already set with a first course of fruit cup and a tall pitcher of iced tea. Fortunately she rather liked iced tea, since people here drank it all the time, even in winter. He seated her and then himself, and inquired, "Did you get through the house? Do you like it?"

"I didn't go upstairs, and yes, I do like it. I'm glad you brought me here. I have another perspective on you after seeing where you live."

"Really? And what is that?"

"Oh, I don't know. I don't somehow think of you as part of a long line of an old Virginia family. And yet you are, obviously. A gentleman and a scholar, as they say. I'm sure the library is your favorite room, where you spend the most time."

"How interesting. Tell me more."

"I suppose my, ah, usual view of you comes from the way we met. To my mind, you belong more to the world I came from. I have this sort of vision of you on a plain at sunrise or sunset, among some standing stones. Not at Stonehenge, but at . . . at Avebury perhaps." Branwen blinked at the bright sunlight. The day seemed quite warm for April, and for a moment she was uncomfortably hot, and her hair felt heavy on her shoulders. She looked across the table at Harry who appeared perfectly normal and cool in a suit and tie. "What an odd thing for me to say! I've never even been to Avebury. I wanted to go, with Jason, when we were on our honeymoon trip, but he said . . ." She let her voice trail off, embarrassed.

"Go on, this is fascinating. What did he say?"

"Well, he said we didn't have enough time to waste any of it on a place where there was nothing but a boring bunch of rocks."

Harry threw his head back and laughed. "Oh, marvelous, that's bloody marvelous! A boring bunch of rocks!"

Puzzled, Branwen said, "How can you think that's so funny? *I* didn't. But of course I didn't argue with him."

Harry sobered. "No, I don't suppose you would argue with him. It's funny because Jason is so obsessed with power, don't you see?"

"No, Harry, I'm afraid I don't."

"Never mind. Someday you will. Ah, here's Mrs. Beecher with the rest of our meal."

Branwen helped Mrs. Beecher unload her tray, and Harry performed the introductions. Mrs. Beecher was small, scrawny, and sharp-eyed. All her motions were economical and deft; her smile, when it broke unexpectedly over her face, was like sunshine. She spoke with a curious accent that sounded almost Scots. Branwen asked Harry about it when she'd gone.

"She and her husband came out of the mountains. There are whole communities of Scots-Irish people up there who've kept to themselves for more than two hundred years, and they all sound like that. They sing songs passed down for generations from parents to children, songs that clearly go back all the way to the Childe ballads and before that. I first became interested in the oral tradition from those mountain people when I was quite young, and I lured Beecher and Mrs. Beecher—her given name is Alice, but I wouldn't dare call her that—down here so that I could pick their brains. Mrs. Beecher took a liking to me," Harry said with a wink, "a rare enough occurrence that I decided to ask them to stay. I put Beecher to work outside, and eventually Mrs. Beecher became both housekeeper and cook."

"She's very good," said Branwen, chewing appreciatively. "And yet she looks as if she doesn't eat more than a bird, herself."

"Don't let her looks deceive you. She's as strong as an ox, and willful and stubborn to match. She keeps me in line, I can tell you." Harry was silent for a beat, a look of affection on his face. "I don't know what I'd do without her. These mountain folk are strong people—I'm sure she could do absolutely anything she set her mind to. When she came here, she couldn't cook at all; our old cook taught her. She'd been with us since I was a baby and she's dead now, rest her soul."

"And your parents? Are you really so all alone, Harry? Have you no family?"

"My father is dead. My mother came from a Yankee family, and after he died she went back up North to be near her own people in upstate New York. I don't see her often. She, ah . . ." He seemed troubled for an instant and disturbingly young, with his pale hair falling over one eye. "She doesn't like me very much."

"I'm sorry," Branwen murmured.

"Oh, it's all right." Harry recovered and grinned his one-sided grin. "I don't like her very much, either. My younger brother John was her favorite, but John's gone, too. He was a Navy man, Annapolis, and he was killed in the China Sea during the Korean War. I'm the last of the Virginia Ravenscrofts, my dear, and as I'm not likely to marry, the line will die out with me."

"It seems a pity. This house, there's been so much happiness in it. It seems, somehow, that it should go on."

Harry shrugged. "There's a branch of the Ravenscrofts in North Carolina. Perhaps I'll leave the place to them. Or perhaps I'll do something unexpected and leave it to someone entirely outside the family. But how in the world did we get on such a dreary subject? I had quite a different motive in asking you here today. Let's talk about that, shall we?"

Branwen eyed him suspiciously. "I thought you just wanted to show me your house."

"Or you might not have come? Keep an open mind, my dear. What I'm about to propose to you will be to your advantage as well as to mine. Here it is: I'm offering you a small part-time job, eight to ten hours a week. I'll get you on the payroll as my research assistant. I've always had one, but when I was in my black period last year, I lost the one I had and didn't hire another."

"I don't know—"

"Wait. I'm not done yet. You'd be working here at the house, in the office next to the library. You saw it?"

Branwen nodded.

"Good. The point is you won't be working for me on the college campus, so there's no reason for Jason to know. No sense looking for trouble. I can pay you the top of the salary scale because you have special skills for my work."

"If you mean the special skills I think you mean . . ."

"Not necessarily," Harry hastened to interrupt. He had anticipated this objection. "Your fluency in Welsh is enough for starters, plus your familiarity with the geographic area of concentration for the project. Your other, ah, abilities, the ones you're so sensitive about, could be useful at some later stage—if you're so inclined. I won't push you. At this stage I expect your intuition alone would make you worth your salary. One last thing I want you to consider before you say yes or no: This is a real job, you'll be paid through Medieval Studies, and I'll keep a personnel file on you and do a written evaluation once a year. You'll have a work history in a field that's a natural for you if, for example, you should decide to go on to graduate school. And you'll have a little income of your own. I can pay for up to twenty hours a week if this works out and you want to increase your time."

Harry waited. Branwen lowered her eyelashes and stared at her plate. None of her thoughts or emotions showed on her face; it was like a porcelain mask. "Say yes," Harry whispered, unable to contain himself. This was so right for them both, he was absolutely sure of it!

Branwen was not so sure, but she was tempted. She voiced her primary doubt, looking up not at Harry but beyond him where in the distance wooded hills held a blue haze. "I'm not sure I can afford the time. I've decided to get my—what do you call it here—my bachelor's degree in as short a time as possible. I've doubled up on courses this semester and plan to do the same in the summer session."

He hadn't thought of that. It was understandable, a wise thing for her to do, and he couldn't argue with it. "Perhaps," he thought rapidly out loud, "I could get you course credit. Independent study, an honors thesis, something like that. I could talk to your adviser."

The truth was that Branwen did want a job; the fact that Jason had all but forbidden her to work was a very sore point. "What would we be working on? The same thing you were doing at Llanfaren?"

"Only in part." Harry pushed his plate aside and leaned across the table, letting his eagerness show. "I decided to let that project lie for the time being, not to rework the grant proposal. Rather, I want to sort through that material, which as you know is original, my own stuff, and make a sweep through similar things others have done. You could be a lot of help there, believe me. And with what we decide to keep of both kinds of sources I'll write a short book or a long monograph with a title something like 'Archetypes of the British and Welsh Landscape: Is Their Power Myth or Reality?' What do you think?"

"I think," Branwen said, laughing, "that your title is too long, but your idea is irresistible. I'd like to do it, Harry, I'd like that very much. Thank you!"

"Oh, splendid! Splendid!" Harry jumped up from the table. "Have you finished your lunch? Yes? Let me show you where you'll be working. Let's talk about hours. When can you start?"

"Easy, Harry, easy." Branwen laughed again, letting him pull her into the house, through the small dining room, and into the office. She dutifully admired the desk that would be hers, the new typewriter, the piles of untranscribed notes in Harry's spidery scrawl. Finally she held up her hand and said, "Have mercy, sir! If you show me anything else today, my head may break."

Harry reined himself in and leaned back against a filing cabinet, folding his long arms. He let a satisfied smile spread across his face. He was immensely pleased to see Branwen at his desk in his house and to know that she would be here often from now on. "Going too fast for you, am I?" he drawled.

"A little. And I have to get back. I told you I have a three o'clock class. Look, Harry, I have to see what's on my calendar at home before I can make a firm time commitment, but let's say I'll definitely do eight hours a week here. If you can get me course credit, I might be able to do more."

"And when will you start?"

Branwen grinned. "Impatient fellow, aren't you? I'll call and let you know. All right?"

"You seem much better, much less tense now than you were back in January," Harry remarked when they were once again in his car headed back to Redmund.

"Um-hm," Branwen acknowledged. She was preoccupied, thinking that she could gain several hours a week to work for Harry by dropping out of the faculty wives group. It would be no great loss; she wasn't making friends there anyway in spite of her longing to have a close female friend.

"I'd guess it's not just the change of season that has wrought this change in you."

"Hm?" Branwen turned her head to look at Harry. "I'm not sure I know what you mean. I haven't changed, I've just kind of begun to make a place for myself here. I'm more comfortable than I was, that's all."

The miles were clicking by beneath the car. Harry didn't have much time, and he was determined to satisfy the curiosity she'd aroused in him on the earlier trip. "You force me to be blunt, my dear. Who is your new friend? The one with whom you went to Monticello?"

Branwen's cheeks pinked, as they had before. "You think my new friend has something to do with this change you think you observe in me?"

"In a word, yes."

"Sometimes, Dr. Ravenscroft, you're too perceptive!"

"And you, Branwen, are sometimes as clear as glass, at least to me. Who is he?"

"He's not from Redmund," she said defensively. Will was her closely cherished secret. Her friendship with him was unlike any other she'd experienced, full of laughter, brimming with discovery—of him, of herself, of a new view of the world. The relationship seemed to her so rare, so fragile, that she was sometimes afraid simply thinking about it too much would cause it to break. And now Harry wanted her to talk about it? Impossible!

"*He.* So I was right. I think, judging from your face whenever you think about this new friend, it's a good thing he isn't from Redmund." Harry felt a stirring in his breast that could be jealousy, or a warning. His voice came out more harshly than he intended. "I see you don't want to tell me his name. Branwen, are you having an affair with this man?"

"No!" she cried. She jerked around so suddenly that her hair whipped across her face. "It's nothing like that. We're just friends!"

"Really?" Harry glanced at Branwen and then wished he hadn't. As he watched, the high color drained from her face and left her deathly pale.

"I'm afraid," she said just above a whisper. There was desperation in her eyes. "I'm afraid that if I talk about our friendship, if I tell you or anyone else about him, I'll lose it. Lose him."

He felt like the worst sort of cad, but still Harry pressed her. "Come on, Branwen, that's a child's game, you know. Being afraid that if you want something too much you're bound not to get it. You have more sense than that!"

She shook her head. "Or being sure that if you do get something you want so very much, you'll have to give it up just as you really believe you have it." She sighed, but her voice was stronger. "All right, Harry. I don't want you thinking this is something it isn't, so I'll tell you. My friend's name is Will Tracy, and he lives in Washington."

"Will Tracy, young Will?"

Branwen didn't even hear the astonishment in Harry's voice; she was so determined to get it all out now that she'd started. "I met him at a party at the Brazilian Embassy, and we got along well right from the start. He's gentle and he's funny and we laugh. We have fun together. That's all."

"And he's about your age," said Harry softly. He was ashamed of himself, touched to the core by what she had said about having fun. She must have had little opportunity for fun in her life, to have sounded so wistful. "I'm sorry I went on at you like that, Branwen. Forgive me—sometimes I forget how young you are. Because I feel that I've known you before, in other lifetimes, I tend to think of you as ageless, but of course you aren't. You need friends your own age, and I'm sure young Tracy is a fine fellow."

Branwen's throat was tight. She would much, much rather not have told Harry about Will. "You sound as if you know him."

"I do. I know his father, the senator, better. Or at least I did until he went back to Kentucky. Still, young Will and I travel in the same social circle, and I see him occasionally. The last time, as I recall, was at Christmas."

They were entering the campus, and Branwen bent to gather up her books from the floor by her feet. Her hair swung forward, and she hid behind it for a bit longer than necessary. She had not expected Harry to know Will, and she hadn't thought about "social circles." The half-dozen times she'd spent with Will she'd felt as if they existed in a magic circle of their own. But they didn't, and Harry had awakened her to that fact. She straightened up. "Harry, you do understand that Will Tracy and I are just friends?"

Harry nodded.

"And that even though I'm not—as you so crassly put it—having an affair with Will, I still can't let Jason know because he would never understand?"

"Yes, my dear, and don't worry—your secret is safe with me. After all, you and I have other secrets from Jason that are far more important—at least to me, they are."

Her hand was already on the door handle, but Branwen stopped. Distress was in her eyes. "You mean renewing our friendship, and my working for you."

Harry nodded. "Um-hm."

"Someday, when he's used to having a wife and when he knows me better, I'll tell him, Harry. I have absolutely no intention of keeping anything from Jason for very long."

"Really?" Harry's skepticism was in his face and in his voice. "And would you care to predict when this 'someday' will come?"

"A few more months, that's all." She pushed her legs out of the car, then twisted around to say, "Surely, at most, a year."

3

————

A year went by and much of another, and Jason did change. But not in the way Branwen had hoped. His ardor for her cooled, and since the sexual act was the only part of his life he had ever been interested in sharing with her, a gap grew up between them and gradually widened. Jason was not unhappy with this estrangement; self-centered as he was, he wasn't even aware of it. Branwen was in his bed at night when he desired her. She ran the house so well on the allowance he provided that he no longer thought to envy Harry for Mrs. Beecher. When he wanted Branwen to accompany him somewhere, which was less and less often, she looked so beautiful that he knew other men envied him; then he would remember why he'd wanted Branwen enough to marry her, and his desire would be rekindled. But not for long. Jason's possessiveness these days was focused on money, not on his wife. He was taking the skills he'd developed and honed in Washington onto a bigger playground, for higher stakes.

For Branwen, Jason's increasingly frequent and prolonged absences were a mixed blessing. She was slow to admit that the passionate physical attraction she and Jason shared would not grow into an enduring married love. But as stubborn as she was, she wasn't stupid. The evidence, well into the third year of their marriage, showed that Jason neither loved her in the sense that she understood love, nor did he have the same expectations of

marriage that she had. His expectations were not that hard to
fulfill, and she met them out of her continuing gratitude.

Branwen's formula for a happy marriage was simple. In the
American vernacular that had become second nature to her, it
was Don't Make Waves. By the end of a year of marriage, she
had understood that Jason was uninterested in her life apart
from him—*except* when it inconvenienced him in some way.
He didn't want to hear how her courses were going or what she
thought of the growing civil rights movement, or even what she
had been doing all day; but if, as she once had done, she went to
the capital to observe a demonstration firsthand and got tied up
in traffic when he expected her to be at home . . . *then* he cared.
Then he would become angry, and handling his anger was so
difficult that Branwen soon preferred to avoid it. At first she'd
been hurt by his lack of interest. Next, she'd made excuses for
him, felt sorry for him as the only child born late in life to el-
derly parents. He'd grown up so alone, she told herself, that it
was no wonder he didn't seem to know how to be close to her
except in bed. So she'd tried to teach him, but to no avail.

Finally she was forced to admit that Jason really didn't care
what went on in her head or in her heart or in her life, apart from
when she was physically with him. It was as if, for him, she existed only when he wanted her to exist. Recently she had realized that Jason's very lack of interest had a positive side: It gave
her freedom. Freedom with one significant limitation. She had
to be at home at night, every night, even if Jason was out of
town. If he called and she didn't answer, or if he returned home
ahead of schedule from one of his trips and she was out, he
would fly into a rage.

Branwen's days were full to the point of bursting. She'd been
quite successful at building a life for herself, and she'd long
since stopped feeling guilty over the fact that the right time had
never come for her to tell her husband about working for Harry,
and about her friendship with Will. But the nights were long and
sometimes excruciatingly lonely. And sometimes they were
frightening. It frightened her to lie in bed in the dark next to Jason and feel lonely, achingly empty inside. She didn't know
which was more terrifying, the empty feeling or the thought that
came with it: *I can't spend the rest of my life this way!*

Will Tracy couldn't stand still. He scuffed with the toes of his
loafers at a piece of litter someone had dropped on the sidewalk

in front of the Georgetown restaurant where he waited for Branwen. Finally he reached down and picked it up—it was a cigarette pack crumpled and stepped on until it had all but lost its identity. He made a face at the thing and carried it pinched between thumb and finger to the waste bin on the corner. Branwen was late and it was something to do, and besides he didn't like to see litter on the streets. Georgetown was *his* town, where he'd grown up, where he still lived on O Street in the federal-style townhouse that had been his father's and was now his. Georgetown hadn't changed much except that there were more shops now—the whole downtown seemed to have exploded with "boutiques," whatever they were. Will seriously doubted anything could force him to go into a place that could call itself a "boutique." Of course there was more traffic now, too, which was probably why Branwen was late. Probably she couldn't find a place to park.

He ambled the few steps back to the restaurant, moving with the lanky, unconscious grace that had come to him in late adolescence when he'd finally learned how to handle his long arms and legs. He glanced at his watch. Branwen was fifteen minutes late now, and that was really unusual. What if something had happened and she couldn't come? He hated waiting for her like this. Not so much the waiting itself, but the necessity for it, the restrictions on their friendship. Which was why today was so important. Today after lunch they were going for a nice autumn walk through Georgetown, and he was going to walk her right straight to a forbidden place: his house. Forbidden because they had, without discussing it, a mutual understanding that to be alone anywhere together was dangerous to their "just friends" relationship. Will couldn't take it anymore. He intended to get her to come inside his house, and then he'd tell her, and maybe *show* her, that he couldn't live any longer with those restrictions. He was more than a little nervous about what he intended to do; he'd had to work himself up to it, which was why it was so all-fired important that today of all days *nothing* should prevent her coming. But of course Branwen couldn't know that. . .

Aahh, there she was! A special warmth spread through Will, and his wide smile spread across his face. Branwen came up the sidewalk toward him, walking rapidly, starting to smile now that she saw him, too. She was wearing tan boots and a longish purple wool skirt that rippled with her stride, and a fringed Guatemalan poncho striped in shades of lighter purple and a turquoise-blue that matched her eyes. He knew the poncho was Guatemalan because he'd been with her when she'd bought it at a Crafts Festival in Rock Creek Park. And he knew what she was wearing under the poncho, too, because once Branwen put together an outfit she liked, she wore it over and over again— unlike most women he knew, who wouldn't be caught dead in the same thing twice in one week. She would have on a white turtleneck sweater and the silver squash blossom necklace with its central turquoise stone that exactly matched her eyes, the necklace that was the only gift she'd ever allowed him to give her. He'd had to force her into accepting it by saying that he was going to buy it anyway, and if she didn't take it, he'd wear it himself. And he would have, too, and she knew it. The memory made him smile. Will was glad Branwen didn't care much about clothes because he was the same way himself; his tweed jacket was so old and beloved that its sleeves were a tad short, and the leather patches on the elbows were there not for fashion's sake but because they had to be.

"Hi!" Branwen was a little breathless when she reached him.

"Hi, yourself." As always when he saw her again, whether they'd been apart for two days or two months, Will had to restrain himself from throwing his arms around her.

"Sorry I'm late." She smiled up at him.

"You don't look the least bit sorry."

"That's because I'm so glad to see you!"

"Well," Will said putting a hand lightly between her shoulder blades and guiding her to the restaurant door, "you can apologize profusely once we've sat down. I trust they haven't given our table away yet."

The restaurant was small, French, and comfortably dim. Will ordered a half bottle of wine to go with their meal.

Branwen protested. "Will! We can't drink in the middle of the day!"

"Sure we can. With French food, wine is practically a requirement. *Comme il faut. De rigueur. Absolument!*"

"I see." Branwen suppressed a giggle. "Another one of those decadent French ideas."

Will opened his eyes wide and raised his eyebrows, making his high forehead seem even higher. "Do I look like the sort of person who would do decadent stuff?"

"Decadent *stuff*?" Now Branwen laughed. She couldn't help it. She shook her head, and her hair swayed about her face. "No.

As a matter of fact, you're just about the most innocent-looking person I know—of your age and sex, that is." She looked at him seriously and realized what she'd said was true. When he wasn't clowning, his face was open and honest, almost painfully so.

"Well, anyway," he said, "I don't think either of us can get in too much trouble with half a bottle of wine. Especially since we're going for a nice long walk after lunch."

"Good." Branwen nodded. "It's a glorious day for it."

Their meal came, accompanied by the wine: Coquilles St. Jacques for both of them, followed by a green salad and dessert from the pastry cart.

Will watched Branwen with her chocolate mousse, and wondered what was wrong. He always got a kick out of the way she devoured anything chocolate, just like a little kid; but she wasn't doing that today. Today she was eating the mousse automatically, without the little satisfied smile and that incredible licking with her tongue that made him hot in places he wasn't supposed to be hot when he was with her. And she was too quiet. In the course of their friendship, each of them had learned from the other. Will had learned from naturally quiet Branwen to enjoy long periods of silence; further, he had learned the subtle difference between Branwen's okay silences and the ones when something was troubling her. Branwen had learned from Will how to come out of her self-containment, had learned that she could say anything that came into her head if she wanted to. Nothing terrible would happen. This silence of hers, particularly with the evidence of not enjoying her chocolate, was the troubled kind.

"Something's on your mind. Want to tell me what's bothering you?"

Branwen made a self-deprecating half smile that pulled the corners of her mouth down instead of up. "It's that obvious, is it?"

"Honey chile, when you don't go into ecstasy over chocolate *anything*, I know something's wrong!"

"Nothing's really wrong. I just had a disappointment this morning and I haven't let go of it yet."

"Tell me," Will urged softly.

"I went to Georgetown University earlier. That's what made me late. I left my car over there, and it was a longer walk than I'd thought it would be." She stopped. It was hard to talk about

something she'd kept to herself for so long, especially as it had
turned out the way it had. "I guess I really should tell you, since
in a very real way I wouldn't have been there at all if it weren't
for you. For the influence you've had on me."

"Uh-oh!" He said it playfully, but his eyes were watchful.

Branwen took a deep breath and plunged on. "I talked this
morning to the Dean of Admissions about coming in as a senior
transfer student. You see, I had this crazy idea that I might get
my degree in journalism instead of English, and they don't
teach journalism at Redmund. I'm almost through with my
course work, and I started thinking: What am I going to *do* with
this degree? I don't want to teach, and I do like to write, and
there are so many fascinating, important things going on now!
Civil rights, the Peace Movement, the whole scene with so-
called hippies, drugs, all of that. This is an exciting, vital time,
Will, and you are the person who showed me and got me started
thinking about these things. Redmund College is still so insu-
lated it hasn't even occurred to anyone that the only blacks on
campus are there to clean the buildings! And I'm sick of it, I really am. So I thought perhaps I could transfer to Georgetown
and get a degree in journalism, even though I wouldn't finish as
soon as I would if I stay at Redmund."

"I agree with everything you've said. So what's the problem?"

Branwen sighed. Her lashes came down and concealed her
eyes. "I'm stupid, that's the problem, I—"

Will interrupted, leaning across the table. He grasped her
hand and tightened his hold until she looked at him. "You are
not stupid, and don't ever say that again, even if you're joking!
If your grades aren't what they want for transfer . . ."

"It's not the grades, Will." Branwen smiled wanly. "My
grades are fine. The dean said they'd be glad to accept all my
courses from Redmund. The problem is that it's too expensive.
I have money saved, of course I knew I would have tuition to
pay, but I never even dreamed it could cost so much! That's why
I said I'm stupid."

"Oh. I see." Will released his hold on her and leaned back. He
didn't know what to say. He made it a rule never to mention Jason Faraday's name between them, and he wasn't going to ask
why Jason wouldn't pay her tuition. So he kept silent and raised
his arm to signal the waiter for coffee.

Branwen, having said so much already, went on. "I was

stunned when the dean gave me that admissions material. I just sat there like an idiot, I was so embarrassed."

"Uh, Branwen, Redmund College isn't cheap. In fact, I always had the impression that it cost more to go there than just about anyplace around here, except maybe Johns Hopkins in Baltimore."

"Maybe it does. I think I get some sort of special rate for being the wife of a faculty member. Jason takes care of the tuition himself. I pay all the household bills, and I've never seen one for tuition, so I have no idea how much it is. Anyway, I sat there like an idiot with the admission papers in my lap, and of course the dean was ready for me to leave, but I was just sitting there, so he asked me what was wrong. I stammered out something about being sorry to have taken his time because I couldn't afford the tuition. I tried to give him the papers back, but he said to keep them, and he sent me to another office. Financial Aid."

"And?" Will could guess what must have happened—no way would the wife of Jason Faraday qualify for scholarships or loans. He saw Branwen's cheeks grow hot and her eyes film over with tears, and wished the dean could have spared her the embarrassment.

"And I saw a woman who wasn't nearly so sympathetic as the dean. She told me flat that if a wife wants to go to school and the husband can afford it, he has to pay. Financial assistance is for people who really need it, not for wives who just don't want to ask their husbands for money!" Branwen's voice cracked, and she swiftly ducked her head and gulped at her coffee. She had been, and still was, bitterly disappointed. She didn't want Will to see how near she was to crying.

They walked in silence along the tree-lined streets, working their way north and east. Will hadn't yet said where they were going. As far as Branwen knew they were just walking, enjoying the fresh fall air and the bright colors of the tall old trees.

"Ah, Branwen," Will said and cleared his throat. He'd be taking his biggest risk of all later, so why not one more now?

"Yes?" She looked up at him.

"Ah, I'd like to see you do the journalism thing at Georgetown."

Again that little turned-down smile and with it, this time, a shrug. "There's no way. Jason would probably accept my going there if he didn't find out until it was already an accomplished fact, and with him gone so much now I might even manage it without him knowing. But he's been more than generous already, putting me through Redmund. I can't ask him for Georgetown, too. I was foolish, that's all. I have to let it go."

"There is a way." Will stopped and faced her on the sidewalk. "You could let me loan you the money."

Branwen smiled. In spite of his serious expression, she was certain there must be a joke here somewhere. "Oh, sure," she said, "a few thousand more or less wouldn't matter to you a bit! You can always live on beans, with maybe a few cockroaches thrown in for extra protein, during all the years it would take me to pay you back. Right?"

He took her shoulders in his hands. "I'm serious, Branwen. I could loan you the money. I have plenty. Heck, I'd *give* it to you if I thought you'd take it. You'd make a great journalist. You have a fine mind and keen insight. I know you do. So often when we talk I'm struck by how you can grasp the big picture of an issue while I get bogged down in details. Say you'll take the money. I'd think of it as a good investment. That is," he ended, lightening up, "assuming you can *write*!"

"I can write." That response came automatically to her; as for the rest of it, she was too surprised to know what to say. For long minutes they stood looking at each other, and then she stepped back, out of his grasp. "I could never let you do that. Never!"

Will shrugged with a nonchalance he didn't feel, and ambled off down the sidewalk leaving her to follow. "Oh, well, that's what I thought you'd say. But I refuse to withdraw the offer. Maybe after you've thought about it you'll change your mind."

Branwen stood glued to her spot. She had so many conflicting emotions that she didn't know how she felt. She was paralyzed.

He looked back over his shoulder, grinning, his head at a rakish angle. He was his old self again, relaxed and easy as ever. Or so he seemed. "Come on, slow poke! We're almost there. You can't rest yet."

Branwen tossed her head and made her feet move. She could just keep up with Will's long legs if she concentrated. She didn't try to talk, didn't think to ask where they were going until he stopped in front of a tall, narrow, brick townhouse with dark green shutters and white trim.

"This is it," said Will. His heart was pounding, and his hands had gone cold. Anxiety. He cared too much. He stuck his hands in his pockets. "This is where we get to stop and rest."

"You've brought me to somebody's house? For a visit?"

"Yeah." He climbed the steps and took the key out of his pocket. He couldn't be casual anymore, couldn't pretend. The intensity of his need was written on his open face. "I brought you to visit *me*. This is my house, Branwen."

"We—we have an agreement, an understanding . . ." Branwen's voice trailed off as she absorbed, fully, the force of his expression. Until this moment she had not known that the keeping of their unspoken agreement not to be alone together was as hard for him as it was for her. Perhaps even harder.

"Please," he croaked, stretching out his hand to her. The yearning in his eyes and in the outstretched fingers pulled her to him, up the steps. Her heart thudded as their hands met.

"I know," he said deep in his throat, "I know what I'm doing." He pushed the door open and pulled her inside. The door closed behind them with a soft click. He brought her hand, captured in his, to his chest. With his other arm he drew her in and held her close, wrapped her to him until her head rested beneath his chin. He felt a faint tremor in her shoulders, felt the silky smoothness of her hair, felt her heart beating as hard as his own.

I should move away from him, Branwen thought. *This is wrong, after all the months we've been so careful. . . .* But the incredible comfort of being in Will's arms for the first time far surpassed self-imposed taboos against touching. She inched closer, and her free arm went around his waist, under his jacket.

Will expelled a heavy sigh, loaded with the release of a thousand thousand restraints. He closed his eyes and simply held the woman he loved in his arms. At last! He didn't think—he'd thought about this moment so many times in so many ways, he'd made himself sick with thinking, and now the time for thought was past.

Branwen heard Will's long, long sigh, felt the slowing of his heart. Her heart slowed, too, and she gave herself into the peace of being newly close in body to this man to whom she already felt so close in many other ways.

When at last Will moved, he bent to touch his lips to her cheek. She turned her head and tipped it up to look at him. He kissed her chin, her other cheek, the hollow of her throat. Her eyes closed, and her lashes lay dark and thick on her fine white skin. Will took Branwen's face in his hands and slowly, gently closed his lips over hers. Lovely, and beloved, so soft, so sweet. . . . He felt her response, the slightest quivering of her mouth under his. With exquisite care he traced the inner curves of her lips with the tip of his tongue. A tremor passed through her whole body then, and he ended the kiss. He felt like a man gone too long without water, who having found the life-giving fluid again must at first be careful not to drink too deeply.

For Branwen, Will's kisses were a revelation. Schooled to Jason's heavy sensuality, for her Will's tenderness was totally new. Each touch of his lips on her skin, on her mouth, brought a warmth that spread through her body until at last his tongue, so delicately arousing, burnished that spreading warmth into an all-pervading glow. That he stopped after the one kiss astonished her; and then she realized the rightness of it. She wrapped both her arms around him and put her head on his chest. She had never, ever felt quite this way before. She felt closer to Will after one kiss than she did to Jason after the most passionate sex. In his arms she felt utterly, completely safe and secure. She searched for a name for this feeling. Not satisfaction, no. *Happiness!*

Will was stroking her hair. Branwen thought muzzily, *This must be how cats feel when they purr.* She said, not moving her head from its comfortable place on Will's chest, "Is that why you brought me to your house?"

Will nuzzled at her hair. "Yes," he admitted, "although I didn't think it would happen when we were only three steps inside the front door!"

Branwen laughed softly, and at last moved away. "I didn't think it would ever happen at all!"

"Hmmm. Yeah. I guess we, uh, broke some new ground there." Suddenly uncomfortable, feeling a restless need to move, to break the spell, Will said, "As long as you're here, let me take you through the house. I grew up here, you know. This has been my home for practically as long as I can remember."

They began on the top floor, in the rooms that had been the nursery and his nanny's room. He'd had an English nanny, Will explained. And a younger sister.

Perhaps it was because she'd been so close to him, or perhaps it simply happened spontaneously, as it had sometimes at Llanfaren years before—but for whatever reason, as Branwen walked through Will Tracy's house she saw the rooms not as they were in the present, but as they had been in the past. She knew Will spoke to her and that she answered, but she was seeing glimpses of a younger Will everywhere. In the nursery was a sweet, fair-haired happy little child who asked too many questions and cried easily. In the hallway was a boy of about six, puzzled by his sister's quick temper and willing to give her anything she wanted to make her smile again. In his old room with the trophies of his school years on the walls was an older boy who had discovered books and could not get enough of reading—he sat in the window seat with an open book propped on bony young knees. Downstairs in the den was a moody, scholarly teenager, gawky and shy, with incredibly long arms and legs; he was telling jokes, having just found that he could make people laugh and that laughter somehow made life more bearable.

All these visions, in such rapid succession, left Branwen drained of energy. In the kitchen she realized she had to sit down, and she asked for a glass of water. Will brought the water and sat with her at the kitchen table.

"Are you all right?" he asked. "You look a little green around the gills all of a sudden."

"Just give me a minute." She wanted to tell him, but Will knew nothing of the psychic, intuitive side of her life. No one in the U.S. did except Harry, and of course Jason—to whom it meant nothing anyway. She was tempted to tell Will that she had such experiences, tell him that she had just been treated to a view of his growing-up years as if in a home movie run by so fast it was almost on fast forward. But she did not. From the visions she had learned a great deal about him, but she would have to digest it later, alone. There was not enough time to tell him today. Though he'd said nothing so far, she knew they had other important things to talk about.

"I'm fine," she said simply. She looked directly at him and saw with electrifying, beautiful clarity the man that Will-child had become. She saw further than mere face and body, she saw the spirit beneath: straight and strong and shining, without a trace of malice, without a hint of pretense.

"Branwen, why are you looking at me like that?"

"I was just wondering how you managed to grow up in this town and work here as an adult, when you almost always say exactly what you mean. How do you survive in Washington without having your own hidden agenda like everybody else?"

"Well," he said with a shrug, "it helps if you've always known, ever since you were a little kid, that you're kind of an oddball. You just accept yourself that way, and after a while other people do, too." He grinned and winked. "Of course, it doesn't hurt if your father happens to be a senator!"

"Not to mention being the King of Kentucky!" Branwen winked back. "And your father the senator, he didn't mind having a son who, shall we say, walked to the beat of a different drummer? Or your mother?"

"What an interesting question! Would you believe nobody ever asked me that before?" Will was, and wasn't, surprised. He'd wanted to have Branwen in the privacy of his home not just so that he could hold her, touch her, kiss her, but also to move their friendship into a new, deeper dimension. She was just naturally doing that—opening him up to her, and to himself, as well—and he was glad.

She smiled at him and waited.

Will said slowly, thinking as he went, "My father didn't seem to mind having an oddball son. My mother may not have noticed. I told you she died of cancer a couple of years ago. Well, she was a very special person, and I didn't realize it until she was gone. She was very kind and loving and had a reputation for being scatterbrained, but she wasn't, not really. Every now and then she'd come out with something so profound, so true, so right on the mark . . . she was, I guess, her own kind of oddball." After a short silence, he continued.

"That's funny. I never really thought about all this before. I'm sure they both knew I was different, but neither of them ever said a word about it. They just kind of let me be."

"How, in what way were you different?"

"Mainly I just felt different on the inside, ever since I can remember. Don't ask me why—I have no idea. I felt things I didn't have any words for. I thought about things other kids didn't think about. I agonized over them, actually. The way it came out to other people was I asked too many questions, I felt things so deeply and cried so easily that my sister called me a crybaby although she's younger than me. Stuff like that. Oh, and I hated competitive sports. All that emphasis on winning always turned me off, even when I did manage to play basketball at prep school. What I liked was reading. Learning to read was the greatest thing that ever happened to me! When I was real little, I had this favorite, favorite story, and I'll never forget how it felt to be able to read it for myself the first time. It was about a dog who belonged to himself. He wasn't a stray dog, or some little orphan mutt, he was this big, slightly scruffy but handsome dog who got along great without a master, and I *loved* that story. It's so silly, isn't it? But I identified with that dog. *The Dog Who Belonged to Himself.* I haven't thought about that in years!"

"I don't think it's silly." Branwen put her elbows on the table and her chin on her laced fingers. "Big, slightly scruffy but handsome—that's a pretty good description of you. You must have known how you were going to turn out."

Will looked embarrassed for a moment, then grinned. He reached across the table with his long arm and tugged playfully at one of Branwen's black locks. "Scruffy? How dare you call me scruffy!"

She batted at his hand, laughing. "I *hate* boys who pull my hair!"

"Oh, yeah?" He reached easily through Branwen's flailing hands and tweaked a long strand of hair on the other side of her head.

She came out of her chair, around the table, after him, crying, "Ya-ya, scruffy, scruffy! I'm going to pull your scruffy ears!" It was the way she'd played with her teasing brothers, and suddenly Branwen was no longer the young woman who always seemed years older than her true age. Her fingers darted, her hair flew, she giggled as she feinted and lunged for his ears. Will, laughing, defended himself halfheartedly while he pleaded in mock terror and an outlandish southern accent, "Have mussy, missy! Land sakes, honey chile!"

He tipped his chair perilously onto its back legs under her onslaught, and then with a whoop he shot forward and grabbed Branwen around the waist. She fell into his lap, squirmed around, reached up, and grabbed both his ears. Eyes dancing, she declared triumphantly, "Gotcha!"

"Ah," said Will, squeezing her small waist in his big hands, "but I also got you!"

In an instant, all playfulness vanished.

"Oh, Will," Branwen said. Her fingers traced the curve of his ears, stroked their soft lobes. His hands moved from her waist, higher, until the swell of her breasts met his palms. On his face was an incredible expression, a mixture of hunger and pain and naked longing.

"What are we doing?" she whispered.

"I believe," he said firmly, "that I am about to make love to you. Unless you stop me."

She didn't stop him. She clung to him in continuing wonder as their kisses lengthened and deepened and the warm glow he kindled through her whole body became a flame that was more than desire. It was a longing for union, as if he were a missing part of herself and she was incomplete until his body merged with hers. When he lifted her from his lap and set her on her feet so that they could walk up the stairs to his bed, she could hardly bear the brief separation.

Will was a gentle, thorough lover. Branwen luxuriated in touching his lean, hard body, as he touched hers. He was all long muscle, with one soft, golden clump of hair, a nest for the maleness of him that, erect, was proportionally long. Will's face, which so clearly showed every emotion, shone with joy as she touched him. His lips and hands seemed to know what she wanted. Or perhaps she simply wanted all he gave.

His coming into her was a request, not a command. He moved over her, with his heart in the depth of his hazel eyes, and spoke one word. "Now?"

"Yes," Branwen whispered.

He took her lips as he entered her in one long, sure stroke. He buried his shaft in her to the hilt, and held. She felt him inside her, and with that joining came a completeness she had never known. She cradled him, rocked with him, rode with him on an ever-rising golden tide of joy. Together they made heat and light and finally a mutual explosion of pure love.

When Will moved to lie at her side, she moved with him, unwilling to relinquish the feel of his skin against hers. "How can it be so different, so perfect?" she murmured, unaware that she spoke aloud.

Will heard her and understood. He had been thinking much the same thing. He brushed her hair back from where it flowed over his shoulder, hiding her face from him. With his fingers along the curve of her jaw, he turned her face up so that he could look into her eyes. Her skin, usually so white, still glowed pink from their recent pleasure. The complete trust in her eyes pierced his heart.

"I think," he said, "it's perfect because we love each other. We've loved each other a long time already, Branwen."

She felt a burning surge in her chest—Will had stabbed her

with the truth. A truth she hadn't wanted to let surface in her mind, not ever, because she couldn't bear to think where it might lead. She threw her arm and one leg over him and buried her head against his neck. He held her tight, both glad and sorry that he couldn't imagine what she was thinking.

He cleared his throat. It was hard to speak, but necessary now. "I didn't mean to make love to you today. I just thought it was time to let you know I couldn't go on any longer pretending to be just your friend." He tightened his arm around her and she, too, tightened her grip on him. But she said nothing, and he went on. "I knew I would have to . . . touch you. Hold you in my arms, kiss you. I've wanted to do those things for so long that I knew when we were alone I would at least try. And I thought you've wanted it, too."

"Yes," she said, her voice muffled below his ear.

Will smiled and began to stroke her hair. Such wonderful hair! It felt like fine, tangled silk. "And then I thought we would talk. About the forbidden subject, your marriage. What it means to you, how much longer you have to stay in it. Because," he said, lowering his voice to a husky whisper, "you know we belong together, Branwen."

It was not until she raised her head and pushed herself away from him that he realized she'd been crying. His neck and shoulder were wet from her tears, and cold now that her warmth was gone; his whole body was cold, and his soul went cold at her next words.

Branwen sat cross-legged on Will's bed, straight and tall, unconscious of her nakedness. She tossed her head and her hair fell back over her shoulders. With her bare breasts and her dark-fringed eyes she lacked only a tall crown to look like an Egyptian queen. Her face was lovely and still, but inside her heart was breaking.

"I have to leave now," she said. "It's too late, too late in the day and too late after what we've done to talk. You're right—I don't love Jason Faraday, and I've known for some time that I never will." Her voice, and her composure, wavered. "I may love you. You are the . . . the best friend, the dearest friend I've ever had. But I'm Jason's wife, and m-making love with you today doesn't change that."

Will reached for her, gripped her wrist, and held it too tightly. "You *could* change it. You could leave him!" He cursed himself for letting the words pass his lips, but he couldn't help himself.

It was the wrong time for such a suggestion, and he knew it, but he felt Branwen distancing herself from him although she hadn't moved an inch. Her wrist felt fragile as glass in his hand.

"No." She bowed her head, and her hair fell forward like a curtain over her face. Slowly, relentlessly, she fisted her hand and pulled her wrist in toward her body. She was not made of glass, but fine-tempered steel. He let her go.

She left the bed. Slowly she gathered her clothes and walked with them in her arms out into the hall to find the bathroom. Every step was pain. Desolation. She couldn't talk anymore, couldn't think, she only knew she had to get home. How strange that Redmund should be "home." Only a little while ago she'd felt the only home she would ever know, could ever need, was in Will.

He was waiting, fully dressed, at the top of the stairs when she emerged from the bathroom. "I'll drive you to your car," he said. She nodded. Her poncho and boots were in the kitchen, and she went to get them. Will followed. She had to sit down to put on the boots, and she couldn't stop him from helping her. He went down on his knees in front of her, and she tried to hide behind her hair and lashes.

"Hey, kiddo," he said softly, "this is me, your best friend. I *know* you, remember? I know how you withdraw when you think something's too much for you, but don't do it with me. Okay? This is too important. This is *us*. Look at me, Branwen!"

She looked at him. She forced herself to say, "Okay."

Will sighed with relief, though the pain in her blue-green eyes hurt him, too. Still on his knees, he reached into the pocket of his jacket and brought out the turquoise and silver Indian necklace. "You forgot this. Lean down." She did, and he slipped the necklace over her head, with difficulty resisting the desire to hold her again. "Talk to me, please. Say something. Anything."

"I . . ." Her mouth was dry. She closed it, swallowed, tried again. "I *can't* talk. I can't think about . . . about *us*!" Her eyes filmed with tears. She blinked them back. "I have to go home, really I do. I know Jason is going to call, I feel it, and I must be there. I *must*!"

Panicky now, she started out of the chair, but Will prevented her. Still on his own knees, he placed his arm across her knees and again compelled her to look into his face. "You're afraid of him! Why? What has he done to you?"

"He gets so angry if I'm not there when he expects me to be. It's not what you're thinking, but I *have* to go! Please!"

Will removed his arm, and she flew from him, out of the kitchen. He caught up to her in the hallway where she stood trembling like a trapped animal, turning her head wildly from side to side. "I—I don't know where your car is!"

Her panic was all out of proportion. He had seen her in many moods, but never like this. He thought fear of her husband was responsible; he didn't realize that he, himself, was even more the cause of her panic. He had forced her to give up the detachment that was her only defense against feelings she could not handle. Will fought down his alarm and took her firmly in hand. "The car is in back. You jumped the gun a little bit, that's all. We have to go back through the kitchen."

They were caught in rush-hour traffic. The car crawled; Branwen sat bolt upright, only the seat belt keeping her from sitting on the edge of the seat. Suddenly she turned to him. "I know where I am, and I can walk the rest of the way faster than you can drive in this traffic. I'm going to get out here. Good-bye, Will."

Will groaned inwardly. He'd been thinking as he drove, and had been just about to put his thoughts into a persuasive speech about how they still needed to talk and he wouldn't take no for an answer. But she snapped the seat belt and was out of the car door so quickly that all he could say was "I'll call you!" The car door slammed on his words. He wasn't sure she'd heard him.

4

Darkness dropped down suddenly, a vast black cloak thrown over the land. Branwen drove on, through Arlington toward Manassas and beyond. She was shaking, shivering, and had endured it for many miles before she calmed enough to realize the shakes were as much external as internal. She was cold. The air inside the car was cold. She switched on the heater and immediately felt a bit better.

When the ego's integrity is threatened, the restoration of that integrity takes on an importance beside which everything, even much-desired and much-appreciated things, becomes secondary. In a usually stable person, this process is unconscious, and so it was with Branwen. She did not savor her brief, revelatory happiness with Will as she drove; nor did she, as she had under his insistence, struggle with its consequences. Just as the land now had its cloak of darkness, Branwen had regained her own cloak of inner silence. For Will's sake she had given it up when he asked, with near-disastrous consequences. Now she assumed it again. Had her silence been a death shroud she would just as surely have done so, for it was her ego's strongest defense.

She drove in inner and outer silence and pushed her Mustang beyond the speed limit. Her mind held only one thought: *Jason will call, and I must be there.* In her state of suppressed confusion, dislike of Jason's anger was no longer her prime motivation. It was, rather, that Jason had once effectively cast himself as Deliverer, and since that time he had come to represent stability in Branwen's life. Jason = Stability: an equation both irrational and invalid for the present day. But since she believed it on a level outside of conscious awareness, it acted on her temporarily threatened ego like axiomatic truth.

Stopped by traffic lights around Manassas, Branwen emerged from her numbed state to notice just how dark it had become. She gunned the car through a newly green signal. There was not enough light from the dash to look at her watch, nor could she afford the distraction of turning on the overhead light at the speed she was traveling. Her internal sense of time was usually quite good, but it had deserted her. She had no idea what time it might be.

"Jason *will* call," she muttered. She pounded the steering wheel with one hand, as if the car were a horse and she could urge it onward. Then, in the extremity of her need to make that irrational security-giving contact with Jason, she did something she had not done since Llanfaren: she reached out with her mind. She cast her mind onto the psychic plane, and threw out her plea: *I must be at home when he calls! Tell me, do I have enough time?*

The assurance came immediately, and she did not question from where. She would be in time; she would not miss his call. Her eyes dropped to the speedometer, and immediately her foot eased on the gas pedal. She'd had no idea she'd been driving so dangerously fast! She didn't question the certainty she felt, although in the normal course of events she would have; in the normal course of events, she would never have allowed herself to reach out like that at all.

Branwen left her car in the driveway and didn't take the time to open the garage. She unlocked the front door and let herself into the dark, still house. Exactly at that moment, the phone began to ring.

"Come, my dear," Harry Ravenscroft coaxed, "you can tell your uncle Harry. What has happened to drive the spark from your eyes and the roses from your cheeks?"

Branwen's responding smile was thin and pale in a thin, pale face. She'd lost weight of late, and she'd had little excess to lose. She'd taken to wearing her hair in a severe manner, pulled back straight and tight against her skull, the length of it coiled 'round and 'round at the back of her head. The style made her face look all eyes, and those eyes were shadowed, melancholy.

She said, "You have been and I expect will be many things to me, Harry, but uncle? No, that doesn't feel right at all. Now if you want me to translate this arcane bit of old Welsh—which by the way is closer to Gaelic, and I'm not at all sure I can make it out—I suggest you leave me alone. Go in your library and read a book. Or go outside and consult your gods and find out if it's going to snow before Thanksgiving."

"It never snows in Virginia before Thanksgiving."

"There's always a first time for everything."

"Don't be trite, Branwen, it's beneath you," Harry grumbled. Clearly she wasn't going to confide in him. She could shut out anyone and anything when she wanted to, and she obviously wanted to shut him out now. This ability of hers to completely isolate herself was psychic ability, whether she knew it or not— she'd had it ever since he'd known her, to some degree. Now she had virtually perfected it in dealing for the past three weeks with whatever was bothering her. When he sent his mind out to probe hers, he encountered a wall that to his own psychic sense felt like foot-thick glass, hard and cold and deceptively crystal-clear. She bent over her task, not two feet from him, but absolutely unreachable. Maddening!

Having no alternative he could think of, Harry got up and left the study. Maybe he would go outside after all. He kept an old, dark gray, loden cloth cape in the vestibule where the kitchen wing met the main house. He went to get it. Branwen was right, the weather was unusually cold for November. The sky had looked like snow, the air had felt like snow earlier in the day, no matter what that lamebrain weather forecaster on Channel 8 said.

Mrs. Beecher popped her wiry little body out of the kitchen as he reached for his cape. "You and Miss Branwen be wantin' tea later?" she asked.

"Yes, I think so. Put it in the library. Oh, and, Mrs. Beecher, do we have any of that excellent shortbread you made earlier in the week?" She nodded. "Good. Put that out, too. In about an hour. I'm going for a walk."

"Bain't a good day for a walk," she remarked, watching Harry with shrewd, birdlike eyes as he swung the cape over his shoulders. "Still and all, I s'pose you'll be warm enough in that thing."

"Yes, I suppose I will," agreed Harry with a wicked grin. He knew his housekeeper-cook did not like his old cape, for precisely the reason he himself liked it very much. She thought it made him look like, as she said, "a witch-man." He preferred to think it made him look like a wizard, which in precise terminology was not quite the same thing; but in Mrs. Beecher's parlance the two were near enough as made no difference.

The wind was cold; it whipped the cape about his legs and streamed his longish silvery hair back from his face. With his height and his high-cheekboned ascetic mien, he was a striking figure. Harry trod an oblique track down the incline beyond the terrace and turned to look up at Raven Hill. Smoke rose from the chimneys, and the house was a picture of colonial squire-ish comfort. The low, leaden-white clouds of earlier in the day were thinning; off to the West there was a translucent brightness where the sun shone through. He put his head back and looked straight up, where the wind drove the low-lying thick cloud cover into a turbulence. He lost himself in the ponderously slow-swirling movement for a while. He wished he could, in fact, change himself into a raven; or better, some bigger bird—an owl, perhaps. Yes. A great, wise, snowy owl with a huge wingspan. He would mount the clouds and ride the very wind—Ah!

Harry put up the collar of the cape and began to walk again. He was restless. More so every day. He did not want to be here; he wanted to be in England. No, where he really wanted to be was in Scotland, in the northern part where all was rocky and bleak and cold. Oh, it would be fine to spend the winter on the sacred Isle of Iona!

At the bottom of his hill he turned and began to walk in a wide circle. He would return to the front of the house. Beecher was out in the meadow on the garden tractor—the old fool was still cutting grass at this time of year. Harry waved, but Beecher didn't see. Harry walked on, rubbing his nose. He was walking straight into the wind now. It stung his nostrils and made his eyes tear.

Yes, it would be fine to spend the winter on Iona. He hadn't been anywhere in a couple of years, and his reserve funds were building up nicely. He could afford it. Could afford to spend the money, yes, but the time was not right. Something was going on with Branwen. Probably with Jason, too, although Jason didn't matter except as he infringed on Branwen. She was under some sort of stress, that was certain, and just at a time when Harry had made some inroads into her reluctance to use her psychic abilities. He flexed his fingers—they tingled with the memory of how it had been in Llanfaren Castle's Fifth Tower, his power and Branwen's in tandem—he had even been able, when they left the Tower, to turn the pivot stone with a raised hand and his mind's command! She might not have been aware that he'd moved the stone, but he'd been very excited about it. He hadn't been able to do anything like that on his own before or since, at least not in this lifetime. And then, after that experience, she had just shut herself off, like turning off a water faucet!

Well, never mind. She'd do it again, perhaps soon. He'd been grooming her slowly, carefully, never using the word "Sight," because for some reason that put her off; remembering, at least most of the time, to say "intuitive" rather than "psychic" when talking of such matters to her. Intuition developed to Branwen's degree was the same thing as psychic power anyway ... the word "intuition" was just more acceptable to most people.

I should get out and walk more, thought Harry. He was at the bottom of the hill at the front of the house now, although the angle of the slope hid it from view. He decided to take the easy way, up the paved drive. Yes, he definitely should walk more, or else when he did get back to England, or Scotland, he was going to find himself in awful shape for all the walking he would have to do there.

Halfway up the drive he had to stop and rest. Maybe whatever was wrong with Branwen could be turned to advantage. The stress she was under was making her use her psychic sense more—Harry could feel it—and he was sure Branwen was unaware that she was doing so. If, for example, he could subtly point out to her what she was already doing, catch her in the act, so to speak. . . . His back was to the wind again as he stood there resting, and his hair blew about his face and got into his eyes. He pushed it back impatiently; in his youth he'd envied men with thick, coarse hair that no amount of wind could blow about. Still did, actually. Jason had such hair.

Jason! Harry got going again. Jason was up to something—Harry wished he knew what. The man seldom bothered to attend faculty meetings or social functions these days. Sometimes he required Branwen to go alone, representing them both; and when he did, she took Harry as her escort. Jason would've been furious if he knew, but who would tell him? He'd distanced himself from everyone by his long absences, even his students, who complained at having so many lectures delivered by the teaching assistant. Bastard would lose his appointment if he wasn't careful. The one thing Jason didn't have on campus was tenure. Then again, he didn't have a regular appointment either, but there he was and there he had been, and there he would most likely stay in spite of abuses other people couldn't get away with. Someday, Harry thought, he'd like to know who was responsible for putting Jason Faraday on the faculty of Redmund College.

Harry mounted the steps from the porte cochere and paused. He turned his back on Raven Hill, as if to survey his land from this splendid site his ancestors had chosen. But he wasn't looking; he was thinking about the complexity of his relationship to Branwen. So she wouldn't call him uncle! He smiled wistfully. He was old enough to be her father—but a lot of men loved and married women that much younger than themselves. It wasn't *her* age that bothered him, it was his own. He felt too old for her, and yet at the same time he was sure that if he were younger, he would have wanted to take Branwen away from Jason and marry her himself. He had been slowly falling in love with her over all the months she'd worked for him. He liked having her in his house. For a wonder, so did Mrs. Beecher. The old lady was positively dotty about Branwen.

Harry took a last look at the sky. He would go in, wearing his cape and looking like a wizard, and tell Branwen he'd made an incantation to change the weather. Whatever his boyish dreams of her might be, he would keep to the role of friend and mentor. The time was at hand when he could push her to use her "intuition," he was sure of it. In her present distress, whatever the cause, her psychic powers could help her. They came out of the strongest part of herself. He must tell her that; in his mentor role, he must make her see. Somehow he would have to get her to tell him what was wrong.

Branwen and Mrs. Beecher were both in the library, waiting for Harry. The drum table, covered with a crocheted cloth in the pineapple pattern, was set for tea. He walked into the room, lifted his arms to spread the cape like great wings, and said grandly, "There will be no snow. I made an incantation and sent the clouds away!"

"Fiddlesticks!" said Mrs. Beecher.

Branwen laughed. "Wherever did you get that cape?"

"Tran-syl-va-nia," said Harry in a Bela Lugosi voice. He took off the cape, threw it over a chair, and said normally, "Really, I did. In my reckless youth."

"Humph," said Mrs. Beecher, "I s'pect in yer reckless youth ye could walk faster than y'do now, even if yer taste in clothes weren't no better. I'll make another pot of tea. Like as not this one's gone stone-cold."

"I never get tired of listening to the way she talks," Branwen said when she was gone.

"You're specially favored," said Harry. "The truth about Mrs. B. is that she doesn't talk much. She talks around you because she likes you. Sometimes she goes for days without even talking to me. I presume she does speak to her husband, but I wouldn't be surprised if she didn't."

"Here ye are," said the lady returning, "nice and hot. If ye like th' shortbread, Miss Branwen, I'll give ye some to take home."

"Well, we'll see." Branwen smiled.

"Come on," said Harry impatiently, "sit, sit. That will be all, Mrs. Beecher."

"I'm sure," she sniffed, and left the library.

Harry chuckled. Branwen poured, and for a while they sat in silence over their tea.

"If you don't eat at least two pieces of shortbread, Mrs. B. will be crushed," Harry ventured.

Branwen nodded, and obediently bit into a tender, golden wedge.

"Why are you losing weight?" he asked bluntly.

Her eyes were wary. "I . . . well, food just doesn't taste very good right now."

"You're not sick, are you? I wouldn't want you coming here if you ought to be resting in bed."

"No, Harry. I'm not sick."

"Well, I'm glad of that."

Silence. She continued to eat shortbread, drink tea, in small bites and tiny sips.

Well, thought Harry, *I'm not getting anywhere like this.* He decided to try something different. He leaned back and let his body slouch carelessly, but he honed his mind to a cutting edge. Over and over he sent the command: *Talk to me!* Her guard was down—no glass wall—he was sure he reached her.

When she began to speak, what she said surprised him. "Harry, do you believe in reincarnation?"

"Yes, of course. Not necessarily the Hindu kind, souls in animals and all that. I believe what your remote forebears believed, Branwen."

"The pre-Christian Celts, you mean?" That brought a small smile from her. So much of their friendship was tied up in the pre-Christian Celtic. Harry nodded, and she said, "Tell me. Tell me how it works."

"Branwen, you already know. You don't need me to tell you. Why do you ask?"

She traced the pineapple pattern of the tablecloth with a slender finger that trembled slightly. She caught her lower lip in her teeth and drew in an irregular gulp of air. Harry kept silent. He continued to send his message: *Talk to me!*

Without looking up Branwen said crossly, "Don't do that!"

"Don't do what?"

"Don't put your words in my head like that, I don't like it!"

Harry blinked. This was progress of a sort. "I was doing it for your own good."

"You'd help me more if you'll just tell me what you believe about reincarnation."

"All right. I believe we humans are merely spirits clothed in a body. The body is born, grows old, dies. The spirit continues. Before birth and after death the spirit lives on another plane that is inaccessible for most people. Some people"—Harry was tempted to say "like you and me," but he did not—"retain their memory, their understanding of their former lives and their ability to function in a limited way in contact with that other plane, while they are living in body. Generally such people, whether their chronological age is three or one hundred and three, are old souls. They have wisdom, or at least experience gained from having lived many times."

"Please go on."

Harry looked at Branwen curiously. How much did she want? And *why*? What was this all about? But she was watching him steadily now, and there was life in those huge, sad eyes. "I tend to be skeptical of people who say they recall a life as someone famous. I doubt for most of us, even the most advanced, the recall is that clear. Under hypnosis, perhaps. I do believe we can have a sense of who we were, where we lived, that kind of thing. Most importantly, we can often retain knowledge that there is no way we could have gotten in our current lifetime. Am I telling you anything new, Branwen?"

"No, and yes. What about destiny, karma?"

"We tend to have the same situations, the same problems, even some of the same people, crop up in our lives over and over again. That's because there is something we have to learn from the situation, the problem, or the person, and we haven't done it yet. In other lives we didn't handle the situation or solve the problem or get the relationship with the person right. That's karma. Destiny is just another word for the same thing. And our strongest personality traits are attributes of our souls, not our bodies. A person who is tenacious in one life will almost surely be tenacious in another, for example. That, too, is karma."

"Ah!" said Branwen. "The same people! How do we know if we've known them before?"

"Usually we can feel it. Even someone who never heard of reincarnation and wouldn't believe in it if it were explained will have a sense on first meeting of having known certain people before. And it seems to be true that we tend to have the same close relationships over and over again because we're naturally attracted to those we've known in other lifetimes. We achieve intimacy with them more easily."

By the abstracted look in her eyes and the halting manner in which she spoke, Harry knew that Branwen had moved from his explanations into her own experience. His ears pricked up as she said, "There are ties that bind us to other people for reasons we don't fully understand. I mean, we can feel . . . all tangled up with them. Confused. Much more than the present reality warrants. It feels . . . it really feels as if it has happened before and has happened all over again whether we want it to or not."

Harry seldom prayed, for the very good reason that he was never sure to whom or what he should pray, but he did so now. He was beginning to understand. He prayed that he would say the truth, and that the truth would be what she needed to hear. "Branwen, the whole purpose of living over and over is so that we should *grow* from one life to the next. Sometimes we've made wrong choices, unhealthy choices—that is, choices that don't help our essential spirit to grow. In our relationships with others, sometimes that bond we feel over many lifetimes is positive, in which case we value it and don't question or struggle against it. But sometimes it's the opposite, it doesn't help us to grow. Sometimes the whole purpose of a single lifetime is to break a bond that has become unhealthy . . . and that's very, very hard to do."

Harry suddenly realized he was sweating although he'd neglected to light the fire in the fireplace, and the room was cool. He'd had to break such a bond once, and he remembered all too clearly. It had been horrible. He still dreamed, on rare and terrible occasions, that the woman—or sometimes it was a man, the same soul in either male or female form—came back and he had to break the bond again. A nightmare!

"And sometimes," Branwen murmured as if talking to herself, "we meet a person, a . . . soul, who is entirely new. Where was he all those many, many years? How is it possible . . . ?" She shook herself out of the reverie and spoke to Harry again. "I've never thought much of religion, Harry, the ancient *or* the modern kind. But reincarnation is the only thing that makes any sense of what's going on in my life right now. I have a terrible problem, and I feel so *stuck*. I've been going 'round and 'round with it."

Harry nodded. This he understood well.

She went on. "Then a couple of nights ago, as I was falling asleep, this thought came in my head: I've felt like this before. Not before, as in last week or last year. *Before*. I was still thinking it when I woke up the next morning."

"That's why you asked about reincarnation."

"Yes. It just . . . . came to me. I suppose I do believe it. I suppose it accounts for my knowing things and not knowing how or why I know them. Karma?" She smiled and shook her head. "I'm not sure I like the word. It sounds so suspiciously foreign. Occult. But if it works the way you explained, it would certainly account for why I feel stuck."

Harry was incredulous. Some things about Branwen he had just naturally assumed, and a belief in reincarnation was one of them. "Do you mean to tell me you haven't always shared in this basic belief of your ancestors?"

"No. I've never thought about it before now. I think you forget something I told you years ago, Harry: that my mother didn't want me taught the old ways. She took me to church, she took all of us to church, and I didn't like it much. I've never had what you might call a spiritual education. Mam actively discouraged my grandmother from teaching me anything, especially after Grandmam told her I had the Sight. I did tell you this, I'm sure."

Harry nodded; he had indeed forgotten. What a shame the mother had not given the grandmother free rein! But then, if she had, then he would not be so strongly in the position of mentor and teacher, which was where he wanted to be.

While he seemed to be lost in his own thoughts, Branwen began to gather up the tea things. The clinking of cups and saucers regained his attention and he said, "Leave all that for Mrs. Beecher and listen to me. I'm concerned about you, Branwen, and you admitted just now that you do have a problem. Won't you tell me what it is? Let me help you?"

She shook her head. "You can't help, Harry. I don't think anyone can, especially not you."

"I don't see why not!" Harry appeared wounded. "Don't you think your old friend Harry Ravenscroft has at least a little wisdom?"

Branwen smiled; she didn't want to hurt him. "I'll grant you that in your great cape you look a bit like a wizard, and wizards are supposed to be wise."

"Well, then . . . ?" He was mollified.

Branwen turned away. She had just remembered something. The memory seemed to come from an old place inside herself, and it came in a flash of brief vision: Wizards, a wizard . . . wizards dazzle by doing tricks. A puff of smoke, a flash of light, shapes in a glass, in a mirror . . . all appearance only. They may not know all they appear to know, may not be as wise as they appear to be.

She left the table and went to stand at the long window so that her back was to Harry. Was this a memory from a former life? Was it why, no matter how much affection she felt for him, she didn't entirely trust Harry? Even if she could trust him, she knew he couldn't help her. She knew, too, that he was more likely to let her be if she went ahead and told him. "If I tell you, Harry," she said, her back still to him, "I believe even you must see why this is something *no one* can help me with."

"Try me." Harry had every sense focused on Branwen. His gray eyes were almost silvery with concentration.

She turned to face him. "Will Tracy says he is in love with me." Her chin came up a notch, but her face grew a shade paler.

"I've had to admit to myself that I love him, too. But I'm married to Jason. More than that, I feel . . . *bound* to him. This is what has me stuck, and I have to handle it my own way."

"I see," said Harry gravely. He did not offer advice because he knew her well enough to understand how profound a conflict this must produce in her. Yet he had to do *something*; he couldn't just sit there and watch the internal suffering written all over her. He picked up his voluminous cape, went to Branwen, put his arm around her, and drew the cape around them both. She huddled against him gratefully.

"Come," he said, "we'll watch the sunset together. The fresh air will revive you. And then you can go home."

Later, when she had gone, Harry built up the fire in the library and sat by it in his favorite wing chair. He thought about Branwen and Jason. Was there a karmic bond between those two? Quite likely. Such a bond would account for a number of things, principally Jason's instant obsession with her. And why Branwen who was in all other ways possessed of extraordinary good sense showed little of it where her husband was concerned. Surely, logically, it must follow that if there was a karmic link between Branwen and Jason, and (as he was certain) between Branwen and himself, then there must be a third link between him and Jason. . . .

Few things in the universe could make Harry Ravenscroft shudder, but now, in spite of the roaring fire, he shuddered. He was no longer concerned with anything so immediate as Branwen's problems. He had lost himself in a timeless void where he struggled with his own angels or demons, not knowing which was which. It had been ever thus, that he could not tell the one from the other. His body quaked until he shook the heavy wing chair. At last the chair's vibrations brought him back, panting and sweating, from where he'd been.

I need a drink, thought Harry—who seldom drank, and when he did, only lightly. His legs refused to support him on the first attempt. He tried again, rising stiffly to his feet, clutching the arms and then the back of the chair for support. The first finger of brandy in the glass he poured right down his throat and scarcely felt it. The second he downed more slowly, still standing with the decanter to hand. The third he took back with him as he sank exhaustedly into his favorite chair. He waited for the understanding he could presume, from other such experiences, would come.

There was movement in the Darkness, that much Harry knew. He had felt it. He felt it still, or the echo of it, like the stirring of a great lumbering blind beast. "And what rough beast," Harry quoted the lines of the poet W. B. Yeats in his mind, "its hour come round at last, Slouches towards Bethlehem to be born?"

"Nonsense!" he said aloud. Not that he dismissed the poem, whose powerful imagery had appealed to him as a student and, apparently, was with him still. Rather, he dismissed the whole concept of the poem's title, "The Second Coming."

"Antichrist, indeed!" Harry snorted. He acknowledged neither God nor Devil in the sense of the world's great religions, and therefore, neither Good nor Evil. No, Harry believed only in the unseen Energy that fueled the "miracles," Energy he was convinced he himself had once possessed and was determined to have again at his command. He knew also that the Energy was invested in the archetypal symbols of Light and Darkness. In all Harry's long existence, he had never discriminated between powers of Light and powers of Darkness—he cared only for the manifestation of the power itself. He made no value judgments.

Harry sipped brandy and gazed into the flames. Great power, a great source of energy was moving. Out of Darkness. Yes, he had felt it. He had moved into that space, been propelled into it really, by acknowledgment of the triangle composed by himself, Branwen, and Jason. Whatever it was would touch them all. This was exciting, was it not? The great wheel of destiny had been set in motion that morning a few years back when he and Jason had first seen Branwen, sweeping the ramp at Llanfaren Castle. She must be aware of it on some level, and so must Jason. Yes, it was exciting.

Then why was he so afraid?

"Nonsense!" he spat the word into the fire, but the fear did not leave him. *I am afraid,* he thought, *because it is Darkness that stirs and swirls with a groping, growing power. Yet I have never feared the Dark before now. We're in for a rough time, the three of us, together or separately.* He gulped the brandy remaining in his glass.

As Harry stared brooding into the dying flames, more of Yeats's poem came to him. He recited, hearing the words in his

own voice drop from his tongue to dissolve in the shadowy
reaches of the room:

> Turning and turning in the widening gyre
> The falcon cannot hear the falconer;
> Things fall apart; the centre cannot hold;
> Mere anarchy is loosed upon the world,
> The blood-dimmed tide is loosed, and everywhere
> The ceremony of innocence is drowned. . . .

5

"A month is a long time to keep me—to keep us both—waiting, Branwen," said Will. They sat in his living room because he had insisted they could not talk about the things they needed to discuss unless they had complete privacy. He'd had to argue, which he hated to do, in order to get her to agree to come to his house, but finally she had relented. She was here, somberly dressed in a gray suit, white blouse, and black shoes. Her hair was parted in the middle and pulled back tightly into a bun on the nape of her neck. A severe style, but he liked it because it reminded him of the way she'd worn it on the night they had first met. His heart ached at the sight of her—but less than it had ached in the weeks they'd been apart.

"I'm sorry," she said. She found it hard to look at him but forced herself. She would get through this somehow. "I didn't think it was safe for me to see you any sooner."

"*Safe?* You couldn't be safer anywhere than you are with me, Branwen! Surely you know that."

"I—I don't feel that way. I'm sorry."

"If you say you're sorry again, I'll—I'll pull your hair," Will said lightly, teasing. He felt anything but lighthearted; his pulse was pounding so loudly in his ears he could scarcely hear himself speak. He knew by everything about her—the clothes she wore, the way she sat, the expression in her eyes, even the hue of her skin—what she was going to tell him. His job would be to change her mind.

Branwen ignored his remark, going straight to the center of what she had to say and do. "You and I have been too close, Will. We went too far. I think you know that, and you know what I meant earlier about feeling safe."

Will found he could not possibly sit still for this. He got up and paced as he spoke. "Yes, I know what you meant, but you chose the wrong word. *You* are perfectly safe with me. It is only your marriage that may not be."

Branwen looked up at him. He was so tall, and yet not the least bit formidable. She loved every inch of that long, lanky body. Her fingertips, her lips and tongue, her very skin, remembered all too well. Her mouth was dry; she had to swallow and moisten her tingling lips and tongue before she could speak again. "I came here this afternoon hoping that if I explain to you why I married Jason, you will understand that I can't walk out of my marriage. But now I realize that you can't ever really understand. There's no point in explanations. You don't know how different life is in Wales. How limited the possibilities are. Arranged marriages still do happen there, and my marriage from that point of view is as good or better than most. Where I come from people marry and they *stay* married." She stood and faced him, squaring her shoulders. "The *fact*, Will, the only important fact, is that I married Jason of my own free will. I made the choice, and I intend to continue to honor it."

"I don't believe you made such a choice of your own free will." Will was seldom angry, but he was angry now. A nerve twitched in his jaw as he fought to keep the anger out of his voice. "The man is a well-known manipulator. He must have manipulated you, taken advantage of you somehow!"

"I'm not going to argue with you. You must simply accept that we can't see each other anymore. If you can't accept it, then—well, you just can't." She picked up her purse from where she had been sitting on the couch. "I'll get my coat and let myself out."

"Wait!" he yelled. More quietly he appealed to her. "Please wait. I listened to you, now listen to me."

Branwen waited, though the strength she'd gathered to face this meeting was nearly gone.

"Sit down again," Will whispered. He saw her exhaustion and gently urged her to the nearest chair. He went down on one knee beside her. His anger had disappeared as quickly as it had come. "Branwen, we've been friends, haven't we?"

She nodded, her head bowed, too miserable to look at him.

"Then let's keep our friendship. I love you, but I won't try to make love to you again."

"I love you, too," she said in a halting, strangled whisper. She raised her head. Her eyes were dark and damp in her white face. "That's why it will never work. It will tear us both apart if we continue to see each other. I wish to God we had never met! I don't understand, if we weren't meant to be together, why this had to happen!"

"Oh, Branwen!" Will drew her forward to rest her head on his shoulder. She looked near collapse. He'd thought he was in bad shape himself, but really she was much worse. All that earlier poise and rocklike calm had been only a veneer. He swayed, rocking her. "There's something my mother used to say at times like this. Well, almost as bad as this. Remember I told you she was supposed to be scatterbrained but she really wasn't? When we were all upset and crying and sure the world was coming to an end, she'd say, 'You are a child of the universe, no less than the trees and the stars you have a right to be here. And though it may not be clear to you, no doubt the universe is unfolding as it should.' I thought she made it up, but she didn't. The original is a much longer piece, and that's only a part of it. By that famous author Anonymous."

Branwen pulled away from him, her lips trembling in a painful attempt at a smile. "That's nice. I'll remember it—it does make me feel better. I think deep inside you must be very like your mother."

"Worse things could happen!" Will got to his feet and helped Branwen up. "You're a little unsteady. Stay a while longer. I'll make coffee, something to eat. You'll feel better. Then I'll drive you home in your car. I can always hitch a ride back or take a bus, or something."

"No. I really have to leave now. I can't stand to stay any longer. I'll be all right. I'll stop somewhere for coffee along the way, and I'll be fine." She backed away from him, her eyes still huge and damp with tears she refused to let fall, their blue-green darkened with inner shadows as the sea turns dark with approaching storm clouds.

"We *are* still friends," Will insisted as he helped her with her coat. "Nothing can ever change that."

Branwen looked up over her shoulder at him with mute appeal. The storm clouds were taking over in her eyes. Slowly, wordlessly, she simply shook her head: *No.*

Will opened the door for her and watched in silent agony as Branwen made her way down the steps and across the sidewalk to her car. In all the time he'd known her, he'd never seen her move so slowly, as if every step brought excruciating pain.

It's not over till it's over, thought Will, *and I'm a long, long way from giving up!*

Jason was, for once, at home for a couple of weeks and observant enough to note that his wife was not quite herself. She said she wasn't ill, though she certainly looked it. The feel of her fragile bones in his hands, against his own hard body, had always excited him and did still, but there was a subtle difference. The curves that bloomed into unexpected fullness at her breasts and hips no longer felt the same. He'd noticed that last night, when he made love to her as he always did, immediately on his return. And across the table at breakfast she'd *looked* sick, damn it, even if she denied it.

This was Saturday, a cold one even for December. He would have to go to his office, but he had no interest in it. Perhaps soon he wouldn't need the cover of the teaching job any longer. Redmund College bored him; even Washington bored him after the new horizons he'd seen. His future was opening up, it was close, so close now. He'd just returned from the Bahamas, and next he would go to Europe—he didn't know where in Europe yet since they wouldn't tell him until he was already on the plane. These new people were even more secretive than he was himself. He might not know where he was going, but he had a good idea what was going to happen. This would be it, the big assignment, the one that would make or break his future with them. They'd been testing him, he knew, building up to this. And he was absolutely sure this would be the making of him in their eyes. No one was going to break Jason Faraday! Not even if these guys were so powerful they made the U.S. Cabinet look like a kindergarten class!

Jason was all the more certain he was about to receive the make-or-break task because the meeting was arranged for Christmas week, and they had a thing about assigning important tasks around holidays. *And* they'd told him to plan to be away for three months. He would have to arrange a leave of absence. It could be done. Fake a medical leave, get a doctor to certify that he needed a long rest, no problem. He hadn't told Branwen yet, wouldn't tell her until the last possible minute. She could handle Christmas alone. It was a good thing, though, that he'd at least been home for a couple of days at Thanksgiving.

Had Branwen looked the way she did now at Thanksgiving? She must have; it wasn't that long ago, but he'd been in and out so fast he hadn't noticed. A surprising tenderness flowered in Jason's breast, and the tiny remnant that was all that remained of his conscience pricked at him. The office could wait—it was time he paid attention to his wife. She was studying in that wretched little breakfast room. Jason strode through the dining room and pushed through the swinging door.

Branwen heard Jason but didn't look up; she assumed he was just passing through on his way to the kitchen. She started in surprise when he squeezed his broad body into the bench beside her. "Jason!"

"Hi." Her hair was loose, long and heavy the way he liked it, and he lifted it away from the near side of her face to nuzzle her neck and nip at her earlobe.

Branwen raised her shoulder as a little shiver traveled involuntarily down her spine. She smiled. "I thought you had to go to your office."

"I do, but right now this is more important," Jason said. She was wearing stretch pants and one of his old cashmere sweaters that was far too big for her. He reached up under the sweater. As he'd expected, she wasn't wearing a bra. He took her breast in his hand, tested the weight of it against his palm, and, because he was holding the breast anyway, rubbed his thumb across her nipple to feel it harden and rise. As the nipple hardened, so did he . . . every time. This woman was better than an aphrodisiac drug!

"What you need, Jason Faraday, is a hobby, like other men. Why don't you take up golf? It's the middle of the morning, and I'm studying for an exam!"

Jason, ignoring her, said, "That's what I thought."

"What?" Branwen was completely baffled.

He gave her breast a final squeeze and removed his hand. "Your breast is smaller than it should be. Quite a bit smaller. You've lost a lot of weight, Branwen. Are you sure there isn't something wrong with you?"

She winced at his choice of words. She could hardly deny that something was wrong, and for a moment she couldn't think what to say. She lowered her eyelashes in the old way and after a tense moment said, "I swear to you I'm not sick. I'm just sort of . . . off my feed. These things happen."

Jason brooded. He rested his square jaw on his fist with his elbow on the table. A thought nagged from deep in the recesses of his mind, something about the way she'd said what she said. . . . At last he had it! His eyes narrowed, and he studied his wife. She had scrunched herself into a corner of the high-backed bench and put her knees up, her arms wrapped around them. Her feet were bare. She was so pale, her skin had lost its translucence, and she looked terribly vulnerable. He felt that heavy ache in his chest he used to feel, the tugging at his heart that had convinced him he loved her. Jason took a deep breath and asked the question: "Branwen, are you pregnant?"

She was so astonished that she couldn't utter a sound. Her eyes widened, and she clutched her knees more tightly and stared at her husband. He had the most incredible look on his face!

"Are you going to have a baby?" he insisted.

She was not pregnant; she'd had her period the previous week. Her mind tumbled. "W-would you mind very much if I were, Jason?"

"Hell's bells!" he exploded, tossing his big head. Sun through the window sparked the red lights in his thick hair. "I don't know!" He put his hands palm down on the table and pushed himself backward and up onto his feet. He worked his shoulders, rubbed his neck, and looked at his wife again. How could she curl herself up like that in such a constricted space? She was . . . so beautiful. "No," he said slowly, finding that his answer was a revelation, "I wouldn't mind. I might like to be a father. Found a dynasty. Is that what's wrong with you, Branwen? I've heard pregnancy makes you nauseous and some women lose weight at first. Of course they gain a lot later!"

He winked at her; he actually winked! And he regarded her with real interest for the first time in months. Branwen said carefully, "I'm not sure yet. It's too soon to tell. I promise that as soon as I know for certain that we're going to have a baby, I'll tell you, Jason. I'm so glad you won't be angry!"

"Angry? Of course not. How could a little baby growing inside my beautiful Branwen make me angry?" He leaned over and kissed her tenderly. "And now I hate to leave you, but I think I'd better go to the office for a while."

"I know. And I have to study." She waved a little dismissal, and he pushed through the swinging door, but he came back and kissed her one last time. She couldn't believe such tenderness, such solicitude.

The door swung shut behind Jason, and this time Branwen listened to his footsteps cross the hall, the front door open and close, his car starting. Her mind raced with new thoughts: *Why not have a baby?* Obviously it would make Jason happy, and that in itself would improve the marriage.

Her thoughts pushed on: *If I have a baby, I won't feel so lonely in this house that has never yet felt like home to me. A baby will fill that aching, empty place inside.*

The more she thought about it, the better she felt. Soon the baby was not just an idea, it was an all-consuming hope, a burning desire.

Hope for a child worked on Jason as well. The possibility of fatherhood tempered his lust and made him once more the skillfully considerate lover he had been with Branwen in the beginning. He would even have abstained from sex altogether if she'd asked him to, but she did not; in fact, quite the opposite. She sought him out and almost pathetically hung on his attentions. Jason was not to know, of course, how often the image of Will Tracy appeared behind her closed eyelids as Jason thrust into her, or how Will haunted her dreams. Branwen was convinced she would become pregnant, and she convinced herself too that in her pregnancy she would be able to forget Will. At last, she would truly feel love for her husband once he was the father of the child she would carry inside. She delighted in Jason's new attentiveness. In those two weeks they were happier than at any time since their honeymoon.

"When will you know for sure?" Jason asked. He noted with satisfaction that Branwen's health was steadily improving, and he congratulated himself that he was the cause. He looked at her as she lay in bed beside him, her dark hair spread fanlike beneath her head on the pillow, and he almost wished he did not have to leave her. Almost.

Branwen opened her eyes. "When will I know for sure about the baby?"

"Um-hm." Jason pulled the sheet and blanket up over her body, taking care of her and of his seed within her.

"It takes a while, Jason. The doctor likes you to have missed two periods, and I'm not that far along yet."

"Oh." He was disappointed. "But *you're* sure. I mean, you know how you feel. A woman can tell, can't she?"

"I think I am," said Branwen. This was true; she'd counted days and seen to it that they made love at least once a day right through her fertile time. She had also thought through what to say, however, just in case she turned out not to be with child. "You want this baby very much, don't you?"

"Yes," Jason admitted. His craggy face showed a sort of avaricious longing.

"Then don't worry." She smiled. "Now that I know you want a child as much as I do, it makes all the difference. If this turns out to be a false alarm, we'll just keep trying."

"Well, sure." Jason rolled away from her and stared at the ceiling. Now was the time to tell her. He'd hoped to know about the baby before he left, but if he couldn't, then he couldn't. His arrangements, including the leave of absence, were all made. Suddenly he dreaded leaving Branwen, wanted to take her with him so that he could watch over her, be sure she was taking care of herself. And of his baby. But of course he couldn't do that. He directed his words to the ceiling, unable to watch her face as he spoke. "Branwen, I have to go away again. I'm leaving the day after tomorrow, and I'll be gone three months."

The import of this announcement didn't sink in immediately since she was so used to his comings and goings. "Oh. Well, you'll come back for Christmas, of course."

"No, I won't." He leaned up on one elbow and risked a glance, since she seemed to be taking it so calmly. "What I have to do will require me to be away the entire three months. No back and forth."

"Jason!" Suddenly she realized what he'd said, and pushed herself up to sit with the pillow at her back. "You've never been gone so long before! And Christmas, Christmas is a family time. We should be together!"

"I'm sorry," said Jason heavily.

Branwen frowned. She didn't know what was going on here. Jason had never, as far as she could remember, said those words before. He never apologized for anything, to anyone, including her. He had a code, he had said once: Never apologize, never explain.

A part of Jason *was* sorry, and that part also wanted to explain. He didn't understand it himself. He weighed and measured in his mind how much would be safe to tell her. "Branwen, I'm going on the most important job I've ever had. I know you don't know much about my work—"

"Jason," she said wryly, "that is the understatement of the decade! I don't know *anything* about your work. And you told me I never would!"

"But you've wondered what I do?" The temptation to tell her more than he should was strong, so strong.

"Of course I've wondered. I decided a long time ago that you must work for the FBI or the CIA or something like that." She reached to the foot of the bed for her robe and put it on. She sensed that this conversation might go on for a while.

"Well, of those three possibilities, you'd be close to the mark if you picked 'something like that.' I make deals for people, Branwen. For people who are for one reason or another unable to do it themselves."

"People in Washington." She watched for Jason to nod his large head in confirmation, and he did. "People who are too high up or too visible to do it themselves, so they pay you to do it."

Jason nodded again, surprised she had figured out so much. As always, he discounted her intelligence. Still, there was the problem of how much he could safely tell her. "When I first came to Washington a lot of years ago, I worked for one man who became very important in government. Then the administration changed, and he was one of the Outs. He parked me here at Redmund College, and I continued to work for him, for his interests. Eventually my circle widened. Even if what you do is secret, some people hear and they come to you—also in secret."

"Is all that secrecy really necessary?"

Jason's brown eyes glowed. Anything clandestine or forbidden excited him enormously. That, coupled with his merciless, manipulative intelligence, was the key to his success. "You may be sure of it. Now, Branwen, with this three-month trip I have an opportunity to break out of Washington. If I succeed in the task I'm given, and I'm sure that I will, the whole world will become my circle!"

"The whole world!" Branwen exclaimed. When Jason looked the way he did at that moment, alight with all the force of his compelling charisma, she could believe he might indeed have the whole world for his playground. "But how? Who would you be working for? The United Nations?"

"The U.N.?" Jason sneered. "The U.N. is a joke, Branwen, a lot of sincere little men who do nothing but talk and work for salaries that prove talk really is cheap." He leaned over her, gloating. His charisma hardened around the edges in a cold, calculated gleam. "You don't really think the United Nations makes the decisions that shape the world, do you?"

Branwen gulped, nodded, and only with an effort kept herself from shrinking away from her husband. His eyes burned, he didn't look like himself, he looked . . . almost insane.

"You're so naive. You probably believe the President and the Congress really run the country, too!"

Branwen nodded again. Jason threw back his head and laughed. He clenched and unclenched his fists, as if he grabbed from the air that personal power he wielded so well. Branwen felt his power swirling around him; it made her dizzy. It made her sick.

Jason felt his power, too; it made him exultant. He forgot that he was talking to Branwen. "I always knew it, always knew that governments are too dumb and too cumbersome to rule the world. The real Movers and Shakers had to be there somewhere behind the scenes, the Puppet Masters manipulating the strings. Year after year I've gotten closer, grown more powerful myself, and now I've met two of them, the Puppet Masters. They're not like ordinary men, oh, no. In Europe I'll meet them all, I'm sure of it. . . ." Jason's eyes glowed like burning coals.

Now Branwen did shrink from him, but at the same time she wanted to bring him back from wherever he was. She sensed danger. "Jason?" she whispered.

He didn't hear her. He was caught in his own grandiose thoughts, which turned in his head like great mill wheels. His voice was a low rumble. "That John Fitzgerald Kennedy, he was almost an exception—he was President but he had too much personal power, which could have ruined everything. But we fixed him—"

"We?" Branwen asked sharply, clearly.

Jason heard. Her question jolted him, and he returned instantly to himself. "Just a figure of speech. We of the opposing party." He frowned. He hoped he hadn't said too much.

"But all this time I thought you worked for President Kennedy, for the government! I thought that was why you said you were so busy after he was assassinated!"

Jason shrugged. These things were no longer important. "There are many agencies in government, Branwen. Forget Kennedy, he's dead. Forget all of that. My point was, if everything works out the way I think it will during this time I'll be gone, *I* can forget the government."

Branwen conceded. "Obviously, then, this trip is as important as you say. Of course you will succeed, and I do see why you have to go." She worked herself down under the covers again, and with an effort, in spite of some of the oddness of Jason's behavior, decided that she was satisfied. She said, "I'll be fine, Christmas or no Christmas. You go. Don't worry about me."

Just as she was falling asleep, a wonderful thought occurred to her. "Jason?"

"Mmm."

"If you do, how did you put it, break out of Washington, could we leave Redmund? Live somewhere else? You and me and . . . and the baby?"

The baby! Almost asleep himself, Jason heard the magic words and rolled over to take Branwen in his arms. "You want to leave Redmund, do you?"

"Yes, I think so."

"Well, not right away. It would, ah, arouse suspicion. But after a while, sure. You give me a son, and we'll go anywhere your heart desires."

Harry Ravenscroft, for all his cosmopolitan manners, could turn a fine country phrase when he wanted to. After all, he'd been born and reared in rural Virginia. So he told himself: "There's more than one way to skin a cat," and he picked up the telephone and called his old friend Ellen Carew.

Ellen was about halfway between himself and Branwen in age; Harry's family and Ellen's family had practically lived in each other's pockets when the children were growing up. For years she'd had a terrible crush on him and was always underfoot, following him around—she'd been rather like a kitten, adorable and something of a nuisance, always pouncing upon him unawares. She'd grown out of the crush to marry an up-and-coming young congressman who had, unfortunately, died in an automobile accident after only a few years of marriage. Ellen stayed on at their McLean, Virginia, estate, her own considerable fortune bolstered by that of her late husband. She knew everybody, including people Harry didn't think were much worth knowing, and she liked to entertain all of them. She was, Harry thought, one of the few truly unselfish creatures God had ever produced. And most important, he and Ellen had retained a genuine, deep affection for each other. She would do almost anything for him, and Harry now presumed upon that affection as one alternate way to skin a cat.

"Ellen? Harry. About that Christmas party . . . I'd like to bring a guest. Branwen Faraday. I've told you about her . . . Yes, Jason's wife. He's gone off for three months to take the cure. Or something. He's supposed to be sick, but I don't believe that for a minute. Anyway, I'd like to bring Branwen to your party. Oh, and one other thing: If you haven't invited young Will Tracy, will you do it as a special favor to me? Good. Thank you."

Harry was satisfied with himself. He had wanted to introduce Branwen to Ellen for a long time, and this long absence of Jason's provided the opportunity at last. But more than that, Harry had been looking for four long years for a wedge to drive between Branwen and Jason. Without success, until now. Now, he was sure that Will Tracy could become that wedge, with just a little help from himself. He intended to put Will in Branwen's path every chance he got.

For days Branwen had felt the pull of the rune stones. Why? Why now? When she closed her eyes and quieted her mind to sink into deeper layers of herself, she did not find the comforting quiet she sought; the sacred bluestones inscribed with the ancient symbols hung suspended in her consciousness and refused to leave. She hadn't thought about the little bag of bluestones in years, except when Harry mentioned them. Now she seemed to think about them all the time.

It was night, and Branwen sat cross-legged on the rug in front of the living-room fireplace. The stereo receiver was tuned to the campus classical/folk station. The floor lamp, on its lowest setting, merely enhanced the golden light that danced out of the fire's flames. The rune stones pulled at her from their hiding place upstairs. Branwen had never shown them to Jason. A woman's voice, both mellow and plaintive, sang of iron wheels rolling in the rain. . . .

Slowly Branwen rose to her feet. *Yes!* said her inner Voice. The voice on the stereo sang on, now telling of hard bells ringing with pain. Branwen climbed the stairs. There was no question of searching for the leather pouch so discolored with age; even if her mind had forgotten where it was, her feet and hands would have drawn her to the place. A feeling of inevitability settled heavily on her. Heavy but sure, like the song: iron wheels rolling in the rain. She moved without hesitation. She had begun, she would not stop. Yes, no matter why the stones had called her, this was right. This was as it should be.

Once more in front of the fire, the stereo silenced now, Branwen poured the rune stones into her hand. Images wavered, like a mist, at the edges of her vision. No one had told her how to cast the stones. No one had told her how to read the runes. She simply knew that the bluestones would speak to her.

As her fingers touched the small, smooth stones, turned them over to feel their markings, the runes she would read chose themselves. Some had an energy she felt in her hands, and some did not. Branwen let the ones she'd chosen form their own pattern on the floor in front of her.

The fire in the fireplace blazed up, crackling, and Branwen saw through its light. She saw the markings of the runes, stick figures, grow huge, tall as trees. Spare and sere, they were like trees in winter, black against a red fiery haze. And she herself stood among them, dwarfed by the naked rune-trees. Her hair and her gown streamed around her, charged with the same energy that courses through the sacred stones. She was alone in the ancient symbolic forest of her vision, and powerful in her aloneness. The runes' message came whole into her mind, neither spoken nor read: *The Power is yours again. Use it well. Begin* now!

The vision faded, not all at once but slowly. The red, fiery haze paled; her own image disappeared, reabsorbed into herself; the rune trees folded into themselves over and over, smaller and smaller, until they were merely black dots and then nothing at all.

Branwen got her journal from the place where she kept it, mixed in with other identical-appearing notebooks from her courses. She wrote: *Tonight I read the rune stones as they are meant to be read, not hesitantly or fearfully, but with a certainty I did not know I possessed. And I felt filled with their ancient energy. My energy and their energy were one and the same. . . .*

6

To Branwen's way of thinking, attending a society party given by a childhood friend of Harry's ranked only marginally above staying at home in her own company. Yet the drive from Redmund to McLean turned out to be exceptionally lovely. A light snowfall the previous night left the gently rolling fields blanketed in white, pure and clean under the blue-purple sky of early evening. Venus, the Evening Star, hung diamond-bright on the horizon.

Harry concentrated on his driving. He didn't mind Branwen's silence. He was not a particularly good driver and he knew it; he could be too easily distracted, too often lost in his own thoughts. Sometimes he would forget where he was entirely, pass his intended destination and have to backtrack. He didn't intend to let that happen tonight.

"Ah, here we are!" he said, pleased when the gates of the Carew property appeared on the side of the road.

"You say your friend Ellen lives here all alone?" asked Branwen, looking out the window at trees on either side of the drive, thick as a small woods. "It seems so big for one person."

"It's only three or four acres. There's a fence and plenty of security, and the gardener has a house on the property—there it is, just through those trees."

"I see it."

"There's a guest house, too. She often has people living in it—some penniless artist or starving writer—Ellen collects such people. But I don't believe there's anyone in residence currently."

"That's too bad. They'd be interesting to meet."

The guest house looked like a miniature of the main house. "Oh, Harry, it's charming!" Branwen exclaimed.

"You mean the little guest house?"

"Well, both of them."

"I suppose so." Harry shrugged, guiding the car into the final curve of the driveway. "Too new for my taste, built in the 1930s. Don't let the quaint farmhouse look fool you. On the inside it's disgustingly contemporary, and you can blame that all on Ellen. For the past few years she's been positively obsessed with taking down walls and poking holes in the roof—opening it up for more light, she says. But come on, you'll see for yourself."

Ellen Carew greeted them in a hallway festooned with fragrant pine boughs and the largest pinecones Branwen had ever seen. Ellen herself was petite and pretty, with blue eyes and short, very curly blond hair. In a full-skirted dress of silver-gray lace with a wide rose-colored sash, she might have been an angel destined for the top of the Christmas tree. Earlier Harry had described Ellen to Branwen as a "fluffy-looking woman with a mind like a steel trap"—an accurate description.

Having made the introduction, he stepped back and watched with interest as the two women approached each other. Physically they were very different. Branwen had left her hair down tonight; secured away from her face by an emerald-green headband that matched her narrow silk dress, her hair hung straight and shining down her back to her waist, like a waterfall made of sheer night. Branwen's beauty was maturing into a classic elegance, never cold, but remote when she chose—which at parties like this one was often. Ellen, by contrast, had retained her bouncy prettiness into young middle age, and was aggressively friendly. Harry remembered Ellen as a ceaseless organizer of childhood games and pranks; now she managed her own considerable business and social affairs with the same unflagging energy. And success.

"Mind the door for me, Harry, there's a love. You know everybody anyway," said Ellen, linking her arm into Branwen's. "I'm going to take Branwen around and introduce her myself!" To Branwen she said as they entered a large, wood-paneled, vault-ceilinged living room, "I think it's simply too dreadful of that fierce husband of yours to keep you hidden away out there in the country in that rock pile of an excuse for a college. How do you ever survive the boredom?"

Branwen smiled. "The truth is, I don't. I have to sneak off to Washington for a day every now and then just to keep my sanity—not to mention my sense of perspective!"

"Just you stick with me, kiddo," Ellen promised, "and we'll broaden that sense of perspective. We have the most interesting people here tonight! Now you be sure and talk lots, let them hear that delightful trace of an accent. Let's see, we'll start at the top so to speak. How would you like to meet a Supreme Court justice?"

Not all Ellen's guests were as well known as the justice, but all of them, men and women alike, were passionately interested in one thing or another. Branwen moved from one lively conversation to the next under Ellen's subtle guidance, and found her intellect and her own interests both challenged and welcomed. She became so absorbed that she didn't notice when Ellen slipped away and left her on her own. Here in this one room was a world so wide, so fascinating, that her own petty problems were forgotten. And then she saw Will.

"You, Ravenscroft," hissed Ellen at his elbow, "meet me in the kitchen in five minutes. I have to talk to you!"

Harry obediently wended his way to the kitchen and waited. He occupied himself with inspecting the various covered dishes that would be set out for the buffet supper later.

Ellen came through the kitchen door and bore down on him like a minor whirlwind. "I know you have a sadistic streak," she accused, "but you might have warned me!"

"About what?" asked Harry in mock innocence.

"About your friend Branwen and Will Tracy the Younger!"

"I was hoping she might become your friend, too."

Ellen glared at him. "I would like to be her friend. I like her very much already, which makes it all the worse. What are you trying to do to her? The poor woman turned white as a sheet when she saw Will, which was pretty hard to do considering she has skin like alabaster to begin with. You're the one who especially wanted Will here, I would have invited him just because you asked, if I hadn't done it myself already. What's between those two? Come on, Harry, give."

"Hmmm. So she turned white. What did he do?"

"He loped across the distance between them in about two strides with those long legs of his. I think he was afraid she was going to faint, and so was I. I think he wanted to be there to catch her."

"Is that all?"

"Well, no. He was practically consuming her with his eyes—talk about your intense looks! She wouldn't look at him. He seems to have persuaded her to talk, though. He put his arm around her shoulders and took her to the inglenook by the den fireplace. I followed and saw them sitting there, and then I came after you."

"Good." Harry beamed, rubbing his hands together.

"Good, my foot! Listen, Ravenscroft, either you're going to tell me what you're up to by bringing those two people together under my roof, or I'm crossing you off my list. And don't lie to me because if you do, I swear I'll go up to Raven Hill and put toads in your shorts!"

"You wouldn't!"

"Of course I would!"

"Yeah." Harry grinned, and his lock of hair fell over his eye as he looked down at tiny Ellen. "So little and yet so fierce, as always. I guess you would. All right, yes, I was hoping they'd see each other here and that it might get them back together. Or at least get them on the road to being back together."

"Together? But . . ."

"Ellen, I think it's safe to assume you have no greater love for Jason Faraday than I do myself."

Ellen's blue eyes flashed, and she crossed her arms in front of her decisively. "You know damn well I don't. In fact, if you will remember, I was the person who jarred you out of that black depression a few years back when I suggested Jason probably pulled strings to keep you from getting your grant."

"Yes, you did, but unfortunately not soon enough for me to prevent him marrying Branwen."

"So?"

"So now I'm trying to do the next best thing. Help her realize that she can and should get out of that marriage. She won't listen to me, but she might listen to Will. They met and became friends a couple of years ago. Branwen never told Jason—she knew he wouldn't understand—and it cost her a great deal not to tell him. She's *too* honest—past a certain point, honesty becomes a fault, not a virtue."

"Hmm. I'm not sure I agree with you on that, but let it pass. In this case Jason would've been right, wouldn't he?"

Harry's face darkened. He drew his brows together. "What do you mean, Jason right?"

"I *mean*, you nitwit, considering that Jason is her husband, he would've been right not to trust the friendship. Will Tracy has one of those faces—everything he feels shows. He'd never make a good politician like his poker-faced daddy. That wasn't pure friendship I saw on Will's face. He's in love with your Branwen Faraday."

"Exactly! Which is what makes him the perfect instrument to break up that awful marriage, and which is why I, with your help, have arranged for them to be together here even though Branwen has said she won't see Will again."

"Uh-huh." Ellen walked around the kitchen's center island, lifting covers off chafing dishes and putting them back again. "We can't talk more now. It's time for me to get the waiters in here to put this supper out. But I can tell you one thing, Harry. It's a mistake to go meddling in other people's lives. No good ever comes of it."

"No, no," Harry insisted, following her to the door. "The mistake was mine, years ago, and I'm only trying to make good. If I'd been in Wales that summer Branwen wouldn't have married Jason. She told me so herself."

"Well, maybe you're right. Jason is a monster, I've always thought so. And you, Harry Ravenscroft"—she took his arm and smiled her irrepressible smile—"are still my dearest friend. I guess I won't try to stop whatever you're trying to do. I may even keep on helping you."

The inglenook was a secluded island in the pleasantly milling sea of Ellen's Christmas party. Will took both Branwen's hands in his, but she snatched them away. He said, "You're looking lovely tonight, Branwen."

"Thank you," she murmured, looking at her toes beneath the silver straps of her evening sandals. Her feet were cold. At first sight of Will she'd gone cold all over, and the fire didn't seem to help.

"I'm glad to see you here. How did you manage it? If you'll forgive my being so blunt with the truth, I'm sure Ellen Carew wouldn't invite Jason Faraday to one of her parties."

This surprised Branwen into looking at him. "She wouldn't?" There was a hint of anguish in the question.

"No, I'm afraid she wouldn't. Yet you're here, and you were having a good time. I watched you. I've never seen you enjoy yourself more. I didn't know you knew Ellen."

"She's wonderful, isn't she?" The burst of enthusiasm was like a ray of sunshine breaking through Branwen's cloudy reserve. "I just met her tonight. I came with Harry Ravenscroft."

"And, uh, Jason?"

"He's . . ." She looked away. It would be dangerous to tell Will that Jason would be gone for three months. "He's not here."

"I see," said Will gravely. "And Christmas is the day after tomorrow. Where is he, Branwen?"

"Just away. I never know where he goes. You should be with your family, too, you know."

"I will be. I'm going home to Kentucky tomorrow." Will spoke softly. Behind Branwen's back he lightly stroked her hair. "You make a very poor deceiver. Your husband has gone off and left you alone over the holidays, isn't that true? I'd like to get my hands on him!"

"He didn't want to, he had to go!" She jerked her head around. Almost too late Branwen remembered what Jason had told her to say. "He was ordered to take a rest by his doctor. He's gone somewhere to do that."

Will removed his hand from Branwen's hair and rubbed it on his trousers. Talking about Jason Faraday disgusted him. Thinking that Branwen was Jason's wife and therefore what Jason must do to her, the intimate ways in which he must touch her, more than disgusted Will—it made him almost physically ill. He said bitterly, "If you're going to lie for that despicable man, he'd better teach you how to do it properly. That's obviously a cover story, and a darn poor one. Is there more? Where's he supposed to be gone to take this cure? And for how long?"

"Since you obviously don't believe me, there's no point in saying any more." Her chin came up a notch.

"No, I suppose there isn't." Will half rose, then sat down again. He controlled his voice, keeping it low. He had a small chance here. He'd almost lost it, but not quite, because Branwen at least hadn't walked away as he'd been about to do. "Forget about him, Branwen. At least for tonight. I *am* glad to see you here, and I know you were having a good time. You belong here with people like these. It's what you want, isn't it?"

She nodded, pain evident in her eyes, remembering what Will had said: Jason would never be invited.

"Good. They're my friends, too. *Our* kind of people, Branwen. Let's go back to the party. The buffet will be laid out soon. Will you have supper with me?"

She couldn't reply. She was torn, utterly miserable. In that dead house back in Redmund, everything had seemed so much simpler. Cleave to Jason, have his baby, be a good wife. Forget Will. But now she had met Ellen Carew; already she sensed that Ellen was the woman friend she'd been missing. Here were all these wonderful people, and Will was a part of this. Not Jason, but Will.

He saw her distress. He couldn't bear to hurt her, even if that hurt was a necessary part of ultimately helping her more. He leaned close and whispered, "Would you rather I left? If you say so, I'll go."

"N-no." She made up her mind. She would enjoy this one night. There could be little harm in that. "I'll have supper with you. I expect Harry will want to join us."

"The more the merrier! Let's go look for that food."

Harry, Will, Branwen, and Ellen sat together at one of the green tablecloth-covered card tables placed around the edges of the room. Ellen believed in combining the casualness of serving buffet style with the convenience of not having to balance a plate on one's knees. When the women were deep in their own conversation, Harry began one with Will, working his way through polite inquiries after his father's health to the question he really wanted to ask: Would Will be in town after Christmas? Will replied yes, that he was working on a report and would return to Washington on the twenty-seventh.

"In that case," Harry said confidentially, shifting his eyes to be sure Branwen and Ellen weren't listening, "call me when you get back. I have something I'd like to discuss with you. About our mutual friend."

Harry noted that Will Tracy, sitting opposite in the matching wing chair, regarded his host with polite, mild suspicion.

"Thank you for coming," Harry said. "I wanted you to come because, frankly, I know how you feel about Branwen, and I want to help you."

Will crossed one leg over the other with exaggerated casualness, but the bald announcement had shocked him. The shock, of course, registered on his face. He proceeded carefully, in a way that reflected his keen intelligence. "There is only one way you could know how I feel about Branwen. She must have told you herself."

Harry inclined his head graciously. "She did."

"I have to wonder why she would tell you something so private."

"I flatter myself that I have a rather special relationship to her. Oh," Harry hastened to reassure as an ominous look came into the young man's eyes, "I'm not your rival for her affections. No, no. I'm her friend and in some ways her mentor. She has been going through a rough time these last weeks, and I persuaded her to confide in me. I want to help you because I know her marriage is a tragic mistake, and I feel responsible. You see, what happened was . . ."

Will interrupted. "I know the circumstances under which she married Jason Faraday. And I know you are her friend, and that she works a few hours a week for you. In what way, may I ask, are you her mentor?"

"I don't think that's relevant to this discussion."

"I think it is." Will's eyes narrowed. "For one thing, a mentor implies an ongoing relationship, and naturally that would be a concern to me. For another, I wasn't aware she needed a mentor."

"Well, ah . . ." Harry was surprised to find himself suddenly on the defensive. He was seeing a side of Will Tracy that few people ever saw, and he didn't much like it. "Ah, Branwen has a highly developed intuitive sense that comes from her Welsh ancestors. She also has considerable background and knowledge in a field that is of special interest to me, pre-Christian Celtic folklore. I intend to help her develop these things into a successful career, one that will be outstanding, I assure you."

"I see." Will was silent for quite a while, and this time nothing he was thinking showed on his face. He knew he was making a decision that could affect the remainder of his entire life. There was a presence about him that revealed an inner strength which would be his in full maturity. Once, when Harry began to speak, Will held up his hand for continued silence. Finally he said, "Dr. Ravenscroft, you are a friend of my family and an acquaintance of mine, and I have no wish to offend you.

If you were as close to Branwen as you'd like me to believe, however, then you would know that her career aspirations lie in an entirely different direction." Will stood decisively. "To be perfectly honest, I don't appreciate your offer to help me as much as I'm sure you would like me to. I feel bound to say that I do not want your help in this matter. Nor, I expect, does Branwen. Good day, sir."

Harry was stunned. He opened and closed his mouth, but no words came out. He found himself on his feet, shaking the hand that Will politely offered.

"Astonishing!" Harry exclaimed when the door had closed behind young Will Tracy. There was a gleam of begrudging respect in his pale gray eyes.

"Let it be," Ellen cautioned when Harry told her over the phone what had happened with Will, "and come down off your high horse. I'm kind of relieved he told you to butt out—it gets me off a hook I wasn't too comfortable hanging on."

"El-len," Harry said warningly, but he got no further.

"Don't you Ellen me in that tone of voice! I've gotten you invited to that New Year's Eve bash the Chandlers are having at the Mayflower, and that's the end of the arranging I'm going to do for you. You can bring Branwen, and I'm sure they'll have invited Will. He's more in their age group."

Harry winced. He was only 52, but he was beginning to feel very old indeed. "Thank you," he managed to say.

"You're welcome. In case you haven't heard, I've invited Branwen here for brunch tomorrow, and I've done that entirely selfishly. I like what I've seen of her very much and I want to get to know her better. Not for you, not for Will Tracy, just for myself."

"And she said she'd come?" Harry was incredulous. Branwen had told him she couldn't come to work because she had to spend all her time studying for the final exams that would begin when the college reconvened.

"Yes, of course she did."

"And I'm not invited?"

Ellen's merry laugh grated on his ears. "No, silly. It'll be just us girls. Don't sound so dejected. Know what I think, Ravenscroft?"

"I can't possibly imagine," he said dryly.

"I think one of your motives for asking Will Tracy to come to your house was so that you could impress upon him the special nature of the friendship you have with the woman he loves. You're being just plain possessive, old friend."

"Me, possessive? Why, I never—"

"Just think about it, there's a love. Got to go now. Ta-ta!" She clicked off.

"Fluff-head!" Harry spat the childhood epithet into the dead line. He was completely out of patience. "Nobody's cooperating," he grumbled to himself. "Nobody's doing what I want them to do!"

He would have to calm down before he called Branwen to invite her to the New Year's Eve party. He stamped through the hall, grabbed his cape off its hook, and went outside, banging the door on purpose behind him.

Hearing the cadence of his tread and the noise of the door, Mrs. Beecher shook her head in the kitchen and said to no one, "Yon man's turned peevish again."

Harry addressed the icy air. "Besides, Branwen won't *let* anybody be possessive of her. She's just not the type to respond to that." A few steps farther across the crunchy frostbitten grass, Harry realized he was wrong. Jason Faraday had always been extremely possessive of Branwen, from the first he'd set eyes on her, and she allowed it. She had accepted his possessiveness from the first, even though it was completely out of her character.

"Karma," said Harry, stopping dead in his tracks. That bond! A feeling of doom settled over him, and with it a bit of wisdom he did not welcome: Only Branwen herself could break that bond. Not Harry, not Will with or without Harry's help.

Harry shivered inside his cape, wondering what it would take to make Branwen break her karmic bond to Jason.

Branwen would not go to the New Year's Eve party with Harry; she said she expected Jason to call wishing her a Happy New Year, and she would wait at home for his call. She would not have lunch with Will on either of the days he asked her. She did have brunch with Ellen, sensed a developing friendship, and encouraged it by inviting Ellen for lunch and an afternoon at the Smithsonian as soon as her exams were over. Branwen spent her time that week between Christmas and the New Year studying for those exams. And when she could study no longer, she took solitary walks or drives and thought about the baby.

She knew she did not, as she had told Jason, have to wait until she had missed two periods; she could be tested as soon as she had missed one. That would be another two or three weeks. She spent a good deal of time telling herself that there were all sorts of reasons why she might not be pregnant. She didn't want to get her own hopes up, but even so she was now convinced that she carried the tiny beginning of a child inside her.

She let herself plan: When these exams were done, she had only one more course to take, and then in June she would have her bachelor's degree. Even if the early stages of pregnancy made her sick, as Jason thought she already was, taking one course would be no problem. She didn't think she would be sick. She had seen her own mother go serenely through many pregnancies—for her mother, the bearing of children had seemed to be the easiest and happiest thing in the world. Having only her mother's example to go by, Branwen was sure it would be the same for her.

She let herself dream: The child would bring joy to her life and to her marriage. Jason was almost a different person already, and after the baby's birth he would be more so. They would leave Redmund, the three of them, a tightly knit, happy little family. Of course, there would be another child no more than two years after the first. There again, Branwen's dreams followed the example of her own family. They would leave Redmund and go . . . where? She got out the atlas and left it on the coffee table. Every day she mused over a different place: Richmond, Baltimore, Atlanta, Boston, Chicago, San Francisco. Not New York City—they'd been there for two days at the tail end of their honeymoon, and the tall buildings were too overwhelming. Maybe they would go someplace totally different, like Seattle or Albuquerque. Branwen looked at pictures of the New Mexico landscape and thought how much she would like to see it. It seemed almost like another planet entirely.

Her Voice cautioned her in the midst of her plans and dreams: *Do not place too many of your hopes in this child—the child is not magic. I know,* she responded. Branwen listened to her Voice these days.

Branwen cast the rune stones. Each time brought her a vision that seemed to come out of some almost-remembered distant past. Always the experience was powerful, and strengthened her. She did not know that the runes were helping her to prepare for a time when all her strength would be required.

At night she slept peacefully. If she dreamed, she did not remember the dreams upon waking. She was very nearly happy. Until New Year's Eve. On New Year's Eve she waited and waited, but Jason did not call.

Panic streaked through Branwen. Jason had a big thing about celebrating the coming of a new year. He didn't make resolutions, he made pronouncements upon what the new year would bring: She would let her hair grow to her waist, and she did. He would have a teaching assistant to help with this one course, and in spite of the fact that no other professor had help with such a light load, Jason acquired an assistant. Jason surely would have a pronouncement for this new year, and she minded only a little that she'd have to hear it over the telephone. . . . Branwen abruptly stopped thinking about Jason. It was doing no good, only making her more nervous. Why hadn't he called? She turned on the television and settled on the couch to watch others at their parties.

A few minutes before midnight, Branwen went to the kitchen. She had been bound to celebrate just as if her husband were at home. She had prepared his favorite stuffed mushrooms and little crabmeat sandwiches and had chilled a bottle of champagne. She removed the cork carefully without letting it pop, the way he had taught her to do, and thought: *Jason must be in a different time zone, and he'll call when it's midnight there.* But it was a feeble attempt to delude herself. She knew in her heart that he would not call now. She had waited in vain.

On the television a ball of light hung over Times Square, and the countdown began. Five, four, three, two, one, Happy New Year, 1967! Branwen raised her glass, drank, and said, "Happy New Year, Jason, wherever you are!" Her voice rang hollow to her own ears.

She turned off the TV and went, as if driven, to get the bag of rune stones from the place she now kept them, in a drawer in the breakfast room. She prepared the room, stoking the fire, turning down the lights. She was wearing a ruby-red velvet dressing gown her husband had given her the previous Christmas, wearing it as she had prepared the food and the champagne, for him in his absence. She sank down in her accustomed place in front of the fire and arranged the soft folds of the gown around her; she tossed her head and sent her hair streaming down her back. Then she took the old leather pouch in her hand. Always, on the other times she'd consulted the stones, she had let them tell her whatever they would. This time was different. This time she commanded the ancient bluestones aloud: "Tell me about Jason Faraday."

Flames flickered in the darkened room. Branwen poured the rune stones into her palm. The air around her felt dead and heavy with foreboding. The stones grew so hot in her hand that she spilled them on the floor. Dazed, she looked at them all tumbled together, as if they did not wish to speak to her.

"Tell me," she said again. She moved her fingers among the tumble, seeking the energy that told her what runes to choose from the rest. All the rune stones felt charged; all were so hot they seemed to burn her fingers.

The more the bluestones resisted her, the more determined Branwen became. She would know what they were holding back! She focused her will until she felt in her own body the same energy she knew in the stones. She felt the energy gather in the center of her body, and when she throbbed with it, she sent the energy down through her left arm, to her hand, to her fingertips. Then she reached out again to the runes. She was seeing now with more than ordinary sight. As she passed her fingertips over the ancient bluestones, a spark of light leapt from her hand to this stone, and to that one, and that . . . Thus she made her choice, six stones in all, and she arranged them as she felt they should be arranged. The runic markings she kept turned down, because the stones themselves seemed to wish it. Then she waited for the vision to begin.

The world around Branwen was gray, all gray, shrouded in foggy, moving veils. She reached to thrust them aside, but they were insubstantial. Like real fog, the grayness yielded to her touch while it continued to obscure. A voice said, *We are not sure you are ready.*

In her place before the fire, Branwen's body rocked. The triangle of chosen bluestones pulsed with a light her inner-focused vision did not see, pulsed in rhythm with her rocking. She was consumed in a process she did not consciously remember how to do, gathering together a power she did not consciously understand. She rocked. In her vision the gray veils billowed and swirled, faster and faster.

"Show!" Branwen cried in a voice mighty with the resonance of command.

The veils parted with a tearing, rending sound. A rushing wind blew them away, and beyond all was dark. All was dreadful silence. Branwen did not see her own figure in that blackness, though she usually saw herself in her visions. Rather she stood at the edge of it, bathed in the energy that was her protection, an observer. She needed that protection because in that Dark was hidden all manner of abominations, creatures who so often had turned from the Light that there was no Light left in their souls.

In the Dark as she stared, a shifting occurred. A huge, massy movement of a bulk awesome in its size, somehow obscene in its gross heaving, blacker than the rest. Then sounds came, jittering, gibbering, demented sounds; and finally insane laughter that became an eerie howl before it died away.

The wind that had moved the veils swept Branwen up, wrapped her hair about her face and neck, filled her ears with its rushing. The wind bore her backward out of the edge of the Dark. At the very last she heard the deep, burnished sound of a gong . . . and found herself abruptly back in the room, her body in the red velvet gown. The fire had died to glimmering ash. On the floor in front of her folded legs the runes lay faceup, though she was sure she had arranged them with their markings facedown. Still pulsing with an energy so strong that it was slowest to fade, one rune stood out from all the rest: the rune of destiny, reversed, so that it signified ill fortune.

Branwen did not want to admit that she understood, but she did. Slowly she gathered the bluestones. They were cold now. With uncoordinated fingers she put them back into their soft old pouch. She felt utterly drained of physical strength, of emotion, of everything. She turned on every light in the room, started to drink a glass of the opened champagne, then thought better of it. Not until she held a steaming cup of coffee in her hand did she allow herself to think what she had seen. In the archetypal symbology of Good and Evil, she had seen the Dark, the place where Evil dwells. There could be no doubt. She had asked to know of Jason, and she had seen Darkness; asked to know of Jason, and she had seen—Evil.

Branwen closed her eyes in weary acceptance. She had brought this unwelcome information upon herself. The stones had resisted, she had insisted, and finally she had Seen. Seen what? Not since the darkest days at Llanfaren had the word "evil" so much as entered her mind. In the ordinary everyday course of events, Branwen did not want to acknowledge the reality of Evil; she preferred to think that some things were only less good than others. But on a deeper level, in that place in her soul where dreams have their origin and symbols derive their unspoken meaning, she knew that Evil does exist. And because she believed without question that each soul is always free to choose its own path, she knew that Jason by his own choice had placed himself in this danger she had seen. Those jibbering things that lived in the Dark were also there by the weight of their own accumulated choices; as was the huge, obscenely shifting mass too terrible to name. They were coming—please God! only the smaller ones were coming!—coming for Jason. They would come wearing their less hideous human forms, but they would still be evil, creatures out of Darkness.

They were coming. Perhaps they were already here!

7

Will Tracy at age twenty-nine was one of the top researchers at the "think tank" where he worked. He had a valuable quality often lacking in his brain-trust colleagues: instinct. Instinct told him when to read more broadly, dig deeper. The projects he was assigned usually dealt with sociological issues. The Parnassus Foundation did not concern itself with espionage or criminal activity or political blackmail—there were other agencies to handle that sort of thing. But Will had assigned himself a project on the day when Branwen made it clear that she intended to stay with her husband, and this self-assigned project took him far afield into the realms of the other agencies. He called it Project Jason.

Will's instinct told him that Jason Faraday was a criminal of the most dangerous kind, that is, the kind for whom the end always justifies the means, the kind who may keep within the letter of the law but who has no personal morality, the kind whose arrogance borders on egomania. That was what his instinct told him, and his project was to prove his instinct right. Or to come as close to real proof as he possibly could. Will wanted the information for one purpose only: to present to Branwen. He had his usual resources, plus personal contacts, his and his father's, in and out of government. He used them all, with a sense of urgency. He knew that time was not on his side. He could feel Branwen slipping further away from him with every day, every hour that passed. He hoped against hope that if she could be made to see what kind of human being her husband was, then she might free herself of the marriage. He wanted this for her whether she would then marry him or not.

Will's own work suffered, but he didn't care. He didn't care that he went around looking more rumpled than usual or that his eyes were bloodshot from nights when he lay awake trying to fit together pieces that didn't fit. Then, in mid-January through one of his father's former staffers, he found the key piece: a man who was willing to talk because he trusted Will's word that nothing he said would be made public. He talked, and after that the rest fell over like dominoes. It was all hearsay; Will could never have taken this information to court, but he could take it to Branwen. And he did, at the end of January.

"Will!" He was the last person Branwen expected to find on the doorstep of the Redmund house.

"Hi," said Will. "Can I come in?"

How could she refuse him? His tall form was hunched against the winter wind, the collar of his overcoat turned up, his hands in its pockets. But she hesitated. If he'd called first, she'd certainly have told him not to come. "Well . . . Jason isn't home. I'm not exactly dressed for company."

"I know he's not here, I wouldn't be here if he was, you look fine, and I'm not company. Besides, I'm freezing! Now can I come in?"

"I guess so," Branwen agreed dubiously, stepping back to let him enter. "It really is cold out there. I have a fire going in the living room. Here, let me take your coat."

They sat warily regarding each other from opposite ends of the couch. Will thought Branwen looked great in jeans, which he'd never seen her wear before, and fringed ankle-high moccasins, and a huge fuzzy yellow sweater. Her hair was in one thick braid that hung over her shoulder, and she fingered it nervously.

She surprised him by saying, "I guess it's good that you're here. I've been putting off calling you, and there's something I suppose you ought to know."

"Oh?" The syllable caught in his throat; she had him off-balance.

"Will," Branwen said, holding his eyes with hers, "I'm pregnant. I'm going to have Jason's child."

"W-what did you say?" His face turned ashen. He felt as if all the wind had been knocked out of him.

Branwen's hands dripped cold sweat. Telling Will was much, much harder than she'd thought it would be. She hurt herself to hurt him like this. But she kept her voice clear and firm. "I said I'm going to have a baby, Jason's baby. I've been to a doctor, and he has confirmed it."

Will turned away. All his hopes were dashed. His life had just been ripped apart. What could he do? He hung his head. His voice came out in a croak. "You want this baby?"

Branwen slid across the couch, reached out to touch him, pulled her hand back. She had no right to touch him anymore. She said softly, "Yes, I do. Very much."

"I . . . see." Will wiped his eyes on his sleeve. Everything he'd come prepared to say had gone completely out of his head. He loved Branwen. He had never quite believed in her marriage; it had never seemed completely real to him. Now he felt as if she had just handed him the most intimate betrayal. He could not bear even to look at her. "I think I'd better leave," he mumbled, pushed himself up, and headed blindly for the door.

Branwen's soft moccasins whispered across the floor in the wake of his long, unsteady stride. "Don't go! I don't even know yet why you came!"

"It doesn't matter anymore," Will said as he stumbled down the steps.

"Will . . ." Branwen murmured, watching through the glass of the storm door. He drove away much too fast. *It's all right,* she thought, *it has to be this way.*

Branwen did see Will again, two months later. Her friend Ellen Carew arranged the meeting without her knowledge. Branwen went to Ellen's house for tea, she thought. At the sight of the tall, masculine figure seated in the sunroom, Branwen's heart leapt, and then sank.

Ellen determinedly took Branwen's arm and pulled her along, explaining as they went. "Now, Branwen, don't you be put out with me. Yes, I've set you up, but you'll understand why when you've heard what Will has to say. And meeting here is lots better for both of you than doing it anywhere else." She pushed Branwen into a chair and beamed at Will. "Don't you let her fuss at you, Will Tracy, you can just blame everything on me. Well, kiddies, I've got some letters to write in my room, which just happens to be clear on the other side of the house. Ta-ta!"

Will had stood when Branwen and Ellen approached, and now he sat again. "How are you, Branwen?"

"I'm fine," she said, giving him a quick glance. He was unusually neatly and conservatively dressed in a dark gray suit, white shirt, striped silk tie. "You're looking well."

Just as she had only briefly glanced at him, he could not let his eyes linger on her for very long. "You, ah, don't look any different. I mean . . ."

"I know what you mean. I haven't begun to show yet, but I will in another month or so."

Awkward silence fell between them. Will was thinking how ashamed he was that he had wished she would lose the baby. Branwen was thinking, also with some vague feelings of shame, that she had lied when she'd said she was fine. She didn't easily accept the fact that pregnancy was hard for her. Not only had she not gained weight, but also she had to fight to keep from losing it. Food tasted terrible and didn't want to stay down, and she felt exhausted all the time. Wearily she pulled herself together and asked, "If you wanted to see me, why involve Ellen?"

Will shrugged. "Just being careful. I know your husband has returned, so I couldn't very well come to your house—even if you were willing to let me in after the way I left last time. I didn't think you'd come to my place, and I had to see you. It made sense to meet here, since we're both friends of Ellen's. I hear you two have become close, and I'm glad. As Ellen said, I think you'll understand why I wanted to see you."

She looked at him, questions in her dark-fringed blue-green eyes.

"I've resigned from the Foundation, Branwen. I'm leaving Washington. To tell you the truth, I'm going because I can't stand to see you having Jason's child."

Branwen stiffened, grasping the arms of her chair. "Where will you go?"

"Wherever the State Department sends me. You know I have contacts, good ones, at State. They helped, and I got hired on. Right now it looks like I'm going to Ireland for a while." Will shifted in his chair, crossing his legs. Words came more easily now that he'd begun.

"As long as it isn't Viet Nam," said Branwen. "I've worried about that, your age and all."

Will raised his eyebrows, and for a moment he looked like his old laid-back self. "Who, me? The senator's son, the prince from Old Kain-tuck? No way! Seriously, as long as I keep having these jobs that are important in other ways to the government, they won't draft me."

"I'm glad of that," said Branwen. She found she could look at him now, though her heart ached.

"Me, too. Anyhow, I get my assignment from State next week and then I'll be off immediately. I discovered I didn't much want to go without seeing you first."

Branwen lowered her lashes to hide her eyes. She was glad he'd wanted to see her, and she was touched, but afraid to say so.

Will continued, "I have some important things to say to you, things I would have said that day you told me you were pregnant. I don't want to leave without having said them. Branwen, I want you to promise that you'll hear me out."

She looked up. "I promise."

"Thank you. The fact is, I'm worried about you staying in your marriage and having Jason's baby. I found some things out about him that I really think you should know, in spite of the fact that you're carrying his child. I've thought it over, and I think I'm right to tell you." Will paused to see how she was taking this. He would edit, not tell her the more gruesome details, only enough to alert her to the possible dangers in her future. She didn't seem to be shutting him out, so he went on.

"Branwen, Jason's job at Redmund is just window dressing, a reason for him to hang around the center of power. And lately it isn't even that. I think by now you may realize that it isn't really the Congress and administration who control what goes on in this country."

"No," she said seriously, "I didn't know that."

"Well, it's true. There are groups of powerful people who work behind the scenes, who have an unbelievable amount of influence. Like everywhere else, among them there are good guys and bad guys. And your husband is in deep with the bad guys. So deep, he may not be able to get out even if he wanted to. He didn't start out that way, but he's been going steadily in that direction for years. He has a reputation, Branwen. He'll make deals for anybody with anybody, if the price is high enough. He doesn't do it for the money alone, he does it out of a need for power."

"He told me some of that, about making deals."

"I'll bet he didn't tell you what sort of deals."

"No, he didn't."

"Well, I'm going to tell you because I think you have a right to know. Don't worry, I'm not going to tell anyone else. I got this information only for you, and I got it from people who only told me because they trust me not to make it public. In telling this to you, I am also trusting that you aren't so far gone in the need to stay loyal to Jason that you'll tell him I know these things. Quite literally, he could have me killed, and probably would."

Branwen's hand went to her throat, and her eyes opened wider. She listened but heard Will through a growing din of anxiety in her ears.

"Okay. Jason has dealt drugs for guns, not once but many times. He's brokered high-priced stolen goods. He's carried false information that has ruined people's lives, maybe even cost lives of people other people wanted out of the way. He's arranged movements of mercenaries, for a profit. There's a well-founded rumor that he was involved in a recent failed conspiracy in South America. And now, Branwen, I hear he's into something that makes my blood run cold."

Her face had gone dead-white, like the knuckles on the hand that gripped the chair. "What?"

Will leaned forward, elbows on knees. Even though they were alone, he instinctively lowered his voice to just above a whisper. "There is a handful of people whose existence as a group is so secret *nobody* will utter a name. They are so powerful that they place themselves above any government of any nation. I know it sounds paranoid—I didn't want to believe such a group could exist when I first started hearing the whispers about them. But once you grant the possibility, then some pretty terrible events that have never been adequately explained otherwise suddenly begin to make sense. This secret group goes after its own ends in any way they choose. *Any way*, Branwen. They destroy, they kill. I heard on good authority that Jason Faraday now works for this terrible group."

"I . . . Will, you must excuse me. I'm going to be sick." Branwen ran for the nearest bathroom. Will followed, worried, not knowing what else to do. She slammed the door in his face and vomited into the sink. He heard her retching and felt his own insides twist, as if they were trying to come up with hers.

Branwen came out apologizing. "I'm so sorry to do that."

"I'm the one who's sorry." Will put his arm firmly around her and led her back to the sunroom. "I didn't mean to make you sick, not literally. I just wanted to warn you, to inform you so you'd know. . . ."

Branwen looked up at Will and tried to smile. "Don't take it so personally. It doesn't have anything to do with you or what you said. Pregnant ladies just get sick sometimes, that's all. Were you finished?"

Will nodded.

"All right." She searched his face and saw only open concern and caring. "I believe you told me those things because you do care for me. Now you must believe me when I tell you that Jason has never harmed me, never done anything to my knowledge that would hurt anyone. He's egocentric, yes, and he enjoys making things happen the way he wants them to happen. But if you could only see the changes I see in him now that he's back and he knows about the baby. . . . This baby is going to make a difference for us, Will. It already has. We're going to be a real family. And if this mysterious group does exist and they're influencing Jason to go the wrong way—" Branwen felt a sudden stab of cold along her spine. She remembered the vision, the shapes moving out of the Dark, coming for Jason. She lifted imploring eyes to Will. "Don't you see that he needs me? If what you say is true, then Jason is in trouble, his *soul* is in trouble, and he needs me and this baby more than ever!"

Will slumped back in his chair and rubbed his hand over his face and his high forehead. He had expected no other reaction from her, but still he felt defeated. Defeated and enormously sad. Privately he thought Faraday's soul was probably already damned. He looked over at Branwen, sitting so tense and pale and earnest. He whispered, "Your husband is a destructive man, Branwen. Don't let him destroy you."

"I won't." Her chin came up.

Will stood, bent, and swiftly kissed her cheek. "Don't get up. I know the way out, and on the way I'll tell Ellen I'm gone. I won't try to contact you, Branwen, but I want you to remember something: I love you, and I'll always love you. If you ever need me, no matter where in the world I am I'll come to you. I'll stay in touch with Ellen, and if you want me, she'll be able to tell you where I can be reached. Good-bye."

"Wait, Will!" Branwen left her chair to reach for Will's arms. With tears in her eyes she sought a last embrace. Both their bodies were at first stiff with tension, but then they melted into each other, clinging, yearning. She lifted her face, and Will kissed her with heartbreaking tenderness.

"Don't forget," he whispered, "if you want me, I'll come."

"I won't forget," she whispered back. "Good-bye, Will. God keep you."

8

It was very, very important to stay asleep. Why it was so important Branwen couldn't remember, it just was. So she didn't open her eyes, she didn't listen to any of the strange sounds around her, and she didn't move. That was important, too, not moving. The warm heaviness might go away if she moved, so she stayed very still. Body still, mind still, sleep. Sleep.

Jason Faraday had had to leave some things unfinished—he didn't like that. He'd had to go through all the tedious complications of waiting on standby to get an earlier flight, and he didn't like that, either. Then he'd had to fight his way through rush-hour traffic, and the overworked air conditioner on his Cadillac had cut out on him in the steamy summer heat. On a scale of one to ten, his anger was at least a nine by the time he strode out of the elevator and down the corridor. Heads turned, and people stepped out of his way as he passed. The barely suppressed violence surrounded his body in an energy field that seemed to plow a path before him.

The white-clad R.N. couldn't stop herself from cringing back as he leaned over the elbow-height counter of the nurses' station and announced, "I'm Jason Faraday. Dr. Nathan called me and insisted that I come here." The nurse nodded and reached for the telephone as Jason continued to hurl words at her. "Where's my wife? She can't have had the baby, it's not due for another month!"

The nurse's anxious eyes darted to and from Jason's darkening face as she spoke softly into the telephone. He reached over the counter and grabbed the instrument out of her hand as she was about to hang up. "You got Nathan on there? Give me that! What's this all about, Nathan? I'm here, and where the hell are you?" But he was talking into an empty line. Jason looked daggers at the nurse.

She took the telephone from his hand more calmly than she felt. She was accustomed to handling distraught husbands, but his thunderousness frightened her. "I just paged Dr. Nathan, Mr. Faraday, I wasn't talking to him. If you'll sit down over there and wait for a few minutes, he'll be here to explain everything."

Jason frowned, clenched his fists and released them, shifted his weight from one leg to another. He was in no mood to wait. "Where's my wife?" he demanded.

"Please wait for Dr. Nathan," said the nurse, rising. "He wants to talk to you first. Mr. Faraday—" Alarmed, as Jason spun on his heel and set off on his own, the nurse ran out from behind the station and after him, her rubber-soled shoes squeaking on the polished floor. "Mr. Faraday, you can't see her until you've talked to the doctor!"

"Like hell I can't!" thundered Jason.

An intern, hearing the commotion, left his charting to intervene. He was a big young man with a football player's build, and the nurse shot him a grateful look as he loped ahead and planted himself in Jason's path. He grinned and stuck out his hand. "I'm Dr. Rogers. Is there a problem?"

"There damn well better not be," growled Jason. He scathingly ignored the young doctor's offered hand and crammed his own hands into his pockets.

"This is Mr. Faraday," interposed the nurse. "His wife is Dr. Nathan's patient. I've paged Dr. Nathan, but Mr. Faraday doesn't want to wait."

"I see," said Rogers, thinking rapidly. Faraday, Nathan's patient . . . Oh, God! They'd had a terrible time with her. He wasn't very good at this yet, but he'd have to do something to keep this husband calm until the senior Ob-Gyn man arrived. "Mr. Faraday, let's just move back here, out of the middle of the corridor. We don't want to disturb the other patients in their rooms."

Jason cared nothing about the other patients, but the intern was big and he was effectively in the way and moving forward.

Jason allowed himself to fall back a few steps. "What did you say your name was?" he barked.

"Dr. Rogers, sir. I'm the intern on this service."

"Well, Rogers, since my wife's doctor apparently lacks the good sense to be here after he insisted that I cut short an important business trip, just for the sake of some cockeyed overreaction on his part—"

"Oh, not an overreaction," the intern hastened to say. "I know Dr. Nathan planned to stay at the hospital until you'd arrived, so it couldn't take more than a couple of minutes for him to respond to his page. I, ah"—he stuck his hand in the pockets of his white coat and rocked back on his heels, trying to appear relaxed, conversational—"I imagine you know Dr. Nathan."

"No," Jason said. "He was my wife's doctor, not mine."

"Oh, sure, but most husbands go in with their wives toward the end of the pregnancy. You know, so they'll know what to expect." A soft bong announced the arrival of the elevator across the corridor. The young doctor's face eased in relief. "Here he is now."

Jason whipped around. Of course he knew by now that something was seriously wrong. His anger had not abated. If Branwen had done anything stupid to endanger his child . . . His thoughts were murderous. He clenched and unclenched his fists inside his pockets.

Dr. Charles Nathan was a mild-mannered, pleasant man of medium height. He was bald except for a fringe of dark hair from his temples around the back of his head, he wore steel-rimmed glasses, and his body was thin as a whippet. The nurse intercepted him as he stepped out of the elevator and quickly explained the situation.

The sympathy Dr. Nathan had felt for this husband all but evaporated as he encountered the angry energy that emanated from the man. Nevertheless, he smiled and offered the usual handshake of greeting. "Jason Faraday? I'm Charles Nathan."

Jason grunted and deigned to shake the man's hand.

"Usually I prefer that we talk in the privacy of my office, but as you seem, ah, rather impatient, let's just have a seat in the waiting area." There was no one in the waiting area; afternoon visiting hours were over, and evening hours would not begin until the patients had been served their dinner. There would be no dinner for Branwen Faraday this night, however.

"All right," Jason rumbled ominously, "get on with it. If my

wife hasn't had the baby prematurely, then what the *hell* could
be important enough for you to call me away from my business?"

"Mr. Faraday, I don't believe anyone has yet said anything to
you about the baby." Nathan's patient, nearsighted blue eyes
narrowed behind his glasses. "But perhaps I'm wrong?"

Jason shook his large head. His blood was beginning to throb
in his veins. A bad sign. "That nurse at the desk—if my wife
had had the baby, that nurse would've said so in a minute. *Get
on with it!*"

Dr. Charles Nathan couldn't figure out how to reach this
strange, angry man. His own heart spilled over with compassion
when he thought of what Branwen had been through, but could
Jason feel it? "Mr. Faraday, your wife Branwen is at the moment heavily sedated, and her vital signs are being constantly
monitored. She has had eight units of blood transfused into her.
She *will* be all right, but from the amount of blood we had to replace, you may realize we thought for a while we were going to
lose her. That is why I asked you to come."

Blood? Jason's own blood screamed like a freight train
through his head. This was it: he'd gone off the top of the scale.
He was no longer in control. He grabbed Dr. Nathan by the la-
pels of his white coat. "My baby? What happened to my son?"

"The baby was stillborn." The doctor blinked, with Jason's
furious, purpling face too near his own. His compassion faded,
rapidly replaced by fear. This man's eyes were crazed. Dr. Nathan feared a psychotic break, but he went on. He had built his
practice on good patient communication, and the habit proved
impossible to alter. "You are correct, the baby was a boy, ap-
proximately thirty-three weeks gestation. After we delivered
the placenta the complications—"

"No!" Jason roared. "No!" He dragged the doctor up out of
the chair, shaking the man's thin body by the grip he maintained
on his coat.

"Please, Mr. Faraday!"

"Where is he? Where's my son? I want to see my son!"

"Mr. Faraday, please believe me, you don't want to see the
baby. The baby was born dead."

"Where is he?" Jason released his grip so abruptly that the
doctor almost collapsed. Jason looked ready to tear the whole
hospital apart in search of the son he refused to believe was
dead. He took a few steps and tottered, confused, not knowing

where to start his search. He turned back and roared, *"You bastard, tell me where to find my son!"*

Valiantly Dr. Nathan tried to treat Jason Faraday the same way he treated all bereaved parents. His soft voice was a marked contrast: "We don't have to talk about that now. You and your wife can decide together about disposition of the baby's body in a couple of days, when she's well enough and can handle it. You should think of *her* now. You haven't let me tell you everything. We had to take her uterus, Mr. Faraday. It was the only way to stop the hemorrhaging, the only way to save her life. She doesn't know yet that she won't be able to bear other children. I'll tell her when she comes out of sedation, or if you prefer, you . . . can . . . tell . . ." Dr. Nathan's voice died, strangled in his throat by the strange light in Jason's eyes.

The two nurses behind the nurses' station looked up, sensing the charge in the air. The intern, who had been discreetly listening, felt his body react to the threat of physical violence before his mind could register it. He moved closer to his superior.

Jason's voice was menacing, low. He advanced step by step. "Get this through your head, Doctor. *She* is not important. Only the child is important. I'm not going to ask you again. Where is my son?"

Nathan swallowed convulsively. "The baby's body is in the hospital morgue."

Something inside Jason snapped, in his mind and in his soul. He felt it give way, and heard the break like a dull thud above, or underneath, the roaring in his head. Morgue, dead . . . the full meaning of the words poured into him. He was enraged beyond recall. With lightning swiftness for a man of his bulk, he lunged for Dr. Nathan and wrapped his hands around his throat. *"You* did it, you killed my baby." He squeezed. "With your incompetence. And *she* did it," he said and squeezed harder. "She killed my baby in her womb! That's why she was sick so much, she wanted him *dead!"*

"Let him go!" yelled young Dr. Rogers. He couldn't believe what was happening right before his eyes. "You're strangling him, man! You'll *kill* him, for chrissake!" He tugged at Jason's wrists and hands, to no avail.

"You . . . can't . . . do . . . that . . . to . . . me." Jason ground the words out from behind clenched teeth, pressing harder, harder.

A nurse, finally understanding that this scene was beyond the ordinary, picked up the phone ever so carefully and called Security.

"Okay, man, you asked for it," said Rogers when Jason had failed to loose his grip. The intern, a head taller and with longer arms, stepped behind Jason and grabbed his head in a wrestler's hold, yanking his hair and applying pressure to the temporal arteries.

The sudden pain in his head startled Jason and brought him partially to his senses. His grip slackened reflexively, and Dr. Nathan, coughing and wheezing, staggered back to collapse on the couch behind him. Only then did Rogers release his hold on Jason. To Dr. Nathan he said, "Do you want to press charges against this man, Doctor?"

Charles Nathan couldn't speak. He rubbed his throat and shook his head.

Jason stood where he was, flexing his fingers, panting, the strange light still in his eyes.

Two hospital security officers, in their subtle uniform of navy blazers and gray slacks, exited the elevator at a brisk clip. The intern said to them, "Escort Mr. Faraday out of the hospital, and tell him not to come back anytime soon!"

In her hospital bed, Branwen stirred. She rolled her head from side to side on the pillow. She was dreaming. A bad dream. She heard Jason's voice, and he was angry. So hard, so hard to stand up to his anger, to act as if she were not afraid, to pretend she didn't care. . . . So hard. But the voice faded, the dream faded. It was very important to sleep. She slept.

Dr. Charles Nathan, speaking in the croaking whisper that was left of his voice, conferred with the intern and the charge nurse. "I want a security officer posted on this floor tonight. If that man comes back, he's not to be allowed off the elevator. Tomorrow I'll see about getting a temporary restraining order. I don't want him anywhere near his wife until she's completely recovered."

The two heads nodded solemn agreement.

"Oh, my God," Nathan croaked, "the morgue! You don't suppose he went there, do you? Dr. Rogers, you see to it. Go down there and make sure he hasn't tried to take that poor baby's body. Tell them what happened."

The intern jumped to his feet. Before he left on his errand he said, "Dr. Nathan, I don't know what we can do about it, but I don't think Mr. Faraday was just suddenly crazed by grief. I think the man's insane!"

The older of the two security officers was a retired policeman. He'd seen that look in the man's eyes, felt that kind of barely contained violence before—in men who committed murder and then claimed temporary insanity. If he were still a cop on the beat, he'd have run the man in, made sure he stayed locked up at least overnight. The best he could do was to bend the rules a little, not simply deposit the man out of the front entrance but escort him all the way to his car. His younger partner looked surprised but didn't protest. The two of them handed Jason Faraday into the Cadillac, shut him in, and watched until the car was out of sight.

Jason's head pounded, pounded, but his mind was preternaturally sharp and clear. His hands thrummed with the need to complete their act.

I wanted to kill him, Jason thought; *I could* have killed him if *we'd been someplace else, if we'd been alone!* Some of the men Jason hired for other people were killers—assassins, the very best. They were paid enormous sums and never got caught. That was the thing, of course, not to get caught. Killing the doctor right there in the hospital would have been stupid for that reason alone.

Jason remembered everything Dr. Charles Nathan had said, every word, every gesture, every nuance. He still jumped to the same irrational conclusion: The doctor, through his incompetence, had allowed the precious baby to die. Perhaps if the doctor had allowed Branwen to die also, then he might be spared. But he hadn't, he had saved her. He had looked after Branwen all through her pregnancy, and then he'd saved *her* instead of the baby. That was wrong, all wrong. That baby would have been the start of a dynasty! And Jason would have been God to the child; the boy would have adored his daddy. Jason thought himself worthy of adoration, now more than ever before. Now that he worked for an international group of people who operated at a level so powerful they were all like gods. . . . Not like his own father who'd been a wimp, a nobody, a great disappointment. Jason would have made the boy into his own image, would have left his child, his heir, as a stamp of the father's greatness upon the earth. But now it was not to be, all because of Branwen and Dr. Charles Nathan. They had let his baby die, so now they had to die, too. That was justice, a higher justice than any man-made law. Laws were for other people anyway, not for Jason Faraday.

Jason drove aimlessly for hours, and inevitably his anger cooled. He realized he would be more comfortable at home, and headed in that direction. He realized that he was hungry and stopped along the way for take-out chicken. He realized that if he killed Dr. Charles Nathan himself, he would probably get caught. Killing with his own hands, no matter how much he itched to do it, was not his area of expertise. But he did not have to do it with his own hands. Something could be arranged. As for Branwen. . . . She should have died there in the hospital. Maybe she still would. That would be easiest.

In the small, black hours of the morning, Jason Faraday awoke sweating and trembling from one of his nightmares. He reached for his wife, but she wasn't beside him, and momentarily he was confused, unsure where he was. Then he remembered—everything. His rage returned. He bellowed: *"My son!"* He felt absolutely bereft, terribly wronged. In panic he turned on the light. Branwen's empty place on the bed mocked him. He clawed off the sheets, beat her pillow against the bedpost until feathers flew. His eyes burned in his head, and the sound of his own heavy breathing rasped in his ears. He felt almost exultant, borne on the force of his tremendous anger, and his near-demented mind clicked to a scene of recent memory. To a time and a place where he'd been in the presence of a force far greater even than this all-consuming rage. Jason's breathing slowed, and his eyes fixed, trancelike, as he remembered: a large room, its ceiling and corners obscured by shadows and in the center, seated in chairs like thrones, a circle of men in strange costumes—long metallic-looking gray robes and hoods that hid their faces. Himself, uncomfortably vulnerable because he was naked under a much plainer robe and had no hood in which to hide. He'd thought at first that he'd somehow made a stupid mistake, that this group—for whom he'd busted his guts for three months—was nothing but some ridiculous cult. He'd gone to Europe and made a diamond merchant "disappear," in the process ruining a too-liberal manager of a South African diamond mine, and this bunch of kooks was his reward? His reward was something as stupid as to learn the name of a bunch of kooks who liked to dress up in long gray dresses? He was supposed to be excited about that? And not only excited, he was supposed to pledge allegiance to that name?

He had wanted to laugh in their unseen faces, but he could not; wanted to turn right around and leave, but he could not; wanted to tell them thanks but no thanks, but he could not do that either. Instead, Jason had felt himself pulled by an irresistible force into the center of their circle, though they hadn't any of them moved a muscle, and he heard himself answering their questions automatically, without thought, as if they had the power to pull the words straight out of his mind. Soon, very soon, Jason had decided that they were not a bunch of kooks at all, and he was glad that they had somehow compelled his feet and controlled his tongue, for they had actually praised him!

Yes, they had praised his work and then they had given him a demonstration of their power. The power had felt, as they gathered it, or generated it, or whatever it was they did, like the surging strength of Jason's familiar anger. Only a thousand, thousand times greater. They had power over life and death, and they had demonstrated that: a servant had brought in a smallish horse, a fine white animal with a graceful curve of neck and glistening eyes, and had tethered it to the iron ring that served as a door handle. The circle of men, with Jason still standing dumb in their center because he had nowhere else to go, hummed with the energy they created. The room grew both warmer and darker; the horse began to stamp and thrash, and finally to rear. The circle rose as one to their feet, and their humming power, like a dark, vibrant cloud, rose with them. Jason's hair crackled, as with static electricity; the short hairs on his limbs stood on end, and his head ached almost past endurance. To this day he did not know whether he had heard or merely felt in his mind the one word: *die*.

The word was hurled from the circle, and with it rushed all the force of their terrible power; Jason felt as if his head were being ripped from his neck as the dark force spun from the circle toward the doomed animal. The horse gave a terrible, shrieking cry, rose on its hind legs and pawed the air, and then abruptly its legs buckled. It sank to its knees, its head dropped. The last of the animal's life-breath whooshed out in a sound like air compressed from a bellows. The white body toppled slowly, slowly, onto its side. The horse was dead. This they had done without so much as lifting a finger—their hands were folded in the sleeves of their strange garments. And Jason, far from being terrified by their demonstration of power, had been exhilarated. He had sensed a kinship between their power and the inner rage that had burned in him all his life long. Eagerly he'd sworn his fealty and learned the name of the group, the name he must never say aloud: Cognoscenti.

It rankled, though, that the Cognoscenti had only made him their agent, not one of them. They had killed the horse to demonstrate what they could do to him if they wished. Once again he was only the hired hand, hired to do the dirty work. Nevertheless, by the rage that ever burned in Jason Faraday's soul, he swore that one day the power and the secrets of the Cognoscenti would be his. He wouldn't be just the hired hand forever, oh, no! He pounded fist on knee and came out of his reverie to find himself sweating, thirsty, trembling.

For the rest of the night hours Jason blundered from room to room, drinking whiskey, alternately missing Branwen and hating her. Whenever that sick, lost feeling came into the pit of his stomach at the thought of life without her, he drowned it in whiskey. By dawn he had unalterably convinced himself that his love for Branwen was as dead as their ill-fated child. She would have to die, too, but her death would be special, would require the most clever planning. . . .

Ellen Carew stood next to Dr. Nathan in Branwen's hospital room. Dr. Nathan, knowing of their friendship, had called her. She whispered, "Is she in a coma?"

"No," the doctor replied, "she's sleeping. We stopped sedating her thirty-six hours ago, but she continues to sleep. All her vital signs are normal and stable, so we removed the monitors. She simply will not wake up! The nurses are baffled. So am I. She responds to painful stimuli—you know, like a pinprick— with the appropriate reflexes, but instead of waking, she goes into deeper sleep."

"Could it be that she just isn't ready yet to face what she'll have to face when she wakes? I mean," Ellen ventured, "she knows the baby was stillborn, and she must be able to recall at least some of what happened after."

The doctor placed a cautioning finger to his lips, shaking his head. He said, "That's a perceptive suggestion. In fact, it's more or less what I think myself, that her sleep may somehow be healing her mind while the bed rest and the antibiotics help her body to heal. On the other hand, excessive sleep can also be a sign of depression. This has gone on long enough. She needs to be taking nourishment by mouth and to have a little exercise. I don't want to force her out of her sleep. I'd rather she gave it up of her own volition. That's where you come in, Mrs. Carew. Sit with her, talk to her, hold her hand. Perhaps she'll wake up for you."

"I'll certainly try." Ellen nodded vigorously.

An hour later, Dr. Nathan returned. The curly haired blond woman was perched on the side of the hospital bed, chattering away; she was so tiny her feet didn't reach the floor, and she swung them back and forth, like a child. But her eyes, as she saw him in the doorway and let her words wind down, were sad. She shook her head.

Branwen Faraday was still deeply asleep.

Ellen joined Dr. Nathan in the corridor. "She moved her head, and for a minute she held my hand real tight, but that was all. You know, I think I just don't know her well enough to know the key things to say. Branwen and I are getting to be good friends, but we only met a few months ago. Dr. Nathan, much as I dislike the man, he's the obvious one. What about her husband, Jason Faraday? Why isn't he in there with her?"

Charles Nathan's hand went involuntarily to his throat, rubbing it. He caught himself doing it and thrust the hand into the pocket of his white coat. "Ah, that's an unpleasant story. He, ah, more or less went berserk in here, and we can't allow him back."

Ellen's eyes widened. With the surprising authority she could command when she wanted, she took the doctor's arm. "I think you'd better tell me all about that. I'm the closest thing to a protector that young woman in there is likely to have, and I think I need to know. Where's your office?"

When the story was told, Ellen said nothing, but sat thinking. Finally she said, "When Branwen is able to handle it, either you or I must tell her what he did."

"I agree."

"I'll do it," Ellen decided. She was in her take-charge mode now, blue eyes snapping with efficiency. "You just take care of Branwen's medical condition, and I'll do the rest."

"I'm extremely grateful," said Dr. Nathan, meaning it, "and more than a little relieved. Thank you."

"No problem. I have an idea who could get her to wake up. Actually there are two people, but one is too far away to get here in good time. Do I have your permission to bring in another visitor?"

Charles Nathan smiled his very pleasant smile. "Mrs. Carew, if it will bring Branwen Faraday out of her sleep, you can bring a whole army!"

"Remarkable!" said Harry Ravenscroft. Take away the ugly hospital trappings and give her a crystal casket instead, and Branwen might have been the sleeping Snow White. Her skin was that white, her hair that black, her sleep that profound. "Leave me alone with her," he said to Ellen. She nodded and left.

Harry stood by Branwen's bed, studying the purity of bone structure in a face uncluttered by any emotion. But what was this? He bent down to see more closely, careful not to touch her. The physical mark of this ordeal, Harry thought, she will carry it to the end of her days: to the right of the widow's peak that gave the heart shape to her face, an inch-wide streak of white was forming in Branwen's hair. At the roots in that inch-wide space the hair had already lost all pigmentation. He had heard of people whose hair had turned gray or white overnight in response to shock or great stress, but this was the first he'd seen of the phenomenon himself. He supposed such a thing was singularly fitting, the body exhibiting marks of a blow dealt to the spirit.

To the spirit. Yes. That was where he would have to go to reach Branwen. Her body slept in this hospital bed, but her essential being had gone somewhere else entirely. Far, far deeper than any meditation. Which, of course, was why no one could wake her. Could he find her? Perhaps. With his gaunt face and angular form Harry Ravenscroft was no handsome prince to wake the sleeping princess with a kiss, but he had other abilities. He could try.

Harry brought a chair near the bed, sat straight with his feet flat on the floor and his hands on his knees, and began to breathe deeply. He had impressed upon Ellen that she must not allow anyone to enter the room, as he was going to try to reach Branwen by what Ellen called with affectionate derision his "mystical mumbo jumbo." Ellen might poke fun at him, but he knew he could rely on her to prevent an interruption that might be not just startling, but downright dangerous.

Harry's breathing slowed. The planes of his face relaxed and smoothed. He focused his powerful mind, in his mind kindled a light, a beacon shining in surrounding darkness, and he became that light. First he was the many-faceted great burning lamp of a lighthouse, sweeping his white path through night and across dark waters. Sweeping 'round and 'round, across dark waters.

Across dark waters Harry went, farther and farther, treading the beam of his own white light into the high-walled labyrinth of Timelessness. His light became a single flame, the flame became a torch that he carried in his hand. The labyrinthine walls were trees, ancient trees, huge oaks, their gnarled trunks so close together that their branches formed an arched living roof above his head. This wood was like a maze that seemed to have no beginning and no end; but Harry knew this wood. He held his torch high and went on.

In the center of the wood, a clearing; in the center of the clearing, a mound; at the base of the mound, an entry; beyond the entry, a down-sloping passage lined and roofed with stone. Not a passage-grave, no. At the end of the passage lay a chamber familiar of old, a place of ritual, where the Initiate sleeps, waiting to be reborn. In the chamber Harry found Branwen. In a bleached woolen robe she lay curled at the base of the Standing Stone that rose through the roof of the tumulus. Moonlight poured through the opening, bathing the Stone and the sleeping woman in its unearthly glow. Harry's torch paled by comparison.

He spoke to her in the old tongue. *Arise,* he said, *I have come for you.*

The woman who was Branwen curled her body more tightly, she pressed against the base of the Standing Stone, threw her arms up over her head so that her flowing white sleeves covered her face.

Life calls, insisted Harry, still in the ancient language. *It is time—you must return with me.*

Slowly, with great reluctance, she uncovered her face. She

rose to her knees and looked up at the Stone. She held up her arms and open hands as if to draw strength from the moon's light. Finally she gained her feet, the woolen robe flowed in folds around her, and she turned to face him. Great, sad eyes consumed her face. An inch-wide streak of pure white was in her hair.

The Raven is a strange harbinger of Life, Branwen said in the old language. But she came with him.

In her hospital room, Branwen opened her eyes. She said, "I think you made me come back too soon, Harry Ravenscroft."

Harry stretched and smiled. He rubbed his hands together, silently congratulating himself. He'd done it, he'd found her *and* brought her back! He said, "Your doctor is concerned for the health of your body, my dear."

She fixed on him eyes as huge and sad as they'd looked in the ancient chamber. "The body would have survived, and you know it," she said accusingly. "The rest of me doesn't feel strong enough yet to deal with—with this *life*. Why couldn't you have left me alone?"

Harry stood over her. "Because if you didn't wake up on your own, they'd have jolted you back into your body with chemicals, or maybe even with electric shock. Far better to do it my way."

Branwen managed a wintry smile of concession. "Yes, I suppose so. I was in the safest place I could find, and yet you found me. I congratulate you, but don't expect me to be happy about it."

Over the next days, while she ate and walked and her body strengthened, Branwen seldom spoke and she never smiled. She accepted all that Dr. Nathan told her without protest and without tears. She signed papers for the cremation of the stillborn child and did not ask how Jason's signature would be obtained. She did not ask after Jason Faraday at all; when Ellen Carew came and told her of Jason's violent behavior and the order that barred him from the hospital, Branwen said only, "I am not surprised."

Her composure was complete, but her physical recovery was slow, and the inch-wide streak of her hair turned completely white down its entire length, from roots to tip.

Late one night, returning from a three A.M. delivery, Dr. Charles Nathan was killed when his car crashed into the concrete abutment of an overpass. They said he must have been exhausted and fallen asleep at the wheel.

Jason came, accompanied by his lawyer, to see his wife. The lawyer was there in case anyone tried to prevent him even though the time had expired on the restraining order. No one did. Jason thought that Branwen should be well enough to leave the hospital—if not at once, then soon—and he intended to take her home. She was his wife, so obviously she belonged at home. That was the first step. Beyond that, he hadn't planned yet. He'd been too busy finding the right professional and arranging Dr. Charles Nathan's "accident." It hadn't been easy to do all that in such a short time, especially to have it go as perfectly as it had done. Not the slightest suspicion, not a hint of doubt, no danger at all of getting caught!

The change in Branwen's appearance shocked him. The sudden white in her hair, the eyes so big in a face so thin it looked mostly cheekbones. Her refusal to go home with him shocked him more. She refused so gently that Jason never suspected the implacable decision underneath. She was not yet well enough to be completely on her own, she said. She didn't want to be a burden, not when his business was likely to take him away for days at a time; she couldn't expect him to give up business in order to stay with her; he could hardly do that, could he? Of course not, he agreed. So she had arranged to stay with a friend, just until she could manage on her own again. What friend? Why, Ellen Carew.

Jason left satisfied. It was a good temporary arrangement that left him free to make more elaborate plans, free to indulge his tastes that were daily becoming more expensive and more bizarre. Branwen's car remained in his garage, and he scarcely noticed when all of her books and some of her clothes disappeared. Jason did not realize that in her lonely sorrow, in her journey into the depths of her own soul, Branwen had at last seen him as he truly was . . . and beyond that, as he would become. He did not know that in her silence as she strengthened her body she also strengthened her will to at last break all the ties—present and from ages past—that bound her to him. Nor did he guess that Ellen Carew's estate had such perfect security that when he did decide to move against Branwen, he would not be able to get near her.

* * *

The deceased Dr. Nathan's partner, Dr. John Halliday, was not satisfied with her progress. She was anemic and underweight and, in his opinion, more depressed than she should be. He transferred Branwen to the Convalescent Wing and ordered a psychiatric consult. Ellen Carew, who did not understand Branwen's unusual degree of silence, approved this decision. Only Harry Ravenscroft understood that in her silence she was completing the inner journey from which she'd felt he brought her back too soon; she was healing her spirit. To a degree, the psychiatrist who examined her also understood, though he would not have described the process in Harry's manner. The psychiatrist concluded that Mrs. Faraday was not inappropriately depressed. He said that withdrawal was for her a coping mechanism, and not severe enough to be unhealthy. He told them to give her food and fresh air and exercise and otherwise leave her alone.

Branwen stayed in the Convalescent Wing for two weeks after her ten days on the Ob-Gyn Service. During that two weeks, Will Tracy came.

The Con Wing was in the oldest part of the hospital and had a small dining room with a wall of old-fashioned French windows that opened out onto a garden patio. The patients were encouraged to spend time in the fresh air and sunshine. Branwen was on the patio, dressed in a long robe of fine handkerchief linen that Ellen had bought for her. The robe was more frivolous than anything Branwen would have chosen for herself. Printed with tiny pink rosebuds in an all-over pattern on a white background, it had narrow ruffles at the neck and along the edges of the sleeves, and a slightly deeper ruffle at the hem. Ellen had provided pink slippers of soft Spanish kid to go with the robe. As usual, Ellen had made wise choices. The pink in the robe heightened the color that daily time in the sun was restoring to Branwen's complexion; the ruffles softened her thinness; the elegant feel of the fine cotton and leather on her skin gently reawakened her senses. She had had her hair washed and brushed partially dry by a nurse's aide, and now she sat in the sun with her hair spread about her shoulders to complete its drying. The new white streak caused much comment among the nurses and aides in the Con Wing. They did not know how recently and out of what trauma it had been acquired, and exclaimed how unusual and striking it was, how amazing that the streak was natural and not bleached! This, finally, had made Branwen smile. She sat now in the sun and closed her eyes, enjoying the feel of its warmth on her head. For the first time in many days her body felt good, and she was glad to be alive.

Wise Ellen Carew had also called Will.

He had come from his post in Dublin with all the speed various forms of transportation and his long legs could muster. Thoroughly briefed by Ellen's long transatlantic call, he thought he knew what to expect. He thought he was emotionally prepared. But when he stopped his breakneck pace to stand at the French windows, seeing Branwen with her face tipped up to receive the sunshine like a fragile flower, her eyelashes frilly and dark on her cheeks, suddenly he couldn't breathe. He backed up a step lest she open her eyes and see him before he was ready. Unexpected tears pricked at his own eyes. He was swamped by a sudden, fierce regret: that he'd ever had to leave her, that he could only stay for forty-eight hours, that he couldn't quit his job immediately and stay with her forever. Will blinked against his burning tears.

His handsome Irish tweed jacket was much too warm, though the weather was relatively mild for a late summer day in the Virginia suburbs of D.C. He shrugged out of the jacket, loosened his collar and tie. *Casual, that's the ticket,* he told himself, swiping at his damp eyes with the back of a hand. Taking a deep breath and hooking the jacket over his shoulder by a long finger, Will strolled out onto the patio. She was lovely as a flower, graceful as a swan with the arched line of her throat. . . .

"Hi, stranger," Will said, grinning.

Branwen's eyes flew open. He had almost forgotten how incredibly blue-green they were. Disbelief was replaced by a joy that lit her face.

"Will, oh, Will!" she exclaimed. She half rose, and he reached for her, letting his jacket fall to the ground as he wrapped her in his arms.

Oh, the feel of her, the smell of her, all clean soap and sunshine! He touched his lips to her cheek. The taste of her skin seared him with a pleasure that was also pain. Her body, her arms that gripped him so tightly, felt as thin as a child's.

"I can't believe you're here!" said Branwen, disentangling

herself from Will's arms. "You're back in Washington. For how long?"

"Just visiting," said Will, stooping to retrieve his jacket. He urged her back to her chair and pulled over another. *Be casual,* he told himself, *don't let her know you want to keep on holding her so badly your heart is about to jump out of your chest.* He slouched in the lawn chair, crossed his ankle over his knee, and winked. "Actually, I came to see you, old friend."

Branwen looked uncomfortable. She wound a strand of hair around and around her finger. "Ellen called you," she guessed, and waited for him to nod assent. "She shouldn't have. I didn't need you to come to—to disrupt your life for this."

"I didn't disrupt my life, Branwen. I'm glad she called me—I only wish she'd done it sooner. I'd have been here for you before now, if I'd only known what you were going through."

"I'm all right. At least, mostly. I'll be better when I can leave here. I'm going to stay at Ellen's. She's giving me the use of her guest cottage for a while, until I can, ah, get on my feet."

"You do look all right," said Will softly, longing to touch her. "In a way, you look more beautiful than ever. But I can see, too, that you've had a hard time."

"Yes, I did." Branwen looked down, then forced her eyes up to meet his. Her voice was just above a whisper. "I lost the baby, Will. All those months, and then something went wrong. I went into labor, and it was born three weeks early, but it was dead. A boy, dead when he was born. The poor little thing never got to live at all."

"I'm sorry."

She swallowed hard. She hadn't tried to talk about this before, not with anyone. "I was, too, but now . . . I think it was for the best. I made a terrible, terrible, unforgivable mistake, Will. Jason and I should never have tried to bring a child into the world. Perhaps I could have taken care of him, but Jason . . ." Branwen's eyes held a hunted look. "Jason became so demanding, so possessive of the child even before he was born. . . . Nothing good could have come of it, you see. I think it must be for the best this way, even for the child. But still I feel responsible. That baby's few months of life inside of me, and his death, are both on my soul."

"Don't say that." Will leaned forward. "You wanted the baby to save your marriage. You did everything in your power, you did what you truly thought was right. So the baby didn't make it—that's fate. It's not your fault. Please, please don't blame yourself!"

"I . . . can't help it. But I suppose I paid the price. I'll be paying it for the rest of my life. That's fate, too."

She went away from him then—her body still sat in the chair, yet she was somehow gone. Ellen had warned him that Branwen was remote and withdrawn for long periods of time. Will let her go, content just to be in her presence. He of all people was used to her silences.

The Con Wing had no set visiting hours, and visitors were encouraged as a way of helping the patients make their transition back to normal life. Will stayed with Branwen all that day and into the evening. He ate with her in the small dining room and only left when it was time for sleep. The next day he was back after breakfast. Overnight the weather had changed. Being out of doors was like being under a hot, soggy blanket. The patio was therefore out of the question; they would have to do their visiting in the sporadic privacy of her room. Will was unpleasantly reminded of all the times past when he'd wanted to be completely alone with Branwen and could not. Always there was not enough privacy, not enough time. Once again he chafed against restrictions. How could he cheer Branwen when he felt lower than the belly of a snake himself?

He tried. He told amusing and highly exaggerated stories about his blunders as a budding diplomat among the charming and eccentric Irish. Slowly but surely he engaged Branwen's attention. Made her smile, made her laugh, especially when he tried out his Irish accent that reeked of a Kentucky twang.

She turned wistful. "When I was at Llanfaren, my favorite place was the wall-walk on top of the North Tower. I could look out across the sea, and when it was clear, sometimes I could see the coast of Ireland. I always thought I'd go there someday, across the Irish Sea. But then I came across the Atlantic Ocean instead, so much farther. I came here, not to Ireland after all."

"You don't know how much I'd like to take you back with me!"

Branwen smiled at him, and he reached over and covered her hand with his. He asked, "What will you do, Branwen? Will you go back to Wales? Have you made any plans beyond staying in Ellen's cottage?"

She looked directly at him. Except for the startling new white streak in her hair, she looked much more like herself today. "Actually, yes, I have made plans. I know everyone around here thinks I'm off in a fog most of the time, but I'm not. I've done a lot of thinking about the future. No, I won't go back to Wales. I belong here now."

"But, ah, surely you won't . . . ?" He couldn't even say the words.

"Go back to Redmund, to Jason? No, but I don't want him to know that yet. He thinks I'm just going to stay on the Carew estate until I'm thoroughly recovered and then I'll come home. Instead, when I'm strong enough, I'll see a lawyer. I don't know what it takes to get a divorce in this state, but that's what I'm going to do. Jason doesn't love me anymore. I had become nothing to him except the living vessel that carried his child, and when the child didn't survive, well, he simply has no use for me anymore." Branwen stopped. Talking to Will, finally getting out of herself some of the many things she had thought so much about, was good. But there were some things she could not tell even Will. Dreams she'd had, vivid visionary dreams of Jason Faraday gone so far in his anger that it had consumed any goodness or kindness left in him. She suspected that he'd somehow had a hand in her doctor's supposedly accidental death. She knew that Jason was dangerous to her now, that she must never allow him near her again. She had no proof, only the testimony of her dreams, but she believed the dreams.

"I won't say I'm sorry to see you so determined," Will observed.

Branwen resumed, her clear voice growing stronger, "As soon as my new doctor gives the word on my discharge, Ellen will use my key and get my clothes and books and a few personal things from the house in Redmund. I don't want anything else, not even the car. I just hope that by the time Jason figures out I'm never coming back, he'll be willing to let me go without a lot of trouble."

"He has an obligation to you, Branwen," Will said, leaning toward her earnestly. "You're entitled to some support. And besides, out there in McLean you're going to need a car."

"I have money in savings. I can buy myself one that will do. It's important to me to be completely independent, Will. *Com-*

pletely. To tell you the truth, I'm not entirely happy about Ellen giving me the use of her cottage. I'd much rather have her rent it to me, even if I could only pay a token amount at first."

"Hmmm." Will leaned back. He supposed, after years of marriage to Jason, she was entitled to feel so strongly. "I hope you didn't mention that about the rent for the cottage. People like Ellen Carew are used to noblesse oblige. She'd be insulted if you tried to pay her mere money."

"I know. I wouldn't dare suggest the idea of rent, it's just that I'd feel better if I could pay my own way." Branwen studied Will's profile. He seemed lost in thought, gazing through the window of her hospital room as if there were something more interesting out there to look at than the parking lot. She called to him softly. "Will? What's wrong?"

"Hm? Wrong? Probably nothing. Probably I'm just hyper-sensitive where you're concerned. Too ready to jump to conclusions."

To Branwen, this was not a mysterious communication; but she sidestepped it for the moment. "I'm glad you came. Your visit has been good for me. I didn't realize how much better I'd feel after having someone I could talk to. There's no one else I can trust the way I trust you. Thank you, Will."

Reluctantly Will looked at his watch. He knew it was almost time for him to leave, and he didn't really want the watch to confirm it. Moodily he said, "I still wish I could take you back to Ireland with me."

The longing in his voice reached Branwen, convinced her that she must deal with what was on his mind. She knew him too well, was all too sure what he was thinking. It would be kinder, in the long run, for her to bring it out into the open now, while they were still face-to-face. "I can't go to Ireland with you, Will. But you should have *someone.* I think you under-stood my meaning when I said I intend to be completely inde-pendent. You should find someone, Will, and marry her. You'll be an ambassador before you know it. You need a wife who will be an asset to you in that kind of life, someone who'll make a home for you wherever you go."

There was genuine bewilderment on Will's face. "The State Department isn't a career for me. I thought you knew that. I'll stay with it until the country is out of Viet Nam for good, and then I'll come home. This war can't go on much longer, there's

too much sentiment against it. More and more respectable people are joining the Peace Movement. It isn't just hippies and
flower children anymore."

"Even so. What I'm trying to tell you, as gently as I know
how, is that when I'm out of the marriage to Jason, I'm not going to marry again. Not ever, not anyone, not even you."

"You don't mean it!"

"I *do*. I can't have children now, Will. I expect you know that
even though you haven't mentioned it. I expect Ellen told you.
I'm not going to live anything like the typical life—you know,
Mommy and Daddy in a detached single family home with two
cars in the garage and two point two children. You want those
things, Will, I know you do. Especially the children, and you'll
be a wonderful father. I want you to have all of that. But that's
not what I can have, and not what I want for myself. I want to be
independent. I want to be on my own from now on."

"Branwen, I don't care if you can't have children. I love
you!"

"I love you, too, that's why I'm telling you this. I've hurt you
enough in the past. I don't want to hurt you more by misleading
you now. I will never marry again, Will. Never."

"Never say never, Branwen." He rose swiftly before the sudden sick feeling in his stomach could take over. He kissed her
cheek. "I have to go or I'll miss my plane. I'll write, and you
can write, too—that's one big improvement for us!"

Later, on the plane, he thought about what she'd said.
Thought about how she'd seemed during the whole visit. Ellen
Carew had said she wanted him to bring Branwen out of herself,
that she was depressed and too withdrawn. He'd found her otherwise. Bits of sadness clung to her, yes; anything else, after
what she'd been through, would have been abnormal. Her body
was still weak, but her spirit was strong. So strong, and so clear,
free of the doubt and confusion and self-deception that had
seemed to plague her in the months before he'd left the country.
It was as if she had walked through a fire that had burned away
from her all that was unessential and left the basic Branwen
clean and strong and shining.

He did not want to believe her when she said she would never
marry again. He didn't want to believe her, and yet he did believe. She had survived marriage to a corrupt man with her own
honesty intact. Will imagined that losing a child and at the same

time losing the ability to have other children must be the worst
ordeal a woman could endure, and she had survived that, too.
He had sensed in her a new purity of purpose, and he could not
doubt her. Branwen had emerged from her ordeal a new and
stronger woman.

PART THREE

———

TRANSFORMATION
Washington, D.C.,
1968–1980

1

"Branwen, honey," Ellen said as she put a glass of mint-sprigged iced tea in front of her on the butcher-block top of the kitchen island, "do you know what a gofer is?"

Branwen was cutting carrots and celery and green peppers into julienne strips under Ellen's eagle eye. On the cook's night out, Ellen liked to try out new recipes, and Branwen was often a willing helper. She said, "Of course I do. I hope you're not planning to cook one! It's a small animal rather like a woodchuck, and aside from the fact they're too cute to kill, I'm sure they'd be too tough to eat."

Ellen made a face at her. "Very funny. Anyway, you're wrong. I don't mean animal gophers, I mean people *gofers*."

Branwen stopped cutting to drink her tea. "Okay, I give up. I never heard of people gophers."

"A gofer is a working person who has the lowest job on the totem pole, so-called because absolutely everyone else is higher and can tell this poor lowly person to *go fer* this and *go fer* that."

"I see." Branwen grinned. "Only in America!"

"Of course it doesn't pay very well at all." Ellen began sorting through a pile of pearl onions, but she watched Branwen out of the corner of her eye. "You probably make more in your job at the public library, but it *is* in journalism. Sort of."

"All right. You've aroused my curiosity and you can stop being so circumspect, Ellen. I know that you know how I feel about using influence to get jobs. So what is this job that's sort of in journalism?"

"Local TV station. Gofer in the newsroom. I'm sure it's a terrible job and I doubt television journalism is what you think you want. But it's a foot in the door, Branwen. The producer is a friend, and he'll see you if you're interested."

"Television," Branwen murmured. She hadn't even considered television. She'd thought that while she worked at the library she'd try some free-lance pieces. It hadn't taken long for her to find out that even the small suburban newspapers were not interested in hiring her on the basis of her degree in English from Redmund College. A thread of excitement ran through her, the first she'd felt in a long time. "Television! Yes, I'm interested."

"Good." Ellen nodded, her fingers flying now as she nimbly rolled the thin, transparent outer skins off of the tiny onions. "Like I always say, a foot in the door is worth two in the bush!"

Branwen laughed.

Three weeks later she was a lowly gofer in the newsroom of Channel 15 in Arlington, and loving every minute of it.

The sense of immediate, intimate involvement was what surprised and delighted Branwen about broadcast journalism. She felt it from the moment of setting her foot in the door, and it didn't seem to matter that she was only carrying tapes and stills and scripts and messages back and forth from the station manager to the producers, from producers to writers, from writers to editors, from editors to reporters and so on, over and over again. The station was a new one, the staff fairly small when she joined it. Branwen grew in experience with the station. There was a lot of bad news in 1968: the assassinations of Martin Luther King, Jr., and Robert Kennedy; the violence against protestors, both for civil rights and the Peace Movement; and late in the year the accidental death of Thomas Merton, monk and writer, a solitary man whose works particularly appealed to Branwen. Dealing with these tragedies in the context of the newsroom, being able to talk and speculate, made them easier to bear.

Branwen's first opportunity to construct a news story on her own came with Merton's death. She offered to put together a piece for the noon news, careful to explain that she only wanted to write it, not go before the cameras herself. She had an angle that seemed so obvious to her that she was surprised that some-

one with more experience hadn't grabbed it: the irony that
Thomas Merton, a Trappist monk long withdrawn from the
world, should be killed in a silly accident with a wet floor and
an electric fan just when he had begun to travel and to lend the
force of his writing talent to the cause of harmony among nations. She had everything going for her in the Merton story: a
unique approach, thorough knowledge of her subject, a reporter
who knew a showcase for his talents when he saw one, and her
secret weapon—technical ability that, now put to the test, surpassed her own expectations. And everyone else's. The piece
was a hit on the noon news, so it was repeated in the eleven P.M.
report. A day later, copycat news segments on the irony of
Thomas Merton's death appeared on other area stations.
Branwen had made her mark. She was soon promoted to news
writer. And though she did not know it, she had established
what would become her personal trademark as a journalist, that
unique, stinging zap of insight inserted into an overall sympathetic treatment of her subject.

Around the newsroom, unofficially, off and on all year they
had speculated about conspiracies. Not since the publication
of the Warren Commission's report denying conspiracy in the
assassination of JFK had so many rumors of that nature been
flying around Washington and environs. Just the word "conspiracy" made Branwen nervous, because it made her think of Jason Faraday. Or rather, it made her have to try *not* to think about
him. *If* there was a conspiracy and *if* Jason was involved in it,
then the whole thing was so monstrously out of control it was
almost beyond comprehension. But it was very hard for
Branwen to get the conspiracy idea out of her head, though she
was careful never to say the word, always to stay on the border
of those particular discussions. Thomas Merton's death seemed
too convenient an "accident" to her. Only by a supreme effort of
will could she ignore an intuitive conviction that Merton's death
was no more an accident than Dr. Nathan's had been. Over and
over again she told herself that she was becoming paranoid, until she more than half believed it.

It was therefore a relief when 1968 became 1969 and
Branwen's divorce was granted on the basis of a year's legal
separation. Perhaps now she could begin to breathe more easily,
dare to go on some day trips by herself, leave the tight security
of Ellen Carew's estate at night. It was over now; Jason had really let her go!

Harry Ravenscroft called on a Sunday morning in late February. "Branwen, do you suppose you could drive out to Raven Hill this afternoon? I have some news that I'm sure will interest you, and also something of a surprise to, ah, give you. Mrs. Beecher sends her regards and wishes me to tell you that she will make your favorite Mud Pie if you'll come."

Mud Pie! Nobody could do that peculiarly southern combination of tender pastry, nuts, and thick, fudgy chocolate better than Mrs. Beecher. "You know, Harry, that Mrs. Beecher's Mud Pie is an irresistible enticement. I'll come, but do you have to be so mysterious? Can't you at least tell me the interesting news over the phone?"

"No, no. This is too important. Shall we say about three? I'll look forward to seeing you, Branwen. It's been a while."

"Yes, it has. Me, too—see you shortly."

Driving the gray Ford Falcon she'd bought used after her release from the hospital some eighteen months earlier, Branwen arrived at Raven Hill at the appointed time. She seldom came out here anymore because the route took her too near Redmund for her comfort, and now she realized she'd missed the place, and Mrs. Beecher. Harry, too, though he did visit her in the cottage from time to time. She drove slowly up the final curve in the drive, thinking that Raven Hill was a good house, peaceful, even if its present owner was so complicated. She liked the dignity and simplicity of the house's architecture. When she left her car under the port cochere, she noticed that the old wisteria, though its gnarled woody trunk vine looked completely dead, was sending out new tendrils that would soon turn green. And soon after that fat buds would turn into fragrant chains of flowers. In a few weeks, she thought, walking across the porch to the front door, all this present lifelessness would be bursting with life—color, fragrance, surging sap, dripping nectar, bird song. . . .

And yet—Branwen's eyes swept the hills—it was so isolated! Involuntarily she shivered and thought, *I'm not over it yet. I'm still afraid to be alone in an isolated place, afraid that Jason will come after me.*

The front door opened behind her, and Harry drawled, "Really, Branwen, don't stand there gawking like a tourist. You've seen my yard a hundred times before. So come in, come in!"

"Some yard," she quipped. "Sometimes I forget how beautiful it all is." She presented her cheek for his greeting kiss as she came through the door.

"Let me take your coat, my dear. Anytime you want to leave Ellen's cottage—which, though admittedly charming, is really rather small—you're more than welcome here. Mrs. B. would be in seventh heaven. Now that you come so seldom, she positively talks my ear off about you before you come and after you've gone. I'm sure she'd like me to either marry you or adopt you!"

"Really."

"Really!" Harry grinned impishly. "After you, my dear, in the library as usual. Later we'll have coffee in the little dining room. I'm democratic and have asked Mrs. Beecher to join us, since she'll no doubt hover over you anyway. It's coffee rather than tea because she says tea doesn't go with Mud Pie. See how henpecked I've allowed myself to become?"

"You *are* in an expansive mood today," Branwen observed as she settled herself in a wing chair. The fire burned comfortably low in its grate.

"That's because I'm simply bursting with news. Ready?"

Branwen nodded.

"You will never guess who called and offered the olive branch."

"I'm afraid I can."

"That's right." Harry's eyes were shining silver as they always did when something excited him. "Your now ex-husband, Jason Faraday. Invited me to join him at the Faculty Club, just like old times. I was curious, naturally, so I went."

"Naturally." Branwen tried to keep her expression neutral, but she was beginning to feel uneasy.

"Jason has resigned from the faculty, Branwen. He said we were celebrating the last time he would ever set foot in Redmund's Faculty Club. Just like that!" Harry snapped his fingers. "He's leaving, not even bothering to finish out the semester."

"Well, I guess that shouldn't be much of a surprise. He's done precious little teaching in the last couple of years. Are you sure he resigned? They didn't fire him?"

"I'm sure." Harry nodded rather vigorously, and his shock of silver-blond hair fell over his forehead. "It takes action of a departmental committee to fire a professor, and if that had been done, I'd have heard. Something's up with Jason, Branwen. He was so full of himself he seemed puffed up to twice his normal size. He positively bristled with goodwill. Said he's selling the house, too. He's not just leaving Redmund, he's leaving the country! Going to live in Europe."

Branwen tried to relax. Perhaps this really was good news. "Where in Europe? Did he say?"

"He said Switzerland. Said he was sorry for the years of bad feeling between us, between himself and me, and that he hoped I'd look him up if I were over there. Now, aren't you pleased? Isn't this good news for you?"

"I . . . think so. I'm more relieved than pleased."

"Why, I'd have thought you'd be jumping up and down with joy to have him so completely out of the way!"

"I don't suppose he said what his job was to be? What work takes him to Europe?"

"No, he didn't. You know he has never talked about that other work of his. I assume it's more of the same."

"I know." Branwen was glad to know Jason would be so far away, and yet she'd gone cold all over. She held out her hands to the fire. "He said when I was expecting the baby that he was working for some new people and that if he did well, we'd leave Redmund and could go—anywhere. That must be what has happened, and he's chosen Switzerland for some reason. B-but something in me doesn't like it. I'm afraid. . . . Oh, Harry, I don't know what I'm afraid of. I guess I've just gotten paranoid. I'll probably never see Jason again. Nor will you, unless you make a point of it." She shook herself, brightened her expression. "Enough of that! Now, what's that surprise you mentioned?"

"The surprise, my dear, comes from that outpouring of goodwill I mentioned. Here you are." Harry reached into his pocket and drew out a set of keys that he dangled from his fingers. "The keys to your Mustang. Jason asked me to tell you that he wants you to have your car. It's in my garage."

Slowly Branwen turned her head. She looked at the small silver keys with a mixture of loathing and disbelief. Her expression did not change as she raised her gaze to Harry's face. "You seem to think this is some kind of magnanimous gesture on Jason's part."

Harry was puzzled. Yes, he'd thought Jason Faraday meant well. "Branwen, I thought that Jason was attempting to leave here a little more gracefully than he has lived for the last year and a half. What earthly harm can there be in him giving you the car? It's a much better vehicle than that piece of junk you've been driving!"

Branwen jumped up out of the chair. Hugging her arms to her chest, she strode away, agitated. "No, thank you, and you'll have to forgive me if I mistrust Jason's motives. For all I know, there's a bomb in the Mustang that will explode with me in it!"

"Really, I think you're being a little extreme."

She tossed her head. She had cut her hair to shoulder length, but still it flew back from her face with the head toss, as it always had. "I don't think I am, and I don't want the car. I don't want anything, not the smallest part of anything that comes from Jason Faraday!"

"Branwen, my dear!" Harry left his chair, thrusting the offending keys into his pocket. "I had no idea you still felt so strongly."

"I do, Harry, I really do. Has Jason left Redmund yet?"

"I don't think so. The house hasn't sold yet, and I expect he'll be around until it does. Branwen, I hope you aren't thinking what I think you're thinking."

She stood with her arms folded, her eyes spitting blue-green fire. "You made yourself the middle man in this, Harry. I refuse this so-called gracious gesture. You can give the car right back to him!"

"Mmm." Harry wrinkled his brow. "I think that would be extremely unwise. Suppose he is as sincere on this one occasion as I believed him to be? You don't want to, ah, rock the boat, do you?"

"I don't trust him. And you shouldn't, either."

"All right, all right. I'll *sell* the Mustang, and you can do whatever you want with the money. Throw it in the Potomac, for all I care. Jason will never know. Does that satisfy you?"

"I don't know. Give me a minute." Branwen went to the fireplace and watched the glowing log with its occasional licking tongues of flame. Was she overreacting? She didn't think so. There was so much Harry didn't know, the things Will had told her, that she must not repeat to anyone. There were her dreams, so full of warnings, and the testimony of the rune stones. Yet in a way Harry was right. It would be best under any circumstances not to provoke Jason. She turned. "I agree it would be better to sell the car. I don't have the title, though it was in my name. I left it in the bank in the safe deposit box."

"Jason said it's in the glove compartment of the car. We can get it, and you can sign it before you leave today. I'll date it when I've found a buyer."

"Harry," Branwen pleaded, "I know you think I'm being foolish, but I don't want either of us to touch that car until a mechanic has thoroughly checked it out. You can get someone out here, tell him you're concerned it may have been tampered with in some way, impress on him to be careful and give it a complete going-over. Please. Promise me!"

"I promise." Harry put his arm around her shoulders. "I promise. Now, let's not keep Mrs. Beecher and her Mud Pies waiting any longer. Shall we?"

On the following Tuesday, Harry got a mechanic out to Raven Hill. He felt ridiculous and sure the man thought he was a little crazy, but he did as he'd promised Branwen. There was no bomb or incendiary device in the car, but the brake lines had been cut almost through. The amazed mechanic said it must have been done deliberately. The damage could not have been from normal wear-and-tear. The Mustang could not have been driven more than a few miles before losing its brakes completely. Out on the highway, a serious accident would have resulted. The mechanic shook his head over such senseless vandalism.

Harry, stunned, agreed that vandalism was a terrible thing. He was glad the mechanic had come up with the idea of vandals, though he wondered how the man could be quite so stupid.

Harry never told Branwen. He had the brakes repaired and sold the car quietly to a dealer in another town. He gave the money to Branwen and never said a word. To anyone.

Afterward, he dreamed. Though he could not know it, his dreams were remarkably like Branwen's: dark shapes humping, slithering, groping blindly toward him and getting closer, making jittering sounds that grated on the ears, tore the nerve endings in the brain. In the dream, a tactile feeling of ugliness that left him disgusted and sick upon waking. Left him also with the conviction that Jason Faraday knew those shapes and had already embraced them.

Branwen did not venture far from her cottage until she was sure Jason had left the country. Then, feeling as if she had been let out of a cage, she took the first real vacation of her life. She went in search of the sea. Alone in her old Falcon, with only a map and her instincts to guide her, she was exhilarated by her freedom. Crossing Chesapeake Bay by the bridge near Annapolis, she drove down Maryland's Eastern Shore and into the Virginia piece of that peninsula, sometimes called "Delmarva." She wandered at her own pace down tiny side roads through a landscape uniformly low and marshy and pocked with miniature bays and inlets. At Chincoteague and Assateague Islands she stopped to see the wild horses, and stayed over a couple of nights at a small house that had been converted to an inn. The feel and taste of the sea were here, though the land and seascapes were so different from what she had known in Wales. She continued her wandering to the very tip of the peninsula where she took a ferry rather than the bridge to Norfolk.

From Norfolk Branwan followed the curve of the shoreline past Cape Henry and into Virginia Beach where she spent a night in an expensive, modern high-rise hotel. Her room was more than comfortable and had a balcony overlooking the beach. She sat for hours listening to the ocean, watching night down-furl veils of darkness, turning the ever-moving waves from purple to black. At dawn she walked the beach in cold bare feet. This beach was wide and clean, yet not quite where she wanted to be. She checked out of the hotel and went on, driving south. After just a few miles she discovered the small community of Sandbridge Beach. It felt right. Satisfied that she need go no farther, she located a real estate office in a house on the main street and rented half of a duplex cottage right on the beach. There Branwen stayed for the rest of her vacation.

Alone and not lonely, Branwen let sea and sand and sky, boats and birds and fish, bring balance into her life. She didn't turn on the television set or read a newspaper or think about her life. She didn't even write in her journal. She did take pictures with a camera she'd bought for the trip, and she read three paperback novels she'd brought along. Her first vacation was a complete success, and she had learned something about herself that would become increasingly important: She liked to travel alone.

Ellen Carew was not a busybody. She was a firm believer in MYOB, even before Ann Landers had invented the acronym for

Mind Your Own Business. So when she received a letter from
Will Tracy asking whether Branwen had moved out of her cottage and if so, would Ellen please send Branwen's new address,
it threw her into something of a tizzy. Will's letter arrived while
Branwen was on her vacation, but having the extra days to decide didn't help Ellen to know any better what to do. It just gave
her more time to stew over the problem. When Branwen had
been back in the cottage for an hour, Ellen walked over with a
casserole in hand, still not sure what she would say. She only
knew she had to say something.

Ellen knocked on the cottage door and waited. "My, don't
you look rested!" she exclaimed when Branwen swung open the
door.

"I am. I had a wonderful time. Come on in."

"I thought you might like to have this for your dinner. It's
chicken and rice, nothing special, but at least you won't have to
cook. I know when I come back from the beach, everything I
own is always dirty and I want to get myself back in order. The
last thing I want is to have to spend time in the kitchen!"

"How thoughtful you are." Branwen smiled, taking the casserole. "And you're exactly right. I'll just pop this in the fridge.
Can you stay for a while and talk? I feel like I need to practice
my conversation after two weeks of solitude."

"You bet." Ellen sat on the wicker couch in the living room
she'd decorated herself and thought, not for the first time, that
she would be sorry when Branwen decided to move to a place
of her own. It had seemed she was gone much longer than two
weeks, and Ellen had missed her.

Branwen had showered and washed and dried her hair. She
was wearing a yellow terry-cloth robe because as Ellen had
said, everything else she owned needed to be washed. The color
of the robe emphasized the light tan she'd acquired on the
beach. Ellen had said she looked rested; Branwen knew she felt
healthier than she had in years. She curled up in the wicker chair
that matched the couch. "So, Ellen. I trust you kept everybody
in Washington on their toes while I was gone."

"Oh, you can be sure of it!" Ellen's blond curls bobbed. "I
missed you, though. Now tell me everywhere you went and
what you did."

Branwen complied, and Ellen listened, silently observing
that Branwen was developing a journalist's eye for detail. When
she was done, Ellen said, "You know, you could make some

great spots for your TV station doing what you've just done—
travel around the state and then talk about it. You notice things
most people don't notice, did you know that?"

"Interesting you should say so. On the way back today, I was
thinking much the same thing. Not about me noticing things
other people don't, but that I'd like to get a cameraman with me
and work up some human-interest bits. Nothing very ambitious,
just five minutes or so here and there. Maybe I'll do a proposal.
First I have to have a unifying theme, and I haven't yet figured
out what that might be."

"You will, though. This idea has grabbed you, I can tell by
your eyes! Do you think this might get you in front of the camera at last?"

"I don't know. It's a problem. I'm a writer, not a reporter. I
don't really want to be in front of the camera."

Ellen grinned. "With your looks you'd knock their socks
off!"

"Thanks for the compliment. I suppose some people don't
ever look at themselves the way they do other people, but let's
not get into that. I know it isn't likely that the station would
give me both a reporter and a cameraman, so if I follow through
on this idea, I guess I'll have to be on camera myself at least
some of the time. But what would I do about my voice, my accent?"

"Your accent is charming. It couldn't possibly be a problem,
unless you forget that most of us around here have southern ears
and can't keep up if you get to talking too fast!"

Branwen grew thoughtful. Ellen was right—this had really
grabbed her. Perhaps it really could work! "You know, Ellen,
maybe my accent could be a part of the theme I need. I'm a new
citizen, I'll be in the process of learning about my new country
for a long time. I could call it Discovering Virginia, or something like that. Sort of a poor man's 'On the Road,' with apolo-
gies to Charles Kuralt."

"Marvelous! I vote for that!" Ellen clapped her hands and
jumped up. "In fact, I think we should drink to it. Don't you
have some sherry around here someplace?"

"How about white wine? It's in the refrigerator."

"Don't get up. I'll do the honors. After all, I do know where
everything is." Ellen assembled a tray in the kitchen with the
wine in a carafe and two stemmed glasses. She returned to find
Branwen scribbling notes on a legal pad. "My goodness, you

are eager to get started! Well, why not? I propose a toast: To Discovering Virginia with Branwen Faraday!"

Branwen laughed as she touched her glass to Ellen's. Then, impulsively, she reached out and caught the older woman in a hug. "You know, Ellen, I enjoyed being alone, but I did miss you. You don't know how important your friendship is to me."

"I missed you, too, Branwen." They hugged again and parted, each a little embarrassed by the unaccustomed display of emotion. It was Ellen who broke the silence that fell as they sipped their wine and thought their separate thoughts. "Branwen, honey, are you simply exhausted from your drive back or could you handle a few minutes more of conversation? There's something, ah, rather serious I'd like to discuss with you."

"I'm not at all tired. What's on your mind?"

"I'm not sure exactly how to get into it. I hope you know that I really don't believe in poking my nose in other people's business."

"Nobody could know that better than I do after living in your cottage for as long as I have. You may be the world's least intrusive person, Ellen."

Ellen expelled a held breath. "I'm so glad you think so. You see, I got this letter and it has worried me because I really care so much about both of you. I feel I simply must ask: Branwen, is something wrong between you and Will Tracy?"

Branwen looked immediately troubled. "The letter you got that worried you—it was from Will?"

"Um-hm. He asked if you'd moved and if I would send him your new address. So you can't have been writing to him, and all this time I thought—well, I thought you and Will were close."

"We are." She brought her knees up to her chest and wrapped her arms around them. "I suppose nothing will ever change that. I don't quite know how to explain—"

"Oh," Ellen said hurriedly, "I don't want you to feel you have to explain anything to me. I have no right to pry. Oh, dear, I'm really botching this up, aren't I?"

Branwen smiled at her friend. "I don't mind talking about Will. What's going on is that I don't want to marry again, and I've told Will that. But when he writes to me, his letters always convey in one way or another that he's waiting for me to change my mind. I'm concerned about that, Ellen. I want Will to have the kind of life he wants, and he wants marriage. Therefore, he needs to find another woman, not me. I don't enjoy not answering his letters, but about six months ago I decided it would be better that way in the long run. In the last letter I wrote to him, I was careful to reemphasize how much I value my independence and enjoy living alone. I don't want him to think I stopped writing because I fell in love with another man."

A tiny worry line appeared between Ellen's eyebrows. "It *is* a difficult situation, isn't it? I always thought you and Will loved each other, that it was just a tragic mistake you had to meet him after you were already married to Jason."

"Yes. And then again, if I hadn't married Jason, I'd never have met Will in the first place."

"Oh, Branwen, I don't know what to think! I suppose I should just shut my mouth and not say another word about it." Ellen got up distractedly, running a hand through her curls.

"Don't go. Stay, please, and help me talk this through."

"Are you sure?" Ellen's frown deepened.

"Yes." Branwen poured a second glass of wine for Ellen and handed it to her, then freshened her own. "Sit, please. That's better. Ellen, you of all people should understand my wanting to live alone. You're obviously content to remain single, and you do it so well. You're a kind of role model for me, you know."

"Me, a role model?" Ellen giggled, her tension eased somewhat. "Good heavens! But seriously, if you'll forgive my saying so, there is a difference. True, my husband was older than I, just as Jason is older than you. In our case, though, we had a happy marriage. I do like my freedom, I admit that, and I've never had the feeling that my life was over just because my husband died, as many widows seem to. I don't expect I'll ever find another man I'll love as much as I did my husband. So far, no one has been able to hold a candle to him. Sometimes I regret that we didn't have children, and now the safest child-bearing years are almost gone for me. . . . Oh, there I've gone and done it again! I have a positive genius for saying the wrong thing today! I'm sorry, Branwen."

Branwen's eyes misted over in a faraway look. Her voice was soft. "I do love Will. If I were going to marry anyone, I would

want to marry Will. I'm not sure how much my being unable to
have any more children has to do with my decision not to marry
again. Probably not much—I simply can't bear the thought of
being in another marriage. I think marriage to Jason permanently traumatized me. One thing I am sure of is that I've already hurt Will Tracy enough. Does that make sense to you,
Ellen? That sometimes if you really love a person the way to
show it is to let him go to someone else?"

"I . . . don't know."

"That's why I think a clean break is best, so that he won't be
hurt anymore. Will is a very eligible bachelor, and a lovable person, and he'll find a woman as soon as he's really willing to
look—which he won't be as long as I do anything to encourage
him into thinking I might change my mind about marriage.
He'll find a woman who'll love him, and she'll marry him and
give him children, and he'll be happy. He'll forget all about
me."

Ellen absorbed Branwen's words and let them settle in. She
thought, *That horrible Jason Faraday has made her gun-shy,
that's the trouble;* but she did not say so. She finished her glass
of wine, stood, and gave Branwen an affectionate peck on the
cheek. "You're a brave woman, and you have a fine life ahead
of you. You are the only person in the world who can know
what's right for you, Branwen. You know I'll always support
you any way I can."

Branwen caught Ellen's hand and gave it a squeeze. "Thank
you. Thank you for everything."

Ellen went back to her own house and, while her determination was fresh, answered Will's letter.

Branwen hasn't moved. She's busy making a new life for
herself and doing quite well at it. I expect her career is really going to take off before too much longer. I know,
though, that the scars from her marriage to Jason are
deep. She certainly seems determined not to try marriage
again.

I can't say why she isn't writing to you, Will. That's
between you and Branwen. Perhaps you need to get on
with your life, as she is getting on with hers. So tell me all
about your life in your next letter. Any idea how much longer you'll be in Ireland? Where your next post might be?

Has the election of our new President made much difference to you folks over there?

I look forward to hearing from you.

Affectionately,
Ellen

2

———

Tiny flames from the candles on the little round table in Ellen Carew's cottage flickered in Harry Ravenscroft's silvery eyes, and candle glow softened his hawkish features.

"You know, Harry," said Branwen, "you've hardly changed at all since I've known you. Certainly not in recent years. You don't seem to age at all."

Harry grinned. A wisp of silver-gold hair slipped over one eye, and he didn't bother to brush it away. "I shall remind myself of that tomorrow morning when my aging joints creak and protest as I get out of bed! But you, my dear, have changed a great deal in the past—let's see, how many years is it since you ended that despicable marriage and began your career in television . . ."

"Eight," Branwen supplied. She pulled a small, suspicious frown. "What do you mean, I've changed a great deal?"

"Oh"—Harry shrugged—"it's not so much how you look. Since you've let your hair grow long again you look much the same as the young woman I first knew at Llanfaren. It's your poise, the way you carry yourself with so much assurance. You've always been a relatively quiet woman—now your quietness has an added air of self-containment. I fancy your successful career has done that for you."

"I don't know," Branwen mused, "sometimes I think the main thing I've learned from broadcast journalism is that I have

200

to keep buying new clothes even when I'm convinced I don't need them."

"Nonsense. You've done excellent work. That series you did, 'Discovering D.C.,' in the middle of all the Watergate mess, was fantastic! Inspirational. You know that—the major networks picked it up, and you've been a local celebrity ever since."

"A very minor celebrity, Harry. You know I prefer to stay behind the cameras and write. If I'm quiet, it's because I'd rather observe and write about it later. I'm an observer, not a performer." She squirmed a little in her chair. This kind of talk always made her uncomfortable.

"Don't tell me you have regrets about your career?" Harry asked her sharply.

"No, not about my work." Branwen bit her lower lip. This talk of past years was doing her no good. She did have one very significant regret, and she wished Harry had not made her think of it: Will Tracy. Will was married now, had been married for a couple of years to a widow with a young son. He'd met her in Iran, where the State Department had sent him after Ireland. He'd written to Branwen only that one time in recent years, to tell her of his marriage to Aletha Khouravi. She sounded the perfect wife for a diplomat—cosmopolitan, European-educated, a distant relative of the Shah—not to mention that she came to Will, the perfect father, with a son, Paul. But Branwen had sensed danger in the letter; and off and on ever since she'd had dreams of Will . . . a Will threatened by violence in a land running with blood. She'd had such a dream only the night before and had tried to put it out of her mind—she had no way of knowing the dream was prophetic, for in 1976 the world still had never heard of the Ayatollah.

"There," said Harry, placing his long cool fingers over her hand, "you've gone off again, like you so often do. But I know how to get your attention: I'm going to let you in on a big secret, Branwen."

She turned her head, then shook off the memory as she shook back the long dark hair that spilled over her shoulder. "A secret! Don't tell me . . . you've discovered the lost secrets of the Druids at last!"

"That's nothing to joke about," Harry grumbled. "It's unlike you and most unkind. Especially since you have for so long steadfastly refused to help me!" Harry's gaze was piercing; for a moment he looked formidable.

"Oops! Sorry." Branwen refused to take him seriously. She supposed they would banter forever about that particular subject. "Here, have some more bread. Do I really want to be let in on this secret, Harry?"

"Oh, yes, yes, I think you do. But first tell me: When did you last cast the runes?"

"Not long ago. I use them as an aid for meditation. I told you that ages ago. Why do you ask?"

Harry chuckled. "I wonder what all those people who watch you on television would think if they saw you bent over your rune stones with your long hair falling around your face."

"They'd think I was nuts. Or worse, they'd think I was a witch"—Branwen grimaced—"and my career would go up in smoke. This isn't the hippy-dippy sixties anymore, you know. With Ford and now Carter in the White House, anything more outlandish than football or peanuts in your Coke is definitely *out*! Besides, my spiritual life is nobody's business. Except perhaps yours, occasionally. Now are you going to tell me this secret? Because if you're not, I have something to tell you, too. I did have a reason for inviting you over here tonight."

"How intriguing!" Harry pulled his one-sided smile. He had finished his meal and pushed his plate away so that he could lean with his elbows on the table. "You tell me yours, and I'll tell you mine."

"You first. I admit you have me dying of curiosity."

"All right. And mind you, this really *is* a secret. There is a fascinating group of people right here in Washington that meets very quietly about once a month to share their common interests. These meetings, and membership in the group, are by invitation only. I've been a member for the past three years, since the publication of my monograph on the Archetypology of England's Standing Stones—you remember that, the one you helped research."

"I remember." Branwen had stopped eating; he had her complete attention. She felt extraordinarily expectant, as if Harry were about to say or do something of great significance to her life.

"This group has no name. At least, no official name. I call it the Psychic Underground."

"Psychic Underground? Here, in Washington?" A tingle

started in Branwen's scalp and tripped through her body. "Harry, that *is* fascinating."

"Yes. A large part of the fascination is the variety, the range of people one sees there. And of course this all must remain underground because, as you observed about your own career going up in smoke, no one wants to lose his or her credibility."

"Um-hm." Branwen was thoughtful. That tingle had contained excitement, and fear, and warning, all at the same time. "Harry, this Psychic Underground. They're not into anything dangerous, are they? Not—not Satanism, or anything like that?"

"No, no. Perish the thought!" Harry leaned back in his chair, waving his hand in a gesture of dismissal. "Satanism is a religion. A cult if you like, but still a religion, with worship and all that the concept of worship implies. We aren't interested in such things. Actually we are more of a study group, not a practicing one—if you understand the distinction." Branwen nodded to show that she did, and Harry went on. "We seek knowledge of the psychic and occult, occult in its true meaning: that which is hidden. We have discussions, guest lectures, demonstrations, that kind of thing. I've secured an invitation for you to come as my guest to our next meeting. You must come, Branwen. Really, it is past time that you should do something with your own abilities."

Branwen looked wary. "You mean you want me to read the runes for these underground friends of yours. I'm to be one of the guest demonstrations."

"Yes, and no. You're invited as a potential member, and as I said, we aren't a practicing group. But most of the members as individuals have their own particular interests and areas of expertise that they will from time to time share with the others in the group setting. Your talent with the runes is the price of your admission, as it were. The mark of your sincerity. After all, you're a television journalist, Branwen. In spite of my vouching for you, you could be present just to get a story, and very few of the Underground are willing to risk public exposure. Once you have demonstrated that you are one of us, that you have your own abilities, which you usually keep hidden, you'll be accepted. After that you can come to as many or as few meetings as you like, with or without me. Believe me, this experience will be important for you. Do say you'll come!"

"Why now?"

"I'm sorry." Harry shifted in his chair. "I don't understand what you're asking."

"I mean, if you have been in this group for three years, why did you decide to tell me and invite me now and not before?"

Harry swiped at the pale hair that had fallen in his eyes. "To tell you the truth, I'm not sure. I didn't think you could be persuaded before, and now . . . the time feels right. Call it psychic, call it intuitive, I simply feel this is the time for you to join us."

Branwen understood. She had the same feeling herself. She trusted the feeling all the more because she had grown accustomed to resisting any pull from Harry in such a direction, and there was no resistance this time. Yet she was cautious. She fixed him with a level blue-green gaze. "The others in this Psychic Underground, do they have so-called psychic powers?"

"Some do. I would guess that most aspire to but actually do not." Harry squirmed, trying to get comfortable in the straight-backed chair. He could feel Branwen's mind probing at him and he didn't like it. He thought of throwing up a block but didn't do it. He let her probe; she wouldn't find any ulterior motive. Nothing any more serious than his natural desire to show her off a bit, to spend more time with her than he had been able to do of late. When he felt her back off, he said, "What we all do have in common is a belief that psychic power and psychic phenomena are real and should be explored."

And harnessed, and used, thought Branwen. But she did not say so because she sensed Harry's sincerity. And she believed that for at least this once, he was right. It was time for her to do this. She placed her hands flat on the table. "You know how I feel about parlor tricks, Harry—using one's gifts only to impress people. Or worse, faking it for the same reason. But in this case I can see the need to establish my legitimacy. I'll do it. There's just one problem. I've never read the runes for anyone but myself."

Harry chuckled. "In this lifetime, perhaps. I have no doubt that you can do it for anyone anytime you choose."

"You're so sure of that?" Branwen smiled mischievously and raised her eyebrows.

"Absolutely. My own area of professed expertise—at least as far as the Underground knows—is an ability to uncover past lives."

"And you can really do it."

"Certainly! Although I myself am not so averse as you to

what you call parlor tricks. In all modesty, I avow, yes, I really can do it. You know as well as I, Branwen, that we two have been on this earth together before. And you know whether you acknowledge it or not that you were no stranger to the blue-stones the first time I put them into your hands. What I do not understand, have never understood, is why you're always so reluctant to explore with me what our past lives together may have been."

Branwen sighed and looked away. The problem with these things Harry proposed was that inevitably it would open doors between herself and him that she had so far successfully kept firmly closed. Well, there was no help for it. She would have to tell him the truth whether he liked it or not. She looked back at him, unconsciously squaring her shoulders. "If you must know, Harry, it's because I'm pretty sure I was a little afraid of you. Maybe sometimes a *lot* afraid of you. But that," she said firmly, rising, "was in another life! Help me clear these dishes, will you?"

"There are advantages to having people be afraid of you, you know," Harry said, winking. "For example, you don't have to help with the dishes. In this case, however, I am willing to be of help. The food was excellent, my dear."

He trekked good-naturedly back and forth from the table to the kitchen while she rinsed and stacked the dishes in the dish-washer. Then he leaned against the counter and watched while she boiled water and ground beans and made coffee in a Melitta drip pot.

"You said you had something you wanted to tell me," he reminded her.

Branwen tossed her hair back over her shoulder. "I can't believe I forgot! I certainly do. Here, let's take this coffee into the living room, and I'll get to it." They settled at opposite ends of the couch, Branwen shedding her slippers and tucking her feet up under her long skirt. "You know Ellen has gone down to Cozumel for a month."

Harry nodded.

"Well, when she gets back, I'm going to have to tell her this, and I just dread it. Harry, I'm moving. I've signed a lease on an apartment in Georgetown. It's a grand apartment, in a triplex near the university. I waited months to get it."

"I can imagine you did. I understand such places are scarce as hen's teeth." Harry looked around the room. Branwen had added shelves in every available inch of wallspace, and still her books overflowed onto windowsills and chair seats and even the floor. The table where they'd eaten dinner usually served as a desk, and her typewriter and a gooseneck lamp and stacks of file folders were crammed into a corner until she could put them back on the table. "You've obviously outgrown the cottage. Ellen will understand. After all, you've been here a long time."

"Yes, I have. She's going to think I purposely waited until she was out of town to do this, but I didn't. The apartment just happens to be available right now. She doesn't want me to move, Harry. She's said so every time before when I talked about it, so this time I just put my name on the waiting list for the apartment and didn't tell her. And that's not all. There's more."

"More?" Harry's eyebrows went up.

"Well, you know I've had job offers from time to time, but nothing I wanted enough to leave Channel 15. This time I, uh, I went after something on my own. That's really why I looked for a place to live in Georgetown. I talked to the PBS station several months ago, Harry, and they didn't have enough funding to hire me then, but now they do. Or at least they will when their fiscal year starts in two months. So I'm taking a new job. I'm going over to PBS."

"PBS? Branwen, you'll never make any money on public television!"

"Honestly, Harry!" She leaned over and put her cup and saucer on the coffee table. "Money isn't what it's all about. And anyway, living here and not paying rent for so many years, I've saved so much it's practically indecent."

"Not to mention," Harry said dryly, "that you drove that despicable old car until it fell apart—when was that?"

Branwen laughed. "Last year. Really, I hated to see it go. It was like an old shoe or something, practically a member of the family. Now listen, you're sworn to secrecy about the move to PBS. I'll give my notice at the station in a couple of weeks, but until then nobody is to know. It was just great luck that the apartment came available right now, too. I'll be able to buy furniture and get moved in before I have to start the new job."

Harry tried to hide his disappointment. He had hoped, once it was clear to him that she wouldn't join him in the academic world, that she would make her mark on a national level in her chosen field. And here she was deliberately putting herself into obscurity. Dutifully he said, "My dear, if it's what you want,

I'm happy for you. Ellen will be, too. In fact, I'm sure she'll understand much better than I do how you could refuse an offer from one of the networks, as you did a while back, and then turn around and badger the Public Broadcasting folks into hiring you!"

"It's really quite simple," she said, reaching across to poke him playfully with a finger, "so simple that even a professor of Medieval Studies could understand. The network wanted me to be a reporter, in front of the cameras. At PBS I'm going to write and produce and maybe direct. For a lot less money, true, but I'll make enough to live on, and the experience will be terrific."

Harry leaned forward, and his hair fell over one eye. "Then what's bothering you? Because something is, my dear. I can tell."

Branwen pulled her knees up and wrapped her arms around them. "I'm not sure. I dread telling Ellen, but that's not really it. We'll miss each other at first, but she knows as well as I do that I couldn't stay here forever. I think it's just that I feel my life moving, taking off in a new direction. I'm excited about it. But I don't quite know what to expect."

Mrs. Beecher absolutely refused to allow Branwen to cast the runes for her. "Them looks like marks o' th' divil, ever' single one. I'll have no truck with that!" she declared. And when Branwen tried to persuade her, she threw her apron over her head.

Harry, leaning in the kitchen door, laughed. "Come away, Branwen. The good woman is not to be persuaded. You'll just have to practice on me."

Branwen agreed reluctantly. She didn't think she dared go into the meeting of the Psychic Underground and demonstrate her ability to read the runes for others unless she had done it at least once for someone other than herself. With Ellen away, her choice of potential subjects was limited to either Harry or Mrs. Beecher, who not only had thrown her apron over her head, but she had now turned her back as well.

Branwen and Harry went into the library and closed the door. She looked around and said uncertainly, "I, ah, usually sit on the floor when I do this."

"How agile of you," Harry drawled. "But *I*, my dear, never sit on the floor for any reason whatever. I assure you that a table will do as well. Shall we?"

They sat at the drum table, and Branwen weighed the bag of bluestones in her palm. She was extremely nervous, and her dark-fringed eyes showed it. "You know, Harry, I don't do this at all the way the book says to do it."

"Book?" Harry asked sharply. "What book?"

"I have it here in my purse. I found it at that little bookstore on the edge of Georgetown. You know the store, it's all right . . ."

"The store's fine." Harry snatched the book from her as she took it from her purse, and without looking at it tossed it onto a nearby chair. "But the book will do you no good."

"I don't see why not," Branwen protested, stiffening. "It's about Viking runes and these are Celtic, but the symbols are almost identical. The process couldn't be very different."

"What on earth would possess you to buy a book on the subject?" Harry was almost angry. His narrow nostrils flared, and his eyes glared silver.

Branwen's chin came up stubbornly. "I wanted to know what the symbols really mean, in case someone asks. Not just what they mean to me. I don't want to seem ignorant! So I memorized them. But the patterns the book says to lay out, they—don't work for me. I tried last night—Harry Ravenscroft, you aren't even listening to me!"

"No, I'm not." Harry shook his head, and his light, longish hair flew about his thin face. "But *you*, my dear, had best listen to *me* before you ruin everything!"

"Then calm down, please!" Branwen put her hands to her temples.

"Right, right. You're right." Harry took several deep breaths, then got up and stood behind Branwen's chair. He put his hands on her shoulders and spoke in a tone peculiarly gentle and compelling. "Listen: The knowledge is not in the bluestone, not in the symbols of the runes carved upon the bluestones. The knowledge, the *intuitive knowing*, is in *you*, Branwen Faraday."

"But—"

"Yes, yes," Harry said soothingly, kneading her shoulders, "the runic stones seem to speak to you. Isn't that so?"

Branwen's head nodded forward in acquiescence. Her hair was tightly braided. Still speaking in the compelling voice, Harry began to undo the braid. "There is a kind of energy in these particular stones. I don't know what it is—I wish I did. I think I knew once. I wish I could remember. There must have been a very good reason for the inner circle of bluestones to have been brought all the way from Wales to Stonehenge, don't you think?"

Again Branwen nodded her head. Harry's voice was helping her. Not just his words, but that certain tone of voice. His hands on her shoulders and now in her hair felt wonderful. She knew why he was loosing her hair; she realized she always did it herself before touching the runic stones. "It's the energy," she murmured, "my energy, too. It feels . . . the same."

"Yes," said Harry, combing his fingers through her heavy, silky hair, lifting it way from her neck, letting it flow free in ripples from his hands. "Yes, I felt that energy from you, through you, years ago in the ruins of the abbey at Llanfaren. That was one of the most exciting moments of my life, Branwen. Do you remember?"

"I remember."

"That energy is your special gift." Harry sat at the table again. He looked at Branwen. Her eyes went through him and his through her. They were, both of them, hovering on the edge between one reality and the next. Harry would keep them there, on the edge. It must be Branwen who took them over. "It doesn't come from books. Forget the book, forget its patterns and interpretations. Let your visions come. Read the runes for me, Branwen."

"Give me your hands," she said. "Close your eyes. See in your mind what it is you want from the rune stones."

Harry complied. Her hands, at first cool, grew hot. He silently formed his question: *When will the Old Knowledge be mine again?* A tremor passed through Branwen's body, and he felt it in his hands, felt the tingling begin that was her energy building. It passed from her fingers into his hands, up his arms, into his chest. He drew in a long, deep breath and held it, in an ecstasy of expectation.

Branwen released Harry's hands. She spilled the bluestones from their pouch. Harry opened his eyes, at first confused, disappointed. She had broken the physical contact. Wherever she was going, he was not going with her. Then he understood. Of course! She was going *for* him, she would read the rune stones for him, that was why she had let go of his hands.

He watched her. Her hair, wavy from its braid, fell about her face as she bent over the bluestones. The white streak was startling—it stood out like a brand. Her left hand, fingers trem-

bling slightly, moved in the air an inch above the array of stones
on the table. The fingers dipped, fluttered, moved on; dipped
again and plucked up a stone.

"I choose the stones that draw my fingers," Branwen said in
answer to the question he had not voiced. "They feel hot, their
heat draws me."

Soon she had chosen seven stones. The rest she moved to one
side with a careful sweep of her hand. "The stones choose their
own pattern," she said. She did not look at him, nor did she
seem to look at the rune stones. Her left hand formed a Y with
the stones, its branches toward him, the trunk toward her. A
tree, Harry thought.

Branwen's eyes were open, her pupils dilated so that they almost consumed the blue-green irises. Her cheeks flamed as if
she were burning up, yet she scarcely seemed to breathe. She
began to speak. "Harry Ravenscroft, your path will split. Not
now, not yet, but soon. One branch is false. I see darkness. . . ."

Her voice cracked. She twisted her head from side to side,
and tension knotted the cords in her neck like rope. In a hoarse
whisper she continued, "I see a confrontation. You and an Old
Enemy. I can't stay in this place! The noise is terrible! There's
too much danger. *I'm* in danger if I stay here!"

Harry was frightened, but he didn't dare intervene. This was
her trance, though she had gone into it on his behalf; since he
hadn't induced it he didn't think he could bring her out of it if he
tried. Beads of sweat gathered on her forehead and trickled
down her face. She didn't blink her enormous, near-black eyes,
and she had stopped breathing.

When he could stand it no longer, when he was about to leap
across the table and shake her no matter what the consequences,
Branwen gasped and then inhaled, a huge, rasping, shuddering
breath. She blinked several times and shook herself, like a long-
haired animal shaking water from its coat.

Her voice was still hoarse, but softer, as she spoke again.
"The other branch of the path is true. It will take you to the goal
you seek. I . . . don't know what sort of place this is, but there's
no danger here. There are . . . *animals*! A wolf, a huge silver
wolf, really quite beautiful. For a wolf! Trees, a lot of trees sort
of woven together in arches at the top. The wolf is gone now,
but . . . there's an owl, a white snowy owl. Oh! He's flying
away—his wings must be six feet across! And down at the end

of this tunnel of trees there's a very bright light. The owl is flying into the light."

Branwen sighed and closed her eyes. "That's all. I'm coming back now."

Harry was beside himself, overjoyed, the fright of the first vision, the false path, completely forgotten. The wolf and the owl were his animal familiars; he had dreams and old, old memories of himself in both shapes. Surely, then, this true branch of the path *would* lead him to the Old Knowledge! If only she could have told him how to find it. . . . But he would know, he was sure of it now.

"What do you want?" he asked as soon as Branwen opened her eyes. "I'll get you anything, anything. You must be exhausted. Brandy, perhaps?"

She shook her head. "No, alcohol is the last thing I want. Water, please, a very big glass of cold water."

"Immediately! Your wish is my command." Harry sped to the kitchen and returned to find Branwen gathering up the bluestones with some difficulty. He handed her the glass of water and made to help her with the stones, but she stopped him.

"Thanks, but I have to put them away myself. It seems to be part of the process. Don't ask why, it just is."

"Whatever you say." Harry sat down and watched Branwen, his eyes shining. She drank all the water, then resumed her task of putting the stones into the bag. When she was done, she closed it with the drawstring and folded her hands on the table. Her hair was in disarray, and her former high color had faded. But her pale skin glowed like pearl. She seemed emptied out, clear, almost transparent. Harry thought she had never looked more beautiful.

She spoke. "Well, did I answer your question? I must say, that smile on your face is almost beatific, so I guess you're pleased by something."

"I'm pleased by you. You were stunning, my dear, absolutely magnificent. Do you remember what you said?"

"Not exactly." She passed the back of her hand across her eyes. "I remember where I was, though. When I do that, I see things. I don't understand why you're so happy—part of what I saw was horrible!"

"Yes, but the other part! Ah, that was wonderful, Branwen. Do you remember the animals?"

"A wolf and an owl. Both very beautiful."

"Yes, and both very special to me. Sacred, you might even say. And they were the answer to my question. The rest is not important."

"I don't know, Harry." Branwen frowned. "It seemed important to me. I almost didn't get out of there. And I wasn't *me* in there, I was you. Listen, can I talk about this with you, or is that against the rules?"

"What rules?" Harry shrugged. "Anyone with your gift can make up her own rules, as far as I'm concerned."

"Honestly, Harry." Branwen was exasperated. Tired as she was, as much as she simply wanted to wash her hands and face and comb her hair and get in her car and go home, she couldn't let that go by. "As far as *you're* concerned! That's why I don't do this kind of thing with you usually, you're so exclusively focused on yourself and what *you* want. There *are* rules, right ways of doing things, whether you want to admit it or not. There's one ancient rule I can think of myself: Do No Harm."

"You're confusing yourself, my dear," Harry said carelessly. "That's Aesculapius. That's for doctors, not for us."

"And what else are wise women, or wise men, but healers? Doctors of a special kind?" asked Branwen heatedly. Again she rubbed at her eyes. "I'm getting the feeling I've had this argument with you before, and I don't mean recently."

"Maybe you have." Harry was irritated. He wanted to stay with the lovely, exciting images of the owl and the wolf.

Patiently Branwen said, "I just feel I have to tell you, for your own good, something that wasn't in this vision. Something out of my own experience."

"So, tell."

"That dark place, and the—the Thing I was fighting with when I was you—I've been there before, Harry. Only I didn't go inside, I stood on the boundary and watched. That Thing is evil. I don't mean it's bad, I mean it *is* Evil. And that's not all." She swallowed with difficulty. Her mouth and throat had gone completely dry again. "Jason is in that black place. Those things have swallowed him up. I know they have! So be careful, Harry. Be very, very careful that you don't choose the wrong branch of that path!"

"I won't, don't worry. After you saw that, you saw the wolf and the owl, didn't you? The wolf and owl represent me, I'm sure of it. Obviously, whatever interpretation you choose to put on your vision, I am going to be just fine and dandy!"

Branwen looked doubtful. Then she put her arms down, folded, on the table and her head on her arms. She felt that she could not move one inch or speak another word until she had rested. There was no sense in trying to get Harry to see that he might be in danger, no sense at all.

"I can't believe I have to do this all over again tomorrow night," she mumbled. And she fell asleep on the drum table in Harry Ravenscroft's library.

Harry sat across from her and watched her sleep. He smiled a glittering, enigmatic smile.

3

The distance between McLean and Georgetown was only a few miles across the river and through the city, but Branwen felt as if she had moved into another world. The world of public television was as different from the little Channel 15 newsroom as her triplex apartment in Georgetown was different from the wooded confines of Ellen's estate. Branwen was ready for the change. She made the adjustment in her usual way, through hard work. Two years passed rapidly, and by her thirty-third birthday in the spring of 1978 she was ready for yet another world: that of the mentally ill. With the help of President Carter's wife Rosalyn, the station had received a grant to produce a two-hour program on the treatment of mental illness in government-supported institutions, and the project went to Branwen.

She did not do her research with books and papers full of statistics; she did it with her whole self, body and mind and heart and soul. Through the summer months Branwen hospitalized herself in one state mental hospital after another up and down the East Coast, from Maine to Florida. The doctors and nurses knew her true identity and mission, but the aides who were the front-line staff on the wards did not; nor did the other patients. Feigning depression, Branwen seldom spoke—she kept her face expressionless in what she'd learned was called a "flat affect," and she observed. Most of the patients moved her, a few frightened her, and a few fascinated her—especially the schizo-

phrenics, some of whom heard voices and saw visions. Silent
Branwen thought: *And so do I, and so do I.* Yet she lived in an
ordered reality, and the schizophrenics did not. Why?

Some of the patients haunted her, and she suspected she
would be concerned about them for years to come. One in particular: a young woman of pale, ethereal beauty, she looked like
an angel painted by Fra Angelico—and then she started to
scream. "Why does she scream?" Branwen had asked the nurse.
And the nurse had replied: "Because she hears voices, and
whatever the voices say to her, it must be terrible!" An aide had
taken the screaming angel away, and Branwen never saw her
again, nor did she ever learn her name; but the face lingered in
Branwen's mind for weeks.

By the autumn Branwen was on the last leg of her project,
following up on those patients who had been released from hospitals into day treatment programs at mental-health centers.
Most of them didn't attend the day programs for very long; they
either went back into the hospitals or simply disappeared.
"Where did they go?" Branwen asked the social worker. "On
the streets," the social worker said. So Branwen, too, went
on the streets. She tracked the particular patients she'd targeted
for on-camera interviews, which was how she learned about
Washington's homeless. She found them all—except Sister Emerald Pearl. Sister Emerald Pearl was a huge black woman who
sang gospel songs and talked to God; only when Sister ran out
of medication or forgot to take it, which was often, she talked to
God in very lewd language indeed, language the social worker
called "inappropriate." Tracking Sister Emerald Pearl was how
Branwen met Xavier.

She stood on a cracked sidewalk in a shabby, dirty, dangerous
part of town. She had not found the Sister, but she had found
something else: an idea for another program, a program on
homelessness, on the ugly side of the city whose beauty and history she had once praised on widely broadcast television shows.
She was thinking that she owed such a story to herself, to the
city, and most of all to the homeless. She was so completely absorbed in her idea that she simply stood there on the street, momentarily unaware of her surroundings.

The man's voice, which fell on her ears before she turned to
face him, was one of the most beautiful she had ever heard.
Deep, full, and rich, it had a texture like an embrace. It was a
voice not so much heard as experienced, and Branwen realized

she had no idea what the words had been. She turned and said, "I'm sorry, I didn't quite get that. What did you say?"

"I said, may I help you? Are you lost?" The man was as attractive as his voice. He was darkly handsome, with thick black hair and eyes as black and deep and shining as a sacred forest pool. His skin was dark and smooth as if perpetually tanned, and the bones of his face were prominent, as if he might have Indian blood. He was about six feet tall, his body of a rugged build, and he was dressed like a laborer: blue chambray long-sleeved shirt open at the neck to reveal a white T-shirt underneath, much-washed denim jacket and jeans, thick-soled brown work boots with yellow laces. Branwen blinked as she looked at him; he seemed to blaze with an inner fire.

"I'm not lost," she said, gathering her wits, "but I'm looking for someone who may be. Perhaps you could help with that."

"Oh?" He had been examining her with a degree of appreciation, but it vanished as surely as if he'd turned it off with a switch. "In that case, maybe I can help you and maybe I can't."

Undaunted, Branwen continued, "Her name is Sister Emerald Pearl. Actually her real name is something else, but that's what she calls herself. She's a black woman, I guess about forty years old, five-ten, three hundred pounds—a really big woman. And she sings, spontaneously, any old time. If she's around here, she'd be hard to miss."

"What makes you think she's around here? You're obviously a long way from your own neck of the woods." A faint smile had played about his mouth at Branwen's description, but it quickly disappeared. Caution and reserve were back in full force.

"She's mentally ill, and I think she's homeless. She was a patient at a mental-health center on the Maryland side and she lived in a halfway house after she got out of the hospital, but she stopped going to the day-treatment program, so they turned her out. It's a requirement, you see, that she attend in order to live in the halfway house."

"I know about that. Go on."

Branwen shaded her eyes with her hand. He was intense now, and looking at his face was like looking into the sun. "I heard there's a house here where people like Sister Emerald Pearl can stay. I mean, in this part of town. I don't know anything about it, not even exactly where it is, but a man back there"—she gestured vaguely behind her—"told me it's on this street. He didn't seem like the most reliable source, but I decided to check it out anyway."

"So you're a social worker, and you've come to rescue this Sister Emerald Pearl, who after all, if she has found a place to live, is neither lost nor homeless." This was said without appreciation or amusement. For some reason, he obviously didn't like social workers. He challenged, "Who told you about the house? Where'd you get your information?"

"I'm not a social worker." Branwen tossed her head and widened her stance. She wasn't going to let him intimidate her, no matter how uncomfortable she might be. And she *was* uncomfortable, understanding suddenly that her good suit of gray-green wool and her tan leather pumps with two-inch heels, even the battered leather briefcase she wore by its strap over her shoulder, marked her as an outsider. "I've been asking around, talking to people on the street. The man who directed me here lives in a big wooden packing crate on a vacant lot back there."

This time there was more than a trace of a smile, and it was genuine. "That'd be George. This early in the day he's still sober enough to talk. Well, you've got guts, if that's how you found us."

"Us?" Who *was* this man? He looked like a construction worker, certainly didn't look homeless, and he sounded like something else again—an actor, perhaps, earning money to stockpile for another attempt to go back on the boards.

"Yeah, us." His smile widened, and he cocked his head the smallest degree, a nuance of movement that made him look both impish and mysterious. "I live in that house George told you about. It *is* on this street, one block down. I can tell you that your Sister Emerald Pearl isn't at the house, but that's all I'll do for you unless you tell me why you're looking for her."

"Never mind," Branwen grumbled, hefting her bag higher on her shoulder. "I have a feeling your help would come at too high a price anyway. I don't know you from Adam's house cat. I don't have to tell you anything." She began to walk back the way she'd come. True, she didn't like to reveal the fact that she was a journalist on a story unless she absolutely had to because it invariably colored what people said to her. But that was not why she walked away. She was leaving because for the first time in longer than she could remember, she felt the stirrings of physical attraction, for a man she'd met on a street in the worst part of town, a man who dressed like a laborer and sounded like an actor and had the face of a new-world god.

He hesitated only a moment before calling out, "Wait!"

Branwen's heart jumped up into her throat, and she reminded herself as she stopped and turned that she was here for only one reason: Sister Emerald Pearl. She confronted him wordlessly.

"I'll trust you," he said. "Sometimes I get overprotective of the people down here. I'll ask around, and if you'll give me your name and telephone number, I'll call and let you know what I find out about Sister Emerald Pearl."

Branwen frowned; it was on the tip of her tongue to ask why *she* should trust *him*. But she nodded, dug in her bag for her notepad, and hastily wrote her name and telephone number. "Okay," she said, handing the paper to him. "Thank you. As soon as possible, I'd appreciate it."

"Twenty-four hours, cross my heart. Branwen Faraday. Branwen? Pretty name. Unusual."

"Not where I come from." What was she doing, standing here making small talk with a stranger? And yet she couldn't take her eyes from the curves of his lips. He'd said her name as if he were tasting it, and again she had felt the texture of his voice, like a caress.

"Oh, and where's that?" He stepped closer.

"Wales, I was born in Wales." Branwen backed away. "But I've lived here for a long time. Years. I'll expect your call, Mr.—you haven't told me your name."

"Xavier Dominguez. Spelled with an X, pronounced like a Z, but everybody around here calls me—" He stopped, suddenly unwilling to tell her.

"Calls you what?" Branwen asked with a small smile.

He shrugged, and the way he did it, it looked both elegant and masculine. His hand went to the collar of his shirt as if to loosen it, though it was open. "I think we're not on intimate enough terms yet for you to know what they call me," he said.

Branwen's insides fluttered. *This is ridiculous,* she thought. *We're both being entirely too mysterious with each other.* Pure habit, the drive to get her story, held her back. She squared her shoulders, determined to leave. "Whatever you say, Xavier Dominguez. I'll expect your call tomorrow evening."

I should have told her, thought Xavier. *I should have told her everybody calls me Father X.* He walked rapidly down the street to the house that was known simply by its number, 622. His mind worked at a furious rate, trying to overtake and suppress the raw, primitive energy that coursed through his body. He reached 622 sooner than he wanted to be there and sat on the front steps to think about the problem he had just created for himself, and maybe also for Branwen Faraday. The tremendous energy coursing through him was sexual; he knew that, just as surely as he knew he hadn't told her they called him Father X because he didn't want her to know he was a Roman Catholic priest. He'd have to tell her eventually, but for the moment he wanted to keep his fantasy. A fantasy in which he, just a man, could love and cherish a woman.

Francis Xavier Dominguez, age thirty-five, was the son of a Mexican-American family that had lived in Southwest Texas since long before Texas became a part of the United States. His namesake, the Spanish St. Francis Xavier, had been a friend of St. Ignatius of Loyola in the sixteenth century, and had helped Ignatius to get the Society of Jesus off the ground. Like his namesake, Xavier, too, had become a Jesuit priest, but he was no saint. His priesthood had been a stormy one so far. His keen intellect and deep spirituality were often at odds with his fiery, passionate temperament. His vows of poverty, obedience, and chastity were all hard for him to keep: poverty, because he came from a moderately wealthy, landed family and had had to give up his inheritance when he entered the Order, yet he was always seeing the good his money could do if he'd only had it to spend; obedience, because of a strong will and a streak of rebelliousness that had been born in him; and chastity because he possessed a sexuality so fierce it often threatened to possess him. Xavier well knew Dr. Freud would have said that the sometimes overpowering energy that drove him to his accomplishments came from sublimation. He was sure Dr. Freud would have been right.

Number 622 was the latest of his accomplishments and the first in his new identity as Father X. Only a year previous, Xavier had solved his problem with the vow of poverty and a good bit of the one with obedience by leaving the Jesuit Order. As a "secular" priest, he still said Mass and administered the Sacraments, and if he'd been assigned to a parish, he would have been paid a small salary. Instead, he remained independent by his own request and had reclaimed the income from his trust fund. With it he had bought and continued to maintain 622 as a refuge for the homeless. He had become a maverick priest; he owed his allegiance only to the bishop who had allowed it.

At first, Xavier had had to go out into the streets and recruit people to live at 622—he had expected the homeless to be suspicious of his motives, and they were. But no more. Now word was out, and they found their way to him, just as Branwen Faraday had. Increasingly he thought of Washington's homeless people, especially the determinedly hardcore homeless, as his own amorphous parish. At least once a month he would dress like the priest he really was, in black suit and Roman collar, and go lobbying on Capitol Hill for his powerless parishioners. Sometimes, if he wanted to impress a congresswoman or needed the cooperation of a female staffer, he would shamelessly don the wide-sashed, long-skirted soutane he'd learned to wear comfortably during his three years of study in Rome—complete with its long cape, if the season were winter. Xavier wasn't vain, but he knew how he looked in that outfit and the effect it had on most women. He told himself that the end justified the means.

Women were attracted to him, and he to them. Celibacy had always been hard for Xavier, and he expected it always would be, unless by some miracle the Church changed the rules and allowed priests to marry. In the late sixties, he'd fallen in love with a young nun in one of his graduate classes, and they'd had an affair that lasted two years. It wasn't all that unusual; many of his contemporaries had done the same. Xavier and his nun had talked about marriage and, in the end, realized that neither of them wanted to give up their faith or their careers. They'd ended the relationship by mutual consent, and the nun had finished her master's and stepped back into her religious life without seeming to miss a beat. Now she was an administrator in the hospital run by her Order in Seattle—she sent him a card every Christmas. Xavier, however, had not gotten off so easily. He'd been deeply shaken, somewhat at war with himself ever since.

"Branwen Faraday." Xavier whispered her name. He should forget her, he knew it, but instead he took the piece of paper out of his shirt pocket and looked at the name and phone number. She'd been attracted to him, he'd felt it and seen it in her eyes. Incredible eyes! The color of desert turquoise. And the hair, so black with the startling white streak—he wondered how long that hair was when it wasn't all bound up in a bun. Such finely textured skin she had, so white. A heart-shaped face. Lips like velvety rose petals, soft and pink, not hard and gleaming with lipstick. Who was she? Why wouldn't she tell him what she wanted with Emerald Pearl?

Xavier groaned aloud. This was one hell of a painful fantasy, and he didn't think he was going to be able to let go of it anytime soon. He'd have to go to the gym where he kept a membership for the very purpose of having a place to work off frustrations such as he was feeling now. He foresaw a long, hard game of handball in his immediate future. But first he'd keep his promise, see what he could find out about the missing woman. Xavier got up and stretched his big, restless body. He predicted he'd be playing a lot of handball in the days to come . . . even if he did as he knew he should and confined his future contact with Branwen to a single phone call to report his findings.

"Admit it, Harry," said Branwen, "these meetings have been pretty boring lately. I don't know why I keep coming."

"My dear," Harry drawled, throwing his arm over the back of her chair, "you've been more absent than present in our Psychic Underground since you joined us almost two years ago, and you know it. If you ask me, you've gotten much too wrapped up in your work. Haven't you finished that dreary project on the insane yet?"

"They're not insane, just mentally ill. And no, I haven't finished it yet. There's one missing piece, and I'll probably know something about filling it in tomorrow. With luck I can do my last interview by the end of the week and can write the conclusion over the weekend." Branwen twisted to look over her shoulder. The room was filling up rapidly. When she'd first started coming to these meetings, she'd been surprised by the variety of people who attended, and particularly by the sides of their personalities they were usually at pains to keep hidden. There were no-nonsense government career types who worked hard on ESP skills such as remote viewing, and others who could recite every UFO sighting since 1952; there were society women with reputations for frivolity who were dead serious about hauntings and poltergeists; assorted diplomats and secretaries and elected officials whose interests ran the gamut of the parapsychological. Branwen had soon learned to accept all this and even to be bored with it. Her own skills with the runes had caused a brief flurry of interest that then subsided, to her relief.

Though it was easier to read runes for strangers than it had been for Harry, she still did not like to do it. Her communion with the bluestones seemed a private thing that she preferred to keep to herself.

She turned back to him, remarking, "There are a lot of people here tonight, quite a few I've never seen before. What is this, Harry? I haven't been away that much to have missed so many new members."

Harry craned his neck to scan the room, nodding and raising his hand in greeting. He was popular in this crowd. "A lot of guests," he said. "This is a special presentation tonight. Didn't you know?"

Branwen shook her head.

"We're to see a trance-channel medium. He's supposed to be genuine—usually does this kind of thing only for friends and family. His name is Melvin Morton. Searles Beauchamp discovered him in some little coastal town where he owns a grocery store or something."

"Really." Branwen looked skeptical. "What exactly is a trance-channel medium?"

Harry quirked an eyebrow. "Surely you've heard of Jane Roberts, who channels Seth? Read her book? No? Well then, think of Edgar Cayce. You *do* know of Edgar Cayce?"

"Yep. Him I know. He lived in Virginia Beach."

"Cayce is probably more responsible than anyone else for the terminology in use today—he called himself 'a clear channel.' The term 'medium' was somewhat tarnished by all the frauds who were practicing spiritualism in the late nineteenth and early twentieth centuries. Cayce acted as a channel for information from many different sources, whereas Jane Roberts channels only Seth. It will be interesting to see what this Morton fellow does."

Branwen agreed, and at that point the convener for the evening walked into the center of the room. The group took turns meeting in the homes of members who had enough space to accommodate them, and the host or hostess acted as convener for the evening. Tonight the chairs and couches were as usual ranged around the living room in a circle, and wide sliding doors to the adjacent dining room had been opened to allow for the larger crowd. The convener began as always by calling for five minutes of silent meditation. Then, referring to written notes, he gave an update on miscellaneous matters pertaining to the psychic.

Branwen let her mind wander. Harry had exaggerated—except for the months when she'd been visiting the mental hospitals, she'd seldom missed a monthly meeting. She supposed she had gotten more out of the Psychic Underground than she usually admitted, either to herself or to Harry Ravenscroft. She absorbed the wide range of material effortlessly, unconsciously sorting and evaluating and adding anything that seemed new and valid to the store of those things she already knew without knowing how she knew them. For most of the people here, the Underground was simply another expression of that all-pervasive Washington obsession with power—in this case, psychic power. Branwen herself was not immune. Her PBS programs had to be funded, and to get funding she had to have recognition. She knew from some place of deep memory that her runes could be used not just for Seeing but also for Binding, which was a way to harness the power of the runes to make what was desired come to pass. But she'd never done it. How many people in this room, she wondered, were spellbinders in the privacy of their own homes?

She sat up straighter. The convener had just introduced Searles Beauchamp, who in turn was telling how he had met Melvin Morton in Trey, Virginia, a little town on the Mobjack Bay just south of the mouth of the Rappahannock River. The man owned not a grocery, but a hardware store. He had been clairvoyant, clairaudient, and clairsentient since childhood, but this fact had been known only to his immediate family. Three years ago Mr. Morton had spontaneously begun channeling a spirit from another plane, a woman from Alexandria, Egypt, named Gracia who had been a healer in the first century A.D.

"A woman!" Branwen whispered to Harry, who raised both eyebrows and grinned.

Melvin Morton made his way through the dining room—he'd apparently been waiting in the kitchen—and into the open space in the center of the living room where the host had placed a plain, straight, rush-seated ladderback chair. He was short and round, with salt-and-pepper hair curled about a cherubic face. Smile lines radiated from twinkly, dark-blue eyes.

He's nervous, Branwen thought, observing that his rather small and chubby hand grasped the back of the chair so hard the knuckles were white. Melvin Morton stood by the chair, smiling and nodding around the room; then he began to speak in a surprisingly firm baritone voice, moderated by the softness of his southern accent. He had a way of ducking his head as he spoke, which suggested shyness or modesty or both.

"It's nice of so many people to come and see me tonight," he said. "Well, I know y'all are really here to hear Gracia and not me. I'm just her channel, so to speak. So to *speak*, heh-heh, I guess that's kind of a joke. I've never done this in front of so many people before so I don't know what will happen, but I'll tell you what usually happens back home. I'll sit down in this chair and kind of open myself up, and after a while Gracia will come. I never know what she's going to say, so don't blame me, please, whatever it is. But the whole reason I told Mr. Beauchamp I'd come tonight is, I guess maybe more folks have a right to know about the things Gracia says. When she's through saying her piece, if some of you want to come up and ask her questions, she'll probably answer them for you. Oh, uh, Mr. Beauchamp, we're going to need another chair in front of this one, for the people who want to ask questions to sit in while they're doing their asking."

An identical ladderback chair was quickly vacated by a spectator in the dining room, and Searles Beauchamp placed it as Morton had indicated. "Well, then," said Melvin Morton, seating himself, "here we go."

A profound silence settled over the room. Branwen, who was only a few feet away, appreciated the quality of that silence. It was both expectant and communal, as if everyone in the room joined with the modest little man in anticipation of his visitor from another plane of existence. Branwen reminded herself that just because he was so harmless-looking was no reason he couldn't be a fraud; but she didn't really believe it. She felt only positive energy, and plenty of it, coming from Melvin Morton.

He had loosened his collar and tie and now sat squarely in the straight-backed chair, feet apart and solidly planted on the floor, hands resting on his knees. His eyes were closed. He was breathing deeply through his mouth; the sound of his breath filled the hushed room. Time seemed suspended, all attention focused to a crux of expectation.

On a long exhalation of breath, Morton's head flopped forward, and his body seemed boneless. Branwen had to restrain herself from darting forward to keep him from sliding off the chair. But he didn't fall. In the blink of an eye, he regained his erect posture, opened his eyes, and smiled. When he spoke his first words, an unconscious gasp escaped from more than half the people in the two rooms. The voice that came from Melvin Morton's mouth seemed anatomically impossible for a man to produce. It was a woman's voice, slightly nasal, clipped, with an indefinable foreign edge to her words.

"Good evening. I am Gracia. I sense many souls here, and this gives me gladness. I come to you through this man who is receptive, a good man, clear with no malice in him. I come because I am a teacher and a healer, and in your time you have many seekers, and much need of healing." The voice fell silent, and then resumed. "I sense there are those present who are aware of this need. I will speak of progress, progress toward the Highest Good. Always it has been generally agreed that individual souls may progress. I tell you now that many, many souls may also progress as a group. The whole civilization may move up another turn on the spiral of progress toward the Highest Good. How is this accomplished? By the action of smaller groups within the largeness of the whole, as the yeast causes the whole ball of dough to rise. No soul, either as you are in the body or as I am without body on the plane beyond, is entirely alone. We are apart yet together. Our groups are like concentric circles within concentric circles."

Melvin Morton's throat worked, his face contorted as Gracia spoke. Physically, this was obviously not easy for him. Gracia did not spare her instrument, nor did she give her audience time to ponder her dense message. She went on. "In your time there are many who are ready to act as the yeast, to move your civilization up to its next level. Others from my plane, and higher, will come in the body to help you; some are already with you. Yet others, who have their own groups, seek to hinder. It has always been so. Progress is hard. Souls are damaged in the effort and must be healed. You see around you material progress, what you call technology. This is good when it does not lead to greed. The technology frees you so that you may seek to penetrate the veil of communication between the material and the spiritual planes. But this has happened before, at a time when greed and arrogance prevailed and progress was lost."

Melvin Morton gasped for breath; his voice, which Gracia used, was becoming hoarse. Still she went on. "I bring you a blessing, but also a warning: Be aware of one another, that we are all made of the same substance, of spirit. Remember that though you may feel isolated in your body, you are not alone. Know that though you may be separated from others of your circle on your physical plane, separated by physical distance, still they are there and working with you, like the leaven in the bread to make it rise. And when you are no longer in the body, you will be with them again. Find one another when you can, draw strength from one another, heal one another, and never cease to pursue our common goal, which is progress toward the Higher Good. This man, my instrument for speech, is tired. I will answer no questions tonight. *Valete!*"

It seemed with Gracia's departure that this time Melvin Morton's limp body really would slide to the floor. Searles Beauchamp, who presumably had seen all this before, was immediately at his side and so was the host with a glass in one hand and a pitcher of water in the other.

Harry was among the first to break the silence. Rather too loudly he said, "If that Gracia is really a healer, you wouldn't think she'd leave her channel in such a state. The poor man looks half dead!"

Branwen ignored his remark. She had pulled out the notebook she always carried in her bag and was making notes while all that Melvin/Gracia had said was fresh in her mind.

Harry peered over her shoulder and commented, "I don't see why you bother. Most of what she—or does one properly say *he*? It's so confusing! Most of what she said was drivel anyway."

"Hush!"

"Very well." Harry rose awkwardly, the muscles in his legs and back stiff with tension. If Branwen had looked at him, she would have seen that he was unusually pale, but she did not; she kept on writing. He looked down at her bowed head, the inch-wide strip of white in her black hair, and thought suddenly: *This is where our paths divide—it's time for me to go my own way.* In a daze, Harry wandered through the buzzing crowd toward the refreshment table.

Branwen was able to recall most of what Gracia had said through Melvin word for word. Writing it down took long enough that the crowd had adjourned to the dining room and kitchen where there was food and drink. The room where she sat writing had grown quiet, but she was so intent that she didn't notice.

"Uh, excuse me, ma'am, but is your name Brand or Brandy or something like that?" Melvin Morton stood in front of her, speaking in his own baritone voice though still with a bit of hoarseness.

"Branwen, my name is Branwen." She looked up and smiled, pleased and curious that he should single her out.

"Branwen, yes, that's it. Branwen Tennant." Melvin nodded his head. "I have a message for you."

"A message?" She thrust her notebook into her bag and got to her feet. Standing, she was half a head taller than he. In a flash she realized that if she had needed proof of Melvin Morton's genuineness, he had just provided it. There wasn't a soul in Washington, except for Harry who was nowhere in sight, who knew her by that last name.

Melvin was looking puzzled, studying her face. "Say, I know you! You're the lady used to be on the TV. Discovering Virginia, that's you. But I thought your name was something else."

"It is. I don't know how you got Tennant. That's my maiden name. The name I use professionally is Branwen Faraday. What about a message?"

"Yeah, it's from Gracia. It's, uh, kind of personal. Private-like."

Branwen glanced around. "There's nobody close enough to overhear. Go ahead."

"Okay. You had a baby, right, but it died. I mean, it was born dead?"

Eyes wide and glazing with the tears that always came when she thought of the lost child, Branwen nodded. A chill ran along her arms. How could he possibly know all these things?

"You see," Melvin explained, his kind face creased with caring, "sometimes when I'm channeling like tonight, Gracia will tell me something that she doesn't say out loud because it's for one specific person, someone who didn't come forward to ask a question. And of course tonight she didn't take questions. She tells me in my head, I just hear her, usually when I'm kind of passed out for a few minutes after she's through speaking. She told me to tell you that the one, the soul who would have been born in your baby, is with her on that other plane. Wherever that is." The little man smiled, his smile innocent rather than self-deprecating. "You know, I don't understand a lot of this. I just let her talk through me. I guess I don't have to understand. Anyway, that one that would have been your baby wants you to know that he left of his own choice. He made his own decision at the last minute not to be born in your child. That's why the baby was dead. I guess he's like a friend of Gracia's, out there wherever they are. They want you to know that it wasn't your fault or anything like that. They don't want you to blame yourself. That's the message."

Branwen's tears spilled over. For a moment she was too stunned to say anything; then, slowly, she smiled. She grabbed Melvin's chubby hand and held it tightly. "Thank you. And Gracia, and the one who would have been my baby. Thank you for telling me that. You can't know how much it helps!"

Melvin Morton beamed. His eyes shone like stars from their nest of radiating wrinkles. "Good, good. That's what it's all about, isn't it? Helping and healing."

Harry had left his car at Branwen's place, and she had driven him to the meeting. On the way back she told him about the message, concluding, "He said 'That's what it's all about, isn't it? Helping and healing.' I'm almost in awe of Melvin Morton, Harry. He has such a beautiful simplicity. He expressed a whole philosophy of life in those few ordinary words!"

"Humph!" Harry sniffed. "If you care for such a philosophy—whether it comes from Morton himself or the so-called Alexandrine healer. That's nothing but fodder for the masses, Branwen. The man is a peasant."

"Harry!"

"Oh, I have no doubt he's a genuine channel, but what can you expect? A peasant channels another peasant. As above, so below. All that ridiculous talk about raising masses of people to a higher level, concentric circles, being part of a group. . . . It sounds positively communistic!"

"Could it be that the man is truly gifted, and you're just a little jealous?"

"Absolutely not! There is a Higher Order, my dear, you should know that. You have only to search in your past lives to know that you have been one of the Elite, as have I. I am virtually certain you have powers that would put any trance-channel medium to shame, if you would only use them. We are individuals, Branwen, we have risen above the common horde."

"And what," asked Branwen through clenched teeth, "would you have us use our supposedly superior power *for*, Harry? To make a big splash, impress people with how great we are?"

"When one gets to a certain level of development, one doesn't have to use it *for* anything, unless one wants to. If you insist on having a purpose, I suppose you could say the Elite are called to be leaders. To lead by example, and by demonstration of our superiority. Gracia's analogy of the yeast in the dough is ridiculous; it would be sheer waste to bury one's talents in that way!"

There was a sneer in Harry's voice. Branwen felt his sidelong glance, and she met it briefly, chilled by the cold silver of his eyes. She said nothing.

Harry felt enlightened, remembering his earlier insight that the time had come for his path to diverge from Branwen. He continued, "But that's what you are determined to do, isn't it, bury yourself in the masses? That's why this plebeian philosophy you heard tonight appeals so much to you."

Branwen braked her car to a stop in front of her triplex. She could think only of Gracia's warning about greed and arrogance. Harry wasn't greedy, not in material terms, but he was certainly arrogant. Yet she was fond of him, and in a way she loved him. She said softly, "What I heard tonight felt true, it felt *right* to me. Harry, please, think back years ago to Llanfaren, the experience you and I had in the Fifth Tower. We've been going 'round and 'round about this ever since, haven't we?"

"Yes, indeed we have." Harry's voice had an edge like a sword.

"I asked you a question back then, and you never answered it. I asked you if we had such power once, don't you wonder why we lost it? Can you answer that question now?"

"*Why* is irrelevant. I've told you before, I don't bother with labels like good and evil; nor with symbology like light and dark, though that's harder to avoid. No, what matters is that our power is being restored to us in this lifetime. I've seen it and felt it. I know this is true."

"All right." The atmosphere inside the car was intense, replete with significance. Lines were being drawn, paths chosen, palpably. Branwen said, "I won't argue that. I'll just tell you what *I* believe. I believe we lost our power because we misused it in some way. Perhaps we've earned the right to have it back again. Perhaps we're simply being given another chance. Or— and I have reason to believe this may be the case—something is going to happen for which we will need the power. I'll tell you the truth, Harry: The runes told me, or I told myself through the runes, that the power is mine again. It has come to me, and I've used it in small ways, almost as if I were practicing. You called Melvin Morton a peasant. Well, peasant or not, he gave me the words for a better way. Whatever power I have, I intend to use it to help and to heal."

"Nothing else?"

"Nothing else."

"I hope you realize, my dear Branwen," said Harry in a voice that burned like ice, "that I have wasted a lot of years on you. I'll wait for you no longer. It's too bad. We could have reached incredible heights by combining our forces. That's what I've always wanted. But, as I said, when we reach a certain level of development, we must act as individuals. I cannot help but feel disappointed in you." He softened, thawed a bit. "I feel I must move on. It has been in the back of my mind to resign and go to live in England for an extended period of time. The British Isles, to be more precise—Scotland, Ireland, Wales. I think now the time has come. Will you not relent and go with me?"

"I can't." She shook her head sadly. "My life is here."

"Then we have indeed reached a parting of the ways." Harry, melting, reached his long arm across to Branwen and stroked her hair. She leaned toward him, and he gently kissed her lips, for the first and probably the last time. "Good-bye, Branwen," he said.

She sat in her car and watched him walk to his Mercedes. She saw around him a crackling aura of ice-cold blue. But surrounding that electric aura was another, dense and black, pressing down on Harry Ravenscroft.

That night Branwen dreamed of Darkness that had a name: the Abyss. The Abyss heaved with putrid motion. Horrid, shapeless creatures groped for its edge and slithered over, leaving nasty trails as they entered Branwen's world. Behind them rose, like a stinking mountain, one too horrible to behold, even in a dream: the Master of the Abyss, the Evil One.

4

Xavier Dominguez Velcroed his Roman collar together at the
back of his neck. It was a lot easier than the old fastening
method, but he felt every time as if he were cheating, like wearing a clip-on tie. He picked up his silver crucifix, automatically
touched it to his lips, and slipped the chain over his head. He
was dressing to go to breakfast with Branwen Faraday, dressing
in his priest's suit because, although she didn't know it yet, after
breakfast they were going to the morgue to identify an unclaimed body that was most likely Sister Emerald Pearl. The
homeless in death were accorded even less dignity than in life,
their bodies filed away in cold metal drawers for a couple of
weeks and then, when no one claimed them, given to medical
schools for students to cut up in their lessons. Xavier would not
go to the morgue in casual clothes; his respect for the dead required him to dress well, and that meant his clerical black.

He went down the hall to the bathroom and looked at himself
in the mirror over the sink. "God," he said, both swearing and
praying, "sometimes I hate being a priest!" He doubted God
had heard him; wondered if He had, would He care. Xavier had
been able to keep his fantasy about Branwen for less than forty-
eight hours.

Branwen was in a dither most unlike herself. She couldn't decide what to wear, didn't even know what she wanted to do with
her hair. The restaurant Xavier had named was downtown, but

he'd said he wanted her to go somewhere with him after, and
that he'd explain over breakfast. She didn't want to feel out of
place as she had the other day, but she *did* want . . . What?

She wanted him to like her. She didn't even know who this
Xavier Dominguez was. He could hang out in that part of town
because he was a drug dealer, for all she knew. But whoever he
was, he was the first man she had been strongly drawn to since
Will.

She decided she was being ridiculous, and besides, she had
no more time to waste. Ignoring the outfits she'd spread out on
her bed, she dug in the closet for the favorite dress she always
wore when she didn't know what to put on—an old, soft corduroy shirtdress that had once been turquoise-blue but through
many washings had faded to aquamarine. The matching belt
had long since fallen to pieces, and she cinched her waist with
one of wide brown leather, so indestructible that she'd had it
since her days at Llanfaren. Her brown leather boots were
newer but comfortable, with low heels. She sat down at her
dressing table and brushed her hair, then braided it in one long
braid. She filled in the open collar of the dress with a paisley
scarf and was satisfied. On her way out the door she grabbed the
trench coat that was her preferred wrap in all but the coldest
weather.

In the end she'd hurried so much that she was early. She
asked for a table near the windows so she could watch for
Xavier, ordered orange juice and coffee, and settled down to
wait. A black-clad priest walked by on the sidewalk, but she
paid no attention to him. She didn't notice that the priest came
into the restaurant, spoke to the hostess, scanned the room, and
headed straight for her table.

"Good morning, Ms. Faraday. I hope I haven't kept you waiting too long." Xavier waited for her to look up and recognize
him before he sat down. He didn't want to startle her, and she'd
seemed completely absorbed in looking out of the window.

Branwen's reaction was almost worth the giving up of his
fantasy. Of course he could have told her over the telephone that
he was a priest and would look like one, but he hadn't been able
to make himself do it. He was glad now that he hadn't. He
wouldn't have missed her reaction for anything. She turned her
head at the sound of his voice, looked up, and for a moment her
face went completely blank. Xavier could almost hear her mind
telling her, *This Does Not Compute*. Then her eyes widened, her

mouth dropped open, and her pale pearly skin flushed with pink until her cheeks blazed.

Xavier smiled, warmed and enchanted by her blush. "I know," he said, pulling out the chair and sitting across from her, "I should have told you."

Still blushing, Branwen started to laugh.

Xavier remarked, "I'm sure I've never seen anybody do that before, blush and laugh at the same time. I don't know whether to be charmed or offended!"

"Oh," said Branwen, stifling her laugh and gulping for breath, "I'm not laughing at you. I'm laughing at myself. When I think what I . . ." She broke off, her cheeks again scarlet, and resorted to her old habit of hiding behind lowered lashes.

God help me, thought Xavier, *she's the most incredible-looking woman I've ever seen!* He forgot why he was there, forgot where they would have to go later. Both things were swept away by a longing that consumed him all the way to his soul. Involuntarily he lowered his voice and leaned across the table. "Don't be embarrassed. There's no reason to be. If you were interested in me, I'm pleased and flattered. You're a lovely woman, and I may be a priest but I'm also a man."

It's not fair, Branwen thought, still not looking at him. *I could be blind and still fall halfway in love with him, just at the sound of that voice alone.* Then the waitress came with menus, giving them a respite they both very much needed. When they had ordered, Branwen felt more composed. She said, "So you're a priest—a Roman Catholic priest?"

"Yes," Xavier replied, his lips curving in a half-smile. "That's right, the *celibate* kind. You realize you haven't told me anything at all about yourself? Maybe you're one of those liberated married women who don't wear wedding rings, and you have a faithful husband and ten kids waiting for you at home."

"No, I'm not married. No kids at home. Not that it ought to make any difference to you in your condition."

Their eyes met, they both laughed, and both sobered at the same instant. Once again the waitress appeared in timely fashion and spared them by serving their food.

Branwen ate in silence, and so did he. She stole little glances at him and admitted that she still felt attracted to him. She didn't know how to handle it. She ventured, "This must happen to you a lot."

"No," said Xavier seriously, knowing what she meant. "Not exactly."

"I don't understand."

Xavier tugged at his collar. He looked and felt uncomfortable. "Maybe we should talk about something else."

Branwen's honesty came to the fore. "I think, unless we want to go straight to the matter of Sister Emerald Pearl and then go our separate ways never to see each other again, we'd better talk about this because we're both obviously feeling something. Nothing remotely similar has ever happened to me before." She started to blush again and pushed on regardless. "I honestly didn't think I could ever be so powerfully attracted to a man on first meeting, *any* man. And then you turn out to be a Catholic priest. That's why I was laughing—it's like some cosmic joke!"

"Only it's not really very funny." Xavier heaved a sigh and shoved his plate aside. "Okay, we'll talk. I should have told you right up front that I'm a priest. There were several reasons why I didn't. For one thing, I've gotten out of the habit of telling people. I used to be a Jesuit but about a year ago I left the Order and now I'm independent. I'm what they call a street priest. I minister to the homeless, and that house you were looking for, it's mine. I bought it with my own money, and it's my base of operations. About twenty people live there now, some of them two to a room. But in the beginning I practically had to drag people in off the street. They don't trust anybody who looks or acts or even smells like any kind of authority, so I stopped dressing like a priest. And I seldom talk about it."

"You don't try to convert these people that you help?"

"No way," he declared with emphasis. "If some of them get interested in the Church later, then that's fine with me. But when I first get them, what they need most are food, clothing, shelter, and medical care. I'm still trying to figure out what to do about the medical care—they don't like to go to the free clinic, and after going there myself a couple of times, I can see why. As for the food, pretty soon I'm going to start a soup kitchen and a free grocery."

"That's terrific." Branwen's eyes were shining. "Really wonderful! There's such a tremendous need for what you're doing. I had no idea how great a need until the last few months. I'd like to know more about it, *everything* about it!"

"Thanks, but let's not get ahead of ourselves. Another reason I didn't tell you anything about me is that you didn't tell me anything about yourself, either. You wouldn't tell me why you wanted the woman you were looking for, and I trust you'll clear that up for me soon. But the third reason I didn't tell you is the most important. . . ." Xavier stopped. He felt as if his Roman collar were strangling him. As much as he had admired her honesty, he didn't know if he could emulate it. He choked out the words, "And it's personal. I, ah, I don't think I can say any more."

"Okay." Briskly, suddenly all business, Branwen reached into her bag and pulled out her notebook. "Just tell me what you found out about Sister Emerald Pearl, and I'll be on my way."

"And I'll never see you again."

"Xavier, uh, Father Dominguez, I really would like to know more about the work you're doing. But I have a feeling that if we can't both be honest with each other from the beginning, it's not a very good idea."

"Not 'Father Dominguez,' please. The street people who know me call me 'Father X.' That's what I started to tell you the other day, and didn't." He paused. It was now or never, and he decided she was worth the risk of baring his feelings. "I think I'd rather you called me Xavier. Okay, the real reason I didn't tell you I'm a priest is that I was as attracted to you as you said you were to me. In a way, you were right when you said this must happen to me a lot. I, ah, I know I'm attractive to women and I guess my greatest failing is that I enjoy it. But I don't ever seriously consider doing anything about it. With you I wanted . . . well, I wanted to see where our mutual attraction might lead. So I held off telling you. That was wrong, and it was dangerous, and I'm sorry."

"I'd rather you didn't think you have to say you're sorry," Branwen said softly. "I felt exactly the same way, that I wanted to see where this attraction might lead."

"Yeah." Xavier leaned back in his chair, an ironic grin on his face. "And it led us right here, into this hellishly uncomfortable conversation. Now it's your turn to talk about yourself. Come on, give. Let me off the hook!"

"Fair enough." Branwen laughed. "I'm a television journalist. I write and produce documentaries for PBS, and I've been working for several months on a two-part program about the mentally ill in government-supported hospitals and mental-health centers. I decided my story wouldn't be complete unless I followed up on the people who won't stay in the mental-health centers, and that's how I began to learn about the homeless. I know I've only scratched the surface there, and I know now that I want to go further—but that will have to be another program or series of programs. You could be a big help, a major source for me if I do that. For now, to finish up with the mentally ill, I need to find Sister Emerald Pearl."

"I see." So she was a journalist, and from all that he could see, a serious, responsible one. Smart. A many-faceted woman, as they say "not just another pretty face." It was no wonder he found her so compelling. "Branwen—if I may presume to call you Branwen—I have bad news. I believe your Sister Emerald Pearl is dead."

"Oh, no! How, what happened?"

"A woman of her description had been staying around Lafayette Park. From what I was told, it sounds as if she had a stroke. Could have been caused by a drug overdose, history of alcohol abuse—that's what usually happens. Or it could have just been a bad heart, or an aneurysm. If you're willing to do it, we should go to the morgue. The woman who died in the park is an unclaimed body. You could at least identify her, if she is the one you're looking for."

"She didn't do drugs or alcohol." Branwen felt defensive on her behalf, though she had scarcely known the woman. She hesitated only a moment before making her decision. "I'll go to the morgue. I have to find out if it is or isn't Sister Emerald Pearl. But you didn't even know her—there's no need for you to come. You've already done more than enough. Thank you." Branwen dragged her oversize bag from the floor and fumbled inside for her billfold. She felt as if she'd been riding an emotional roller coaster. First, wanting a man she couldn't have; now learning of the untimely death of a woman who had been vitally alive. All she could think of was that she'd never been to a morgue and she dreaded it.

While Branwen was getting out her credit card, Xavier counted out cash to cover the breakfast bill and put it on the table. He closed his hand on hers, curling her fingers around the credit card, and said, "Let's get two things straight. One, if you think I'm going to let you go by yourself to identify that body, you're wrong. I am definitely going with you. Two, when I ask you out, I pay. If you happen to ask me out, then you can pay. Deal?"

"Yes, deal." She was registering the fact that he talked as if he did intend to see her again. She didn't dare ask on what basis. Didn't dare so much as think about it.

Xavier drove her to the morgue where she identified Sister Emerald Pearl and said she would have the social worker at the mental-health center try to find next of kin to claim the body. It was not an experience Branwen would care to repeat, and she was grateful that Xavier had insisted on coming with her. He had been sensitive, kind, and something more—something that was new in Branwen's experience. As he prayed over the woman he had never met, his spirituality emerged. She would never have guessed that Xavier Dominguez might be a deeply spiritual man, but he was. He did not put on the mantle of his priesthood like an actor assuming a role. Rather, the sacredness of his calling welled up from deep inside him and poured forth, transforming the man, marking him as one consecrated to God.

By the time he returned her to her own car at midday, Branwen was sure that she would never understand Xavier Dominguez until she understood the depth and complexity of his religious faith. And she knew that she wanted very much to know and to understand him.

Many people in the Psychic Underground were fond of saying, "there are no accidents." Branwen was inclined to believe the statement was true, especially after Xavier Dominguez came into her life at precisely the same time as Melvin Morton came with his message of helping and healing. When she visited 622 and Xavier shared with her in detail his self-chosen mission, Branwen was immediately in complete accord. She wanted to help. She knew that ultimately she could help most by making a documentary, but first she wanted to know these powerless people in the same way Father X knew them. She wanted them to accept her, as they did him. There was only one way to make it happen, and he had no objection: She began to work by his side virtually every hour she did not have to be at the television station. She left jeans and old shirts at 622 so that she could change her clothes without wasting the time to go by her own apartment. An unusual intimacy grew between Branwen and Xavier, an intimacy they both cherished all the more for its nonphysical nature. The attraction between them was no less powerful, but they chose to ignore it.

Branwen's life had been transformed in the space of a few weeks. Or so it seemed; in reality the changes had been occurring over a period of years. Now in the fall of 1978, she was ready and able to grasp the concept of "service" and to embrace it for herself. She understood that when Xavier Dominguez said, "The highest purpose in life is the service of God," and demonstrated that by literally serving his homeless fellow human beings, he meant exactly the same thing as Melvin Morton when he said, "That's what it's all about . . . helping and healing." That Xavier lived out of a Catholic Christian framework and Melvin functioned through the paranormal made no difference—they were doing the same things, pursuing the same ends. And so was Branwen.

There was only one problem: She had no time to see her friends, and she especially missed Ellen Carew. Ellen knew nothing about Xavier because Branwen felt her relationship with the priest was entirely too complicated to explain on the telephone, and she hadn't seen Ellen in person for weeks. Finally, just before Christmas, Branwen called her and asked if she might come out to the McLean estate on Ellen's next free evening.

"Oh, come on now," said Ellen when Branwen arrived, "you don't have to apologize to me. I know how busy you are. Whenever I don't see you for a while, I know you're working on something. Is it still the mentally ill thing or a new project?"

Branwen followed her friend's bouncy step into the living room. Though she'd been in that room hundreds of times over the years, its soaring high ceiling—the result of Ellen's having removed the second floor over this part of the house—and huge expanses of glass always took her breath away. As Harry had said on her first visit, it only looked like a farmhouse on the outside. Her house was like the woman herself, full of delightful surprises.

Branwen joined Ellen where she'd been sitting on the rug before the fireplace. With the ease that comes of long friendship she automatically began to help Ellen with what she had been doing before she arrived: stringing fat red cranberries on heavy green thread. There was no need to ask what the cranberry ropes were for. It was Christmas, and Ellen always made all her own decorations for the house. The women worked as they talked, and Branwen began by answering the earlier question. "I'm doing a little of both. I've finished writing the mentally ill thing, as you called it. I still have to supervise the production crew and re-create portions of the interviews I've already done, but for me the hardest part is finished. And I am doing something new that's taking almost all my time. What about you, Ellen? Been up to anything new?"

"Well, you might say so," Ellen said happily. "Would you believe that this old lady in her late forties is getting married?"

"Married, you? No! I don't believe it! Don't hit me, please, I'm only kidding. Seriously, Ellen, I'm really happy for you!" Hugging each other while on their knees in the midst of a lot of cranberries wasn't easy, but they managed. Branwen urged, "Tell me all about him. Is he someone new? Why haven't I guessed you were up to something like this? What is this, a whirlwind romance?"

"You could say so. He's been in Washington for years and years, but I never met him until three months ago. His name is Jim Harper, he's a widower, and he's FBI but due to retire in six months. The wedding will be right after his retirement. It will all be done very quietly, nothing fancy, and no formal announcement of our engagement. We're both too old for all that."

"Ellen, at the moment you don't look too old for anything. You look about fourteen." This was only a slight exaggeration. Ellen wore a green velour jumpsuit, and in it she was tiny and trim. The more recent strands of silver-gray in her hair were mixed in with the curly blond like a good frosting job, and her face sparkled with happiness.

"Thanks, sweetie. I admit I feel like a kid."

"Will you live here, in this house?"

"I don't know. We haven't gotten that far yet in our plans."

"Uh, I hate to sound like your mother or something, but . . . You do know him well enough to be sure? Some of these FBI types can be, uh—"

"Tough?" Ellen giggled. "Yes, Mother, I do know him well enough. It's not as if I haven't been looking all these years. I just thought I'd never find anyone. Jim has that special quality I've been looking for. I can't put a name to it, I just know he has it. Sure, he's tough, but with me he's a pussycat." She winked. "He wants to do a lot of traveling after he retires, and that's fine with me."

"Speaking of traveling," Branwen said, tying off a three-foot length of threaded cranberries and rethreading her needle, "have you talked to Harry Ravenscroft lately?"

Ellen frowned. "Yes. He's already told them at Redmund that he's leaving at the end of the semester. I don't know, Branwen, he sounds too keyed-up or something. He's not really thinking clearly. I had to persuade him not to close up Raven Hill. I can't imagine why he didn't realize for himself that the Beechers have nowhere else to go! He talks as if he's never coming back, but of course he will. And besides, you just don't turn away people who have worked for you years and years, like the Beechers have done for Harry."

"I should hope not! He's still upset with me, you know, because I wouldn't go along with him to England."

"Maybe you should go with him, Branwen. Just for a little while." Ellen paused in her cranberry stringing, as if for emphasis. "You could visit your parents and keep an eye on Harry at the same time."

"No, no." Branwen shook her head. Her hair, which she'd left loose, swung back and forth. "I've never really been able to explain to my mother about the divorce—she adored Jason. You know how he could be with people. Especially women. Our relationship has been a little strained ever since, even over the telephone with an ocean between us. I really don't want to go back, Ellen, and even if I did, I can't right now. There's too much going on in my life for me to leave."

"Branwen, there's something more. Something I'm sure you don't know about."

The serious note in Ellen's voice made Branwen look at her. "What is it?"

"Harry has been in touch with Jason."

Why that information should make her blood run cold Branwen didn't know, but it did. She said, "For some reason that doesn't surprise me."

Ellen's cranberries were completely forgotten. "Actually, Jason started it. He wrote to Harry a couple of months ago, bragging about some fabulous estate he's bought in Germany, complete with ancient *schloss*. Harry showed me the letter. He was incensed, said Jason was only writing in order to impress him, and after I'd read the letter I agreed. Jason has gotten quite a lot of money somehow, and he's playing lord of the manor."

"Well, Jason has had ten years of doing God only knows what." Now Branwen's cranberries, too, were forgotten. "Obviously it pays well." She stared into the fire, not seeing its flames, unwilling to tell Ellen what she had seen more than once in the runes: that Jason had been entirely corrupted. That she and Harry were still in some way tangled up with him. That one of these days, or one of these years, Jason would come back into their lives, bringing a wall of Darkness with him.

When Branwen said no more, Ellen resumed. "It's crazy, Branwen. First Harry is totally ticked off at Jason, and then the next thing you know he answers the letter and just like that"— she snapped her fingers—"they're writing back and forth, buddies again. Harry isn't planning anymore to go to England. He says he's going to visit Jason in his castle. I thought, if you said you'd go to England after all, you might get Harry to change his mind."

"I see your point." Branwen brooded. Finally she said, "No, I won't interfere. I'm not going to try to be Harry Ravenscroft's keeper. I agree with you that he isn't making wise decisions right now, but it's *his* life." With an effort she smiled and changed the subject. "Let's get back to stringing these cranberries. What would you have done if I hadn't showed up to help you? It would take you days to do all this by yourself! You must tell me what decorations you have planned for Christmas this year. . . ."

When Branwen left Ellen's much later in the evening, she realized she hadn't said a word about Xavier Dominguez or about the work she was doing with him. She had let the talk about Jason and Harry drive Xavier right out of her head. Just another example, Branwen thought grimly, of how successfully bad news can overshadow the good.

5

Branwen spent Christmas alone by her own choice. On New Year's Eve she went to an informal dance with Xavier in the parish hall of the church in his neighborhood where he said Mass and heard Confessions . . . but she pleaded a headache and left before midnight. In her car driving back to Georgetown, she felt like a fool. She'd turned down other considerably more glamorous invitations in order to be with Xavier. But then, like a bent Cinderella, she'd run away before midnight because she was afraid of what she might feel if he kissed her on the stroke of twelve.

That, however, was not the only reason Branwen had left the dance. For days a sense of foreboding had been hanging over her, and in the midst of the simple parish celebration she had remembered how Jason always celebrated the new year. How Jason did not make resolutions but rather made proclamations of what, in accord with his wishes, the new year should bring. The sense that Jason was at that very moment pronouncing ill fortune upon herself and Harry Ravenscroft, and perhaps others, had been so strong she'd felt sick and disoriented. She must have looked sick as well because Xavier had willingly let her go.

New Year's Day 1979 found Branwen at 622, knocking on the door of Xavier's room, wanting to apologize and needing to talk.

The door was vigorously jerked open, and Xavier's voice

said, "Hang on a second—I'll be right with you." But he was nowhere to be seen.

Branwen had spent as much time as a person could spend in the house without actually living there, but she'd never been in his bedroom. Usually they sat and talked at the kitchen table, and usually that was where she'd find him—in the kitchen or in the closetlike room he used for an office. This morning he hadn't been in either place, and a resident had directed her here. She stood on the threshold and looked around the room. To her surprise, it was no better furnished than any of the others in the house. In fact, it looked much worse, but perhaps that was because it was so messy. Books and newspapers were scattered around; clothes were all over the room, and the bed was unmade. Well, if she thought about it, such untidiness was typical of the man: he was always focused on something other than his own personal comfort.

Branwen lingered in the doorway holding her tongue, glad that inside the room a half-open door of what must be the closet hid Xavier from view. She must have interrupted him in the process of changing his clothes. Sure enough, he was tucking a plaid flannel shirt into his jeans as he stepped away from the cover of the closet door and kicked it closed with a sock-clad foot.

"What's up?" he asked as he turned his head in her direction. Then he saw her. His face registered surprise and then pleasure, not a trace of embarrassment. "Branwen! I didn't expect to see you today!"

"You sound as if you were expecting someone else. Have I come at a bad time?" asked Branwen uncertainly. She let Xavier lead her into the room. She envied his cool. Never once in any circumstance had she ever seen him at a loss, yet she herself felt distinctly uncomfortable to be in his bedroom.

"I thought you were one of the guys from the house, that's all. I'm not expecting anybody, but you know how it is around here." He held both her hands in his and smiled down at her. "It isn't possible for you to come at a bad time, Branwen. Having you here automatically makes it good."

That voice! Before she lost her courage, Branwen said, "I came over to apologize, to say I'm sorry I left so abruptly last night."

"How are you feeling this morning?" His eyes, dark as onyx, scanned her face. "Better?"

"Much better, thank you." She stepped back, but he didn't release her hands. Instead, he moved with her, only he took a bigger step that brought him closer still.

"In that case . . ." he said, and deftly one hand was at the back of her head while the other folded her hands against his chest, and he kissed her. An excellent kiss, pleasurable yet stopping short of arousal. Expertly done, yet somehow for her . . . disappointing.

He let her go, backed off, and said, "You owed me that. Happy New Year, Branwen."

"Happy New Year, Xavier." She felt odd and decided she'd rather be honest than polite. She tossed her head, and her braided hair bounced on her shoulder. "All the same, I wish you hadn't done that."

"Why? New Year's kisses are allowed, even expected. Besides, I thought I did it rather well, with just the proper degree of restraint. . . . Uh-oh." Xavier had been so surprised and pleased to see her that he hadn't acted with his usual care. He'd taken her at her word when she'd said she was feeling better. Maybe she was, physically, but something was wrong.

"Yes," Branwen said, "uh-oh." Suddenly everything felt too much for her. If she couldn't turn to Xavier, to whom could she turn? Her shoulders slumped inside the bulky green sweater she wore over gray slacks.

Xavier came to her side and put his arm around those dejected shoulders in firm, comradely fashion. "I didn't mean to be insensitive. Tell me what's wrong."

She sighed. She felt close to tears. "Sometimes I just don't understand your rules, *Father*."

"Ouch." Xavier winced. "Did I deserve that?"

"I don't know," she said helplessly. "You've got me off the track. I came here to say I was sorry for running out on you last night, but also because I need to talk about something, and you . . . you . . ."

Branwen wrenched away from him, turning her back. Xavier heard someone out in the hall and closed his door, never taking his eyes from her. He thought of Branwen as an extraordinarily strong woman. Already in the three months he'd known her she'd plunged fearlessly into many of the unpleasant situations he dealt with routinely; she'd done things most women wouldn't think of doing, like stripping and bathing a man who was infested with body lice and too weak from hunger and cold to do it himself. Xavier had come to think she could handle anything, including him. But he had never seen her as she was now—the very curve of her neck cried out that she was vulnerable. His mind tumbled even while his body yearned to comfort her. What had she said? Rules . . . she didn't understand his rules. What rules? Damn!

Suddenly he understood. It was the kiss, the calculated kiss that had come from his head, and not from his heart. He'd thought only of himself, that he could in fact get away with kissing her for the New Year. He hadn't been thinking of her at all. He stopped thinking, let feeling take over.

Branwen's head drooped like a flower too heavy for its stalk. Xavier felt blinded by the white, tender nape of her neck. He went to her, wrapped his arms around her from behind, locked them under her breasts. He let his lips fall on the exposed nape in a kiss both yearning and achingly sensual.

"I'm sure that kind of kiss is not allowed," she whispered.

Xavier rested his cheek against her temple. His lips and tongue burned with the taste of her skin; his voice came from deep in his throat. "Right now I care more about you than I do about what may or may not be allowed." He closed his eyes. The effort of keeping his hands clasped about her rib cage was almost too much—what his hands wanted to do, what *he* wanted to do, was to hold the fullness of her breasts and feel the nipples bloom and harden against his palms. He swallowed a groan and said, "You need something from me, Branwen. I should have seen that sooner. Tell me what you need, what you want from me."

She moved. She turned her body under his hands and for a sweet, agonizing moment Xavier thought she would tip her head up, parting her lips, inviting him to kiss her again. But she stepped back. Xavier opened his hands and let her go.

"I don't know what I want," she said. "I thought I knew when I came over here, but you've confused me."

Xavier was not confused. Every fiber in his body throbbed with wanting to touch Branwen, to hold her. But he waited, searching her serious face for clues, answers. "I'm sorry," he said simply, "I didn't mean to confuse you."

"I know you didn't."

The priest in Xavier was, after all, stronger than the man. The priest took over. "My first kiss was selfish. I've wanted to kiss you for a long time, and I was thinking only of myself. The other—when I held you just now—was less selfish, I hope, yet still not what you needed. Isn't that so?"

Branwen nodded, beginning to feel better. She remembered the other reason she had come. "What I need is to talk to you, Xavier, about something really serious. And not—not personal. Do you have time?"

"Um-hm." Privately both the man and the priest thought she needed more than talk; she needed to be loved, physically loved. But perhaps that was only a projection of his own desires. He squared his shoulders and forced himself to speak lightly. "It's about time I gave myself a day off from this place anyway. You know what will happen if we try to talk here."

Branwen knew all too well. She smiled. "We'll be interrupted. Could you come to my apartment, is that asking too much?"

"Not at all. I'll get my jacket." Xavier grinned, lifting a socked foot and wriggling his toes. "And my shoes!"

Branwen drove. Halfway between Southwest Washington and Georgetown Xavier asked abruptly, "Branwen, do you want me to have an affair with you?"

Traffic was light. She took her eyes from the road and looked at him. He was, she saw, quite serious. She let her glance linger on the planes of his face, move over his body. Then she returned her attention to her driving. Once she had physically desired this man; only with effort had she forced desire out of their friendship and all too easily, as she had just found out, it could return. Unable to be anything but honest, she replied, "Maybe. And maybe not, if an affair is all it would be. I don't do affairs very well, Xavier. I found that out years ago."

Xavier looked out of the window, thinking, weighing, judging himself. "Probably that's all it would be. I can't be certain, but in the end I probably wouldn't leave the Church."

"Have you done it before? Had an affair?"

"Once, yes," he confessed. "It happened a long time ago, in the sixties."

Branwen fought with her curiosity, biting her lip, telling herself she didn't need to know more. She thought of that other woman and couldn't help herself. She had to ask. "How did it end? What happened to your—your lover?"

Xavier turned from the window to study her pure profile. He wished he'd paid more attention in his pastoral counseling courses. He was having trouble understanding his own feelings, much less hers. He rubbed his hands on his thighs, as if he could rub away the memory of pain. "How did it end. Ah . . . amicably. She was a nun, still is. She went back to her vows and her Order, and I went back to mine." *But I hurt for a long time after,* he thought. *A long, long time.*

Thinking of herself and Will, Branwen said slowly, "Sometimes it's hard to know if love is worth the pain."

"Amen," Xavier murmured.

They finished the drive to her apartment in silence. As Branwen removed her key from the car's ignition, he caught her hand. Their eyes met. He said, "It is worth it, Branwen. Love is worth the pain."

Their habit of talking at the kitchen table prevailed at her apartment as well as at 622. Xavier was not a tea drinker, so Branwen made coffee.

"Okay," said Xavier, "what's on your mind that's so serious?"

The sense of foreboding returned and threatened to overwhelm her. She plunged into the heart of the matter. "Xavier, do you believe there is such a thing as evil? I don't mean as an abstract concept. I mean real, objective *Evil.*"

"Wow. You don't kid around, do you? When you say serious, you mean serious! I can't answer that off the top of my head." He grew contemplative. His handsome face with its broad, high cheekbones settled in solemn lines; his dark eyes were fathomless. At length he spoke. "Yes, I do believe in the existence of Evil. I think we're doing ourselves a disservice these days with our moral relativism, things like situation ethics. Sure, there are a lot of shades of gray, but there are also, very definitely, black and white, good and evil. I could say more, but that's probably enough. The rest is pretty esoteric, Christian Catholic stuff."

"Please tell me. I can handle that."

Xavier looked doubtful. "All right, but I warn you it's heavy. Things I almost never talk about. You know me as an activist priest, a down-to-earth sort of guy, and after this you'll probably think I have a crazy streak."

Branwen placed her hand on his arm. "Xavier, when you're done, I'll tell you why I'm asking. And then we can toss a coin to see who's the craziest. Please go on."

"That sounds interesting! Okay. Branwen, I don't only believe in God the Father, Son, and Holy Spirit. I also believe in

angels and demons, and the Devil. God help me, I believe all
of it, including demonic possession. I was in seminary with a
guy who's now an exorcist, and I've seen him work, seen and
heard things that bend credibility beyond the breaking point. I
know that sounds fantastic, but it's true. Not quite so dramatic
as in that movie *The Exorcist*, but actually it was *worse* because
it wasn't a movie. It was real, all right. I saw what I saw and
heard what I heard. I know how it feels to be in the presence of
the Devil, Satan, the Other—or one of his lesser demons. It's
hard to tell them apart.

"That is real, absolute Evil, Branwen. Nothing the least bit
abstract about it. Evil doesn't just float around free in the universe, settling at random here and there. It takes a—a
consciousness—a *soul*, I guess I'd call it—to generate the evil
act. Malevolence is palpable. As love is palpable and is its opposite. The hard part for me was admitting that these souls can
exist in forms other than the way our souls exist, in our bodies.
But witnessing an exorcism made a believer out of me. I have a
tape of the exorcism—I'll play it for you sometime if you
want." Xavier sat back in his chair. A fine sheen of moisture had
appeared on his forehead, and he wiped it away.

"I believe you." She crossed her arms and leaned with her elbows on the table. "I don't like it, but I do believe you. I don't
need to hear the tape. In Wales where I grew up there are people
who remember, and some who still practice, the Old Religion—
they say that the Christians invented the Devil. I remember my
gran saying that Christianity brought the idea of Evil into the
world. I know that in many ways Gran was wise, but she may
have been wrong on that particular point. What do you think,
Xavier, as a Christian? What's your explanation about where
Evil comes from?"

He laughed and threw up his hands. "You're asking *me* about
the origin of Evil? I'm no theologian. Theologians have debated
that question for centuries."

"This isn't an oral examination in theology. I just want your
opinion. I assume you have thought about it. You couldn't very
well have had the experience you describe with the exorcism
and not think about it."

"Yeah, I thought about it." Once again Xavier's face went
grave. He was far more serious and scholarly than those who
had come to know him after his leaving the Jesuits could have
guessed. "There is a myth that offers an explanation. A Chris-

tian myth, probably the one Milton drew on when he wrote *Paradise Lost*. I believe myths endure because they contain an element of truth we recognize, consciously or unconsciously. So for what it's worth, here it is: God, the Energy and Source of everything, created other Beings before He created Man. Like us, these Beings have separate identities, personalities, and free will. They think, and act, and communicate. Unlike us, they are bodiless. They are spirits who live in a spiritual realm. We call them angels. Lucifer was an angel who, with his free will, decided he didn't like God or the way God did things. Lucifer attracted a lot of followers. In some versions of the myth, Lucifer leaves God's kingdom of his own accord after earth has been created—Lucifer takes over the earth, and God lets him have it. The Gnostics, among others, believed that version. The orthodox Christian version says that God cast Lucifer, or Satan, out of Heaven—the place of Light—and created for him and his followers Hell—the place of Darkness. And incidentally, Branwen, the way that business got started about Christians inventing the Devil: In the Dark Ages when Christianity was spreading through Europe and Africa and the Near East, the Church made an unfortunate but effective practice of stomping out old local religions by assigning the names of the various local gods to the Devil and his demons. The same with the practice of magic—if 'miracles' were done outside the sanction of the Church, they were called works of the Devil."

"Um-hm. That's interesting, especially the part about God creating angels first with free will, et cetera. I hadn't heard that before." Branwen took their neglected coffee cups, in which the coffee had grown cold, and refilled them. Then she sat down again. "Xavier, I have apparently inherited from my Welsh ancestors an ability for which your Church Fathers would have burned me at the stake. I have the Sight. I'm sensitive about it, and I don't normally go around telling people, any more than you go around telling them you believe in demonic possession. I was brought up to deny having the Sight, though my gran would have encouraged and taught me if my parents had let her. And until the last few years I denied it myself, or ignored it. I don't have a strong religious belief the way you do. What I have are spiritual beliefs that seem to have been born in me—I didn't *learn* them so much as I *uncovered* them, am still in the process of uncovering them. I know such a thing isn't supposed to be possible. We're supposed to be taught such things from our culture, but that's how it feels to me."

"Fascinating! Are you familiar with Jung, Branwen?"

"Not really, not in any depth."

"What you just said about uncovering beliefs—it reminds me of Jung's theory of the Collective Unconscious. If spiritual truths were stored in the soul, and the soul is immortal . . ."

"And if there is such a thing as reincarnation . . . But you as a Catholic aren't supposed to believe in that, Xavier."

"Maybe yes, maybe no. But I don't mean to distract you. Please continue."

"Okay. To condense everything down to what really seems most important at the moment: Increasingly over the last few years I've had this sort of nagging awareness that has something to do with evil. Yet intellectually I haven't wanted to say that evil is real—I've wanted to say that what we call evil is simply less good, and it might get better."

"I would say that evil is the absence of good, and absolute evil is the complete, total absence of good. My God, this is a heavy discussion!"

"Yes, it is." Branwen paused and smiled at Xavier. "I told you it was more serious than whatever you and I were doing."

"I hate to admit you were right, I so much prefer to be the center of my own small world," he said, his black eyes shining, "but you were."

"I'm afraid that's not all. It gets worse. The Sight has shown me things symbolically, and I've put them out of my mind in the same way that you manage to forget a recurring nightmare—until it comes back and grabs you again. I don't want to be specific right now, Xavier, I can't. I only know that my dreams and visions are filled with Darkness and the presence of what I must call evil—there is no other word for it. I can't go on any longer thinking of it as 'less good.' Talking with you has helped more than you can possibly know. Thank you."

They had talked for hours and were both depleted by the subject. She proposed that they go into the living room and listen to music. He agreed, with the stipulation that she let him take her out to dinner later. For the first few minutes they sat decorously apart; then Xavier wordlessly held out his arms to her, and she came to him. They neither kissed nor spoke, they simply rested in the safety and security of each other's arms while the mellow-bright sounds of Mozart's Horn Concerti soothed their souls.

When the music ended, Xavier turned Branwen in the crook of his arm. He touched his lips to her forehead where the white streak began in her hair. He whispered, "Why you, Branwen? Why must such a strong awareness of evil come into your life?"

"I don't know," she replied. "I guess one of these days I'm going to find out."

Jason Faraday had lied to Harry Ravenscroft. His was not a castle but a manor house; not ancient but merely some two hundred years old. Of course, that was the least of the lies he had told him in his letters and would tell him in person as soon as he had the opportunity. Jason sat at an antique fruitwood desk and looked out of a huge mullioned window that ran from floor to ceiling in the beautiful room, looked at the green lawns of his estate and wove his elaborate plans, like a fat spider weaves his web. And he *was* fat; he had gained weight in the manner of many squarely built men, massively. He looked and moved like a block of granite, and was as implacable.

Jason had drawn Harry to him as easily as a fly to sugar water. Cunningly he had extracted the man's secrets, and soon he would dispose of him. But not by his own hand, oh, no. Jason was far beyond the need to soil so much as the tip of a finger.

Jason chuckled—the coffered ceilings of the chamber reverberated with the harsh, evil sound. So Harry wanted to develop and use his magical powers, did he? And he was willing to pay out of that considerable old Ravenscroft fortune. Very well. Harry would arrive in a few days, and Jason would lull him and woo him . . . and then he'd send Harry to the Cognoscenti. They would train him. And then they'd use him, and use him, until they'd used him up. Jason didn't have to do a thing to destroy Harry Ravenscroft—that arrogant Virginia aristocrat who had looked down his long narrow nose at him for years; who had somehow protected his ex-wife from a car accident that should have been fatal. No, Jason didn't have to do a thing, the Cognoscenti would do it for him. Not that they would know they were doing it for him. They would drain Harry dry; they'd leave him nothing, not even his soul.

The beauty of it was that Harry would thank him for it, he would fawn and grovel in gratitude for the coveted introduction. The existence of such a group was rumored in occult cir-

cles, but the name was not even whispered. The name
Cognoscenti was known only to a select few. Jason had earned
the right to know. Jason had worked for them for years, con-
ducting their affairs in areas even the occult circles would have
never dreamed of. Jason had grown rich and powerful in their
service. Now he would give Harry, who had no right to it, the
forbidden name—and thus he would seal Harry's doom.

Branwen would be next. Branwen he would take care of personally. The Cognoscenti would not prevent his return to Washington, not now that he was as powerful as they. And he was as
powerful. Not in the Black Arts, no, but in ways the world better
understood. Now at last he could go back after Branwen. As
soon as he had disposed of Harry. He chuckled again, and the
chuckle grew into a monstrous laugh of fiendish glee.

There was a strange car parked in Branwen's assigned space
in the short crescent drive of her triplex. She saw it from half
a block away. At first she was merely annoyed by the inconvenience, thinking that the new couple in the center apartment had
been inconsiderate enough to allow their guests to take her
place. Well, the guests would just have to move because it was
late and dark and cold, and there was no way Branwen was going to hunt for a space on the street. But then, as she approached
the crescent, her headlights picked out a figure sitting in that
car. A man, judging by the width of his shoulders and the short-
ness of his hair. Who would be waiting for her, sitting in her
own parking space? She wasn't expecting anyone and she knew
her friends' cars. Alarmed, she hit the button that automatically
locked all four doors of her Volvo. She decided to drive on
through and call the police from the nearest pay phone.

Closer to the strange car, she noticed it was a Lincoln, black,
with government plates. The kind assigned to visiting digni-
taries. She slowed, more curious than frightened now. The man
moved. The lanky grace with which he unfolded himself out of
the door on the driver's side was hauntingly familiar. He raised
his head, and she saw his face.

Will! Will Tracy! She hit the brakes, killed the motor, and
without the slightest compunction left the Volvo blocking her
end of the crescent drive.

"Will!" She flew to him, into his arms. "Oh, Will, it *is* you! I
can't believe it!" How wonderful his long body felt against

hers, and how familiar, even through the bulk of his long overcoat.

"Hi, Branwen." For a ridiculous moment it was all he could think of to say. Then he added, "I've been waiting for you. I went to the PBS station, and they told me you'd left. I tried calling, but you didn't answer, so finally I decided to come on over here and wait. Looks like I took your parking space. There weren't any others. I'd better move the car—"

"Oh, hang the parking problems. If anybody objects to my blocking one end of the drive, they know where to find me. I just can't believe you're here! Come on, let's go inside. We've got years of catching up to do."

She gave him brandy because he looked half frozen; then gave herself the same because she discovered she was shaking right down to her toes. Finally, as they sat on opposite ends of the couch, she allowed herself to take a long look at him. Will had aged, that was what she noticed first. But age became him; he'd grown into the character his strong features demanded. His hairline had receded to the crown of his head, which emphasized the noble sweep of his brow and made his eyes seem larger. The eyes were the clear, warm hazel-brown she remembered, and as kind. The wide mouth was less quirkily mobile, more sculpted. In repose his face had a hewn solemnity, as if he had seen and felt many things of which he would not speak. His hands, so familiar that her own fingertips tingled as she looked at them, warmed the brandy snifter with long fingers.

But Will was pale, unhealthily pale; and his body radiated tension.

Of course, he had been examining her, too. "You still sit like that, with your feet under you," he observed.

His voice was gentle, the smile so kind. She had not forgotten his gentleness or his kindness. Not forgotten, no; but she had not thought she would ever feel those things from him again. Now she felt them, all the way from the other end of the couch. She said, "You seem tired, Will. I wish I'd known you were coming. Nobody told me, not even Ellen."

"Ellen doesn't know I'm here." Will sipped the brandy. "Nobody knows. When I've gone, you won't have seen me. I'm supposed to be at the embassy in Paris, and I have to fly back to Paris tomorrow. Then back to Teheran."

"For heaven's sake, why? You haven't gone CIA, have you? The last I heard, Iran was a friendly country."

"Yes. And the next you hear, that may no longer be true. And I didn't say that, just the same as I wasn't here." Will rubbed his forehead, a familiar gesture. "There's a plot to overthrow the Shah, and we aren't supposed to know about it. Nor should I tell you, but I trust you, Branwen, and if I don't talk to someone, I think I'll go mad. I'm not a spy, but I have friends who are. I haven't gone CIA—just the opposite. As soon as I get back in this country again, I intend to stay here for good. I'll get out of government service so fast it'll make their heads spin!"

"Oh." Branwen was shocked by the change that came over Will as he spoke. He looked broken, and she wanted to kill whoever or whatever had done that to him.

He continued to speak. "I came over to arrange my own return and to get permission for my wife and stepson to come with me. She's a distant cousin of the Shah and she's Christian. The boy, too. If what I think is going to happen does happen, they will both be in danger." He tossed off the last of his brandy. "And I guess I will be, too. So we've got to get out, but it has to look as if we have compelling, nonpolitical reasons to leave."

His hands were shaking. Branwen asked, "More brandy?"

"No, thanks. I shouldn't have come here. I mean *here*, to see you. But I needed to talk, and I haven't seen you in so many years. . . . I just wanted to look at you again. No, more than that. Talk to you. Oh, God, how I need to talk!"

"I can see that." She gripped the sofa cushion, hard, stopping herself from going to him. "I'm glad you came. I've missed you."

"I've missed you, too. More than I like to admit. You look well. A little tired yourself, maybe. This is a nice place. Ellen wrote that you'd moved." He was babbling.

"Relax, Will. I'm fine—don't talk about me. Talk about yourself. Tell me exactly what's wrong. I get the feeling it's more than just the political situation."

"Yeah." Will bent over and put his head in his hands. There was anguish in his eyes and his voice when he raised his head again. "Damn near everything is wrong. I've got to get out of the State Department, Branwen. I'm just not cut out for it, I never was. It isn't Iran, it's the job itself. It's killing me!"

His suffering tugged at her. She inched closer, to the middle cushion. "Will, if it's that bad, why don't you just stay here? Don't go back. Turn in your resignation and send for your wife and the child. State will understand—they know what a high burnout rate their people have."

He avoided her eyes. "I guess I, ah, I do want more brandy. You stay there, I'll get it." From across the room with his back to her, Will said, "I wish I could do it that way, but I don't think she'd come. My wife. She doesn't want to admit there's danger in Iran, none of them do. Worse than that, once I tell her that I intend to resign from the State Department, I'm pretty sure my marriage will be over."

"What?" The cry escaped Branwen's lips involuntarily.

"You heard right," said Will, returning to the couch. "Aletha didn't marry *me*, Will Tracy. She married Wilbur F. Tracy, Jr., a wealthy American diplomat. Only I turned out to be somewhat less wealthy and a lot less of a diplomat than she thought. It hasn't been much of a marriage, but I've tried. I swear to God, I've tried!"

"I'm sure you have," she said softly. "You would. I know you would." There was so much sadness in that big, gentle man. Her heart ached for him.

"We have this huge house and so many servants I sometimes forget their names. Not my first choice for a life-style, you may imagine. Of course she has her own money—I couldn't support all that on my salary. Anyway, we live in the style to which she was accustomed, and I soon found out that meant she has a whole section of the house that's *hers*, and I have a section that's mine. We don't live the way I always thought a man and wife would live. We never have."

"You mean you don't sleep together."

Will smiled. It was rather wan, but a smile nonetheless. "I see you haven't lost that relentless honesty—I'm glad. Yes, that's what I mean. And it's more than that. It's a whole cultural kind of thing that I just didn't understand when I married her. I hardly ever get to see the boy. He lives in his mother's part of the house, and he idolizes his dead father, the pilot. He won't let me be any kind of father to him, and his mother has never done anything to change that. It goes without saying that there haven't been any other children."

"I'm sorry." She waited, and when he said no more, she asked, "What are you going to do?"

"Well, if it weren't for the political situation in Iran, I'd just tell her I've decided I don't want to live abroad anymore and I'm miserable in the diplomatic corps, and that would be that.

I'd leave, and she probably wouldn't, and eventually one of us would get a divorce. The quiet acceptable kind of divorce. But I can't do it that way. I've got to try one last time to persuade Aletha to leave Iran and take Paul. I'll go back and stay in Teheran for as long as I dare, or as long as it takes to persuade her to leave with me—whichever comes first. I'll have to rely on my friends to let me know if things start to blow up suddenly. The arrangement I've worked out in the last two days here is that as soon as I let them know I'm ready to leave, or if it's about to blow and they hear about it, I'll get an urgent call to come home, my father is dying. He won't be—he's as healthy as one of his horses. I'll ask Aletha to come with me and to bring Paul, too. She won't know the call is a fake; it wouldn't be safe for her to know. But I will be honest enough to tell her that once I'm out of Iran I won't go back. And that I'm going to resign. Oh, damn." He rubbed his forehead and swallowed more brandy. "This is the most god-awful mess."

"So it would seem," Branwen murmured.

He looked at her, and she read hopelessness and defeat in his eyes. "My wife won't go for it. The only thing she likes about me is my job, Branwen. The marriage is as good as over, but I just don't like to admit it. I've been over and over this in my mind. If I tell her the truth, that I'm resigning and not going back to Iran, she'll never leave. The only chance I have to get her to leave is if I lie to her, trick her into leaving. I can't bring myself to do that. I just . . . can't . . . do . . . it!"

"Stop it, Will. Just stop it." Branwen began to rub his shoulders. He was so tense! Understandably. "Let go, you've gone 'round and 'round with this long enough. You aren't responsible for whatever happens in that country. And it looks to me as if you've stayed much longer than is good for you in a job you hate. You've done enough, now let go. If you must return and try one more time to get her to leave, then do it. But stop torturing yourself. I can't bear to see you this way."

Will turned to her, and her arms went around him. He buried his head in her shoulder and cried, apologizing for his tears over and over, declaring that he was ashamed. Finally Branwen had heard enough. She was angry and didn't know where to direct her anger—at the woman who was his wife, at his job, or at Will himself. She said sharply, "What has happened to you? The Will Tracy I remember and thought I knew so well wouldn't have been ashamed to cry. That Will Tracy would have known when enough was enough. He had more common sense than any ten men put together! What happened to you, Will, to make you this way?"

He blinked. Slowly, visibly, he pulled himself together. "I honestly don't know," he said. "I think I may have tried too hard, for the wrong reasons. I know I said I needed to talk, and I thank you for listening, but damn it, Branwen, I do hate for you to see me this way!"

"Hush, it's all right." She held him and stroked him, and eventually he fell asleep on the couch, his head on her lap. She sat there for what remained of the night, and as gray predawn light came through the windows, she slipped away to her own bed.

Sometime later, Will joined her there. He woke her with his kisses, and she responded to him. She felt his need and gave herself to fill that need. They made love, at first tentatively, and then with increasing joy as they found that the closeness they had once shared was so easily rekindled. Their bodies moved and fit together as if none of the intervening years, none of the intervening sorrows, had ever happened. Branwen knew him so well, she had loved him so much. She loved him still.

Later, the memory of that closeness would fade, become a memory she mistrusted out of her awareness that she wanted it so much. She would not forget, though, a promise Will made as he left her. "I'll come back," he said. But he didn't. The people of Iran revolted and threw down the Shah from his Peacock Throne. They raised up the Ayatollah, and he denounced the United States. Many people died, many disappeared. Among those who disappeared were Will Tracy and his wife and stepson. Something had happened, and Will's plan for escape didn't work. Something had gone horribly wrong.

6

The vision came uninvited, demanding to be Seen. At first Branwen resisted. She wanted to relax in her bath full of soft bubbles, to let the warm flower-scented water soothe her tired body and restore her mind to peace, but as soon as she emptied her mind of the day's cares, the vision came. She pushed it away, yet it came again in a swirl of color and light. So she gave up and watched as scenes without words or sound unfolded before her closed eyes.

This was a land of dazzling, blinding brightness. A land like nothing known on earth, although the sky above was blue. Everything shone: tall buildings, skyscrapers, faced with gold, copper, silver, steel; people in form-fitting clothing in myriad colors, all of which gleamed with a metallic sheen. Huge, shining machines rose into and descended from the sky. Smaller machines, triangle-winged, darted like colored birds along the canals that divided the precincts of the richly metaled city. The air crackled with crystal clarity; the sun was mercilessly bright. It was all very beautiful. But it was also somehow very cold.

From the boundary of the bright, busy city an avenue of steely-gray metal monoliths ran through fields whose grass was not green, but the pale-gold color of straw. At the avenue's end rose an immense pyramid of white stone, like marble. Inside, the pyramid was honeycombed with many, many rooms. The vision entered only one, where a small group of men and women stood in a circle in whose center, suspended in midair, was a large clear-glass ball. These men and women wore loose, sky-colored robes that lacked the metallic sheen of the city people's clothing. The room, though otherwise empty, hummed with energy—a familiar energy. The people raised their hands, and the glass ball rose in the air; they turned their palms, and the ball revolved, slowly, then faster until it was spinning and shining and glowing with blue light.

The glass ball shattered. The men and women staggered and fell to their knees. The pyramid shook and came apart, stone by stone. Outside, the straw-colored fields heaved, the metal monoliths toppled. The great, shining city exploded, and the blue sky turned red with its burning. Into the fiery sky rose three of the huge metal machines . . . and there the vision ended.

Branwen lay in the now-tepid tub, baffled by the feeling of déjà vu left in the vision's wake. Had her overtired brain just replayed for her entertainment scenes from a science fiction movie she had seen once and then forgotten? No, she didn't think so. She added hot water to the tub and finished her bath, all the while puzzling over the experience. It was like nothing she could remember, and yet it resonated with memory's ring through the intuitive part of herself. Frustrating and tantalizing. Like a name on the tip of one's tongue. Or like an unyielding Chinese puzzle box that, turned over and over in the hands, ever presents a deceptively smooth surface. She got nowhere. She simply did not understand.

The night air had a late-summer softness that felt vaguely, pleasantly sensual on the skin. While not exactly cool, it was a welcome relief after the heat of the day. Branwen and Xavier sat on the grass in the park in shared silence, at rest. Several evenings a week they walked together through the streets and the parks where the homeless stayed, simply talking, greeting old faces and getting to know the new ones, whose numbers increased daily. Through these walks they built trust, trust that would enable them by day to get a sick person to accept a ride to the clinic, get the hungry to visit the soup kitchens. And when fall came and then winter, those who trusted enough might be willing to come off the streets and into one of the shelters. The trouble, Xavier knew, was that there was not enough shelter space to accommodate them all.

Branwen had another reason for needing the homeless people to trust her. She had begun the filming of her program, starting with the interior shots at 622; any day now they would be moving out into the streets, and without the people's cooperation she'd be sunk. She didn't think that would happen—she was optimistic. This whole project had a right feel to it, and she was more confident than she had been of any other since "Discovering Virginia." She gazed through the trees in the park and thought that knowledge of its ugly underside had not altered her opinion of Washington. It was still a beautiful city. Similarly, knowledge of the uglier side of life didn't dim her enthusiasm. She'd spent an apprehensive spring, and the summer hadn't been much better, brightened only by Ellen's wedding. Now Ellen and her new husband Jim were celebrating with a honeymoon trip around the world, with no definite return date, and for some reason Ellen's absence made Branwen more apprehensive.

Not that she spent a lot of time looking over her shoulder, feeling paranoid. She didn't. Only in Will's case was there anything specific to worry about, and because there was absolutely nothing she could do for Will, she tried not to think about him. As for the rest, it was about as nonspecific as a landscape seen through fog. And elusive. Which made Branwen all the more grateful for her daily time spent on the homelessness project. That was tangible, that was real, that was positive. All in all, Branwen was content. For this one evening at least, she was in a mellow mood.

Xavier interrupted her reverie. He put his hand on her blue-jeaned knee and said quietly out of the blue, "There's someone else, isn't there?"

"Someone else what?"

"Not someone else what, someone else *who*. A man in your life, someone else besides me. My competition. My rival for your affections."

"A lot you have to complain about," joshed Branwen, poking him in the ribs with her elbow. "Your whole church is my competition, and you don't hear me complaining! You *are* kidding, aren't you, Xavier? I thought we were beyond all that."

"No, I'm not kidding. I don't recall that we ever resolved anything." His hand increased its pressure on her knee.

She turned her head to look at him, his face carved by the shadows, his eyes reflecting the park lights like dark stars. In a hushed voice she said, "If you're talking about what I think you're talking about, that time you asked me if I wanted to have an affair with you, that was months and months ago! I thought you had forgotten. I thought we had, more or less by default, mutually agreed to forget."

"No, I haven't forgotten anything. You said 'not if an affair was all it would be,' and I haven't forgotten that." His hand left her knee and moved to cup her face. "I think about you, about us, far more often than I should. So tell me, please, is there another man, someone you're involved with?"

"Ah. . . ." Words froze in Branwen's throat. Images of that intense winter night with Will flickered through her mind, images caught in her memory like freeze-frame after freeze-frame on a videotape she could not bring herself to edit. She had resolved not to think about that night until when and if Will returned; when and if he was free of his marriage. She could not speak, and her silence was for Xavier confirmation of his fears. Through the shadowy dark she saw the lines of his face draw down. His hand left her cheek, limp, resigned.

"I knew it," he muttered. He turned away and threw himself full length on his stomach on the grass. Before burying his head in his arms he barked, "Go away, go on home! You can walk back by yourself. You'll be safe enough—these people would kill before they'd let anything happen to you!"

Branwen was used to Xavier's volatile temper, though he seldom aimed it at her. He was an emotional man, as passionate in his moods as he was in his beliefs. She hadn't meant to hurt him, but there was no use trying to tell him so until his anger had passed. She knew it would pass as quickly as a summer thunderstorm. She stretched out on the ground next to him and said only, "I don't think I'll leave just yet."

As she lay there, her mellow, even mood returned. She felt close to Xavier Dominguez. She had learned to be untroubled by the lack of the physical element in their relationship, which in every other way was as intimate as she could imagine between any man and woman. Now she realized that she'd been untroubled because she trusted him to keep that side of things under control. She understood that he was conflicted in some areas of his priesthood, and he had his times of vulnerability, as she had hers. That he had been thinking along the lines he'd revealed was news to her.

Eventually Xavier rolled onto his back and talked up into the trees. "I was in the soup kitchen the other day, sitting out at the tables, and you came in and went behind the counter to help serve. Two men, one of them a new guy, went through the line and when they'd sat down, I heard them talking. The new guy said, 'Who's that gal, the looker with the two-tone hair?' And the other one said, 'Don't go getting any ideas about her, that's Father X's woman.'"

Branwen turned on her side and leaned up on one elbow, her head on her hand. She was smiling. "Oh, really! Well, I don't mind if you don't mind."

"Mind!" Xavier's voice exploded into the trees with its intensity. "Those words opened something up in me, some place that before I'd always kept closed off. Father X's woman—*my* woman. I went all funny inside, kind of warm and mushy. I had to get up and leave. I didn't dare be around you right then. I've felt that way off and on ever since. I've wondered if . . . if this is how husbands feel."

After an interval in which she could think of nothing safe to say, Branwen asked, "Is that why you wanted to know if there was another man in my life?"

"I guess so, yes."

"You thought, when I didn't deny it, that meant there is one."

"Well, sure I did. Hell, you've been divorced a long time, and you're gorgeous and talented, and even if you do spend a lot of time with me, you're not with me twenty-four hours a day. I'd be a fool not to think there's someone else! Actually, I *am* a fool, the way I've been letting my thoughts run wild."

"Xavier," said Branwen carefully, "there *is* someone else, but not the way you think. It's not an active, ongoing relationship."

He rolled on his side to face her. "Well, what is it, then?"

"Somebody I loved once but first couldn't and then wouldn't marry. He married someone else, which is what I wanted him to do. They live halfway around the world. I never thought I'd see him again."

Following the nuances of her words, and some of his own observations, Xavier stated, "But you did see him again."

"Yes. Just one night, months ago. In the wintertime." It had been such a strange night, so emotionally exhausting yet in the end so sweet. The tone of her voice was both wistful and intense.

Xavier knew her so well. He didn't want to ask, didn't really have to, but he needed to hear her confirm it. "And . . . did you sleep with him?"

"Well, yes, sort of."

"Sort of?" He bolted up into a sitting position. "Branwen, you know damn well what I mean. You can't sort of have sexual intercourse with a person. Either you did or you didn't!"

Branwen balked. "I could tell you it's none of your business."

"You'd be right to tell me that," Xavier grumbled. "It's just that I'm having all these feelings I haven't had before, not like this. I suppose it's jealousy—that's completely new to me. Damn it, it's eating me alive!"

Her deep caring for him forced her to speak, forced her to open herself to the memory she had barred. "That night, actually by then it was early morning, we . . . it wasn't like having sex, not quite. He was here only for the one night, and he was hurting. A lot. When he came to my bed and we—we touched and kissed, I didn't feel that I was having sex with him. I felt that he was in pain, and I could give him my body, could use the touching and the kissing and all the rest, to heal him. Not so much to give pleasure, but to take away the pain."

"Oh. Now *that* I can understand. Not that I've ever taken it that far, but I've come close. I've held women, even kissed them, for the same reason."

Branwen scarcely heard him. She had gone too deeply into thinking about Will to be able to pull out. She said miserably, "I don't know if I'll ever see him again. I don't even know where he is right now."

"Do you want to see him again? You said he's married. Look, Branwen, I guess I can handle it if you're in love with someone else, but I'm not going to stand around and see you hurt by a married man!"

"I don't *know* if I want to see him again, but that's not the problem. The problem is"—her voice caught on a sob as tears of fear and desperation broke through at last—"I'm *afraid* for him! Oh, Xavier, he was in Iran when the Ayatollah took over, and now he's disappeared. Along with his wife and stepson. Nobody knows what happened to them! Not the State Department, or his father, or anybody!"

"Oh, my God!" Xavier pulled Branwen to him, into his arms. "Cry," he murmured, "go ahead and cry all you want." Softly, he continued to speak. The soothing tone of his voice was for her, but the words he spoke to himself. "You've been holding this back, haven't you? No wonder there were times when I felt you'd gone off somewhere inside yourself, where I couldn't reach you. You've been worried out of your mind and keeping it all inside. Oh, Branwen, love, I'm so sorry."

He held her and rocked her and thought, *What a pair we are! Her with her lost love and me locked in my love-hate relationship with the Church.* He stroked her head, the jealousy he'd felt earlier vanished, forgotten. She trembled in his arms, and her tears were so copious he could feel that she was wetting his shirt clear through to his skin.

In order to ignore his own physical stirrings, Xavier went up into his head. Branwen was in love with this man. That she still loved him was obvious, whether she herself realized it or not. Well, he'd asked, and he'd gotten his answer. Did that resolve Xavier's dilemma? No, not really. His problem was that he really believed his Church was wrong in not allowing priests to marry. He knew now, had known for weeks, that he loved Branwen enough to marry her—*if* that were possible for him, and *if* she would have him. The irony was that loving her as much as he did, he couldn't simply have an affair with her, as he had at one time thought she might have wanted. The Church frowned mightily on priests having affairs, but they didn't kick them out of the priesthood for that. In addition to being in love with Branwen, Xavier was restless. He didn't really know what he wanted to do with his life; he only knew that he wouldn't be Father X, the street priest, forever. He'd thought maybe, if he and Branwen could open up their relationship and explore together, see how far they wanted to take it . . . Well, that would make a difference. What bothered Xavier most was that he suspected, in spite of his restlessness, that the only reason he would ever give up the priesthood was so that he could marry. He was a deeply religious man, but he was also a loving man. The truth was that he didn't know what the hell he was going to do.

Branwen moved out of his arms. "I got your shirt all wet."

He forced himself to get up, forced himself to smile. She would never know how much he wanted to do as she said she'd done, use his body to ease her pain. "Believe me," he said, "a wet shirt is the least of my problems at the moment. Let's go back to the house and have something cold to drink. A beer, maybe. I think we'd both feel better."

"Yes. Xavier, thank you. I think I must have needed to cry."

They walked hand in hand to his car, an old Chevy he kept running like a dream. He could have afforded a newer one but thought a new car wouldn't look right sitting in front of 622.

Branwen was quiet, pensive, during the drive. At the house she went to wash her face while he checked his phone messages, then went into the kitchen and opened two cans of beer. He got a bag of pretzels from one cabinet and a glass for Branwen from another; he preferred to drink out of the can. While driving home he had decided that he had to talk to her about all of this, now, tonight. He hoped she was willing and that the house would stay quiet so that they could talk without interruption.

One look at her face when she entered the kitchen changed his mind. She was so pale that her black eyelashes looked like marks of soot in her face. The white streak in her hair stood out like a beacon, and he suddenly remembered how she'd told him she acquired it. Without consciously making any decision, he heard himself say to her, after giving her time to swallow a few sips of beer, "You're still in love with that man, Branwen. You know that, don't you?"

She said, "Yes, but I don't deserve him. I've caused him so much unhappiness. If only I hadn't thought, so arrogantly, that I knew what was best for both of us, he'd be safe at home now. And truly, Xavier, I didn't realize how I felt until he came back that one time. I've tried to forget. I believe I could have forgotten if he hadn't returned."

"You didn't forget anything, you only denied your real feelings, shoved them down. When you do that, the real feelings tend to get bigger, not to go away. They can get distorted, too. It's much better to get your real feelings out into the open and keep them there—it's less painful in the end." Because he sounded to himself like he'd been preaching, he grinned and winked. "At least, that's what they taught us in priest school. Not that I'm any good at it myself."

Branwen tried a smile and found that she could do it. "I don't think I've ever heard anyone say 'real feelings' so many times in such a short space of time in my life. You're right, of course. You're also better at it than you're giving yourself credit for. As I recall, until I went to pieces, you were doing a pretty good job of talking to me about your real feelings."

"Yeah." He swigged at his beer and looked over her head, unable to meet her eyes.

"Xavier . . . ?"

He swallowed down the rest of his beer in one long gulp and got up to get another can from the refrigerator. Behind him

Branwen said, "You know I always do better knowing the truth. How are you feeling right now?"

"Not feeling," he said gutturally. He returned and sat with her again. "Thinking. I'm thinking the best thing I can do for both of us is offer to help you find your, ah, friend. As soon as Congress is back in session, I can go to see some people. I have my contacts, too. So, will you let me help? You can start by telling me his name."

"Will Tracy. He's the son of Senator Wilbur F. Tracy. I doubt there's anything you can do, Xavier. His father has more clout and more contacts than you could ever hope to have, and his father hasn't been able to find out a thing."

Xavier said doggedly, "I can try. It can't hurt to try."

Jason Faraday moved with ponderous steps from room to room of his manor house . . . the house that had been a reward from the Cognoscenti for years of faithful service. Say rather, Jason thought, years of *effective* service; he was willing to be faithful to no one other than himself. Such a grand place this was! He had felt like a lord in these rooms. He'd never guessed that the Cognoscenti had intended their noble gift to be his prison. He might never have had to know, if he hadn't decided to go back to Washington after Branwen.

In every room he checked the things he'd rigged to make it appear that he was still at home: timers on lights, on stereo receivers, on television sets; tape recordings of conversations to be played on the telephone and into the air of empty rooms; drapes pulled back just so to let in morning and afternoon light. There was no way to make the ruse perfect—for that he'd have to have help, and he couldn't trust anyone anymore. He wouldn't fool the Cognoscenti this way for very long, but all he needed was long enough to get well away on the complex route he'd worked out. Once he was back in the United States, they wouldn't dare touch him—he was too well known.

Jason was supposed to be retired, and in fact he *was* retired from the work few people knew he'd done. He had enough money in Swiss bank accounts to live out the remainder of several lives. He didn't need to work anymore. For anyone. He had waited years to be able to pursue his own agenda, and then as soon as he'd had the ball rolling to go back for Branwen— boom! They'd come down on him. The Cognoscenti hadn't given a shit when he'd lured Harry Ravenscroft over here to

Germany, but he couldn't do that with Branwen. Nor would he eliminate her from a distance, although it would have been easy to arrange. On, no. He had to *be* there, hands-on, had to see everything with his own eyes.

That guy, the so-called Archon, who'd been his main contact with the Cognoscenti had showed up, and Jason found out his manor house had strings attached. Archon reminded Jason that he had agreed, after taking on certain jobs with high-visibility results, that he wouldn't ever return to the U.S. Jason had said, "So what? I lied." Archon had had the nerve to say he shouldn't lie to the Cognoscenti. Jason had laughed, asked what did they expect from the best liar in the world? Archon had not been amused, however, and Jason had had to appear cooperative, much as it galled him. He'd said he was sorry, didn't realize it was such a big deal, etc. etc. ad nauseam.

Months of delay followed, while Jason continued to appear docile; months during which he unmade one set of arrangements and made new ones in secret. Now, finally, he had it all set up: the devious travel route, the succession of tickets, the alternate identities, the perfect rental house waiting at the other end of the trip. The house had been the hardest part because he had very particular requirements. The one he'd had to cancel hadn't been easy to find. He'd found it through an international property broker. How could he find such a place on his own? He couldn't. He used a different broker, carried on the whole transaction by mail, and after all the necessary papers had been signed, the unfortunate man had had an accident. A fatal accident of the sort Jason arranged so well.

His tour completed, Jason went last to his bedroom and changed his clothes. No disguises for him. He might change his identity but he would never change his appearance—a figure as striking as his had become, as memorable, couldn't be disguised. Or so he thought. In his arrogance, it never occurred to Jason that he might have dressed as a common laborer, a farmer, or a tradesman. He smoothed his hand-tailored Italian suit over his massive girth, looking at his image in the full-length mirror with pride. He liked his bulk, liked looking the fat and prosperous retired man. A significant man of significant bodily proportions, that was him. His face, though jowly, was still leonine; his hair, still thick, was a silver-streaked russet mane. Branwen would be impressed by him. Anyone would.

Going by the devious route he'd plotted, Jason wouldn't arrive at the rented estate in Silver Spring for many days yet. But he wasn't worried, not a bit. No, he wasn't worried because not only was he smarter than any of the Cognoscenti, but he'd also stolen one of their magic tricks. Stolen it as retirement insurance. He'd never have used it if they hadn't tried to turn him into a prisoner in his own house. They'd never guess what he'd done because they thought he wasn't capable of doing their tricks. But he was, he had, and now Jason had the Protector. Too bad the Protector couldn't travel with him, but never mind—Jason would call him up when he got to Silver Spring. He could call up the Protector anytime he wanted, and the Protector would do what his name denoted: he would protect Jason.

There was only one thing Jason didn't see when he admired himself in the mirror. He didn't see how much his eyes had changed. They were still brown, but other than that the eyes were not Jason Faraday's eyes at all.

Branwen's desk phone rang. She answered it only half listening, her mind still on the production costs for her new documentary on the homeless. She was thinking of calling it "Father X's Powerless People," but she knew in the end she wouldn't—the Father X part would have to go. You couldn't use a name in a title unless it was somebody famous.

Suddenly she realized what the voice on the phone had said, and she snapped into alertness. "Beecher? Harry Ravenscroft's Beecher?" She had never heard the man's voice before, never so much as seen him at a distance of less than a hundred feet. "Is your wife all right?"

At the other end of the line Beecher said, "Well no, ma'am, she ain't hardly. She's purely beside herself over Mr. Harry, and she can't make no calls from the house on account of he'd hear. So she says to me, Beecher, you go t' store an' call Miss Branwen at that TV place where she works, an' ask her can she come out, 'cause like as not Miss Branwen be th' only person can talk sense inta Mr. Harry. An' here I be a-callin' ye."

"Of course I'll come out to Raven Hill. Wait a minute—don't hang up! What's going on? You mean to tell me Harry is there, at the house?"

"Yes'm. He come up right smart in a taxi cab early this morning! He weren't expected but there he be. My wife says he's actin' real strangelike, even for Mr. Harry. I don't know zackley what he be doin', but Miz Beecher ain't one to get upset less'n there's a reason . . . an' she's plenty upset, I can tell ye!"

"All right. Beecher, you can tell your wife I'll be there in about an hour. I don't know what I can do, but I'll certainly try. I'm glad you called me."

Branwen called 622 and left word for Xavier that she couldn't be there at the usual time. She told the receptionist at the station that she had to leave for a personal emergency, and on impulse she swung by her apartment to pick up her runes. She made good time, and in less than an hour was turning into Raven Hill's long private drive. On the way she'd alternated between two persistent thoughts: what "acting strange" meant when applied to Harry; and a fervent wish that Ellen Carew, who was now Ellen Harper, would stop gadding about the world with her new husband and get home to McLean where she belonged. Branwen was sure that Ellen could handle Harry much better than she could herself.

Except for one thing, Branwen thought, and placed her hand on the deep pocket of her full skirt where she carried her bag of bluestones. Except that she had a special kind of connection with Harry that she'd rather not use—but she would if she had to.

Not sure why she was being so cautious, Branwen turned her Volvo into the secondary graveled portion of the drive that led around to the back of the house. She left the car in the shed next to Beecher's battered four-wheel drive vehicle, crossed the terrace, and entered the house through the kitchen wing. She had hoped to find Mrs. Beecher in the kitchen, but she did not. At the end of the main hallway, Branwen paused. She felt a change in the atmosphere of the house. She knew this house well; its very walls customarily radiated a placid contentment so strong that it remained undisturbed by Harry's erratic moods. This was no longer true; whatever disturbed Harry was strong enough that it also disturbed the house itself. Not good, Branwen thought. On a psychic level the only thing she had ever encountered that created a similar disturbed energy field had been a malevolent spirit that had once invaded the Psychic Underground through a Ouija board. The naive woman who'd brought the board to the meeting had learned that the Ouija was not a toy or a game; and Branwen had learned, in an instant's intuitive reflex, how to protect herself from such spirits. She did it now: She visualized a light in the center of herself, a clear white light that was her own strong spirit and her connection to other positive spirits like herself. Calling forth the light from herself was, for Branwen, a palpable experience. She called the light outward from her center until it surrounded her in a glowing ball. Although she could "see" it only in her mind's eye, she could actually feel the light in her body—first as a warm glow just beneath her rib cage, then as a spreading, tingling warmth that coursed along her bones and through her flesh until at last it reached the crown of her head and from there poured down to surround her with its protection. When the process was complete, she went to look for Harry and Mrs. Beecher.

She found the thin little woman on the stair landing, gazing upward. Relief flooded Mrs. Beecher's eyes as Branwen approached. "Thank the Lord ye've come, Miss Branwen!" she whispered.

"He's upstairs?" Branwen asked, also in a whisper. Mrs. B. nodded, and Branwen drew her back down the stairs and into the powder room where they could talk privately. "I'm glad you had your husband call me, but what in the world is wrong?"

"Oh, I'm sure I don't know. I seen Mr. Harry in a lot of ways ever since he were a devilish handsome young man, but I ain't never seen him like this!"

"Uh, Mrs. B., can you be more specific? What exactly is he doing?"

"It ain't so much what he's doin' as the way he's doin' it—if you take my meaning. All kind of wildlike, with such a look in his eyes! And the way he talks . . . over half what he say makes no sense a-tall! He say he come home to sort through his things, only he be tearin' the place apart in the sortin' of it. I says to him, Mr. Harry, you leave off an' eat you a meal or take you some rest, an' he say he don't have to eat nor sleep no more. Miss Branwen, he's pitiful thin! Why do you s'pose he would say such a thing?"

"I can't imagine."

"The worst was when he looked all 'round with his eyes so wild and did say he might as well burn the house down on account of he don't need it no more. And I says, Mr. Harry, this be yer family place, ye can't burn it up! He just laughs an' says me an' Beecher'll be taken care of, an' he throws this money at me. Looky here, Miss Branwen." From the pocket of her apron Mrs. Beecher took two crumpled bills, smoothed them, and handed them to her. Branwen had never seen so many zeroes on a piece of currency—they were thousand-dollar bills. Mrs. Beecher said, "Now that there be a powerful lot o' money, but I say it ain't normal and it ain't right to throw it around, and I wisht you'd give it back to him."

"No," Branwen said, handing the money back, "you keep it. I doubt he's out of his head enough that he really would burn down the house, but if he did, you'd have something to tide you over in an emergency. Besides, think of it this way: The way Harry is acting he'd only waste the money, which is wrong, whereas you and your husband will put it to good use. Now I guess I'd better go talk to him. Does he have a doctor that you know of? A medical doctor?"

Mrs. Beecher nodded.

"Well, get the doctor's phone number handy. We might need to get poor Harry some tranquilizers or something. Then make a good, big lunch. I'll try to get him to come down and eat something. Is he in his bedroom upstairs?"

"Was the last I heard. I give up follerin' him around. It grieves my heart sore, Miss Branwen, to see him this way!"

"I know." Branwen gave her a quick hug. The woman's body felt like sticks, she was so thin. "Wish me luck."

"Bless you, Miss Branwen!"

Harry Ravenscroft's bedroom looked as if vandals had struck. He had always been a rather elegant dresser, and it was shocking to see silks and fine linens and wools and cashmeres pulled out of drawers, jumbled on the floor, strewn across the bed, and heaped on chairs. More shocking still was Harry himself. His pale hair, uncut and straggly, hung down his neck and into the grayed collar of his shirt. He looked as if he had not washed or changed his clothes for days. His vest hung open, and his jacket sat his shoulders like a scarecrow's. He stood at his bureau, leather accessory box open, tossing gold cuff links and other items carelessly to the floor. Occasionally he pocketed one that took his fancy. He muttered words to himself that Branwen could not understand. She feared her old friend had gone completely insane.

The disruptive presence was strong in the room. Branwen reassured herself that the protection of her light still surrounded her. She clutched the rune stones in her pocket through the fabric of her skirt and walked into the room. She said, "Hello, Harry. Do you need any help with what you're doing?"

He whirled abruptly, and she was relieved to see recognition in his eyes. "Branwen! Oh, my dear, you are the very one I wanted most to see! But I thought it wouldn't happen. Because, you know, we're on different paths now, you and I. We had the parting of the ways, didn't we?"

"Never mind that." Branwen suppressed a shudder, nearly overwhelmed by the disturbance that either came directly from Harry or hovered around him—she couldn't tell which. Determinedly she walked toward him with her hands outstretched. "I'm so glad to see you! I've missed you. I want to know everything you're up to, everything you've been doing." As she talked, she took Harry's hands and began to lead him out of his bedroom. "We'll go downstairs and have lunch together, just like old times, and you can tell me everything."

What followed was the strangest afternoon of Branwen's life thus far. Harry's conversation and behavior were erratic, full of contradictions. He said he was not hungry, but when Mrs. Beecher put food on the table, he devoured it like a starving man. He said he was ecstatic about some new people he'd met; yet other things he said suggested that he'd left them without their knowledge, suspiciously as if he'd run away, He had felt an urgency to get to Raven Hill, but now that he was here he could no longer remember why he'd come. This last seemed to be the reason he was tearing the place apart, a vain search for he knew not what, but he was sure he'd remember as soon as he found it.

Branwen deliberately kept Harry long at the table, giving Mrs. Beecher time to restore order where he'd created the most chaos, in his bedroom and in the library. Harry babbled on and on, but she stopped listening. Instead she concentrated on using her own protective light to drive away whatever it was that threatened and confused him.

Gradually Harry calmed. He decided on his own that his state of dress was deplorable and excused himself to take a shower and change his clothes. When he joined Branwen in the library, he looked and sounded very much like his old self, except for a certain new wariness in the depths of his gray eyes. "My dear, I've been positively babbling, haven't I?"

Branwen could feel the difference immediately. Whatever had disturbed Harry was gone. She tilted her head to one side, smiling, as if considering how she should answer him. She was sure that the Harry she knew would hear her answer, whereas earlier she hadn't been sure of anything. "Yes, Professor Ravenscroft, you certainly have."

A lovely soft light came into his eyes. Swiftly he came to her, took her hands, and led her to the high-backed Victorian love seat. "My dear, you haven't called me that in such a very long time!" He lowered his voice. "I wasn't myself. You must disregard everything I said and listen to me very carefully now."

"I will."

"Did I say the name Cognoscenti, or anything about a man called Orson?"

"I think you did, but I don't remember what you said. Frankly, I was concentrating too hard on driving out this thing that was troubling you to pay attention to what you were saying."

"So," Harry said, beaming, "you did help! I can never thank you enough. Branwen, you will be in danger if you ever so much as speak the name Cognoscenti. I should not have mentioned it. It is the most secret of all occult groups; knowledge of its existence is forbidden and punishable by death. Only those whom the members themselves invite may know of them. Your ex-husband told me about them, Branwen—I believed he had arranged such an invitation for me. He hadn't. When he sent me to them, he was sending me into a trap."

Branwen said nothing. She was alert in every sense she possessed, hanging on Harry's words in dread anticipation.

Harry grinned out of one side of his mouth. His hair, which he had dampened to tidy it, nevertheless escaped and strayed over one eye. "I am happy to report that Jason underestimated me. They all underestimated me, and I am turning the trap to my advantage. Forget the name, never allow those syllables to touch your lips, and we will be simply one old friend telling another what he has been doing. Agreed?"

"Agreed."

"I had heard, through the sort of grapevine you will be familiar with from the Psychic Underground, that there existed a group of practicing Adepts—people who have mastered the old skills, recovered the old secrets. I was jealous, as you may imagine, to learn that others were doing what I so much wanted yet had failed to do myself. Of course such a group would have to be kept hidden. I let my interest be known on the grapevine and waited. I was amazed when Jason Faraday not only knew of these Adepts, but had a direct contact! The heart of the matter is that I have been brought in as a sort of trainee, and if I say so myself, I'm doing very well."

Branwen, who was feeling nothing but vibrations of danger, protested. "But, Harry, the danger!"

"I admit the experience is taking a lot out of me. The, uh, the way in which they have achieved their power is not necessarily the way I would have chosen, but the point is that the skills are returning to me. I'm stronger than they realize. The proof of that is my presence here now."

"Harry, leaving aside the condition in which I found you—if you aren't supposed to be here, what will happen to you when you return?"

His gray eyes went opaque. "Nothing. I will create a screen of obscurity and confusion. They will never know I was gone. Provided, of course, that I can finish my business here and leave at first light tomorrow."

"What business? You really must give an explanation to Mrs. Beecher. Do you know you told her you were going to burn the house down?"

"Did I? What a bizarre idea! Especially when I intend the very antithesis of that." Harry gave Branwen a long, considering look. "Perhaps it's just as well that someone in addition to my lawyer should know. I will tell you, Branwen, and after I've gone you may tell Mrs. B. as much as you choose."

"All right," she agreed.

"My teachers are greedy. They will take as much money, and whatever can be converted into money, as they can, from whatever source they can wring it. I think it is fair that I should pay a reasonable amount for my training, but I will not be deceived into devastating the entire Ravenscroft estate. This is why I came home to Raven Hill. When I went upstairs to shower, I called my lawyer, and he will be here around five o'clock tonight. I am going to put everything in trust, and he will be the executor. The trust will be revocable only by me, and then only if I am of sound mind. You see, my dear, I do realize that I'm putting myself in danger. I know my mind is under assault."

Branwen was so distressed that her voice broke. "Th-then why don't you stop it?"

"I can't." Harry's grin was as impish and engaging as ever. "I want what they have—only I want it for *my* purposes, not theirs. If I lose my sanity or my life in the process, I don't care. The knowledge is worth the risk. Now, Branwen, you must assure the Beechers that they will continue to receive money every month for themselves and to keep up the house. If I die, they're provided for in my will."

"Harry—"

"Hush, my dear. I know what I'm doing. I have a good deal of cash I took out of my account—more than I intended, but as it works out, that's all to the good. I'll drive my car, the Mercedes, back and sell it there. By the way, how exactly did I get here?"

"You don't remember? You came by cab. Harry, where is *there*? Won't you at least tell me how I can reach you?"

"By cab!" Harry stared across the room, a faint smile on his gaunt face, his long bony fingers splayed on his knees. "How very resourceful I am, even when not in my right mind." He turned to her. "No, my dear, I can't tell you any more than I have already. I do wish I could demonstrate my increased powers for you, but I fear that would draw the attention of my, uh, guardian, and I do not wish that."

At the mention of a "guardian" Branwen felt dark and cold. Her alarm showed in her eyes.

Harry held a warning finger to his lips. He whispered, "No more. To name is to call."

Branwen nodded. She understood. Without a word she wrapped her arms around Harry. His shoulders were all bone. She poured her love into him, and her will that he might survive.

"I'm so glad you came," Harry said. A film of tears glistened in his silver eyes.

"So am I." She sensed that it was time to leave. As she rose from the love seat, she felt the heaviness of the rune stones in her pocket. Her impulse to bring them had been correct, and she knew now what she would do. She reached into the deep pocket and took out the leather pouch. Even through its soft old skin she could feel the positive energy invested in the sacred bluestones. She said, "Give me your hand, Harry Ravenscroft, my old friend."

He stood and gave her his hand, which she held for a moment. Then she turned it palm up, placed the bag of runes in the palm, and closed his fingers over it. "I return the sacred bluestones to you," she said. "I suggest you keep them with you at all times. Carry them in your pocket. Sleep with them under your pillow. Keep yourself—and the sacred bluestones—*well*, Harry."

The rune stones felt saturated with Branwen. He could feel her energy there in his hand. Harry squeezed his eyes shut, and two large tears gathered in the corners and dropped down his cheeks. She could not have given him a more perfect gift, unless she had given him her very self.

7

The German tourist who got off the charter fishing boat in Key West and rented a car to drive to Miami was a massive block of a man with the unsteady gait and jaundiced complexion of a poor sailor. It had been just an ordinary charter fishing trip—unless someone happened to observe that the German tourist had not been on board when the boat went out at dawn that morning. And no one had. The boat's captain had been well paid to pick the German up at Puerto Plata in the Dominican Republic. This same German tourist, poor sailor that he was, had nevertheless made his way to Puerto Plata from Rio by a series of similarly chartered boats. It was clear that he was thoroughly sick of traveling by water. He had flown to Rio from Johannesburg, having changed his nationality and reason for travel to German tourist from Italian businessman during a bumpy bus ride somewhere along the border of Mozambique.

This Italian—Milanese, actually—had begun his trip at a certain manor house in Germany. From there, driving a car ostensibly his own, he had crossed through Switzerland into Italy and stopped overnight in his supposed hometown of Milan. He had then proceeded to wind his way down through Italy to Naples where he sold his car and flew a short commercial flight across the Mediterranean to Tunis. Only a genius travel agent or a very patient police detective could have followed his hops and skips through Africa to Johannesburg—by which time, of course, the Italian had disappeared and the German went on in his stead.

In Miami the German tourist turned in the car he had rented
in Key West, hailed a cab, and at last began to speak English.
The hotel room he rented in his own name, just as he registered
the car he bought the next morning: Jason Faraday. On September 30, 1979, Jason began to drive north on I-95.

Also on September 30, Xavier Dominguez, spectacularly
dressed in his long-skirted, wide-sashed soutane, returned to
622 from a long day on Capitol Hill.

Branwen, sitting at the table, looked up when Xavier entered
the kitchen. She had never seen him in that outfit before and she
said what most women only thought: "Wel-l-l, look at you!
Xavier, you're gorgeous! I'm glad I waited for you. Where have
you been?"

He went straight for the refrigerator and popped open a can of
beer before he answered. "Visiting folks I know on the Hill. I
didn't tell you I was going because I didn't want you sitting
around on pins and needles all day, wondering what I was finding out."

She tensed, unconsciously pulled a strand of her hair over her
shoulder, and began to wrap it around her finger. "And . . . ?"

"And I have some news. *Not*," he said hastily as he saw hope
begin to light in her eyes, "of your friend Will, but of his wife
and the boy." He sat down then, twisted in the chair so that he
could reach through the slit in the seam of the soutane into
the pocket of his trousers beneath. "Here. You recognize the
name?"

Branwen took the piece of memo-sized white paper, unfolded
it, read the name, and nodded her head. Her heart thudded.
"Yes. He's a good friend of Will's. I met him once at a party. At
some embassy, I think it was. He's with the State Department.
You know him, too?"

"Not really. I got to him in the usual way, through a friend of
a friend."

To lighten her tension, she teased, "These friends and their
friends, they wouldn't be female, would they? That would account for the costume."

Xavier shrugged and looked at her from the corner of a sparkling dark eye. "Could be. Anyway, you call him tomorrow, and
he'll see you. Not in his office—he'll set up a meeting somewhere. What he tells you won't be official, but at least it will be

something. He remembers you, too. That's why he agreed to see you."

"Thank you, Xavier." Branwen grew silent, her head bent so that her hair fell forward around her face. She creased the slip of paper over and over again, folding it to a sharp edge with her fingers.

"I like your hair loose like that," Xavier ventured. "You should wear it that way more often."

"It gets in the way," she said absently. She was wishing she could call Will's friend now. Perhaps he would know why the escape plan had failed. Maybe, even if he didn't know exactly where Will was, he would have a good guess. What he did know could be bad news, so she mustn't get her hopes up. But at this point, even bad news and good guesses were better than nothing.

The news about Will's wife and stepson was as bad as it could be: They were dead, slaughtered during those first few days of terror in Teheran. This was not official but was still reliable information. U.S. Intelligence had learned that their bodies had been identified.

As for Will himself, he was neither dead nor held as a hostage, so he was assumed to be in hiding, perhaps working his way out of the country very slowly, probably on foot. Will's friend had known about the escape plan, had in fact been the person who had tried to make that crucial call. But the uprising had come on too swiftly, and the phone lines had been first saturated and then cut off. He could not get the call through. He had sent a cable, but it had arrived too late. He blamed himself, and Branwen ended their meeting by comforting him.

She went home to her apartment and rummaged through the top drawer of her desk, looking for Ellen's last postcard. Ellen was good about letting Branwen know her itinerary a couple of weeks ahead, even though she and Jim were making it up as they went along. There it was on the card, the name and address of a hotel in Istanbul and the dates of their stay. A letter sent off today by Priority Air should reach Istanbul while Ellen and Jim Harper were still at their hotel. Branwen sat down and wrote the letter quickly. Maybe she was completely crazy to think that Ellen and Jim, since they were already in the Middle East, might help to find Will. And maybe she wasn't. Jim was ex-FBI, so perhaps he wouldn't be daunted by looking for a human needle in the haystack; and Ellen was always amazing. There was no telling what she could do if she put her mind to it.

Branwen pushed aside the thought that the Harpers were on their honeymoon and in all fairness should be left alone. Fairness was not an issue where Will's life was concerned. *If* he was still alive. Branwen felt strongly that he was.

She was at the door on her way out to the post office when she noticed the time. It was midafternoon and she hadn't yet been to the studio. Her documentary, for which she had finally settled on the title "Powerless in the Shadow of the Powerful: The Homeless in Washington," was in the editing stage. She was doing the editing herself, just as she had done almost everything herself—not to gratify her ego, but for lack of money. Homelessness was not a popular cause. Her only sponsor was the local PBS station, and their main contribution was her time. She supposed she could afford not to go in today since nothing would suffer but her own work. Xavier would be waiting at the house to hear what she had learned, and tonight was one of their regular nights to mingle on the streets—that had not stopped just because Branwen had completed her filming. She felt a little panicky at the thought of all she had to do.

Branwen tossed her head, impatient with herself. *What's the matter with me?* she thought. *It's not that unusual for me to need to be in more than one place at a time.* She went to change out of her navy linen suit into the jeans and shirt she habitually wore in Xavier's part of town, thinking: *What is unusual is for me to feel so worked up about it.*

Later, grocery shopping for 622 after she had mailed her letter, she had the same too-rushed feeling. She felt as if she were running downhill out of control, and she didn't like it. By the time she had unloaded the groceries she knew what was wrong. Too much had been happening in her life, and much of it she couldn't understand, much less control. She couldn't remember when she'd last had a vacation, but it was before she'd even met Xavier. She needed to get away for a few days, be by herself. Put everything into proportion. In fact, she needed it badly.

"Well, what did you find out?" Xavier asked as he helped put away the groceries.

"The wife and child are dead. Killed during the takeover."

"I'm sorry."

"So am I. But the authorities do think Will got away. At least they know his body wasn't found and he's not a hostage."

Branwen shuddered inwardly. "That hostage thing is so awful! What do you think will happen to them, Xavier?"

"I don't know, I can't imagine. All I know is"—he reached his hand down for one of the cans Branwen was handing him to put on the top shelf of the cupboard—"if *I* were a hostage, I'd go stark, raving mad!"

"No, you wouldn't." She looked at him, at the big muscular body that was as strong as his soul was passionate, and said, "You'd probably get yourself killed for trying to escape or for refusing to obey your captors, but you wouldn't go mad. Seriously, Xavier, thank you for what you did to help me learn that information. As bad as it is, at least it's something, and there is some hope for Will."

"I'm glad I could help." He closed the cupboard doors. "There. Want a beer?"

"I'd rather have a Pepsi. I'm kind of tired, and beer will only make me sleepy. Uh, Xavier—there's something else I'd like to talk to you about, if we could take the time before we go out tonight."

"Sure. We'd better do it in my room, though. Now that we have food in here again, the kitchen is likely to be overrun with people at any minute." He handed her a can of Pepsi and took a beer for himself. He'd forgotten her glass again, but she let it go. Drinking from cans was only one of the many unexpected things she'd learned from Xavier.

His room was slightly neater than it had been the only other time she'd been in it: the bed was made. Picking her way across the floor, she commented, "I don't know where I ever got the idea that all priests must be neat."

"Most of us have housekeepers," Xavier responded, unperturbed, closing the door behind him.

Seeing no other alternative because the one chair was piled with dirty clothes, Branwen sat on the bed. "You need one. Honestly, Xavier, I don't mean to be critical, but I don't see how you can live in this mess."

He tucked the beer can under his arm and scooped the dirty clothes from the chair, dumped them unceremoniously on the floor of the closet, then shut the closet door. Grinning like a kid, he said, "How's that for instant neatness?"

Branwen laughed. "I'll bet you've been doing that all your life."

He sat on the chair. "Pretty much. So you think I need a

housekeeper. You don't want a job, do you? Free room and
board, the pay is low, but the staff relations are terrific."

"Cute, Father X, real cute. If I told you that only male chau-
vinists can't pick up after themselves, you wouldn't like it.
Would you?"

"Uh, no. I wouldn't. You're a damn difficult woman, you
know that? I get you in my bedroom, you're even on the *bed*,
and all you can do is sit there and tell me the uncomfortable
truth about myself."

He was joking, of course, but the truth of his remark struck
home. They knew each other too well, that was the trouble;
even their bantering lately cut close to the bone. Suddenly serious and more than a little weary, Branwen raised her can of
Pepsi in a mock toast. "Score one for you. You've just picked
out one of my more unfortunate traits."

Xavier recognized that Branwen was in one of her vulnerable
moods, and he leaned forward, elbows on knees. "Hey, we were
only kidding around, weren't we?"

"Yes, but when two people are as close as we are, it's awfully
easy to go too far, and then it isn't funny anymore. I *do* do that,
Xavier, I always have to go for the uncomfortable truth. I've
wrecked more than one relationship that way." She added,
thinking of Will and speaking so low he could barely hear her,
"One in particular."

"Branwen, I love you but I haven't the slightest idea what
you're talking about!"

She allowed a small silence to stretch before asking softly,
"Did you hear what you just said?"

"Sure I did, I said. . . ." But his facial expression showed that
he hadn't, and now he realized. Xavier's hand went to rub his
neck, tugging at the clerical collar he wasn't wearing. He
looked at her with naked eyes. "It slipped out. I'm not going to
say I'm sorry I said it. But I hadn't meant to tell you yet, to say
those words. I've been waiting."

Branwen sighed a heavy sigh. She said enigmatically, "The
truth is I'm not any better at this than you are. I'm really much
worse because you have a great excuse and I have none. No excuse at all."

Xavier could usually follow her through the most convoluted
discussions, but right now he was lost. What did she want, what
did she need? "What is it that you're no better at than I am? I'm
afraid you lost me."

"Intimacy, Xavier. I'm talking about intimate relationships. And that wasn't what I started out to talk about with you at all. You got me off the track."

She looked so dejected sitting there on his bed, and he wasn't in the least prepared to talk about a subject like intimate relationships. With an almost superhuman effort of his will, Xavier had set all that aside until her lost friend could be found; he had armored himself against his own feelings so thoroughly that even now he wasn't sure how he felt about his slip of the tongue. He decided to ignore it, pretend he had never said the three fateful words. He wasn't at all sure how to help Branwen at this moment, but he knew techniques. He had been superbly trained, and he fell back on that. He echoed her words: "You think you're no better at, uh, intimate relationships than I am."

"Uh-huh." Suddenly it seemed funny to her, and she giggled. The giggle turned into one of her clear, bell-like laughs.

The laugh gave Xavier the clue he needed. For all the purity of its tone, under the circumstances it was inappropriate and bordered on hysteria. He set his beer can on the floor and went to her, sat next to her, and put a supportive arm around her shoulders. In a voice that would have made a rock respond, he said, "The main thing going on here is that you're exhausted."

Branwen stopped laughing. She came back from the edge of hysteria, into an awareness that his arm was strong. She could lean on him, and she did. "Yes. That's what I wanted to tell you. It's not that I'm physically exhausted, it's that so many things have been happening. I need time out, breathing space. I'm going to go away for a few days—that's what I wanted to tell you."

"I see. That's probably a good idea. Where will you go, and when?"

"I'll go to the coast. When I get like this, I need to be near the ocean. As for when, I'm not sure. Our project on homelessness is so nearly finished that I can leave it for a while, but I do have other jobs at the station. I expect anything I can't postpone or juggle, someone can cover for me. I won't know for sure until I get to work tomorrow. Maybe I can leave the day after."

"The day after tomorrow?"

"Mm-hm." Branwen let out a long breath, sighing deeply. Just thinking about the long drive alone in her car, with the sea her goal, calmed and relaxed her.

Xavier felt much of the tension leave her body with that sigh and pulled her closer against him. "That's right, let go," he whispered. Her head dropped to his shoulder. Her body, which had been brick-hard with tension, became all softness. After a few moments he began to wish they were sitting anywhere else in the world except on his bed. His mind flashed him a picture of Sister Maria Dolorosa, teaching him and the rest of the third-grade parochial school class about "occasions of sin." The deal about occasions of sin was that you were supposed to avoid them. He wondered if they still taught that. Himself, he'd never been too good at avoiding occasions of sin; he'd rather see how long he could hold out. It had always been a kind of contest for him, a matter more of pride than of virtue. Ever since child-hood, Xavier had been at war with himself, unwittingly de-manding more of himself than he would of anyone else. On this particular occasion he won the immediate fight and capitulated the larger battle. He said softly, "Branwen, I want to go with you."

She raised her head and pulled away from him. "You want to go to the coast with me?"

"Mm-hm."

"Xavier, you can't do that!"

"Sure I can. I haven't been away from this house since I started it over two years ago. I'm entitled."

"But how would it look? I mean, wouldn't you get in trouble or something?"

"I expect to most people it would look like we were a couple vacationing together. As for getting in trouble"—he flashed a very white, tempting smile—"not necessarily. That would de-pend on what we do. I wouldn't announce it to the world, Branwen. I'd just like to go with you and see what happens."

She withdrew into herself, thinking about what he'd said. Xavier watched her. He was always surprised by her ability to do that, to seem as if she had somehow folded herself up. She even seemed physically smaller, and she was not a small woman in spite of her slenderness. When she withdrew, her lovely, heart-shaped face became still—as it was now—without a line or a trace of expression. And she lowered her thick black lashes. He had never known anyone who could more perfectly focus her attention inward. Experience had taught him that she would not stay withdrawn for long, and that nothing he might say would bring her back sooner than she chose to come. So

Xavier waited, as focused on her as she was within herself. He yearned—ached—to be able to influence her thoughts.

At last Branwen raised her lashes and gave him the fullness of her blue-green gaze. She said, "Xavier, it's very hard for me to say no to you, about anything, but I have to say no to this. It's not because I'm worried about your reputation or about what people might say. And it's not that I don't like you enough to be with you . . . alone with you. It's that no matter how close we are or how close we might ever become, there will always be times when I have to be by myself. No one else, just me and the sea. This is one of those times."

"I understand." The ache inside him gathered into one intense burst of pain and then was gone. He reached out and stroked her hair, smoothing the white streak back from her forehead. She looked worried, and he understood why. Now that the pain was gone, he could tell her what she needed to hear, and it would be the truth. "Don't worry, you haven't hurt me. I really do understand. *Vaya con Dios.* Go with God, Branwen."

Branwen decided to leave Washington after work the following day. She knew as soon as she'd left Xavier that her first destination would be the little town of Trey on the Mobjack Bay. She wanted to see Melvin Morton. The sooner, the better. And she had done enough roaming around the state to know that getting there would be interesting but not necessarily easy. Driving to Fredericksburg after work and staying the night there would give her a head start the next day. She could call from her motel and ask Morton for an afternoon appointment, being reasonably certain of reaching Trey around midday. So she left in the evening, and the next morning Jason Faraday waited in vain outside her Georgetown triplex apartment.

Melvin Morton was as round and friendly as she remembered, but Branwen was nervous. She had to overcome a natural tendency to feel foolish about what she was about to do. She was always questioning her own psychic ability; how could she not question his?

He showed her into a large but very plain office behind his store, put a Do Not Disturb sign on the door, and closed it. Branwen liked the feel of the room. It felt as clean and uncluttered as it looked. The floor was bare boards, scrubbed and oiled; the walls were papered in an old-fashioned all-over pattern of tiny blue flowers on a cream background; and wide windows across one end of the room looked out onto a grassy verge and the bay beyond. There was a big roll-top desk of golden oak and a matching swivel chair in the middle of the wall opposite the door, a long wooden table in front of the windows, and in one corner of the room, facing each other on the diagonal, were two fan-back rockers painted blue. Smiling and bobbing his salt-and-pepper head, Melvin gestured to the rockers.

"This is where we sit, please, ma'am," he said.

"Thank you," said Branwen, sitting in the comfortable rocker. "I appreciate you seeing me on such short notice. Would you mind if I tape this, uh, interview?"

"Reading, it's called a reading," Melvin said, rocking slowly, his eyes twinkling. "I don't mind a bit, and I'm sure Gracia won't either. How may we help you?"

Branwen took a minicassette recorder from her bag and switched it on. "I had a kind of vision a while back that I didn't understand, but I can't forget it. It's almost haunting me. I thought perhaps if I told you about it, you or Gracia could interpret it for me. Also, I'm just in general concerned about a lot of things and I felt that somehow you could help."

"Not me, Ms. Faraday, but I'm sure Gracia can. I'll get her and tell her you're here. You relax, now, and when she comes through, you talk to her. All right?"

"All right."

As she had seen him do once before, Melvin Morton placed his arms on the arms of the chair, his feet flat on the floor, and breathed deeply. He closed his eyes. His breathing ceased, and his body went limp, but the chair supported him. After what seemed an excruciatingly long time, he gulped in a noisy, ragged breath, straightened up, and opened his eyes. The change in his voice was startling though she expected it. Gracia said, "Branwen."

"Yes," she acknowledged.

"I am Gracia. We are glad that you have come. We know you, we recognize you as one of us." Branwen would have liked to ask about "we" and "us," but Gracia did not give her the opportunity. She seemed to have her own agenda. "Two things you must always remember when you open yourself to the spirit plane. First, you should protect yourself. You should do this automatically, it must become second nature to you. You should no more open yourself to spirit without protection than you would cross the road without looking both ways. I mean you no harm, but you should be protected, even with me. Call your protection—do it now."

Astonished, feeling a bit like a child who has forgotten her homework assignment, Branwen did as she was told. She closed her eyes and said silently, "I surround myself with the Light that is my protection," and then she did so.

Gracia approved. "That is good. The second thing to remember is that if you will call on us, we will help you. This is important because the time will come when you will need our help."

Now she could ask. "Gracia, of whom do you speak when you say 'we' and 'us'?"

"We are, to use the language of your world, your friends. Though we are at present out of the body and living on the spiritual plane, we share your beliefs and your goals. We are all at or beyond your own level of development. I repeat, if you call on us, we will help you. What may we do for you now?"

Branwen recounted her unasked-for vision of the shining, metal-sheathed city, the monoliths, the pyramid, the glass ball, the explosion, and the huge machines rising in the air. She asked what it meant and if the vision had any connection to other things happening in her life.

"What you saw," Gracia said, "was both a vision and a memory. You saw the place men have since called Atlantis. They seek it on Earth but will not find it there, because Atlantis was on another planet, long ago. The memory of Atlantis lingers in the race of humanity like a dream. The shapes you saw in your vision have meaning rooted in the Atlantean time. The ships you saw, the metal machines rising in the air, escaped the destruction of that planet and eventually brought the survivors of the destruction of Atlantis to Earth. There were already humans living on Earth then, and the Atlanteans joined them. There is much more to this, but for now and to spare my friend Melvin's throat, I will speak of the significance to you. Atlantis was a civilization far advanced in what you call physics. They could do things that are still only hypothesized on Earth. The majority of the Atlanteans became so focused on their material world, however, that they forgot their spiritual essence, and their souls did not progress. The loss of their world was not, as some have suggested, divine retribution—but rather the result of their own arrogance and carelessness, an error of vast proportions. Many of us, including you, were in Atlantis then. We would like not to see the same mistakes repeated on Earth, and the time to guard against it approaches."

Gracia paused. Melvin's eyes closed, and his head turned from side to side, stretching his neck. Branwen was concerned about the strain on his voice, and could only assume that Gracia would know when to stop. Melvin finished his neck exercises, opened his eyes, and Gracia resumed.

She said, "I am not sure why the vision of Atlantis came to you at this particular time. We did not send it. Perhaps it was only a memory. But it could have been sent by the Others, meaning to distract you."

"Others?" Immediately Branwen felt the Darkness she so often saw in meditation. She felt it as a frisson of fear that invaded her body in spite of the protection of her Light.

"It is well to fear the Others," Gracia observed.

Quickly accepting and assimilating the fact that Gracia knew her feelings, Branwen asked, "Who are they, Gracia?"

"We here are sure that you know them." Gracia's voice ceased. Melvin's eyelids descended, and his head lolled on his neck. Branwen was torn between her concern for the man whose body was being used and her own need for reassurance. Gracia solved her dilemma by speaking again. "We see that you need clarification. Very well. The Others are spirits, souls if you prefer that word, in or out of the body, who of their own will have chosen to move away from Light, away from pursuit of the Highest Good. Their path is not our path. They do not heal but hurt and destroy; they do not free but dominate and enslave, do not teach but confuse, do not love but hate. Their form of communication is deception. By their lies you will know them, on any planet in the universe, on any plane of existence."

"They are evil," Branwen said, barely breathing the words.

"Yes," Gracia confirmed. "Some are more powerful than others, as they are older souls and more practiced in their deceit. You, Branwen, are also an old soul and have the power to confront and withstand the Others. That is your task, one you chose for yourself, whether or not you consciously remember the choosing.

"I must leave you now. Remember to protect yourself and to ask for our help when you have need of it. Farewell."

Branwen held off her own thoughts so that she could attend to Melvin Morton. She remembered he had needed water and she scanned the room for it, but there was none. From the corner of her eye she saw him move and turned back to him. Melvin was rocking in his chair with a peaceful smile on his face. "I'll be all right in a few minutes," he said, with just a trace of hoarseness. "It's always much easier at home."

Smiling, clicking off the tape recorder she held in her lap, Branwen too leaned back in her chair and began to rock. Melvin's own presence was comforting, tranquil, whereas the soul who spoke through him was charged, dynamic. Gracia had departed and left her medium in peace. Branwen rocked, letting the peacefulness enfold her.

Later when she thanked Melvin again for his time, Branwen wanted and expected to pay him. He refused, saying, "I don't do anything. It's Gracia who does it all. She comes through me like a gift, and gifts are free."

In the interest of saving time, Branwen took the most direct route from tiny Trey on the Chesapeake Bay to Sandbridge, south of Virginia Beach on the open ocean. This route took her along a busy highway many miles through the largest naval installations in the United States. In the midst of the huge military and industrial complex, she felt a sudden, sharp stab of longing for the wild windswept Welsh coast, for Llanfaren with its rocky cliff plunging down to the sea.

The restless longing stayed with her at Sandbridge as she walked the wide, flat beach. The sea nourished her as it always did, but she would gladly have traded its calm susurrations for salt spray flung high in the air of some treacherously rock-clogged little bay.

I need a change, Branwen thought, *I'm ready for it.* But that was immediately followed by a flood of reasons why she shouldn't leave Washington, and she put the thought away.

The remaining two days of her short vacation she spent going deep, deeper into herself. She found she did not need the runes to use the Sight. Her visions came easily, sharp and clear. She took long naps, and while her body rested, she went in spirit to visit her friends and family. She asked for information about Will and saw him in a vision: thin, pale, dirty, but blessedly alive; and when she probed for *where* he was, the vision vanished. When she tried to call it up again, she could not. So she did the only thing she knew to do—she called up the Light of her protection and sent it to Will wherever he might be. All of these experiences strengthened and rewarded her.

One disturbing thing happened: Branwen had a Visitor. He looked like a man, he looked real. Dressed in a dark gray hooded sweat suit and running shoes, he came out of nowhere and walked up to her on the beach. She watched him come, and as he came she clothed herself in her Light. He greeted her by name; she did not answer. From the kangaroo pocket of his sweatshirt he drew out a small leather drawstring bag that looked like the bag of sacred bluestones she had given back to Harry Ravenscroft. Branwen knew the bag did not contain her runes. She knew the man, the Visitor, was no man but an evil spirit. She refused his gift. Feeling the protection of her Light pulse in and around her, she sent the Visitor away, and he vanished before her eyes.

8

Jason wanted to frighten his former wife. Not so badly that she would take steps like calling the police or carrying a gun, but just enough to put her on edge. That was to be the first step. Then he would have her abducted and brought to the house he'd rented in Silver Spring—a big house with a finished basement, as he'd specified; on spacious grounds, as he'd specified; with an up-to-date electronic security system, as he'd specified. She wouldn't be able to get away, and she could scream all she wanted to. More than anything else, he wanted Branwen to beg and cry and scream. When he had broken her, he would kill her with his own hands.

Jason ran into a problem right away: Branwen wasn't easy to scare. He hung around the little Georgetown triplex where she lived until one of her nosy neighbors came out and told him to get lost or he'd call the police, so Jason left. He had by then deduced that she must be out of town anyway, so it was no big loss. He called her office at the PBS station and found out when she was coming back. He was determined to follow her everywhere, so that every time she came out of a door or turned a corner or looked in her car's rearview mirror, she'd see his large, imposing figure. He presumed that would intimidate her, but it didn't. The first time she saw him she stopped and talked to him, very politely until the end, when she'd said, "Our marriage is long over, Jason, and I have no desire for us to be friends. I don't want to see you again. Good-bye." He followed her anyway, but from that point on she ignored him. Looked right through him, the bitch! His ex-wife had developed nerves of steel.

Another thing he hadn't counted on was that she had so damn many friends. How had that happened? And how had quiet little Branwen ended up on TV? Of course it was only public television but still. . . . She looked different. Not just older but *different.* Somewhere along the line, Branwen the Welsh village girl had gotten class. Maybe it was the white in her hair that did it; that white streak was really unusual. He had a nagging feeling that he should remember something about that white streak, but he didn't.

Her friends were a big problem. She wouldn't look at him, but *they* did—they gave him dirty looks. That big foreign-looking guy from the bad part of town had actually threatened him! It turned out that Branwen did some kind of volunteer work over there, and the day came when Jason, having followed her, realized there were dozens of these out-of-work types hanging around, and all of them were giving him dirty looks. They might be derelicts but they were mean sons of bitches. So he couldn't follow her there anymore. He took to waiting outside her apartment at night, and the nosy neighbor did call the police. Jason damn near got caught. After that he grudgingly admitted he wasn't going to be able to frighten Branwen, and he prepared to move to step two: the abduction.

Xavier was trying to teach a few basic self-defense moves to a reluctant Branwen. "Honestly, Xavier," she complained, "I don't need this! Jason isn't even following me anymore. I know him—he was only trying to get some sort of rise out of me. The one thing in the world Jason Faraday can't stand is being ignored, and I ignored him, so he gave up. I repeat: I do not need this!"

"I disagree. I saw the look in that man's eyes. I'm sorry to say this about a former husband of yours, but that man is nuts. Judging from everything you've told me about him, he's not just a nut, he's a rich, powerful nut, and they're the worst kind. So come on. If the nuns can learn this stuff, you can."

"Nuns? *You* taught self-defense to a bunch of nuns?" Xavier flashed a knowing smile, and Branwen laughed. She gave in. She learned to kick, whirl, punch, jab, and yell. Actually, she was pretty good at everything except the yelling, and Xavier assured her that if the time were right, she'd have no trouble yelling. As an additional precaution, he gave her a little earsplitting whistle on a silver chain and insisted she wear it around her neck.

Within a week Branwen was mugged as she walked between 622 and the soup kitchen. She whirled and kicked and blew her whistle, and the mugger ran off. Three homeless men charged out of the soup kitchen and took off after the mugger. They caught up with him and beat him within an inch of his life. That was one mugger who wouldn't be attacking anyone again anytime soon. Branwen had come to no harm. The only thing she couldn't figure out was why should she have been mugged in the first place? She hadn't even been carrying a purse.

Orson. Branwen knew she had heard the name somewhere, and it wasn't Orson Welles. This Orson was a self-proclaimed bicoastal psychic, and he was coming to do a demonstration at the October meeting of the Psychic Underground. Orson, Orson, Orson—for some reason the very name made her uneasy. She decided to go to the meeting and find out why.

He didn't use a last name; he was introduced simply as Orson. He waited out of sight in a hallway while the evening's host made introductory remarks: Orson was a phenomenon who had already taken the West Coast by storm and soon would do the same in the East. He had gained his powers literally by accident—an automobile accident. Orson's car had plunged off a bridge and into a river, and Orson drowned. He was brought back to life, however. He had had a classic near-death experience that he recalled in every detail, and there was more: Orson came back to life with the ability to access all knowledge from all of his former lives, even though up to that point he had never believed in reincarnation and had had no interest whatsoever in the spiritual world. Orson had come back to life also with the ability to move his consciousness freely from this plane of existence to the next, and thus he could communicate with not just one Spirit Guide, but many. Prior to his accident, Orson had had a successful career as a business executive, but he had given up everything, preferring to start a new life of sharing his newfound wisdom with the world. "Ladies and gentlemen," the host concluded, "Orson!"

He was the most dramatic-looking man Branwen had ever seen. More dramatic even than Xavier, who was striking in an entirely different way. Orson was at least six and a half feet tall. His hair was black, full, swept back from a high forehead; his eyebrows were black and thick and sharply arched; his eyes were so pale a blue they looked almost colorless. His nose was hooked like a predator's beak, and his cheeks were broad. He had a full black beard and mustache, and he wore a charcoal-gray single-breasted suit, white shirt, crimson tie, and black shoes. Branwen thought he looked like Rasputin, the mad Russian monk—he would have seemed more at home in long, brocaded robes. And he did look mad, especially around the eyes. Those eyes were chilling.

Unsmiling, Orson surveyed the room. There were about fifty people present, a good crowd for the Underground, but his expression suggested that he was used to more, better. Coldly and deliberately he made eye contact with each individual in his audience. When the roaming eyes touched her, Branwen felt that she had been assessed and found wanting. She would not have been surprised if others had felt the same way; if indeed this strange man had found them all wanting, and turned on his heel and left without so much as speaking one word.

But he did speak, in a voice as deep and resonant as a bass bell. "I am honored to appear before this select group, though I cannot imagine what I might say that you do not already know. My friends—"

Branwen shivered. She did not want to be called "friend" by this man. Suddenly she remembered where she had heard the name Orson. She lowered her eyelashes, lest he see the recognition in her eyes. She called up her Light and surrounded herself with it, not raising her eyes until she felt its warmth from the crown of her head to the soles of her feet. Harry Ravenscroft had said Orson's name. Only once, but that was enough, for he had said it in the same breath with the forbidden Cognoscenti.

Orson was continuing. ". . . I am here to draw back the veil for you so that you may know what I now know. I, who have died and come back to life with access to the wisdom of the Plane Beyond, will share that knowledge with you. Know, then, the great secret: *You Are God!*"

He waited to let this statement take effect. "You are God, you are the Creator, the creator of yourself. You can do whatever you want to do, can have whatever you want to have. You can transcend the petty restrictions of this culture in which we live because you are limitless!"

Orson went on in this vein for a while, and Branwen heard in the sense that she monitored him, but she kept his words at a distance. At the same time, she acknowledged the man's magnetic appeal. The Psychic Underground had a jaded edge to their credulity, but he held them enthralled. Her attention sharpened when she heard him ask:

"How is this possible? How can you have whatever you desire? Recognize that the restrictions of convention and the prohibitions of religion were made for the masses, but they need not apply to you. There are two keys: openness and visualization. Open yourself to the power of the universe, and that power will be given to you. Visualize your heart's desire, and you will achieve it. You are no doubt already aware that we humans use only about one tenth of our brain's capacity. Add to that pathetic figure the fact that most of us use less than one tenth of one percent of our spiritual capacity, and you will see why we so often feel helpless, victims of Fate, Fortune, the weather, the so-called gods! Through visualization, you create your own reality. By opening yourself to the power of the universe you link your own untapped power to that infinite source. Pay close attention, now. I will teach you an ancient technique of visualization that was taught to me by one Sartor Sartoris, apprentice Adept of the great Trismegistus. . . ."

Branwen, like everyone else in the room, was sitting on the edge of her chair.

She ended that evening with mixed feelings about Orson. As was her habit when she could not tape, she made thorough notes, as near word-for-word as possible. When days went by and Orson lingered in Branwen's mind as if demanding that she resolve her ambivalence, she asked Xavier to come to her apartment—she would cook for him in return for his help with a problem.

Branwen had not cooked for anyone in months, and she had forgotten how much she enjoyed it. She also enjoyed dressing in clothes quite different from the jeans and old shirts or sweaters she usually wore when she was with Xavier. She chose a long skirt of soft beige wool and a pale yellow silk blouse; for a belt she wrapped her waist in a scarf striped in shades of yellow, rose, and gold. She washed and brushed her hair to shining smoothness, then held it back off her face with a narrow gold headband.

I don't look too bad for a woman closer to forty than thirty, Branwen thought. *I'm too pale, but I've always been too pale.* She brushed blusher on her cheeks to fix that problem, added a bit of rose gloss for her lips. She doubted that Xavier would notice how she looked but she didn't mind; she had dressed for herself, not for him. Changing her clothes and cooking a good meal had lifted her out of a rut. The doorbell rang, and she was ready.

"Hi!" said Xavier, stepping through the door. "I was going to bring wine but I forgot to ask what we're having, so I brought these instead." In the hand he'd kept behind his back he held a bunch of lavender chrysanthemums wrapped in green florist's paper.

"How lovely and how thoughtful! Come on in. Make yourself comfortable, fix yourself a drink—you know where everything is. I'll just put these in water."

Xavier looked around the room appreciatively. There was a fire burning in the fireplace, the lamps were glowing golden on a low setting, and there was a fat pillar candle flickering its flame on the coffee table. Very nice, he thought. Branwen, too, had seemed to glow in her yellow blouse, with the gold in her hair. He sneaked a peek into the dining room and smiled. Yes, the table was set, and there were candles—no eating in the kitchen tonight. He wished he'd known she was going to make a fuss. He'd have worn something a bit better than old jeans and a green sweater! He had settled himself on the couch near the fire when she returned.

"I put the flowers on the table where we can enjoy them with our meal," she said.

"Do you want me to fix a drink for you?" he asked.

"No, I'll do it. You sit there and relax."

Xavier watched her, admiring the way she moved, the graceful sway of her long skirt. Her hair fell free like a cascade of black satin. He was disappointed when, with her drink in hand, she went to her desk instead of joining him on the couch. He reminded himself this was not a date; he didn't have dates with Branwen. Or anyone else. She had asked him here to help her solve a problem. Nevertheless he said, "You look unusually pretty tonight, Branwen."

She turned her head quickly, which sent her hair flying, and pink flushed into her cheeks. "Thank you," she said simply and returned to riffling through the papers on her desk. "Sometimes

I think I have gremlins in this house," she muttered. Then, "Oh, here they are."

Xavier took a long swallow of bourbon and water and wished she hadn't found whatever it was, wished she had invited him for some reason other than a problem. She was handing three sheets of paper to him, all covered with her own handwriting. He took them, resigned to the inevitable. "The problem, huh?"

"Background material. These are notes on a talk I heard several nights ago. This man Orson is a psychic. He claims to have received some, uh, special abilities after he drowned in an auto accident and was brought back to life. I thought you might use this time to read my notes while I do a couple of things in the kitchen. Dinner's almost ready."

"I can't sit in the kitchen and talk to you while you cook?"

"Not tonight." She smiled. "Tonight we're going to do this dinner business by the book. The trouble with both of us is that we've been spending entirely too much time in soup kitchens!"

Her smile was infectious. He grinned in return. "I won't argue that." His smile soon faded as he read what she'd given him.

Branwen lit the candles and admitted to herself that she was tempted to tell Xavier she'd changed her mind, she didn't really have a problem. Staring into the glow of the candle flames, she realized that "tempted" was the operative word here. She couldn't capitulate; she had to maintain her ambivalence. At least they didn't have to talk about it until after their meal.

She had prepared a feast: boneless chicken breasts on a bed of wild rice seasoned with onions, green peppers, and chopped crisp bacon; a casserole of green beans and sliced mushrooms; soft, light-as-air rolls she'd made herself from scratch. After the main course she served a salad of Bibb lettuce and mandarin orange segments with a sweet-sour dressing. With the meal she poured a chilled Grey Reisling wine. Dessert was thin slices of cheesecake from Xavier's favorite bakery, and coffee.

Over the second cup of coffee Branwen finally spoke of her problem with Orson. "I guess the main thing is that I can't get the man out of my mind. I may have been unfairly prejudiced against him at first. Someone I know well—it's Harry Ravenscroft, you've heard me speak of him—mentioned Orson's name in an unfavorable context. But I may have been mistaken in what I heard Harry say, or Harry himself could have been wrong. You've read my notes?"

Xavier nodded gravely. He was not yet sure what she wanted of him. It was hard for him, after one of the best meals he'd had in his life, produced by a woman he hadn't known could cook like that, to leap right into anything.

She said, "The notes are objective. I want to know what you think about the things Orson said, as I've reported in my notes, Xavier."

He pulled himself together. "All right, but first I'd like to hear a little more about your confusion. It isn't like you to be confused, Branwen."

"I know." She sighed. "I think part of it comes from my being so worried about Harry, and now I've seen and heard Orson and I know Orson could have some connection with the mess Harry's in."

"What kind of mess?"

"I can't tell you. He made me promise not to talk about it. Harry's situation is very secretive, and he said I'd be in danger if I told anyone that he had confided in me."

Xavier frowned. "He might have thought of that before he said anything to you! I don't like anyone putting you in danger, Branwen, and it's happening. First your crazy ex-husband, now this Harry—"

"All right. Be calm, Xavier. Nothing is going to happen to me. The point is that Harry still means a lot to me, and if Orson has some connection to Harry, I'd like at the very least to make up my mind what I think about Orson. But I can't. At first I didn't like where he was coming from at all, but the longer he talked, the more I began to think I'd misjudged him. He said some things I know are true. And maybe he really does have a source of information that's superior to what the rest of us have."

"Hah!" Xavier snorted. "You want to know my opinion, and I'll tell you. My opinion is that this Orson is a crackpot or worse, and I hope to God he doesn't get much publicity. I wouldn't want a whole lot of people to be exposed to the stuff he has to say. I've never heard of him and I hope it stays that way!"

"He's already supposed to be big on the West Coast. At the conclusion of his talk he said he is setting up a base of operations in New York State, and he plans an East Coast lecture tour."

"That's bad news." Xavier shook his head. "You remember

that talk we had here one night several months ago, the talk about Evil?"

"Yes."

Xavier's eyes were dark, his face solemn. "The things Orson said, as you reported objectively in your own notes . . . those things are dangerous, Branwen. Just think: If *you* can be swayed by him, then he's either an absolute genius of a con man, or he's getting outside help from a source I wouldn't want to name. After all, he did confuse you, didn't he?"

Branwen nodded.

"The best liars always mix in the truth—it throws an honest person off their scent. That whole lecture of his is filled with I, I, I. It's a supremely selfish life-style he's advocating: you can do anything you want, have whatever you want, make your own reality. A lot of people want to hear those things, but they aren't true." He paused, having seen one source of her ambivalence. "Well, maybe people *can* live that way, but what kind of world would we have? It would be hell, Branwen. Sheer living hell. In that kind of world, where is there room for love and compassion and helping others?"

"You're right. Of course you're right!" She felt as if she had been tangled in a net and Xavier had cut it away. "Why didn't I see that?"

"Because this Orson is a deceiver. He probably has a lot of charisma. He turns you on to him and gets you so focused on what he wants you to believe that you forget you know better. However, *you* didn't completely forget. You didn't accept what he said, you became ambivalent instead. How he got to you when he started out with something as ridiculous as 'You are God,' I'll never be able to understand."

"Most of the people in the group he was speaking to don't believe in your kind of God, Xavier. Even so, I admit that statement kind of jolted me. Later on, I thought what he probably meant was that we're all spiritual beings in essence, like God."

"That's not what he said. If you want to get theological about it, this guy started off his pitch with the same argument the Snake used in the Garden of Eden: Eat the fruit of this tree and you, too, can know everything, as God knows everything—you can be God! Like the Snake, who represents Satan, Orson delivered a seductive, insidious message. You can call it what you like. I call it evil."

"You and Gracia," Branwen murmured. She was appalled

that she had not been able to see this for herself, and was grateful for Xavier's clarity. She was also fascinated that once again Xavier and Gracia/Melvin, coming from different belief systems, were nevertheless in complete accord. He should know about Gracia, she decided. "Let's take our coffee in the living room, Xavier. I have a tape I want you to hear."

She explained as she set up the minicassette, "This is a recording of a session I had with a trance-channel medium named Melvin Morton. You know what a trance-channel medium is?"

"I've heard of them."

"Melvin is absolutely genuine, you can take my word. You're going to hear just a little of his voice, and then the female spirit who speaks through him. Her name is Gracia, and her last life on earth was in Alexandria, Egypt. I've forgotten what century—first or second A.D., I think. You'll also hear me."

The quality of the tape was excellent, so clear that the changes in Melvin's breathing could be heard. As Gracia began to speak, Xavier's amazement showed on his face. When Branwen reached out to fast forward through the part about Atlantis, saying "What I want you to hear is near the end," he stopped her.

He said, "I'd like to hear all of it."

Branwen listened with him, humbled by her fresh realization that everything she needed to know about Orson was there in Gracia's words. Right down to the confusion Branwen herself had felt. She thought she had protected herself, but apparently Orson had been powerful enough to partially penetrate her protection.

"Amazing!" Xavier fell back on the couch when the tape was done. "That's one of the most amazing things I've ever heard in my life. She's got Orson's number, all right. He's one of the Others, obviously."

"Yes," Branwen agreed. She kicked off her shoes and settled thoughtfully in her corner of the couch with her feet up. "I hate that I let him get to me and confuse me the way he did. I'd feel better about myself if I'd recognized him as one of the Others on my own. I should have, Xavier. I shouldn't have needed your help, but I'm grateful for it. Thank you."

"De nada." The tape had really knocked him on his ear. He was reminded of the exorcism he'd witnessed, the alien voice of the possessor speaking from the mouth of its possessed victim.

But the woman speaking on the tape had been clearly coming from the opposite end of the spectrum.

Xavier looked over at Branwen who had curled up, hugging her knees, lost in thought. He was struck anew by her beauty. Twice struck, as the tape had brought home to him the realization that her soul was as beautiful as her body. He said, "The woman on the tape, Gracia, has a high opinion of you. And so do I."

Branwen looked up, met his eyes, and smiled, then quickly lowered her lashes. They were so thick they made crescent-shaped shadows on her cheeks.

Xavier repositioned himself so that he faced her. An irresistible urge was building in him, an urge to deal with matters long suppressed. He tried to shove it down but it wouldn't go. He needed release. He cleared his throat. "Er, um, are we done talking about Orson and all that? Can I talk about something else?"

"Sure," she said. "A change of subject would be welcome."

"Ah. . . ." He made one last desperate attempt to regain his old equilibrium, though he knew it was futile. "That was the best meal I've had in a long time. Years. I didn't know you could cook like that."

"I like to cook, but ever since I got involved with you, Xavier, I've been too busy to do much cooking. As I said, we've both been spending too much time in soup kitchens." Smiling faintly, she rested her chin on her hand, which in turn rested upon her drawn-up knees.

She looked adorable. Xavier felt his final restraint dissolve in the blue-green sea of her eyes. He was going to do it, jump right in with both feet. His voice turned husky. "Branwen, what would you say if I were to ask you to marry me?"

Her head came up, her eyes widened. She looked like a graceful doe, alert, poised, waiting yet ready to fly. She moistened her lips with the tip of her tongue. "I—I'd say something completely silly, like oh, my goodness!"

Xavier could feel his pulse beating in his throat. "Could we talk about it? About us?"

Still alert, Branwen drew in a deep breath. Wheels of thought turned behind her eyes. "Are you thinking of leaving the priesthood, Xavier?"

"I would have to if you would marry me."

"I think," she said cautiously, feeling her way, "that you may be going at this backward. If you decide that you no longer want to be a priest, and if you get released from your vows or however it's done, then you'd be in a position to talk about marriage."

Xavier sighed and rubbed at the throbbing pulse in the side of his neck. He confessed, "I find it hard to make any decision at all without knowing how you feel about me. I thought I could wait until your friend Will is found, but the waiting gets harder every day." The proud planes of his face softened. "I love you. Do you love me, Branwen?"

They sat sideways at opposite ends of the couch, facing each other, only their glances touching. Branwen said, "I do love you, Xavier. One thing I've learned in thirty-five years of life is that there are different kinds of love. The way I love you is unique. There has never been anyone, I think will never be anyone, I love in the way I love you. I gave up trying to analyze and just accepted it, months ago."

Xavier's finely shaped lips curved in an ironic smile. "I see this big word hanging in the air there between us. The word is *but.* . . . Say it, Branwen, tell me what's in your heart. I need to know."

She looked away. "It's not that simple. There are things about me you don't know. For example, you don't know that after I ended my marriage to Jason I decided that I would never marry again."

Now Xavier moved closer, sliding his arm along the back of the couch. As far as he was concerned, her ex-husband was a horrible human being. Just looking at the man gave Xavier the creeps. He couldn't bear to think of Branwen married to him, of the things they had done together. "It was that bad?"

Branwen nodded, hanging her head. Her hair obscured her face. "Did I tell you I can't have children? Did I tell you that when I lost my baby something went wrong, and they had to take my uterus to save my life?"

"No. You told me you lost the baby, but you didn't tell me the rest." He reached out and took her chin in his hand, turned her face to look at him. "I'm sorry for your pain, but if I marry you, it wouldn't be because I want children. It would be because I want *you.*"

"Don't, Xavier," she whispered, sensing that he about to kiss her, "please don't." Swiftly she got up from the couch and moved away. She wrapped her arms over her breasts and swallowed hard as a great, sweet sorrow welled up inside her. Then she turned to face him, the coffee table between them. The expression on his face, hope in his eyes warring with anguish in the carved lines of his mouth, threatened to make her mute. She swallowed again and asked a question. "Do you remember several weeks ago when I told you I needed to go away, and you wanted to go with me, you said, 'to see what would happen'?"

Xavier frowned. Where was she going with this? He answered, "Of course I do."

"And I went alone. When I came back, we went on with our friendship the same as always. So how did you get from wanting to be alone with me to see what would happen, to asking me to marry you—how did you get from that to this all by yourself, and in such a short time?"

"I've been wrestling with my feelings about you for months. Months, hell, years! Sure, I wanted to go away with you, but . . . well, it wasn't necessary. I know I love you. I know that if you'll marry me, I can leave the priesthood. I wasn't sure of that for a long time, but I am now."

Branwen took a deep breath. She hated doing this, but she had to. "Don't use me to settle your doubts about the priesthood, Xavier."

His face darkened, as she had known it would. But at least he didn't explode. "You think that's what I'm doing? You doubt I really love you?"

"No, I don't doubt that you love me, and yes, I think that's what you're doing."

Now Xavier's anger came, swift and terrible, like a rushing wind. "Damn you!" he cried, smashing his fist on the coffee table. The pillar candle jumped and extinguished itself at the force of his blow. He surged up from the couch like a thunder god and glared at her. "How dare you say such a stupid, self-righteous thing to me?"

Branwen bit her lip and stood her ground. She said nothing. She waited while Xavier strode back and forth across the room, wearing down his anger. Finally he came and stood in front of her, with his hands shoved in his pockets. The sudden storm was over.

"I'm sorry," he said. "You know me too well."

"No need to be sorry," said Branwen softly.

"You're right, you know."

"I thought so."

Xavier smiled, but his smile was weary, tinged with suffering. He reached out his hand and with the tip of a finger traced the gold circlet in Branwen's hair. Then he looked into her eyes and said honestly, "I don't know what to do."

Branwen sighed. She caught his hand and held it in both her own, over her heart. "Maybe I can help you, at least a little. I love you, Xavier Dominguez, in a most extraordinary way. You're a most extraordinary man. I hope we'll always be friends. And if you were ever to ask me to marry you, I would say no."

The dark pools of Xavier's eyes welled but did not spill over. "Ah, Branwen," he groaned, and pulled her into his arms. He held her so tightly that she could scarcely breathe. She made herself boneless, absorbing his hurt.

There, crushed in Xavier's arms with his pain pouring into her, Branwen saw into his soul. She saw how inextricably Xavier the Man was bound up with Xavier the Priest. Saw, and knew, that she was right to tell him she would not marry him; right for him as well as for herself. And gradually she became aware that another pain, her own pain, was mingled with his. Her pain was for Will, for missing Will and loving Will and for knowing now, probably too late, that Will was the only man she could ever marry.

9

The weather in Washington was peculiarly ominous that fall; it had everyone on edge. Thunderstorms so heavy they turned day to night roiled across the skies well past their usual season. Lightning cracked, and hail fell. The storms did not clear the air but left in their wake a smothering humidity. Heavy gray fog hung over the Potomac even in daylight; at night it left the river to twist sinuously through the streets, shrouding all in obscurity. There was no autumn air crisp and bright as new apples. Week after week, even when the heat at last released its relentless grip and the first frost came, all remained leaden and soggy. The trees bravely tried to show their colors in spite of a lack of sun, but cold, hard rain drove the leaves from their branches to deposit them on the streets and in the gutters in brown, sodden masses.

Everyone was depressed—even the Republicans, who could look forward to Ronald Reagan's inauguration in January. Xavier Dominguez was depressed by that election of 1980; he said social problems like homelessness would only get worse; he felt as if he'd taken two steps forward and now would have to take ten steps back. Branwen was depressed because Xavier was depressed, and also because there was no news of Will. Ellen and Jim Harper had returned home from their long honeymoon depressed because they couldn't find him. Probably the only person in the Washington area who wasn't depressed was Jason Faraday.

Jason was enjoying himself. He enjoyed himself so much that he was willing to put his plans for Branwen on hold. The "mugger" he'd hired to kidnap her had failed and been so badly beaten in the attempt that he refused to try again. Not only that, but all of Jason's sources for hiring a replacement seemed to have dried up, and he couldn't understand why—unless *they* had done it. If they had, well, never mind; he couldn't be bothered with the Cognoscenti. Sometimes he wondered what they'd done to Harry, but other than that he never thought of them at all. He didn't have to because his Protector was always with him now. The Protector never left him, night or day, stayed so close that Jason sometimes felt the Protector was inside of him. That was a fine feeling, exciting, because the Protector was wise as well as powerful. It made Jason feel even more wise and powerful than he already was, to sense the Protector inside, joined to him.

Life was grand for Jason, so good that he forgot his original Washington game plan: Lie low, take care of Branwen quietly, return to the manor house as soon as possible. Far from lying low, he was highly visible. Prowling around Georgetown, he'd run into a couple of old acquaintances, who had invited him to parties, and the next thing Jason knew he was being asked everywhere. He could still do it, draw people to him, wrap them around his little finger. Keep them hanging on every word. In his own eyes, he had become a celebrity, the hit of the season on the party circuit. It was true that he was sought after, that fashionable hostesses wanted him on their guest lists. But his celebrity was of a strange nature: He was an oddity, a curiosity. Jason Faraday had become something of a freak. He would not have liked what was said about him behind his back, but he didn't know. So he enjoyed himself. Oh, yes, he was much too busy being entertained to concern himself with how to carry out plans of revenge against his former wife when he couldn't hire anyone to help him. The fall in Washington was the busiest social season, right up through Christmas to the New Year. He decided that Branwen could wait until the season was over.

The Cognoscenti, however, were not the waiting kind. They knew exactly what Jason Faraday was doing, and they would decide how long he could keep on doing it. He was not so invulnerable as he thought, nor was his Protector the true protection he thought. True, they had been surprised that Jason had been able to call the Protector, but that was only a minor inconvenience—they had far more powerful Forces at their command. From their far-flung individual empires the Cognoscenti came together in secret. The question they asked of themselves was not *if* but *how* they would take Jason's life. They decided that he would die as he had lived, in a bizarre and cruel fashion.

Branwen sat at her office desk, as unable to work as she had been unable to sleep the night before. In an attempt to lift herself out of the doldrums, she'd gone to a party with a colleague from the station, and Jason had been there. His presence itself didn't surprise her—she'd heard he was being asked everywhere, which meant she was bound to encounter him sooner or later. She'd thought if she found herself at the same gathering as her ex-husband, she would just very quietly leave. Last night it had happened, but leaving had not been as easy as she'd thought it would be.

The party was at the home of a woman who liked to mix culture with politics; for this reason Branwen usually enjoyed her parties. She had been looking forward to the evening and had gone determined to have a good time. Yet as soon as she'd walked through the door, she'd known something was wrong— very wrong. There was a Dark Presence in the room that leapt out at her and drew her inexorably, like a bit of passing star stuff to a black hole. She was completely unprepared, so off-balance that she had neither time nor thought to kindle the Light of her protection. The dark thing was with Jason.

Branwen had been frightened, unable to hear Jason's familiar voice over the horrid gibbering sounds the Thing made. The closer she got, the more horrified she became . . . for the Thing was not just with Jason, it was *inside* him. If she had allowed herself to look, she knew she could have seen It, crouched in the depths of Jason's eyes. She didn't look. She turned deathly pale and backed away. Jason hadn't yet seen her, but he would in a moment, she was sure, because It knew she was there. She felt insanely panicked that It might detach Itself from Jason and come after her, if she called any attention to herself in any way at all. So she moved slowly though her feet wanted to run, slowly, slowly inching backward. Not caring or hearing who spoke to her, back, back. . . . Until at last she judged that she could turn and hurl herself out of the door.

Safely outside, she had closed the door and leaned against

it—sick, weak, drained. She could not move and she had no energy to call her Light. Then she remembered Gracia's counsel,
and she pleaded aloud, "Help me!" The help came. She could
move again, down the steps, up the sidewalk, to her car. The
sickness passed. Her hand was steady as she put the key into the
ignition. Driving away, she had felt the warm, tingling sensa-
tion that accompanied the spreading of her Light—her unseen
friends had called it for her. At home she'd turned on every light
in the house and stayed up until dawn, afraid to close her eyes,
afraid to sleep, afraid to dream.

Now, rationality bolstered by daylight and the mundane reality of the PBS offices, Branwen was no longer actively afraid.
The memory of that fear was nevertheless imprinted on every
nerve and sinew. She could understand that unrelieved fear
may, finally, result in despair. She had been close to that; she
had walked on the edge. It was one thing to have seen visions of
obscene shapes moving out of Darkness to envelop Jason, another thing entirely to have encountered one of these horrors, Its
purpose accomplished, in real life.

Why had her fear been so great? Because she had been so
completely unprepared. As if she were an audio/video receiver
turned on without her knowledge or consent, she had simply
walked into the range of a power transmitter that had broadcast
pure Evil and aimed it straight into her soul. Her fear had not
been for Jason—he had courted Evil and reaped its benefits,
must have welcomed the evil entity around and into himself.
Her fear had been for herself—primitive, heart-stopping fear
that left her helpless; a child's pure irrational terror of the dark
unknown.

In retrospect, there had been recognition, too. She *knew* that
Blackness Jason harbored, recognized it as her enemy. And It
had recognized her as well. *Aha,* Branwen thought, *now I'm really getting somewhere! Now I'm getting a handle on that encounter.*

Yes, the Thing, Entity, evil spirit, whatever, must at the very
least have recognized that she could perceive its nature and its
presence. Why else had It reached for her and tried to pull her to
It? Why else for Branwen alone of all the many present had the
light dimmed and the voices died in that bright, noisy room?

Branwen shook her head vigorously. No, she did not want to
fight the Thing. Old enemy, or not. True, she had helped Harry
Ravenscroft to rid himself of his Disturbance, which had felt

something like whatever had Jason. But Harry's had been smaller, weaker, probably because he was fighting it himself. Briefly she considered Harry, how courageous or foolish or both he must be to willingly engage himself with the thing she thought of as Harry's Disturbance. Jason, though, wasn't fighting. He had joined the Others willingly.

Suddenly an enormous, overpowering grief swept through Branwen, dangerously akin to that despair she desperately held at bay. The grief was for Jason. No matter what a travesty he had become, at one time she had believed she loved him. He had been good to her for a while, in his own way. She had joined her body with his more times than she could count. How could she not grieve for him? And what would become of him?

Branwen got up from her desk and paced around her office. It was so small she could go no more than ten steps in any direction. She didn't want to think about any of this anymore. There was nothing she could do for Jason; he didn't want anything done. She had already done what she could for Harry, and she continued to go out to Raven Hill every couple of weeks to visit the Beechers. If there was anything else to be done at present, she hadn't the foggiest notion what it might be.

Time to get on with life, Branwen thought. *Do some work, earn a living.* She sat at her desk again and determinedly sorted through the morning's mail. With the "Powerless" documentary completed and scheduled to air locally, she was on the lookout for two types of mail in particular: requests from other PBS stations to preview "Powerless" and any correspondence from any source that might spark an idea for the future. One letter stood out above the rest. It was from a major network TV station in San Francisco, written by a man Branwen remembered because he had been impressed enough by her program on the mentally ill that he'd come to see her when he'd been in Washington a few months before. She had told him about her project on the homeless, and he'd seemed excited, interested; now he wrote asking for a progress report and sample tapes if they were available. He said he was very interested in her work, which was gratifying. Branwen set his letter aside.

Later in the day she read the letter again. Why not send him one of the preview tapes of "Powerless"? He wouldn't be able to buy it for his network station because the program wasn't Branwen's to sell. Fifty-one percent of it belonged to the local PBS station, and they had decided that the program should be offered only to public television stations. Branwen had fought that decision because she had wanted the broadest possible exposure for Xavier's work, but they'd remained firm. Still, Branwen was proud of her work on the homeless. She knew it was one of the best things she'd ever done. She decided to send a tape to San Francisco with a note saying that this was only a sample since unfortunately the program was not available to network TV. She packed up the tape herself in a padded bag, addressed it, and threw it in the mail basket. Then she forgot all about it.

Jason Faraday's body was found on January 2, 1981, by the caretaker of the estate in Silver Spring, Maryland. The caretaker had been so horrified by what he'd found that he'd voluntarily gone for psychiatric help. The police and the news media called Jason's death "a bizarre ritualistic murder." His body had been gutted, internal organs removed, all the blood drained out by a remarkably neat murderer. Not only had there been very little mess, considering, but also the organs and the blood had been completely removed from the site. Several feet of Jason's own intestines had been wrapped around his neck—according to the autopsy—while he was still alive. Cause of death, however, was not strangulation but exsanguination.

What the autopsy did not say, and the news reports did, was that Jason's body had been laid out on his living-room floor in the center of a circle—a circle drawn in red chalk with strange markings at points North, South, East, and West. The newspapers, having dug up Jason's Washington past in the first flurry of investigative activity, suggested that the trappings of occult ritual were a ruse designed to obscure the fact that this was a political killing. Branwen knew better. She did not have to see the circle or read its markings with her own eyes to know that they were made to contain the Dark Thing, which would have left the body along with the leaving of Jason's life breath and blood. Was It still there, bound within the circle? Or had the murderer sent It back to the Abyss? Or, worst of all, did It now roam the world on Its own, seeking another willing host?

Abruptly, two days after the discovery of the body of Jason Faraday, all news coverage of the murder ceased. Realizing that he'd had no living relatives, Branwen called the Maryland Medical Examiner's Office to see if she might make arrangements to have the body cremated. She was told that the body had been claimed by "an agent of the deceased's estate who had power of attorney." Surprised but glad to be relieved of that unpleasant responsibility, Branwen waited for the police to question her in their investigation. The police did not call. She went forward voluntarily and was interviewed by a detective who obviously could not have cared less, and would tell her nothing about the progress of the investigation. Days went by, and still there was nothing in the news.

Branwen felt uneasy; she didn't understand why nothing was being done. Jason might have been a horrible person in his last years, but still he had been murdered in a most brutal fashion. She complained to Xavier, who advised her to pray if she wanted to do something, but otherwise let it go. Finally Branwen called Ellen, knowing that Ellen could find out most anything worth knowing; but this time Ellen, too, came up against a blank wall. It was Ellen's husband Jim, the former FBI man, who had the contacts that eventually yielded the truth: The news coverage had ceased because it was ordered to cease by someone high up in the newspaper world. Who? That, Jim or anyone else could not discover.

Branwen's unease turned to disgust. A cover-up! Her every instinct told her that even if Jason's murder had been political, there was also more to it. She might have tried to pursue an investigation on her own but she hadn't the heart for it; her disgust was too monumental.

When the San Francisco network television station issued an invitation for Branwen to fly out at their expense to talk about a job, Branwen went. The nation's capital, which had for so long been her home, was no more a welcoming and nurturing place. California called, and Branwen was ready to hear and respond.

PART FOUR

———————

CONFLICT
California,
1981–83

1

————

"Of course you must go to San Francisco," said Ellen Carew Harper. "It's such a marvelous opportunity for you. I have only one concern: I know how you are about the money side of things, Branwen. What about salary?"

"It's so much more than what I've ever been paid before, it's embarrassing," Branwen acknowledged, "but I didn't object! They said they'd pay my moving expenses, too."

"So what's the problem? The money is better, they're offering you network exposure for the kind of programs you do best, and it's understandable that you might be ready to leave here—especially after Jason's awful murder. A fresh start will be good for you."

"It's that I feel so much here is, well, unfinished." Branwen left her chair in Ellen's living room and went to gaze out of the wide window at the snow-covered lawn. The new job, the new place, tugged at her. If she took it, there would be no more snow, but something better: the Pacific Ocean. In the brief stay for her interview, she had discovered the northern California coastline, and it had reminded her of Wales, of Llanfaren. The rocky shore, the clifflike bluffs plunging down to the sea, the mist, the cool temperatures—all had the look, feel, scent of her native land. She had loved it on sight, and she'd been fascinated with San Francisco, and Sausalito, and the wonderful little island of Tiburon. . . . Branwen turned from the snowscape to face her friend. "I admit I want the job *and* the move, but if I take it, I'm going to have to leave some things hanging."

"I hope you're not still thinking of trying to break through that cover-up." Ellen frowned, and the lines of distress looked out of place on a face that usually reflected the new contentment of a good marriage. "You can't, you know, not when it comes from that high up. And besides, if you'll forgive my saying so, Jason isn't worth it—even if he was your ex-husband."

"No. I'm willing to let that go." Branwen returned to sit in her chair. "It's Will Tracy and, to a certain extent, Harry Ravenscroft."

"I understand." Ellen nodded, her blond curls a nimbus around her head. "And I think I can help you there. I promise I'll let you know the minute there's news about either of them. My husband Jim is still working on finding Will. As for Harry, I'm sure he's all right. He's just off on some eccentric wild-goose chase and he'll return to Raven Hill eventually. You'll see."

Branwen wished she could be as sure as Ellen that Harry was all right, but she knew things Ellen did not know. Often she'd been tempted to tell her friend about the mysterious Cognoscenti, to enlist Ellen's help in finding out who those people really were, what they really did. But she had not done so, out of concern for Ellen's safety. And her own. Branwen sighed and unconsciously stroked the braid of hair that fell over her shoulder. "I suppose I could give Mrs. Beecher a phone number, and she'd call me if Harry shows up without warning. I'd have to persuade her that California isn't the end of the earth. But as for Will. . . . I'm convinced he's alive, Ellen. What does your husband say these days?"

"Same old things. Oh, I guess he's refined his thinking since you and I last talked about it. Jim thinks the most likely place for Will to try to get to is Kuwait. There are undercover people looking for him, Branwen. If you're right and he's still alive, then he's keeping himself well hidden, and that's all to the good. It can't be easy for him to disguise himself, and if he had any money, he's probably run out of it by now, so it's no wonder this is all taking so long. We can only wait."

"And keep on hoping," Branwen said.

"Yes." Ellen leaned forward and placed a solicitous hand on Branwen's knee. "Listen, I promise you I'll keep in close touch with everyone who's likely to know when Will is found, especially his father. You go on and take this job. Why, good heavens, all sorts of people commute back and forth from here to the West Coast all the time! When Will comes home, you can get here in a jiffy. You'll be here for him. That's what worries you most, that Will Tracy will return to Washington and find you gone—isn't it?"

"Yes, it is." Branwen's dark-fringed eyes were sad. "I want another chance with him, Ellen, but it may be too late."

"Nonsense! I'm living proof that it's never too late."

"If—no, *when* Will comes back, I don't want there to be a whole continent between us—and there will be if I take this job. They want me to sign a three-year contract, which makes sense considering the way I prefer to work. First I have to get to know the area well, and then any in-depth program is going to take at least a year to get off the ground. Once I sign I'll be committed—"

Ellen, afraid that Branwen was going to talk herself out of a good thing, interrupted firmly. "You can't put your whole life on hold for Will, Branwen."

Her eyes went to Ellen's face, and she did not like what she read there. "You think Will is dead. That's what you really believe."

"I haven't wanted to say so, but yes, I do believe he must be gone or else we would have heard something by now. I hope I'm wrong. One thing I do know—even if Will is alive, he's going to come back a changed man. You have to get on with your life and deal with these other things when and if they happen."

"You're right. I don't agree that Will is dead, but you're right about the rest." Branwen took a deep breath and mentally made the plunge. "I'll do it. I'll go home and call to tell them I'm accepting the job."

"Great!" Ellen leapt up to give Branwen a hug. "Come back tonight when Jim is here. Have dinner with us to celebrate!"

"No, thanks. Let's the three of us go out somewhere instead, but another time. Tomorrow? There's something else I have to do tonight."

The something else that Branwen had to do was tell Xavier Dominguez that she was going to leave Washington.

She hadn't expected that telling Xavier would be easy, and it wasn't. She hadn't expected him to like it, and he didn't; but he didn't storm at her either, and that was a surprise.

"That's all," Branswen asked, puzzled, "that's it? You're not going to blow my head off? Not going to try to change my mind?"

Xavier leaned back in his chair. They had met for dinner at a Georgetown restaurant, and because he'd been hearing Confessions into the early evening, Xavier wore his black suit and Roman collar. His shapely lips curved in a weary smile. Since the night she'd said she would not marry him, and virtually accused him—rightly—of using her as a way to resolve his struggles with the priesthood, Xavier had not been comfortable with Branwen. He was even a little bitter. He asked, "Do you want me to try to change your mind, Branwen?"

"No, but I didn't expect you to take this quite so calmly."

Xavier shrugged with a nonchalance he didn't feel. His bitterness was very close to the surface. "I'm tired, that's all. My inner resources are low. I've been hearing Confessions all afternoon, and that always takes a lot out of me. I don't expect you to understand."

Branwen shook her head wordlessly.

Xavier went on. He had pushed down his feelings for weeks in order to be there for her, especially after Jason's murder. He knew he shouldn't blame Branwen for the conflicts he felt in her presence; he had been the one to say that they would go on with their friendship as before. Nevertheless, he felt as if he had been on an emotional roller coaster. He was tired now, and he wanted to get off, but not before he let her know something of what he was going through. He leaned toward her and spoke with intensity, just above a whisper. "No, you don't know anything about Confession, do you? For instance, you have no idea what it costs me to hear Confessions when the whole time I know that I haven't yet made my own Confession. About you."

Branwen was concerned and baffled. "But, Xavier, there's nothing to confess! You and I never did anything wrong."

"I know you didn't, but I did. I knew I was falling in love with you but I continued to see you. Day after day, week after week, month after month, year after year. . . ." Exhaustion overcame him, and he covered his face with his hands.

"Xavier?" Branwen inquired softly. "Look at me, please."

He dropped his hands and lifted his head.

She said, "I can't believe there was anything wrong with the way you and I have loved each other. You taught me so many things about compassion and service to others. You taught me that I can be close to a man and trust him—and that wasn't easy, after being so traumatized by marriage to Jason that I even pushed Will away."

Xavier smiled sadly. "We weren't that close, Branwen."

"Yes, we were. We are. Always will be. Physical intimacy isn't so important. In fact, it may be the least important kind of intimacy."

"No," he said, slowly understanding; and as he understood, the lump of bitterness dissolved and released its grip on his heart. "It's not, is it? But I've been so tangled up in wanting physical intimacy with you, and not being able to have it, that I lost sight of what we did have. Do have."

Branwen shook her head. "Maybe you did at the last, but only then, Xavier. For quite a while you were the one in control, and I was the one always in danger of losing it, as far as the physical attraction thing was concerned. Why, I learned from you how to be close without having to have sex."

Slowly Xavier smiled. There was sadness still in his smile, but less of it. He was beginning to feel better. "I didn't mean for you to learn that from me, didn't know I was teaching it. I was just being a priest. And a bad one at that!"

"You're a good man, Xavier," said Branwen with conviction, "and an even better priest!" She remembered what she had seen when she was crushed in his arms, the Man and the Priest so inextricably bound together. "And you are likely to continue to be so, in spite of all your passionate struggles. So if that means you have to make a confession about me, about us, then you should do it."

"I will," he said solemnly. Then he brightened. "Enough of that. Tell me about your new job. Are you sure it's worth going all the way to California for?"

"Definitely," Branwen affirmed, and she told him about it. By the time they finished their meal, all the comfortable old camaraderie between them had returned.

They left the restaurant, and Xavier walked her to her car in the next block. The night was cold, clear, and windless. Branwen stopped on the sidewalk and looked up at Xavier. "I'll miss you, you know. You've been a big part of my life for so long."

"Likewise." His dark eyes gleamed in the light from a street lamp that made a chiaroscuro of his face. "You're not leaving yet, are you? I mean, we aren't saying good-bye?"

"Of course not. Never."

Xavier thought about the future, hers in California and his . . . *Yes.* In the priesthood. He would make that confession.

He took her in his arms for a moment before handing her into the car and allowed himself the briefest taste of her lips. He said, "I told you once, a long time ago, and it's still true, Branwen: Love is worth the pain."

2

———

Branwen wrote to her mother:

Dear Mam,

I wish you could see this northern California coast now, in winter. Maybe you and Dad could come for a visit, now that all the children are grown. Even little Rhys—how old is he now? Twenty-two or three? I'd send you money for the trip, if you will come. Surely by now you understand about Jason, or even if you can't understand, you must have forgiven me. You must realize he wouldn't have died the way he did if he hadn't been a very different sort of man from what you thought, and I thought, when I married him.

Anyway, I do wish you could see this. It is very like parts of Wales, but in truth it's even more beautiful. Inland there are forests of giant redwood trees—Sequoia sempervirens, they are called. Trees so old and majestic and so tall that they are as awe-inspiring as any cathedral; walking beneath them I feel closer to God than I ever felt in church. Can you imagine a tree over 100 meters tall? And they grow nowhere else on earth. If you want to see them, you have to come here.

Another thing: At certain times of year you can see whales just off the shore. I haven't seen them yet, but watching for them is more than half the fun. My favorite spot for whale watching is a lighthouse at a spectacular place called Bodega Bay. That's where I used to go on my weekends off, but this time I drove farther north, through a town called Albion . . . which reminded me of home and made me think of you. Just a few miles north of Albion is Mendocino, where I am now. I've fallen in love with this place, Mam. There's something very special about it, and I know already that I'm going to come here as often as I can. . . .

As often as I can. Branwen looked at the words she had just written, and an idea was born. Too excited to sit in her room any longer, she put aside her letter to finish later. She pulled on a gray-hooded sweatshirt over her jeans and white cotton turtleneck, and over that she threw a forest-green blanket-cloth cape that reached almost to her ankles. She had bought the cape because it was exactly what she needed for her weekend wanderings along the coast. Her boots were black, sturdy, good for walking. She had already explored the headlands of Mendocino, pleased to find that there were trails for walking along the bluff tops. The sea pounded against the rocks and rushed into tunnels it had carved in the cliff face, making wonderful, wild sea sounds. Where a river, identified as the Big River by a neatly posted sign, flowed into the ocean, there was a little bay bordered by a sandy beach. Best of all, this whole magnificent seaside approach to the town was preserved as a state park for people to enjoy and roam to their heart's content. A wonderful, wonderful place! She had walked long and returned tired to her hotel, but now she was out again, this time fired by her idea.

She wanted to find a little house, a cottage, a cabin—no matter how small, as long as she could rent it. A place of her own here in Mendocino, where she could come as often as she could get away. Most weekends, surely, and she had a whole week off between Christmas and the New Year. Winter was the off season in any seaside town, so she should be able to find a place for rent. Branwen flew through the streets with her dark green cape billowing behind her, past weathered picket fences around little Victorian-style houses equally weathered to genteel shabbiness. And not a single For Rent sign anywhere.

The next day Branwen took a more logical approach and bought a regional newspaper. Seeing the rents printed right there in black and white gave her a moment's pause, and she almost gave up her idea. Then she looked out of the window of the little restaurant where she was having breakfast, across the open area of scruffy grass to the bluff tops, up at the gulls wheeling in the misty gray sky, and she forced herself to be realistic. She *could* afford some of these rents, the ones on the lower end of the scale; she only felt that she couldn't because the salary she now earned still seemed more like a dream, and she'd been half afraid to spend it. She wanted to rent a place here more than she'd wanted anything in years. What else was all that money for? More excited now than scared, Branwen gave the newspaper her full attention, circling ads and making notes in the margins.

By nightfall the deed was done, the first month's rent and deposit paid, and a lease signed for a whole year! Her place was called McClosky's Cabin, McClosky having been a fisherman now long dead, according to the present owner, Mrs. Simmons. The cabin was on the outer limits of the town, but it was at the ocean end of its short street, with nothing to obstruct its view to the bluff tops. In warmer weather with the windows open, she would be able to hear the pounding sea. Branwen checked out of her hotel so that she could spend the remaining night and day of her three-day weekend in her own cabin.

She immediately took to calling the place simply McClosky. It was one big room, plus a narrow bedroom and a bathroom in a sloping-roofed lean-to addition. On the outside it was the same silvery-gray weathered cedar as most of the houses in town, but it was plain, shaped like a box, with no porch or architectural embellishments. It had windows, though, large for the size of the house, many-paned. Inside it was cozy, with a huge wood-burning fireplace the owner said she would need to use most of the year. Wood was provided regularly as part of the rental. One corner of the big room was fitted as a kitchen with butcher-block countertops and a breakfast bar that served as a room divider. A motley collection of pots and pans hung on a circular wire rack suspended from the ceiling. There was a stainless-steel double sink and a large frost-free refrigerator that matched a recent-model electric stove. The furniture was a hodgepodge of colors and styles but comfortable and clean. An oval braided rag rug added yet more color. The windows had curtains of coarsely woven soft off-white cotton, hung from wooden rings on a wooden pole, to be drawn by hand. The bedroom had only a long narrow window running horizontally near the eaves; since it was too high up to see directly out of or into, it had no curtain. The bedroom was cramped, all right, with its one double bed pushed into a corner, but Branwen didn't mind. She lay in the bed looking up through the window and wondered if on a clear night she might be able to see the stars. She fell asleep thinking of Will, thinking that he would like McClosky. He would like the unpretentious warmth and the nearby healing presence of the sea.

The rental of McClosky contributed further to the solitary life-style Branwen adopted in California. Unlike Washington, D.C., with its relentless social pressures and people's insatiable need to know what everyone else was doing, San Francisco seemed to encourage individualism. The city was both cosmopolitan and just plain fun. People smiled a lot—at the cable cars, *on* the cable cars, at the flower carts where one could buy a bunch of violets for three dollars, at dogs and cats, and at each other.

Branwen lived in an apartment on Green Street near the top of the hill. Every morning she would climb the one block to the top, up a sidewalk angled to about forty-five degrees, and catch a cable car to work. The trolley went down the hill, past Union Square, bumping through a maze of tracks over to Market Street. There she would hop off and walk the rest of the way to the television studios in a high-rise building near the financial district. Even in this more staid part of town, tolerance for individual differences was evident—mostly in the way people dressed. Gradually Branwen realized that the variety of clothing she saw on people in the district and on the elevators in her building did have certain rather interesting limits. Though both men and women often departed from the gray-suit/white-shirt norm, they did not depart into casual dress; rather they wore clothes with a kind of quirky elegance, a careful carelessness. Branwen's own naturally eccentric manner of dressing fit in very well.

She had been hired to write and produce material on social issues, in both long and short format. She was given carte blanche with one exception: She was not to cover homosexuality, which the station directors felt had already been overdone. Branwen worked hard. For the first several months she was out on the streets daily, picking up short pieces for the noon or evening news, or both. This was her way of getting to know the city. Since, like most sensible San Franciscans, she left her car garaged during the week, she learned to get around on buses, BART—Bay Area Rapid Transit—and an occasional cable car. She hailed a taxi if there was an emergency or if she ran short of time. Sometimes in a crunch she would have to tape her own piece; when that happened, she found that she did not mind being in front of the camera as much as she had in the past. She thought she must be mellowing with age.

Experience had taught Branwen that out of the short pieces a larger picture would emerge, and from that larger picture eventually one or two issues would leap out and grab her. Then her real specialty would come into play, and she would do a one-hour program. Or she'd produce a series of shorter programs on the one issue. That had not happened yet. There were the usual homeless mentally ill, drug problems, poor people dispossessed out of their homes by developers, and more disgruntled well-organized subgroups than she had seen in Washington, but nothing stood out and demanded her special attention.

To find that something special, one had to have an instinct, had to both talk and listen to people—all sorts of people. Branwen did that, day after day. Weekends she was off on her own exploring; once she had found Mendocino and rented her cabin, she was off to McClosky every chance she got. She gained a reputation as an insatiable worker and a loner. She didn't mind. She enjoyed hard work and at least for now she wanted no new close friendships. In her heart she knew she was waiting, waiting for Will. But as more months passed with no word, she tried to forget and devoted herself more diligently to finding that one issue she could really sink her teeth into.

When she had been in San Francisco almost a whole year, she found her issue. She had gotten permission to spend two days accompanying a police social worker on her rounds, and she discovered how much of the woman's time was spent answering calls or complaints about aging people living alone. These people, almost always women, had fallen through society's cracks. They were not on welfare, so the regular social workers knew nothing of them; they had no family to look after them, and all their close friends had died, leaving them alone. They would be ignored until some kind of crisis occurred, and then the police would be called. Branwen decided that a one-hour program on this subject would be overwhelming, so she did a series of shorts instead.

The short spots, usually five minutes, were easy to organize.

She did it by neighborhood, since this was a city-wide problem, one that knew no barriers of geography or social class; even the wealthiest did not escape, as they were often at the mercy of those they paid to look after them . . . and in this they did not always use good judgment. Branwen served as her own reporter and made the tapes herself, doing her interviews and commentary.

In one of San Francisco's oldest and most elite neighborhoods, through a tip from a newspaper vendor, she discovered a poignant situation that she knew could be the highlight of her series. In an elegant old townhouse that looked closed but well tended, as if the owner seldom visited, there lived five old nuns. The house was their convent, and it was identified as such by a narrow brass plaque on the door, much too unobtrusive to be read from the sidewalk. These nuns were the last of their Order and lived together in a poverty they were too proud to disclose. When Branwen persuaded one of them to admit her, she was astonished both by the once-elegant austerity of their home and by their age—all were well over eighty. For years the only human being to lay eyes on them had been the priest appointed as their spiritual director, and for his visits they saved their best tea and gave him costly treats they would not buy for themselves. They were literally starving and baffled by a world in which the most vital of their Sisters had left the Order, and no new young women had been interested to take the places of those who had left.

Branwen ended her series with two segments on the old nuns, unforgettable in their voluminous, medieval-looking habits that almost, but not quite, hid their emaciation. In soft voices they told of their plight factually, without a hint of complaint or self-pity; their faces shone with the light of their faith—thin, translucent skin stretched over features starved to bone—while they declared that their God would sustain them. The images of that final piece were burned into the brains of all who watched; everyone had to be moved. Best of all, donations poured in to the station, and the nuns and many others had food again.

Branwen had scarcely had time to catch her breath from this success when Ellen's call came.

Will Tracy was found. He had been taken to a military hospital in Germany for a routine medical checkup. After that he would be flown to Washington for debriefing. Since he had no military or Intelligence connection, the debriefing should take only a few days, and he did not have to stay in "secure" quarters. He could stay at Ellen's, and he was expected. Branwen must come, Ellen said, as soon as possible.

"I will," Branwen breathed into the telephone. "Oh, yes, I will!"

She made her preparations in a strange sort of daze. She had waited for this for so long that now she was almost superstitiously afraid to feel elation. At one point in her packing she found herself tiptoeing from bed to closet as if the slightest misstep might eliminate the fragile good news. The night following Ellen's call she was on an eleven P.M. flight from San Francisco International direct to Kennedy in New York, where she would take an early-morning commuter flight to Washington.

Branwen had been gone only a little over a year, but it seemed longer as she sped in her rented car along the McLean road, looking for the familiar gates of Ellen's estate. *Slow down!* she warned herself. Her pulse was racing, much like the motor of the car. The gates appeared on her left, and she turned in. Ellen's woods were denser than she remembered, thick with evergreens, and the drive was narrower. She felt claustrophobic after the wide California spaces to which she had so quickly grown accustomed. She spared the barest glance for the little guest house as she passed it. Now she began to think of Will in earnest. Her heart pounded. Could he have arrived before her? Or was he still at the hospital in Germany? Was he en route, at this very moment flying above the Atlantic . . . in a plane that could crash into the ocean so that she would never, ever get to see him again?

"Don't even think such things!" Branwen chided herself. She pulled her car into the parking area and took time out. Closing her eyes, she forced herself to take deep, slow breaths. She prayed silently: *God, and all my friends out there, bring Will safely home!* She had prayed these same words many times before, but now, she hoped, would be the last. Then she slung her big leather purse over her shoulder, along with her carry-on bag, and draped the dress bag over her arm. With one knee she urged the car door shut, then walked up the flagstone path to the front door.

Ellen herself, in a fuzzy blue dressing gown with a blue ribbon in her unruly curls, answered the bell. "Hi, sweetie! You're bright and early." She hugged and chatted, deftly relieving

Branwen of her burdens and shepherding her toward the break-fast room. "We're just finishing breakfast. You come and join us. I'll bet you didn't eat a thing on the plane. You didn't sleep either, did you? Your eyes look positively hollow! But some food and a nap will fix you right up. Look, Jim honey, here's Branwen."

Gratefully Branwen let Ellen take charge—something no-body could do better than Ellen Carew Harper.

"I see my wife has already taken you in hand." Jim chuckled, rising to greet Branwen. "Glad to see you again, glad you could come."

"Thank you," Branwen acknowledged. She was always a lit-tle embarrassed to realize, as she did again now, that in between the times she saw Jim Harper she invariably forgot what he looked like. His disarmingly ordinary appearance was, she knew, one of the things that had made him an outstanding agent for the FBI. He was average height, average weight, with a face neither handsome nor plain. His eyes were medium brown and so was his hair, though tastefully touched with the gray his age had earned for him. One had to look closely to discern the deci-sive firmness of jaw, the economy of movement, or the rock-hard musculature that were also marks of his former profession.

"Here you are, and don't say you can't eat because no one can resist Ada's biscuits. And her scrambled eggs are heaven," said Ellen, putting a full plate in front of Branwen while Jim poured coffee from a thermal carafe on the table.

"Smells wonderful," said Branwen, "but who is Ada?"

"She's our new cook. She lives in. That way I have more time with Jim, and there's someone here when we're gone. Now to the important stuff. How long can you stay, and why didn't you tell us when your plane got in? We'd have met you at the air-port."

"I wanted to rent a car. I thought I'd need one—for one thing, I'll be driving out to Raven Hill to see the Beechers while I'm here. I can stay for a few days. I said I had a personal emer-gency, that I didn't know how long it would take. Uh, I take it Will hasn't arrived yet? Do you know when to expect him? Is there anything else you didn't tell me over the phone?"

Jim answered, "He'll be on an Air Force jet into Langley by midafternoon today. I'll go pick him up. I expect we'll have him to ourselves for two to three days while he's debriefed, then they'll have to let his father know he's back. He's being treated very much as if he'd been undercover—aside from giving him the okay to stay here—but Ellen says he wasn't an agent to her knowledge. Of course, she wouldn't or shouldn't have known. What about you, Branwen, do you think Will was an agent?"

"No. In fact, he told me he wasn't."

"Well, maybe. Yesterday I talked to the CIA man here who was instrumental in getting Will out. He also denied that Will was one of theirs, but of course where I came from we wouldn't take the word of CIA for much. Anyway, this CIA guy said one of their people in Saudi Arabia learned there was an American hiding in a little village on the coast of the Persian Gulf, offering to pay to be taken across to one of the American-run oil fields. It was the kind of break our people had been hoping for, and they got right on it, got Will out before the Ayatollah's men could hear the same rumor. We hear Will's in pretty good shape physically . . . as for the rest, we'll have to wait and see. Don't forget, your friend was alternately on the run and in hiding, his life under constant threat, for almost two years."

The food in Branwen's mouth tasted as if it had turned to ashes. She had tried never to think how long it had been. She gulped and murmured, "I can't imagine what he's been through."

Ellen reached out and squeezed her hand. "Whatever he's been through, he'll come out all right. Will Tracy is made of strong stuff, and he has us. He has *you*. We'll just have to do all we can before his father gets hold of him."

"Wh-what do you mean?" Branwen asked. "Don't you like the senator? I never heard anything about Will not getting along with his father."

Ellen shrugged. "Their personalities are very different, that's all. I don't think *I'd* want to recuperate from a traumatic experience with the senior Wilbur F. Tracy hanging over my shoulder."

"You just want the young man here"—Jim smiled at his wife—"so you can play Mother Hen and cluck and fuss over him. Not that you aren't good at it."

"As one who has been clucked and fussed over"—Branwen also smiled at Ellen—"I can testify that she's *very* good at it. The best. Anyway, Will isn't really a young man anymore—he's over forty. I expect he'll have something to say about where he does his recuperating."

Jim's bland face looked doubtful. "I don't know. I've seen

men come out of similar situations and after initially being kind of up, they often sink into a lethargy. Will may not be able to make many decisions for quite a while."

Branwen and Ellen were not allowed to go with Jim Harper to meet Will's plane; his arrival was to be kept as quiet as possible. The two women gave up trying to talk to each other and simply waited. Ellen thumbed through magazines, while Branwen sank into a semimeditative state to counter her anxiety.

At last the moment came. They would have known him, of course, in spite of his near emaciation. But Will's ordeal had changed him to a shocking degree. His careless slouch had become a stoop. His eyes had the slightly glazed, inward-turned look of one who has seen too much of things better never seen. They flickered when he saw Branwen, like a candle with too short a wick trying and failing to keep a flame. "Branwen," he said. "You're really here."

"Yes, Will, I'm really here," she affirmed, and went on to say as she had long planned to say, "From now on I'll always be with you, as long as you want me."

They stood a short distance apart, filling their eyes with each other. Ellen and Jim faded tactfully into the background.

Will smiled, a ghost of the old shy gentle smile, his head cocked a bit to one side. Branwen's heart lurched, and she went to him. She took one hesitant step, and then as his arms came up to reach for her, she flung herself forward and wrapped her own arms around his too-thin body. She buried her head against his chest, and warmth rushed through her when she heard the reassuring thump of his heartbeat. He clutched her to him, at first awkwardly, and then his hands began to stroke her as if he were teaching himself anew the contours of her body.

"You're really here," he said again. "Bran-wen—" His voice broke on her name.

Branwen raised her face, tears streaming down her cheeks. "Will, oh, Will!"

"Don't cry," he whispered. The flame flickered in his eyes again and held. Burned. He bent his head to her as she yearned upward. With agonizing hesitancy his lips sought hers—the taste, the touch, the feel of her so fine, so familiar. He tasted more, shifted his weight to mold her body fully against his length, and slowly, surely, found his way into a lover's kiss.

Branwen kissed him back, her lips moving under his, all the longing in her soul reaching out and giving herself to him, drawing him into her. Time had no meaning; her whole world turned on the point of this one reuniting kiss.

Ellen and Jim Harper, who had not known quite what to expect, saw that their presence was not needed. Hand in hand, by mutual unspoken agreement they left the room.

Branwen and Will did not speak for a long time; their hearts were too full for words. Eventually they moved to one of the two couches that flanked the fireplace and with arms entwined sat in shared, silent wonder.

Finally Will spoke, sounding much like his old unassuming self. "You know how in those corny movies some guy has been in prison or lost in the desert or something, and he says to the girl, 'What kept me alive was the thought of seeing you again'? Or he says, 'I kept remembering your face, and it was the only thing that kept me from going insane'? Well, that was what happened, Branwen. I knew I had to stay alive so that I could see you again."

Tears started fresh in Branwen's eyes; she blinked them back. She murmured, "I always believed you were alive. I kept on hoping that somehow you'd find your way back here. Back to me." She moved a bit apart to look at his dear face. "Do you want to talk about it? I don't mind if you'd rather not. It's enough that you're here, safe."

Will countered with his own question. "Did I hear you right before? Did you really say you'd be with me as long as I want you, or was I dreaming again?"

"You weren't dreaming. I had a long, long time to think, to look back over all the years and, with that famous clarity of hindsight, see the mistakes I made with you. I promised myself that if I could have another chance, I'd stay with you for as long as you'll have me."

With long, thin fingers that trembled slightly, Will traced the outline of her face, from the widow's peak to the temple, the delicate curve of ear, the firmness of jawline to chin. Hesitantly, he said, "I can't believe there hasn't been someone else for you all these years. Ellen's husband told me you've moved to San Francisco. I was afraid to ask if you'd gone out there to get married. I didn't hear much of what he said after that—I kept on thinking you must have met someone out there, and how did

you meet. Or you fell in love with someone here, and he was
transferred so you followed him. . . ."

"No." Branwen captured Will's hand and laced her fingers
through his. "It's work. A very good job, nothing more. I didn't
know a soul when I got there, and I've kept pretty much to myself ever since. I found a place I like on the coast north of San
Francisco, and I've rented a cabin there. I go alone as often as I
can. It's a wonderful place—you'd like it."

"Is it cool? I think I've heard that part of the country is cool
all the time."

"Yes, it's almost always cool, seldom really cold. Lots of
mist that feels cool and fresh on your skin."

"It sounds like heaven. Where I've been, I sometimes
thought I'd never want to be out of walking distance of an air
conditioner—that is, provided I got out—for the rest of my
life!"

Branwen felt encouraged by Will's joking tone. She had preferred to remember Will that way, with his easy temperament,
always ready to laugh at himself—not as the tense, self-blaming
man who'd spent a difficult night at her apartment before returning to Iran. She squeezed his hand and waited to see what
else he would say.

He said, "I grew a beard and wore a turban, like a Sikh because Sikhs are tall. You know, to disguise myself. I never want
to wear a beard again, either." He raised their interlocked hands
to his lips and kissed her knuckles. "Suppose I tell you the rest
when we're all together. Ellen and, uh—"

"Jim."

"Thank you. Ellen and Jim—it's hard to believe Ellen is married, isn't it? She got married, not you. So much is hard for me
to believe. Anyway, Ellen and Jim will want to hear it, too, and
I don't want to go over it more than I have to. Branwen, you do
know about—about—"

"About your wife and son? Yes, Will, we know. I'm sorry."

"So am I," he whispered. Will untangled his fingers from
hers and, in a daze, stood up. "I think maybe I might, uh, rest for
a while. Uh, before dinner. I'm not even sure what time it is. I
sold my watch about a million years ago."

"Come on." Branwen was beside him, taking his arm and
steadying him. "We'll buy you a new watch tomorrow. I'll take
you shopping, or else Jim will if you prefer. For now, let's go

upstairs, and I'll show you to your room. You have plenty of time to nap before dinner."

"I can't believe I'm here," Will said, shaking his head as they climbed the stairs.

After dinner the four of them sat in the den, a room Ellen had seldom used before marrying Jim. It was his domain, masculine, full of leather and books and photographs, a cozier place than the living room with its large expanse of glass. Jim started to light the fire laid in the small fireplace, but Will stopped him.

"Do you mind if we don't have a fire? I know it's—what is it, October? But I, uh, I—"

"He prefers the cold," Branwen supplied. "He was too hot for so long. And, yes, Will, it's October."

"Yeah, I was too hot," Will agreed. "How did you know that?"

"You told me this afternoon before you went up to rest."

"Oh, yeah." Will rubbed his hand across his forehead and up to the shining bald crown of his head. He seemed different than he had been just after his arrival. All through dinner he'd been a little vague, often at a loss for words, and his eyes had had again that inward-turned look.

He's just tired, Branwen thought, *of course he's tired.*

Ellen, who wore a long, soft dress of gold-colored cashmere, curled up beside her husband on a leather two-seater couch. Branwen, in a skirt of purple wool and a pale green cowl-necked top, sat somewhat anxiously in a deep leather chair. Will, in a similar chair, rubbed his head again and cleared his throat.

"I'd like to tell you what happened," he began.

"If you're sure you want to," said Jim in a carefully neutral voice. "You're going to have to tell your story over and over for the next couple of days. We don't want to put any pressure on you here. We want you to regard this as your home."

"I want Branwen to know," Will said, looking directly at her, "and I thought I'd just, uh, tell all three of you at the same time."

Ellen and Jim both inclined their heads in understanding, and Will told his story.

"We didn't have the warning I'd hoped we'd have before the revolt. I'd been trying for weeks to persuade Aletha to leave Teheran with me and bring Paul, too, but she wouldn't budge. I

was frustrated and nervous, and I went ahead making plans anyway but I wasn't as on top of things as I thought. That morning,
everything seemed to happen all at once. Noise, people breaking in and running all over the house. They had guns, rifles.
They shot Aletha and Paul and some of the servants who got in
the way. She'd gone after Paul as soon as all the commotion
started. They were in her bedroom, that's where they were . . .
shot. I was in another part of the house, getting money and pass-
ports and all that. I don't know why they didn't come after me,
but they didn't. One of the servants, a woman, ran in and told
me my wife and son were dead. She kept pulling at me, saying I
had to get out before they came back, and she would take me
where it was safe. But I wouldn't go until I'd seen my wife and
the boy. . . ."

Will broke off, his hands digging into the arms of the chair.
His face was haggard but otherwise without emotion. His voice
throughout all of this was flat. "They were just—just so dead! I
didn't know what to do, I couldn't think. Before that I'd been
pretty organized, mainly concerned about having enough
money to buy our way out, and after I saw them lying there everything sort of clicked off."

"You were in shock," Jim said.

"I guess so. Anyway, the woman, whose name I couldn't remember, took me by the hand and led me out of the house. I
think she threw some sort of robe or cloak or something over
me but I'm not sure. She had hold of me, and we just kept walking, walking, through all the noise and the killing. To this day I
don't know why I wasn't killed."

"If they'd caught you, they'd have used you as a hostage,"
said Jim.

"Maybe. I remember walking through the streets, and then
there's just a blank, like I blacked out or something. A couple of
days later I came around and I realized I was in this woman's
house, in a tiny little room with no window, hot as blazes, and
that she'd probably saved my life. I tried the door, and it was
locked, and then I thought she was keeping me a prisoner—I
didn't think hostage, I thought prisoner. I didn't care. She'd
bring me food and water and some male in her family would
take me out of the room to use the bathroom a couple of times a
day. They'd talk to me in Farsi—I understand the language but
I didn't listen and I didn't talk to them. I suppose I ate the food.
I don't remember. Most of the time I slept.

"After a while they started leaving the door open at night. Their house had a small courtyard in the middle, open to the sky. I guess the fresh air sort of revived me. And it was cooler at night. I'd crawl out there and look up at the stars. Finally, days or weeks later, I figured out they were hiding me. I couldn't be their prisoner because they hadn't taken anything. I had a lot of money I'd been wearing in a money belt, and I'd taken it off when she gave me one of those things the natives wear, looks like a dress, you know, loose—and I wore it because it was cooler than my own clothes. I'd tossed the money belt in a corner, and it was still there with all the money in it, and a ruby and two diamonds I'd put in there for heavy-duty emergencies. I began to get better after that, after I realized I wasn't their prisoner after all. I ate more, asked for something to read, and the woman brought me magazines. But I still didn't talk much—for some reason I couldn't talk."

"Of course you couldn't!" Ellen cried sympathetically.

"I lost track of time very early on." Will hadn't heard Ellen; he was lost in his story now. "I still had my watch, didn't sell it until a lot later, and the watch had the days and dates and all. But I just didn't look at it, didn't want to know. So I have no idea how long I'd been in that house when one night the woman came with a man she said was her cousin. He gave me more clothes, native clothes with a burnoose-looking thing for my head, and said I was to come with him out of the city to a village where I'd be safer.

"After that it was much the same wherever I went. I'd stay in a village, only go out at night, and when I'd been in one village for a while, I'd offer money to be taken to another. I was afraid to stay in one place too long. Somewhere along the line I got enough sense back to realize I didn't know where the hell I was, and I paid a kid to get me a map. The kids were the best, they always could get you things—food, a knife, whatever. Anyway, that map was a nasty surprise. I'd been moved along in the direction of Afghanistan, which I figured was the wrong way to go. I became more active, took more risks. I went out in the daytime, got the right clothes and a cloth for a turban so I could dress like a Sikh. I already had the beard, and Sikhs are tall—it was the best way I could think of to disguise myself. I could get by as long as I kept my mouth shut. I started to walk back the other way, toward the Persian Gulf, with my map to guide me. A lot of the time I couldn't find the name of whatever village I was in on the map, but I kept going. I never saw a single American, never heard a word of English. When I got tired or sick or scared, I'd pick a village and hole up for a while. I ran out of money and sold my watch, and then the diamonds one at a time for a lot less than they were worth. I knew it was dangerous to sell them because it attracted attention to me, but I was lucky. I got away with it.

"Finally I made it to a village within a few miles of the Gulf. I was going to use the ruby for payment to get me across to one of the American-run oil fields, but I didn't have to. You know the rest. It was good to find out that people had been looking for me. I know, actually, that a lot of people were good to me and helped me along the way, but I didn't *feel* good about it. Not at the time."

"How *did* you feel," Branwen asked, "when you were going from one place to the next for so long?"

"Hot. Tired. Discouraged. I just kept on going, wanting to survive." Will's eyes locked on hers. Unashamed in front of Ellen and Jim, without joking this time, he said, "I thought about you, Branwen. I wanted to survive so that I could see you again."

"And you did survive," Ellen cried, jumping up from the couch in a swirl of gold cashmere to put both arms around Will, "and we are so very proud of you!"

"I'm more than proud, I'm impressed," Jim declared from the couch. "I don't know how you did it, but you did a damn fine job staying alive and making all the right moves to get yourself out of there. What say we all have a drink to that, eh? I put some champagne on ice earlier. I had a hunch we might be wanting it."

"That's a wonderful idea." Ellen made to move from the arm of Will's chair where she'd perched, but Jim stopped her.

"You stay where you are and keep Will company, love. Branwen will help me, I'm sure."

"Yes, of course," Branwen agreed, but she was puzzled. How much help could a grown man need with one bottle of champagne and four glasses? She followed Jim to the kitchen where she found that things were still as she remembered. With no trouble at all she located tulip-shaped glasses and a small silver tray.

"I'd like to tell you something about your courageous friend," said Jim, twisting the wire on the cork of the champagne bottle so that it came out without popping. "And I hope you won't take offense."

"Why should I?"

"I noticed during dinner and in the den with that business about not lighting the fire. . . . Damn, there's no easy way to say this, but it has to be said. You're being too protective, Branwen. You're hovering too much. Haven't you noticed that when he's temporarily at a loss for words, you finish his sentences for him?"

"I know what he's thinking," she said defensively, "and I want to help."

"That's a mistake, believe me. I've seen men, women, too, coming off of experiences not one tenth of what Will Tracy has been through, and there's a pattern. When he finally and completely understands that it's all over, he's home, and he's safe, he's going to crash. Come unglued. Hell, he's close to it already, he's beginning to come unraveled at the edges. You aren't quite real to him now because he's idealized you. Everything you do or say takes on a magnified importance to Will right now, and it will be that way until he's fully recovered. That's a strong man there, Branwen. Maybe, as he says, he was lucky. But mainly it was strength of character that got him through. Ellen has told me a lot about Will Tracy, Jr., and about you, too. Now that I've met him, I suspect people helped him because there's an innate kind of goodness in the man, and people respond to that. Even I do, hardened old G-man that I am!"

Branwen smiled. "Yes, Will's a good person. And in a strange way, all he's been through confirms my belief in his strength. I wasn't so sure—I thought, when he was here in the winter before all this hell broke loose, that the marriage and the years in the State Department had somehow broken him. He wasn't himself at all then."

"He was *here*?"

"Yes, briefly. He didn't tell anyone because he was making arrangements to get himself and his family out, but his plans fell through. I saw him for just one night."

"Hmmm. Well, let me finish what I was saying. They'll wonder what's taking us so long. Will is going to crash, it's only natural. Because everything you say and do has an exaggerated importance, if you treat him like a child or like an emotional invalid, he'll believe that's what he is. He could even conclude that he's not man enough for the goddess he's made of you, and

that could ruin your relationship. When he falls, so to speak, let
him pick himself up. Or let Ellen help him, he can take it from
her. *You* look the other way. Give him space. If he withdraws
from you, let him go. He'll come after you when he's himself
again."

"Not help him?" Branwen's eyes were clouded with doubt.
"You're sure you're right about this?"

"I'm certain. Now let's go back. We'll drink to the reunion of
two lovers. I didn't say not to love him, you know!"

For the next two days Branwen saw little of Will, and from
what she did see she had to admit that Jim Harper had been
right. Will's crash took the form of a gentle, bemused abstrac-
tion. Jim drove him to and from his debriefing. Jim drove him to
Bethesda for a psychiatric evaluation. Ellen took Will to buy the
clothes and other things he needed, and she reported to
Branwen that it had been like outfitting a child. Branwen paid
dutiful visits to the Beechers, to Xavier and the folks at 622, to
her former colleagues at PBS, but her heart wasn't in it. She
wanted only to be with Will.

On the third day, Will did not have to go anywhere; they were
finally through with him in Washington. He wandered about
Ellen's house in his new clothes, a blue cable-knit sweater and
gray slacks, looking pale, handsome, and lost. Warnings or no
warnings, Branwen had had enough. She tracked Will down sitting in the inglenook and staring into the empty fireplace.

Slowly Will looked up; slowly he smiled. "Hi."

"Hi. Do you have any plans for today?"

"No, I don't think so. Not really. I guess I really should call
my father, but I don't feel like doing it yet."

"There's somewhere I want to go, and I could use some company. Want to come?"

"Well, maybe. Where are you going?"

"To see somebody who reminds me of you. Come on, come
with me."

Branwen drove her car across the Potomac, into the Tidal Ba-
sin where she parked. The weather was fine, crisp with advancing autumn. Will walked docilely at her side. From the corner of
her eye she saw that Will's interest perked up as they walked.
He sniffed the air, and his shoulders straightened. *Good,* she
thought, *this isn't a mistake.* Boldly she reached out and took his

arm; with her other hand she pointed to their destination, shining white in the morning sun.

"There," she said. "That's where we're going."

"The Jefferson Memorial?"

"That's it! I thought I'd pay a call on Mr. Jefferson."

Will actually grinned—he was pleased. And that pleased Branwen.

They stood before the tall statue. Will said, looking around and up into the domed roof, "You made a good TV show here once."

"You remember."

He put his arm around her. "Of course I remember. I remember everything about you."

Branwen looked up at Will, then farther up at Jefferson. "I always thought he looked like you. Don't you think so?"

Will looked up, squinted, and then chuckled. "I guess so," he said, "except that he has more hair than I do." And then he kissed her.

Branwen returned Will's kiss with all the desperate hunger she had been feeling for the past three days. Her arms went around his neck, and she clung to him.

Barely separating his lips from hers, Will whispered, "Do that again!" Branwen kissed him again, with even more desperate passion. Will held her tenderly, his long-fingered hands pressing her to him at the small of her back and between her shoulder blades. He was so moved by her kisses that his whole body shook. At last he said softly, "You don't know how long it has been since I felt what I've just felt from you." He moved her out of his arms so that he could search her face. His own face was alight with wonder. "You want me, that's what I felt in your kiss. You want me, don't you, Branwen?"

Her eyes were darkened by the intensity of that wanting. "Yes, I do. You have no idea how much."

"Ah-h-h," Will breathed, closing his eyes. Lines of strain faded from his face on that sigh. "I was afraid. I thought when you always seemed busy and it was Jim or Ellen who went places with me, I thought you were just being kind that first day. That once you'd had a good look at me and heard the whole story, you were . . . turned off."

"Oh, no! I was giving you space. They said I should let you find your own way—" Branwen broke off as a party of tourists came chatting up the steps of the Memorial.

"We need to talk," Will said swiftly, taking Branwen by the hand, "and this obviously isn't the place. Let's walk up the Mall—we ought to be able to have a private conversation in all that open space."

As they walked, Branwen recounted an abbreviated version of the advice Jim had given, without identifying him as the source. Will listened, nodding now and then. When she was done, he said, "The psychiatrist in Bethesda told me much the same thing, about crashing, being unable to make decisions, and so on. It really threw them when I turned in my resignation. I'm not supposed to be able to make any decisions but I was hard-nosed about that one. I made them take it. That more or less blew their minds. You realize, of course, that Washington, D.C., has more experts per square inch than anywhere else in the Western Hemisphere—they'll tell you how to brush your teeth if you let them."

Will stopped talking and turned to Branwen. "You don't know how glad I am, now that I know it wasn't for another man, that you've left this place. I can't wait to get out myself."

"Really?"

"Yeah," Will said, grinning, "really. The trouble with all the experts is that they're suspicious of anyone who doesn't fit their pattern. I don't, and it had me going there for a while, reexamining myself. Especially since you seemed so distant."

"That's why you were so quiet?"

"Partly. Mostly it was plain old readjustment. You see, Branwen, according to the experts, once I believed I was really here I was supposed to crash, but I don't think I'm going to crash at all. I had a lot of trouble believing I'm really here, though; it has been pretty disorienting. I kept thinking, What if I'm hallucinating this whole thing and I come out of it to discover I'm still in Iran? Last night was the first time I went to bed and didn't think: I'll wake up in the morning and I won't be at Ellen's, it was all a dream."

"You believe it now?"

"Absolutely." The grin was now a wide smile. "The funny thing is I knew I finally believed it yesterday when the debriefing was over and those assholes at State didn't want to accept my resignation. The runaround they gave me was so typical—it was like Wham! Welcome back to bureaucracy, buddy! I didn't feel disoriented when I woke up this morning, either. And, like I said, I don't think I'm going to crash—at least, no more than I already have. I just want to get on with my life. That's what I was thinking about when you showed up this morning. You came at the perfect time, Branwen."

"I'm so glad! You do seem a lot better. Less, well, stunned. Less confused. I don't have to stay away from you anymore?"

"Don't you dare stay away any longer than you really have to! Shall we sit on one of these benches and rest before we hike back? I forget everybody isn't as used to walking as I am."

"No, I walk a lot. Let's go on back to the car. We can go get some lunch. Or we could sit here and finish our conversation and then go into the Smithsonian and wander around, and have lunch there."

"Yeah, what a great idea! I haven't been in the Smithsonian in years! We could look at the dinosaurs like I used to do when I was a kid."

Branwen laughed. Will was coming back to her by leaps and bounds this morning. She recalled his enthusiasm for the Smithsonian from when she was new in Washington and he had introduced her to that vast storehouse of knowledge. Her heart was filled with joy. "If you think the dinosaurs can wait for a few minutes, there is something I'd like to talk about. Especially since you mentioned earlier that you have to call your father."

"I don't think the Big Guys are in any shape to run off. They can wait." Will led Branwen to the bench and they sat. "Talk. I'm all ears."

She didn't know where to start. She felt shivery with expectation and so happy just to be sitting there next to him that she was almost speechless. Looking into the warmth of his hazel eyes, Branwen caught her breath as her heart leapt in her chest. She reached out and touched his cheek, traced the contours of his mobile mouth with a gentle finger.

"Unh-h-h," Will groaned. "You don't know what it does to me when you touch me like that! You know what this reminds me of? That first couple of years when we went all over the place and I was on fire for you half the time, but there was nothing I could do about it. We were never alone together."

"I was thinking much the same thing, only now it's better. It's wonderful, like the greatest possible gift. We've been given another chance with each other, Will. That's what I want to talk about. Is it too soon for me to ask if you'll come back to San Francisco with me? We don't have to, ah, live together if you don't want to. I don't know how close you want to be, and I'd understand if you aren't ready. I have two bedrooms in my apartment, so you could stay with me until you find your own place. I just thought, since you said yourself you don't want to stay in Washington . . ."

"Branwen." He clasped both her hands and said solemnly, "I want to be as close to you as you will let me be. I love you. I've never really loved anyone else but you."

There was silence between them for the space of several heartbeats. Then Branwen said, "I love you, too, Will. There hasn't been anyone else for me, either."

Will raised her hands to his lips and kissed each in turn. "I must say something important to you. The deaths of my wife and stepson were horrible, but that's over now. My marriage, like yours, is in the past. One good thing that came out of all the months I walked from village to village across Iran was that somehow, during all that time, I got over my guilt. I stopped feeling like a failure. You must remember how I was when I spent that one night with you—I'm not even ashamed about that anymore, and I certainly was for a long time after. I guess the hot Persian sun burned all the guilt and the shame out of me. I feel that I come to you clean, Branwen."

Branwen's face shone with her happiness. "Then you will come back with me!"

"I will. I can look for work in San Francisco as well as anywhere. I do need to see my father, though. How soon do you have to go back?"

"I'm not sure. I left it indefinite. I think I can manage another week. Is that long enough?"

"Yes, it's enough. I'll call Father tonight. We could go there, but it will be easier for me if I go on and invite him here, as Ellen has suggested. He's going to want me to stay at home in Kentucky with him until he's checked me out to his satisfaction, and I don't want that anyway. I've been trying to figure how to get out of it, and you solved that one for me! Father will make less of a fuss about me going to San Francisco instead of Kentucky if he's here. I wonder what you'll think of the senator."

"Maybe we'd better wonder what he'll think of me!"

"He'll be nuts about you as soon as he sees that beautiful face. I haven't told you, have I, that you're every bit as beautiful as I remembered?"

"And you, Will Tracy, are in every way *better* than I remembered. As soon as you've gained a little weight, you'll be perfect. Let's go see those dinosaurs now so that we can get to lunch and start putting the weight on you."

Laughing, holding hands, they crossed the street to the Smithsonian. As they climbed the steps of the castle, Will slipped his arms around Branwen's waist and bent his lips to her ear. "I love you," he whispered.

3

Ellen Carew Harper, in a Victorian-style nightgown trimmed with ribbons and lace, sat at her dressing table brushing out her curls with necessary vigor. She paused, brush in hand, when her husband emerged from the master bath with a towel wrapped around his waist.

"You know what I think?" she asked.

"No," he said and eyed her with amusement, "but I'm sure you're about to tell me."

"You bet I am. I think something happened between Branwen and Will today. I think they reached some sort of understanding and just haven't told us yet."

"Why do you think that?" Jim whipped off the towel and stood naked without self-consciousness, drying his hair.

"Because ever since they came back from their morning outing—which, by the way, they didn't do until the middle of the afternoon—they've been looking at each other the way people look when it's all they can do to keep their hands off of each other."

"I know how *that* is," said Jim, dropping the towel on the floor and advancing toward Ellen. "I've had a hard time keeping my hands off you since the first time I saw you!"

"Silly!" Ellen kissed and caressed him, and then playfully pushed him away. "You're such an impatient brute! Didn't you really see how it is between those two? And do you think it's all right? I remember what you said about Will's state of mind, and to tell you the truth, I don't want either of them to get hurt."

Jim, who always slept naked and delighted in divesting his wife of the confections she insisted on donning every night, turned his back on her and headed for the bed. He knew that she would soon follow. "Yes, love, I saw what you saw. There has been a remarkable change in Will Tracy in the past twenty-four hours. Whether the change will hold or not, I don't know. He is an unusual man; his experience seems to have strengthened him rather than shaken him. Then we must consider that, from what you've told me, Will and Branwen have loved each other for a long time. I think love is always right, and if you'll come over here, I'll be glad to give you a demonstration. . . ."

In another wing of the large house, Branwen was wishing she had brought something sexier to sleep in than the long T-shirts for which she had developed a preference through her many years of sleeping alone. Or that she had had the foresight or the optimism to go out and buy a pretty nightgown. But she hadn't. She sighed and pulled the pink T-shirt over her head. It dropped to the tops of her thighs. She unpinned her hair and let it fall, tossing her head. She hadn't cut her hair, except for trimming the ends, in almost as many years as it had been since she'd bought a real nightgown. It was almost as long as the T-shirt. She took her brush from the top of the chest of drawers, sat down on the bed, and began halfheartedly to brush her hair.

Perhaps I read the signals wrong, she thought. *Perhaps Will won't come to my room tonight.* If he didn't, should she go to him? No, she couldn't, not tonight. Maybe tomorrow, after she bought a new nightgown, something really beautiful, with ribbons and lace. . . .

There was a soft tap on her door. Branwen thought it *might* be Ellen—but in the space of that thought, the door opened soundlessly, and Will slipped inside the room.

"Hi," he said. He looked a little unsure of himself, and he was very fully dressed in all his new nightclothes: beige silk pajamas, a golden brown velour robe that almost matched his eyes, and tan leather slippers. "Mind if I come in?"

"Please do. I was hoping you'd come." Now that he was here, Branwen didn't care what she was wearing. She pulled her legs up under her, Indian fashion, and dropped her hairbrush, forgotten, beside her on the bed.

"I brought us this rather unusual nightcap." Will held up a quart bottle of mineral water he'd had behind his back. "I seem to have gone off alcohol—that champagne we had the other night disagreed with me. But if you'd like something stronger, I'll go back downstairs and get it for you."

"Mineral water is much healthier. I'd love some."

"Good. Uh, I've got a couple of glasses in my pockets."

Branwen's heart thumped as she watched him. How could he be both so strong and so ingenuous, so awkward yet so graceful? She felt she was getting to know Will all over again, and that the process was infinitely better the second time around. Better for the maturity they both had. Just as, somehow, with the hair gone from the top of his head and his features carved by the strong bone structure, Will was now a much handsomer man than he had been ten, twelve, fourteen years before. Had she known him, loved him, so long? She had.

"A toast," Will said, handing her a glass of the mineral water. His voice wavered a little as he proposed, "To us. To tonight, may it be the first of many, many nights together."

"How beautiful," Branwen said. She touched her glass to his, and they drank.

Will felt as nervous and as sexually charged as a seventeen-year-old. He hadn't been with a woman for two years. He knew he wouldn't be able to last, wouldn't be able to make it good for Branwen. He backed up, looked around, spied a chair, and sat in it. "I reached my father a while ago, after we all came upstairs."

"And?" Branwen knew his father had not been at home when he'd tried to call earlier in the day.

"And he wasn't totally surprised. He'd been notified that I was being brought back to Washington and that he'd be called as soon as the experts were through with me. He was his usual demanding self at first. Then he broke down and sounded glad that I'm alive. He's coming. He won't stay here, though. He likes hotels. Even when I had the Georgetown house, he'd always stay in his favorite suite at the Mayflower. That's where he'll stay. He'll drive, or, to be more precise, his driver will drive, and he'll arrive sometime tomorrow. I'm to have dinner with him alone at the Mayflower."

"Ellen will be disappointed that he isn't coming here. So am I, a little. But I suppose it's better for you to see him alone the first time."

"I'd rather have you with me. But there's so much to tell

him. . . . I hate to think about it. I hate to think about having to tell all that again, just when I feel I've begun to put it behind me."

"Then don't think about it. When the time comes, you'll just do it, and that will be that."

Gratefully Will looked across the room at Branwen. Once again, as had happened that morning, lines of strain faded from his face. "How simple you make it! You are so good for me! I feel like the luckiest man alive—oh, God, what a cliché. But I do."

"We're both lucky. It's like being able to fall in love twice with the same person, the *right* person. How many people get to do that?"

"Not many." Will's voice was husky. He approached the bed and picked up the brush. "I've always wanted to brush your hair. May I?"

"It's heavy work," Branwen teased. "Are you sure you're up to it?"

"Oh, I think so." Will sat next to her, and she turned her back. With long, sensuous strokes Will pulled the brush through her thick, silky hair. He smoothed it as he stroked with his other hand. The white streak had a different texture, slightly coarser than the rest. His fingers lingered on the streak, as he recalled her sorrow and her courage at the time the streak was made.

"That feels wonderful," Branwen murmured, "don't stop."

She had not meant to be provocative, but another meaning, an intimate, suggestive meaning for those particular words, leapt into Will's mind. He was fired to a growing desire. With each stroke of the brush his uncertainty faded. Each stroke of the brush became, in his mind, another kind of stroke.

Branwen was melting inside. She wanted him so much that she ached with an awareness of emptiness only Will could fill. She longed for him to take her, to fill her up until she brimmed over with him.

Will put the brush aside and lifted her heavy hair in his hands, spilling it through his fingers. The length and weight of it amazed him. "I love your hair, Branwen," he said. He moved closer to her, buried his face in the curve of her neck, working his way under that dark, silky curtain to kiss the softness of her skin. His hands moved down the contours of her slender arms. Her breath quickened. He felt her desire, and it urged him on. His hands moved to cup her breasts through the soft cotton shirt she wore; through the material he felt her nipples harden. She turned her face, seeking his kiss. He bent over her and his mouth claimed her seeking lips.

He could not be gentle for long in that kiss. He wanted her too much, and when her tongue touched his lips like sweet fire, he groaned, lost control, and devoured her. The organ of his manhood, so long unused, swelled and strained to a throbbing hardness. He gathered Branwen in his arms, his mouth still locked on hers, his tongue plunging ever deeper in a meaningful rhythm. His clothing and hers was a restriction he could no longer endure. She understood, she was with him, her fingers tore at his belted robe, flew to the buttons of his pajama top, and then in a swift movement her mouth left his to trail burning kisses across his chest.

"Branwen, Branwen," he said thickly, falling back on the bed. In heated wonder he let her remove the clothes she had loosed. Everywhere her fingers touched he burned; his skin was on fire with little rivers of flame. He could endure no more. He grasped her hands and rolled her onto her back. Somehow, while she had undressed him, she had also undressed herself. The sight of her long, white body, the shimmering globes of her breasts crowned by the exquisite pink buds of her nipples, brought tears to his eyes. "You are so beautiful," he whispered, and he bent to take a budding nipple in his mouth.

She gasped as his mouth touched her breast, as his tongue flicked the sensitive nipple to hardness and then delicately his teeth nipped, and he suckled hard and long. His hands moved, one beneath her, one above, and she could not help but writhe and moan under that arousing touch. Her legs parted. He moved his head to her other breast, to tend it as he had done the first, and as he did so, one hand slipped under her buttocks and the other through the damp triangle between her legs, slowly, slowly. She gasped as his fingers found and parted the folds of her sex, brushed and circled that most sensitive of spots. She was dying for him. "Will!"

He moved over her then. For a moment he hung above her, supporting his weight on his arms. Never had she seen so much passion in a face, so much love as she saw in his eyes. She opened her mouth to say his name once more, but his tongue plunged in, as in the same instant he plunged his shaft deep and hard inside her. He filled her completely, pushing, holding. He withdrew and plunged again, groaning as he did so, plunging deeper, harder. Again and again. Branwen cried out with joy. She wrapped her legs around him, met and matched every convulsive thrust. This was no gentle mating. It was a passionate, primitive celebration of love once lost, now found. An explosion of primeval bliss.

Panting, exhausted, glowing with happiness, Branwen and Will both fell instantly asleep, tangled in each other's arms. It was a profound rest they both deserved, hard-earned.

Branwen climbed carefully down an almost invisible track on the cliff face to a special spot she had discovered, a scooped-out place in the rock that accommodated her body as perfectly as if it had been made for her. There she could sit and gaze out across the ever-moving Pacific, while all around her, murmuring and moaning through its unseen, mysteriously carved passageways, the sea spoke. Today the ocean was quietly restless, almost but not quite contented. As Branwen was herself. She curled up in her rocky seat and looked out to the horizon. In a rare deep-blue sky, little clumps of jewel-colored clouds—amethyst, alexandrite, tourmaline—vied to cover the sun and make the water beneath reflect their colors. A flock of small brown-and-white-speckled birds dipped and wheeled, tossed on the salt-scented wind. It was good to be back in Mendocino.

Will was back at the cabin, at McClosky, trying to adjust to yet one more time change. And, she knew, he was trying to adjust to other things as well. All had not gone well with his father. The senator had opposed his son's decision to come to California, but Will had been adamant. Thus the senator had returned to Kentucky earlier than anticipated, gone off in a huff without visiting Ellen and Jim, without meeting Branwen. In fact, Will admitted that he had not even told his father about her; he had said only that he needed a completely fresh start and was going to California with "a friend." "He'll come around," Will had said to Branwen, "eventually."

In the meantime, with the senior Tracy's departure there was no reason for Branwen and Will to linger in Washington. Will swiftly concluded his affairs there, the only matter of any complexity being the sale of his Georgetown house to its renters. They had long wanted to buy the place and were anxious to close as soon as papers could be drawn up. Branwen had thought that she would introduce Will to Xavier before they left, but she changed her mind when she saw that dealing with his father had set Will back considerably. There hadn't been time, anyway. Instead of staying in Washington for another week, they had stayed only three more days.

It had not been an easy leavetaking. Jim Harper had looked doubtful about Will and Branwen going to California together, and he had been unable to hold his tongue even while his wife looked daggers at him. Ellen, as if to make up for her husband's skepticism, overdid her enthusiasm to the point of becoming flustered enough to ask, "When's the big day going to be, you two? When are you going to get married?" Branwen, shocked not only by the question but because Ellen of all people never got flustered, had blurted out, "We're not—that's not an option." Later, privately, she had taken Ellen aside and explained, "Will doesn't need that kind of pressure now. We haven't talked about marriage. It's enough that we'll be together."

It is *enough,* Branwen insisted to herself, hugging her knees. A flock of noisy gulls, like harbingers of discord, came wheeling on the wind. They seemed to fly right at her. Alarmed, she instantly and automatically threw up an invisible shield of the sort she had used to protect her thoughts when Harry Ravenscroft, or anyone, had tried to enter her mind. *Now why did I do that?* she wondered, watching the gulls veer away.

"It's enough that we're together," she said into the wind. The sea, sighing unseen through tunnels in the rocks beneath her, agreed. Add to that the happy surprise of being able to spend the remaining four days of her time off in Mendocino rather than in Washington, and she should be happy.

When she was with Will, she *was* happy. But when she was physically separated from him even by a short distance, as she was now, she felt uneasy. Perhaps that was only natural after all they'd been through. *Well,* she thought, *I'll just have to get over it. We can't be together all the time, even if we were married. . . .* She paused in her thoughts as the sun broke through the muted jewel colors of the clouds in a blinding burst of radiance. It was a moment of revelation, in which Branwen knew with certainty that she wanted more than just to live with Will—she wanted to marry him.

It's too soon, Branwen thought as she climbed back up the cliff with the same care she had used in her descent. Will had a long, long way to go before he'd be ready to talk marriage. Maybe he would never be ready. Maybe that's where her uneasiness was coming from.

Then again, perhaps the uneasiness had nothing to do with Will at all . . . except that the joy of his presence could drive the uneasiness away. She'd had a respite for more than a year; perhaps now it was over. She could, as she had done after Jason's murder, close her mind to the Abyss. But she could not close the Abyss itself, as she was about to find out.

The last two segments of Branwen's TV program, the ones about the aging nuns, had generated some strange mail in her absence. There were several letters that insisted the nuns were not the holy women they appeared to be, but devils in disguise. One letter asserted that the nuns were not simply the last survivors of their Order, but rather they had been cast out of the Order because they were evil, sealed into the abandoned convent. And now, the letter went on, Branwen had broken that seal; she had done worse than let the evil out, she had put it on television! That letter in particular bothered Branwen. All day long she could not shake it. And that night in her apartment, when he had finished telling her about the job interviews he'd had during the day, Will noticed her preoccupation.

By way of an answer, Branwen played the videotape of her program that she had made for her own archives, all the segments one after another on the same tape. Ending with the two segments on the nuns. Then she told Will about the letters and the one that bothered her most.

"That's silly," said Will. "There's nothing remotely bad about those old women. Just the opposite. I don't understand why you're letting a crank letter bother you—that doesn't seem like you at all."

"There are things you don't know, Will, things that happened while you were away. I suppose I thought I'd escaped by coming to California, but I should have known there's no geographic cure for this. I told you Jason was murdered and that the prevailing opinion was that his death was politically motivated. You said that made sense, and it does, but I'm afraid there was more to it. . . ."

Branwen told him everything in detail, just as she had once told Xavier Dominguez. She held nothing back, in spite of an increasing concern that Will might think her mad and walk out, horrified, then and there. She had underestimated him.

"You know, Branwen," he said thoughtfully when she was done, "if I didn't know you so well, and if I hadn't spent almost two years living among villagers who believed unshakably in the supernatural, I'd think you were nuts. But it just so happens I know you are *not* nuts. I saw things in my wanderings that I wouldn't have believed if I'd seen them here. I'm not the skeptic I used to be. So, what do you think? You think those nuns could be, what do you call it, possessed? Like Jason?"

Branwen frowned. "I didn't say Jason was possessed, not exactly. Though I suppose to argue that point would be quibbling over semantics." She broke off and used intuition rather than rational thought in order to find an answer to his question. When she emerged, she said definitely, "No. I believe those nuns are pure, good. But people who are good can attract the Dark Force. It wants to discredit Goodness, if It can't corrupt. If there are evil spirits around, then they certainly don't want Goodness publicized. Which is what I did."

"I hope that doesn't put you in danger," said Will solemnly.

"Um," said Branwen. Then she sighed. She felt like one who has put down a heavy burden and now must pick it up again. "I thought I was involved in those things because of my connection with Jason and Harry. They are neither of them present in my life anymore. I could do without this feeling I have that everything I told you about is resurfacing, Will. I really could do without it!"

"More stuff stirred up by those old nuns," said Branwen's secretary, tossing the mail she had screened down on Branwen's desk.

"I don't understand it!" Branwen complained.

"You don't?" The young woman, whose name was Jessica but half the staff called her Jennifer and she didn't seem to mind, sat herself on the corner of Branwen's desk. "Well, geez—I do."

"Then please explain it to me."

"Anything occult is big right now, especially here in California. Lots of people really go for the spiritual stuff, and those nuns with their bony faces and weird clothes, they were like hyper-spiritual, you know? You should do more. It would go over really big. I mean *big*!"

Jessica was, unfortunately, not Branwen's favorite person—because she shared her secretary with three other writer/producers all of whom were men, and all of whom got more of Jessica's attention than Branwen did. Certainly Branwen would never have thought of seeking Jessica's advice, but in this case . . . "You're right," Branwen agreed. "Thanks. I'll look into it."

"You need help, you let me know. I know lots about the occult."

"Thanks," said Branwen again, dryly. Jessica's performance to date gave Branwen ample reason to be skeptical of the quality of her knowledge about anything. Since the secretary remained perched on her desk, Branwen added, "I'll remember that."

Jessica didn't budge. "You should check out this really excellent psychic guy named Orson. He's over in Oakland at the Aud. I saw him last night. My girlfriend and I saved up for *weeks* because he's like superexpensive, but I knew he'd be worth it. I mean, this Orson is like totally incredible! He'll be there two more nights. He's supposed to be sold out, but I'll bet I could get you tickets if I said it was for the station."

Branwen's grip on her ball-point pen was so tight that her knuckles were white. "If you think he's really that good, Jessica, you might try to get me one or two tickets. But don't use my name, and don't make any promises about news coverage."

"I gotcha. You want to be like undercover, right?"

"Right."

"No problem." Jessica hopped off the desk, flipped her skirt back in place where it had hiked up. Showing more savvy than Branwen had given her credit for, she said, "I'll tell them to hold two tickets for the station and I'll send a messenger to pick them up."

Reminding herself that she should know better than to judge a book by its cover, Branwen smiled. "That's brilliant, Jessica. Absolutely brilliant."

Knowing what he was, Branwen was irked to have to pay Orson's exorbitant price for the tickets, but she didn't want the station to absorb the expense. So she gritted her teeth and wrote a check for $500.

The Oakland Auditorium was already filled almost to capacity when Branwen and Will joined the crowd. Seats were not assigned—but through Will's persistent hunting from his superior height they found two seats, not together but only one row apart and fairly close to the stage. Remembering the effect

Orson had had on her before, Branwen mentally distanced herself from her surroundings and called up the protection of her Light, well before Orson appeared.

The houselights dimmed but did not go out. Orson would want to see his audience, though Branwen could not imagine how he could make eye contact with so many people in the same way he had done with his small audience at the Psychic Underground. So many people. . . . At $250 a head, considering the capacity she guessed for the Auditorium, Orson could gross a half to three quarters of a million dollars in one night! In Jessica's words, that was "totally incredible," all right! Branwen thought about the last time she had seen Melvin Morton, when she had wanted to pay him and he'd refused. "Gracia comes to me as a gift," he'd said, "and gifts are free."

A hush fell over the crowd as the stage lights came up. Two plain wooden chairs were placed center stage against a deep red backdrop curtain. That was all, not even a microphone. Branwen, who was knowledgeable about such things, knew that a microphone would be necessary in a place this size; but there were cordless hand-held mikes, or tiny lavaliers powered by quartz batteries. She felt anticipation growing in the huge room with its double-tiered balcony. For a moment she closed her eyes, strengthened her protective Light.

Orson entered from the wings and strode across the stage. His appearance in every detail was exactly as Branwen remembered. Somehow on the vast stage he seemed even larger than he had a few feet away from her in a private home. So impressive was he that the audience, like one giant creature, drew in its collective breath in a gasp of huge proportions. Orson stood on the stage apron and stared at them with his colorless eyes.

He's doing it, Branwen thought. She turned her own gaze from Orson and looked at the predominantly female crowd instead. She would have bet her life that every person there felt that Orson had looked directly at her or him. Surely he could not accomplish the same with those in the balcony tiers, but he lifted his head. Orson's mesmerizing gaze flowed in a stream above them, she could almost see it. From the corner of her eye, taking her unaware, she did see Orson's aura. It was red and black and crackled in spikes around his head and shoulders. A menacing, powerful aura.

The perusal of the audience took minutes, and Orson did not rush. Restless anticipation built again in the room. Whether he

really needed the sense of personal eye contact he took the time
to engender or was simply working the crowd to a fever pitch,
Branwen could not tell. He had mastered the technique and
spoke at the precise moment when further delay would have irritated rather than whetted his listeners' desire for him.

"I have come to tell you a great secret," said the deep bronze-
belled voice. "You . . . Are . . . God!"

The thousands of mouths gasped, like a waking or dying
beast.

"How do I know this secret and the others I will share with
you tonight? I have been given a rare privilege: I died, and returned to life. . . ." Orson went on, reciting his credentials, giving the audience the information that she had heard in his
introduction to the Underground. The difference tonight was
that he told his own story in greater detail. With the spell of his
own great voice Orson's tale of death and rebirth and the time
between when he had walked on the Other Plane became an he-
roic saga. Branwen felt herself reinforcing her Light repeatedly
as she resisted him. To the many in this room who were like
Jessica, longing to believe, the man must have seemed a Lance-
lot or a Siegfried by the time he had finished this verbal autobi-
ography.

Next he went on with the same theme Branwen had heard in
Washington: You can do whatever you want, be whatever you
want. He used virtually the same words he had used then,
though his examples were less elitist, tailored to a broader spectrum of people. "How do you do this?" Orson asked. "First, by
visualization. Second, by opening yourself to the Power of the
Universe. I will teach you how to do both before you leave here
tonight."

Branwen froze. All the alarms in her mind, in her soul, cried
"Danger! Danger! Danger!" Oh, how utterly devious and subtle, she thought, and no wonder she missed the danger the first
time. No danger in visualization, a benign technique and so
helpful that its results could seem miraculous. But the second . . . ! Orson did not say Universal Energy, he said Power of
the Universe. And there was a difference. A telling difference.
That there is an invisible energy coursing through all things was
undeniably true; as it was also true that individuals can learn to
tap into, amplify, channel that energy. But in the language of
Spirit, "the Power" can be wielded for good or for evil, and further, the Power can itself be good or evil personified. For an ig-

norant, unprotected soul to be *open* to the Power without specifying *which* Power was the same as saying to the Others, "Here I am, let me be your door, come on into the world through me." Hadn't Gracia cautioned Branwen against this very thing? "Do not open yourself to Spirit without protection," Gracia had said. And here was Orson, either intentionally diabolical or abysmally ignorant, teaching three thousand people how to open themselves to a Power he had not called by name. He did not say a word about the need for protection, much less did he teach his audience how to protect themselves.

Branwen was appalled. Could Orson be that ignorant? She thought not. The omission was surely deliberate, especially since calling protection was not that difficult. Anyone could do it. And Orson had just given a lesson in visualization, a more difficult technique than calling protection. Anyone who could visualize could learn to protect themselves in the same way Branwen did: by visualizing and feeling the Light in their own centers, finding and kindling that point of Light and then sending it through their bodies until it poured out around them, a shell of protection made of Light. People who were more verbal and aural than visual could achieve the same purpose by making the declaration: "I am of the Light and I am surrounded by the Protection of the Light."

What was Will thinking of all this? Branwen wondered. She wished Xavier were here, too. Then she realized she knew already what Xavier would say: Of course Orson knows what he's doing. His failure to teach people how to protect themselves is deliberate. He wants them to be open to the Power he, Orson, chooses—the Power of Evil!

Having thought of Will and Xavier, Branwen now thought of Harry Ravenscroft. Was this Orson the same person whose name Harry had mentioned? More than likely. How many psychic Orsons could there be in the world? Suddenly, sharply, Branwen longed to know what Harry knew about the man on the stage who at this moment seemed to loom much larger than life.

Orson had finished his presentation, but the evening's "entertainment" was not over. Holding up a large hand for attention, Orson said, "Ladies and gentlemen. My dear friends. We will now have an intermission, after which I will introduce you to a charming young woman I have discovered, a natural trance-channel medium whose name is Miriam."

The crowd's murmur at this announcement grew to a tumult as Orson left the stage. Most people, including Branwen and Will, stayed in their seats for the break. Branwen turned her ears to the comments of those around her. "Isn't he amazing?" "So handsome!" "That face, that beard, that voice—my dear, he is to *die* for!" "The things he says really do work. Why I know a woman who tried it last year, and now she has a new car *and* a mink coat!"

The houselights dimmed; this time they went completely out. The light came up on the stage. The many mouths of the audience sighed with enough collective breath that the earth seemed to heave. Miriam presented so great a contrast to Orson that one's senses were jarred almost to disorientation. Where he was a huge, dark Rasputin of a man, she was an ethereal blond wisp, looking as if she had stepped straight out of the canvas of a medieval painting. No doubt to enhance her angelic appearance, the child/woman wore a long white robelike dress with full sleeves that covered her hands, and a slim gold circlet upon her head. Orson led her to the center of the stage and introduced her simply. "This is Miriam. She channels several spirits. We will soon learn who speaks to us through her tonight." He turned his back to the audience and conducted Miriam to one of the two chairs. When she had sat down, he hovered over her, blocking her from the audience's sight; Branwen was alarmed until she realized he was merely arranging Miriam's lavalier microphone. Then Orson sat in the other chair.

Branwen was extremely skeptical, even while her sympathy was engaged by Miriam's delicate beauty. For one thing, Miriam hadn't said a word in her own voice—how could they know that another entity spoke through her, that Orson hadn't merely hypnotized her? For another thing, Branwen was sure she had seen Miriam somewhere before. Where? Someplace to do with television was most likely. Was she an actress? A model? Where had Branwen seen her? It was maddening to be unable to remember.

Miriam was entering a trancelike state. Her body rocked back and forth. Orson sat as immovable as a black volcanic rock. Miriam's body went rigid, and she sat very straight in her chair. In a voice as pure, clear, and sweet as a child's, she said, "I bring you blessings from the Convent of St. Catherine, she who died a martyr on the wheel."

Orson leaned forward, his deep voice surprisingly gentle. "What is your name, my child?"

"I am Sister Druscilla."

"And I am Orson, your friend."

"Yes. I know you, Orson. Greetings."

"There are many people here tonight who wish to hear whatever message you bring. Speak to us, Sister Druscilla."

"I would not wish to live in your time," said the childlike voice, "for all your many riches. No, I prefer my own times, which your history books call the Dark Ages." She sighed and went on in a non sequitur. "Have you seen God's angel? I have seen him. He of the six wings, who folds two across his eyes and two across his breast and two across his feet. God's angel is bound and silent, and it is you who have bound him. God's angel does not sing or cry, he cannot move. It is your world, not mine, that has wounded the angel. It is so sad, really, so sad."

"What must we do, Druscilla, to loose the angel's bonds, to set him free?"

The entity Druscilla laughed, a tinkling peal of laughter that was somehow more eerie than merry. "Why, we must wake him up! Noise will wake him up—music, loud music. You should play loud music, tell funny stories, and laugh. Celebrations, explosions. Making love, yes, men and women make love, women and men, men and men and women and women, all must make love. A little death. Not killing. You know the little death, friend Orson?"

"Yes, I know, Sister Druscilla."

Branwen was extremely uncomfortable. She felt her Light around her, but even so this spirit or entity speaking through Miriam made her soul crawl.

Miriam, or Druscilla, went on prattling in that deceptively clear, pure voice. "Make love, and the angel will unfold his wings and show his terrible face. Celebrate with laughter and wild noise, and the angel will lift all his six wings and fly away. Six and six and six, the Number of the Beast. Apocalypse will come, London Bridge is falling down!"

While Miriam sat catatonic, another voice issued from her mouth, close on the first. This voice was still female but older, harsher. "Go away, Druscilla, foolish child. These people do not want to hear your prattle!"

"Tell us who you are," said Orson.

"I am Eleuthera, older and wiser. I have little to say. I was only tired of listening to that silly girl."

"Will you favor us with your wisdom, Eleuthera?"

"I think not."

"There are many people here, all of whom have paid money—much money—to hear what you would say. Reconsider."

"Very well. To them I say: Look around you. You live in a material world. So it was in my own time, the time of the Greeks, and so is it in yours. Do not postpone your pleasures, for life in the body, where you can enjoy your pleasures, is short. Make your material goals, and do not stop short of them. That is all I have to say. Good night."

After this, Miriam's body again began to rock. Orson got up, put his hands on her shoulders, and she stopped rocking. He bent and whispered into her ear. She looked up at him, recognition in her eyes, and smiled—a heartrending, beautiful smile. Orson bent and whispered again, and removed her microphone. He left her in the chair and advanced to the center of the stage.

"One never knows," he said, a severe look on his face as if he dared criticism of his woman/child, his creation, "what the spirits will say through Miriam. I have presented her to you tonight so that you may see and hear for yourselves that it is possible for any of us to have a direct connection, as Miriam does, to the spirit world. This concludes our presentation. Miriam does give readings, and she will be available in our hotel suite for this purpose all day tomorrow, Saturday, and Sunday. You will find flyers in the lobby as you leave, giving more information. Thank you for coming. Good night."

Branwen lost sight of Will in the crush and waited for him by the outer lobby door through which they'd entered. When he showed up, he held one of the flyers Orson had mentioned. His facial expression was grim.

"Well," she prodded as they went down the steps and into the night, "what did you think?"

"I think that Orson is the worst sort of charlatan! I don't know how much you had to pay for our tickets, but whatever it was it's a rip-off. Passing off that garbage as spiritual wisdom— there ought to be a law against it!"

"You don't know how thoroughly I agree with you. But just

how many other people do you think there were in there who
would agree with us, Will?"

Will's generous mouth was pressed into a disapproving line.
"Not many, unfortunately."

"Don't be too hard on them. Orson does such a good job of
telling people what they want to hear. The first time I heard him
he had me wondering if he might be right."

"Huh!" Will snorted and then grew quiet. He did not speak
again until they were in the Volvo, Branwen driving, halfway
across the Bay Bridge. "Are you going to do a piece on this guy
Orson, is that why we went? Going to expose him for the crook
he is?"

Encouraged though she was that Will had seen through Orson,
Branwen was still surprised by his vehemence. She answered
slowly, "I'm not sure yet what I'm going to do. I hate to say this,
much less think it, but Orson could be part of a much larger picture. He may not be the independent agent he appears to be."

Will took the flyer out of his pocket, unfolded it, reached over
to the dash, and flicked on the map light. Branwen glanced
down. Miriam's ethereal face, illuminated by the map light,
looked back at her, and she shivered. Where had she seen that
face before?

"What's a reading, Branwen?"

"It's kind of like a counseling session, one on one, only the
counselor is a psychic instead of a psychologist or a psychiatrist."

"At these prices, it ought to be good." He tapped the flyer
with a finger.

"Well, at least you can't accuse Orson of being cheap!"
Branwen's attempt at humor went right past Will. She could feel
his anger in the close confines of the car.

"This girl," he said. "Miriam—Orson's exploiting her,
Branwen. You know about these things. Is she really one of
these channelers?"

"Maybe. Let's hold off on this discussion until we've got the
car back in the garage. It's a heavy subject, and I'm still not
comfortable on these hills. I need to concentrate on my driving."

They left the car in their rented garage space and began to
walk the two blocks up the hill to Branwen's apartment. Will
said half apologetically, "I don't know why I'm so stirred up

about Orson and Miriam. I guess it's the girl. She seemed so helpless, so innocent."

"Not to mention so blond and so beautiful."

"That has nothing to do with it!" At her skeptical look, he said, "Well, maybe it has a little to do with it, but damn it, Orson is exploiting her, and he ought to be stopped. Maybe I'll go have a reading with Miriam. Maybe I can get a clue how to stop him that way."

"I'm not so sure that's a good idea." Branwen didn't try to talk anymore. She had too many thoughts in her head, too many warning bells going off all at once. Finally, back in her apartment, she decided to take a stand. "I'd rather you didn't get involved with Orson, Will. And you will if you try to help Miriam."

"What's that supposed to mean?"

"Miriam may look innocent, but looks can be deceiving. Did you listen to what she said? All that stuff about the angel was just loaded with a—a kind of depraved sexuality."

"That wasn't her, that was What's-her-name. Druscilla."

Branwen shook her head. She had unpinned her hair and it tumbled about her face. "You asked me if Miriam was really channeling. If she was, then she has opened herself to an entity that's unhealthy, if not outright evil. Make that two unhealthy entities—the second one, Eleuthera, was no enlightened spirit. I really don't want you getting mixed up in this!"

"What's the matter, you think I can't take care of myself?"

"You know I don't think that."

"Good. I'm going for a reading. Tomorrow."

"Will, don't. Hold off until I figure out what I'm going to do."

Will shook his head stubbornly. "I can't hold off. I think I'm about to be offered a job, and tomorrow may be the only chance I'll get to go."

"A job?" Branwen was beginning to think she didn't know Will as well as she'd thought. "I know you've had interviews, but I had no idea you were that close to an offer, much less to taking a job. Why didn't you tell me? Who's it with?"

"If they offer, and I accept, I'll tell you. I don't want to talk about it unless it happens. Anyway, the point is, whether you like it or not, I'm not going to be able to get Miriam out of my head unless I see her again, and the only way I know to do that is to have one of these readings, *and* I'm going to do it tomorrow because it may be my last chance. I'll take a tape recorder, and you can hear the whole thing. Heck, maybe you can use it in your investigation."

"Oh, so you're not only going for a reading with Miriam, you're also mighty sure all of a sudden that I'm going to investigate Orson."

"Yeah." Will grinned and reached for her. "I'm sure, and job or no job I'm equally sure I'm going to help you. We're partners, Branwen. Besides, I know you, I can see all those gears turning behind your beautiful blue-green eyes. Don't think for a minute I'm going to let you go confronting any of this evil crap all by yourself!"

Branwen snuggled against Will's shoulder. This was the closest they'd come to a fight, and yet it was all resolved so easily. The "evil crap" could wait. Right now, in the arms of the man she loved, Branwen was content. "And all this time I thought you were only interested in Miriam because she's blond, and I'm dark, and she's young, and I'm not."

"Why, Ms. Faraday," Will said as he nuzzled her cheek, "could you be jealous!"

"Who, me? Not a chance!" Smiling, she raised her face for his kiss.

4

Will accepted a job as a researcher for the California Chapter of the Nature Conservancy. His old think-tank credentials and his knowledge of the legislative process helped to qualify him for the position, but he had a lot to learn. He was excited about it. Orson and Miriam quickly lost out to the environment as the focus of Will's attention.

He had taped his reading with Miriam, using Branwen's minicassette recorder. The quality of the tape was poor because he'd recorded illegally, without permission, and the microphone had had to pick up her voice through the fabric of his jacket pocket. Branwen, with her memories of Melvin and Gracia, thought the reading was pathetic. But Will had not been interested in content, only in Miriam herself. The recording did not reveal the fact that Orson had been present throughout, but Will had come back outraged, completely convinced that Orson treated Miriam like a slave. The girl had haunted Will, so that Branwen was not sorry to see the new job claim almost all his attention and his time.

On her part, Branwen had begun an investigation of the psychic/spiritual scene in California that threatened to take over her life. The amount of material she had to work with was mind-boggling, and Jessica was a big help. No one at the station, not even Jessica, was aware that Branwen intended her emphasis in the program to be on the Dark Side of her subject. While Jessica happily plowed through reams of material on subjects like crystal healing, Kirlian photography, remote viewing, and out-of-body experiences, Branwen found links between a ritual murder at the Stanford Memorial Church and New York's Son of Sam murders. She found whispers of Satanism surrounding the Hillside Strangler. She uncovered evidence that spirits of dubious nature were being summoned in places as disparate as an L.A. ghetto and the proper streets of San Francisco's Pacific Heights. All this and more, without ever touching on the whole business of Charles Manson and Family.

She kept patiently on. She did not want to do a sensational program about Satanism and was frustrated that there should be so much of this. It was bad, but she didn't know what to do with it. She was after something far more subtle, far more insidious. She wanted eventually to be able to show how the sunshiny Californians in all their bubble-gum innocence might unknowingly be opening the gate to unspeakable evil. She had time, Jessica's impatience not withstanding. Branwen's reputation for painstaking research was well established, and no one expected her to put together a major program in less than a year.

The months went by, her material mounted, Jessica's enthusiasm flagged and then faded away. Branwen, too, felt like giving up. She had been unable to accomplish the one thing she wanted most: the unmasking of the Cognoscenti and the exposure of Orson. She had a strong intuitive hunch that the man was linked to the group, but she could learn nothing of it, and Orson had dropped out. The most Branwen had been able to learn was that Orson had changed his emphasis from large public gatherings to small private seminars and retreats, by invitation only. He was supposed to have a lodge in some remote area of northern California where these took place.

At this point Branwen once again enlisted Will's help. He had bought a Jeep Cherokee, in anticipation of the one thing he wanted most on his job: to be appointed to a field-study team. In the Cherokee Branwen and Will spent several weekends fruitlessly searching for Orson's Lodge. In the fall of 1983 when she had been researching for almost nine months, Branwen finally called a halt. She missed Mendocino and McClosky, which she still leased year-round. She was ready for a rest. She traded in her heavy Volvo for a lighter, if less fashionable, Camry wagon with four-wheel drive; now Will could take the Cherokee, and she would have her own four-wheeler if she wanted to do any more hunting. She didn't think she would. She intended to hole up at McClosky with all the material she'd amassed and begin, at a leisurely pace, to put her program together. Without, unfortunately, ever having found out what she wanted to know about Orson and the Cognoscenti. Without remembering where she had seen Miriam before. She got permission to be away from the office for an extended period, for the express purpose of readying her program.

Branwen piled all her books and notes and tapes in her station wagon, ready to head for Mendocino, ready for a rest and a change of pace in her work.

She got neither the rest nor the change of pace. What she got instead, just as she was about to leave San Francisco, were two phone calls. One from a frantic Mrs. Beecher, and another from a calmer but no less alarmed Ellen Harper. Harry Ravenscroft had come home to Raven Hill. They thought he was dying.

"It's all right, Will," Branwen assured him. "I don't mind going alone. You hardly knew Harry, so no one expects you to be there. I'm going to stay at Raven Hill and help the Beechers through this. I'll call your office, and someone can get word to you wherever you are when I've arrived. Then you can call me whenever you have access to a telephone."

"If this wasn't my first field-study assignment, I'd cancel in a minute," said Will. He took Branwen's shoulders in his hands and studied her face intently. "You do understand, don't you? You know how long I've wanted to get out of the libraries and the archives and be a part of a field-study team."

"Of course I do." She looked into Will's hazel-brown eyes and loved the deep caring she saw there. She realized how much she would miss him, how much she relied on him.

Will folded her against his chest. He murmured, "I'm going to feel strange without you."

Branwen wrapped her arms around him and lifted her head. "Don't be silly! Our jobs have kept us apart a lot these last months. This is no different."

"It feels different. Washington and Virginia are a whole continent away. We promised we'd always be together, Branwen, that nothing would separate us ever again."

"I know, but we were being a little unrealistic. This is an emergency. My ties to Harry are old and deep. He's important. Your job is important. No two people can be together always. It isn't as if I'm not coming back."

"Yes," Will whispered, burying his face in her hair, "you will come back to me."

Branwen rented a car at the airport and drove straight to Raven Hill. The countryside, the outskirts of Redmund, the house itself—nothing had changed. Raven Hill was as well tended, as stately, and as beautiful as it had ever been. She pulled into the porte cochere and left her bags in the car. Beecher wouldn't object to bringing them in, and she wanted to go straight to Harry. As she left the car, she noticed the gnarled old wisteria vine, autumn-bare and sere, and it reminded her of the solemn purpose for which she had come.

Her steps seemed loud as she crossed the front porch. A palpable hush enshrouded Raven Hill. The door opened silently before Branwen could knock. Beecher stood there, soberly dressed in a dark suit, the first time Branwen had ever seen him out of work clothes. A lump formed in her throat, and she feared she had come too late.

Beecher bobbed his head. "Afternoon, Miss Branwen. Thankee fer coming." He stepped back so that she could enter the hall.

"Hello, Beecher." She swallowed the lump with difficulty. "I hope Mr. Harry is no worse?"

"No'm. He be the same. He stays in the liberry day an' night, had me to move his bed in there. I'll go get the wife. She be cookin' supper."

"Don't disturb her. I'll go straight in to Harry. I left a small suitcase and a canvas bag in the car. Perhaps you might bring them in?"

Beecher bobbed his head again. He touched her arm as she reached out to open the library door. "Miss Branwen, best prepare yerself. Mr. Harry be in pitiful poor shape, an' he don't talk hardly a-tall."

"I understand." She squared her shoulders and smoothed the skirt of her gray wool suit. Then, with Beecher looking on, she opened the library door. She stepped in and closed it behind her.

The large high-ceilinged room was gloomy; where before there had been airy white curtains at the long windows, now there were heavy drapes of an indeterminate color. The drapes were drawn, and only a feeble ray of sun, pencil-thin, struggled through. Branwen did not see Harry. She took a moment to get her bearings. Not only were her eyes unaccustomed to the gloom, but the room itself seemed strange, somehow wrong. She decided it was because the furniture had been rearranged to accommodate Harry's four-poster bed that was pushed against the far wall.

Branwen jumped, startled by a visual perception of movement. Dark shadows wavered on the ceiling and on the book-lined walls. Now she realized that the shadows were thrown by a fire burning in the fireplace. One wing chair faced the fire; the other was nowhere to be seen. Branwen walked over to the fire and went down on her knees beside the wing chair.

"Hello, Harry," she said.

He did not move, did not look at her, did not appear to have heard. Harry Ravenscroft looked as if he were already dead. His hair was completely white, long and scraggly, as if it had grown out inside the coffin. His hands, resting on the arms of the chair, were bent and clawed. His skeleton of a body was covered by a dark tartan bathrobe, his feet encased in black velvet slippers. His nose stood out like a beak; his eyebrows were wild tufts. He was frightening to behold.

"Harry?" she inquired softly.

Nothing, no response.

She inched closer and looked up into his face. His eyes had gone completely silver. He was almost blind. Her heart filled with love for him and spilled over, even as tears welled and flowed from her eyes. Branwen threw her arm across Harry's sharp knees, put her head in his lap, and sobbed.

A claw, too bony to be comforting, came down on the back of her neck. It was recognition of a sort. She continued to cry as the claw struggled to shape itself into a hand, tried and succeeded to stroke her head with a semblance of gentleness.

"Branwen?" The voice was hoarse but recognizably that of Harry Ravenscroft.

She raised her head to find those silver eyes, strangely pupilless, looking down at her. And the face was not the death's head she had expected. True, there was little flesh under skin and over bone, but Harry's face glowed with an inner light. "Can you see me?" she asked.

Harry tried to smile. The effect on the fleshless face was grotesque, but she had never loved him more. "I . . . can . . . see," he croaked. "Not very well, but well enough."

"Don't try to talk, don't waste your strength. I've come to be with you. I'm going to stay right here in the house. You'll get better, stronger, and then we can talk. For now, let me just sit here with you."

Harry sighed. The sound of his sigh was like the wind rustling through dry leaves. Branwen curled up at Harry's feet, leaning her back against his chair, resting her cheek upon his long, hard thighbone. She watched the fire dance as it licked life from the log in the grate. She was grateful for the fire's warmth, as no doubt Harry was also. She sat with him for a long time, knowing that he drew on her strength as the fire drew its flames from the log that had once been a living tree. For her old friend she gave her strength gladly.

"Have you seen him, Ellen?" asked Branwen over the telephone.

"Yes, once. Briefly. Mrs. Beecher called, and I went out. I was shocked. He didn't want a doctor, and I respected his wishes. The Beechers don't know where he's been or what happened to him. Do you, Branwen?"

Branwen drew a deep breath, knowing she was about to take a great risk. "Harry has been with some people who call themselves the Cognoscenti."

"The *who*?"

"Cognoscenti. It means 'the knowing ones' in Latin. You might ask your husband if he has ever heard of them. I believe these Cognoscenti had a hand in Jason's death, and now they've all but killed Harry. I'm going to track them down if it's the last thing I do!"

"Branwen, no! They sound like a secret society, and that can be dangerous. Whoever they are, if they really did do what you just said, you'll be getting yourself in awful trouble. I told you before that whoever made the move to cover up the facts about Jason's murder is very, very powerful. Leave it alone!"

"I left it alone before, and now look what's happened to Harry. I'm a journalist, Ellen. I know how to do investigation, and I swear to you I'm going to track these people. I don't care if it's dangerous. Where would we be if nobody ever did anything dangerous?"

"I'm not going to help you because I don't want you to get hurt."

Branwen ignored that. "Listen, Ellen, I'm really serious. I intend to expose the Cognoscenti on national television. Ask Jim for me, and while you're at it, ask him if he knows anything about a psychic named Orson."

"Branwen Faraday, I'm not going to ask Jim one single thing! I'm not, repeat *not*, going to help you get yourself in big trouble. You stop all this nonsense, you hear?"

Yes, Branwen heard. She knew that tone of voice in Ellen, knew that to insist any further would be useless. "Suit yourself, Ellen. I've got to get back to Harry." She was bitterly disappointed.

"Wait, Branwen. Shall I come out?"

"Not yet. He's getting stronger, but I don't think he'll ever be himself again. Just stay in touch, okay?"

"Okay," said Ellen doubtfully.

Each day Branwen widened the opening in the library drapes to let in a little more light, but Harry shrank from the sun. He lived—perhaps existed would be a more accurate word—in a shadowy world that seemed to be halfway between this one and the next. He seemed never to be entirely awake nor completely asleep. Food and drink did not interest him. Sometimes he would talk a little. Branwen judged his increasing strength by a concurrent strengthening of his voice. He improved in tiny increments.

On the fourth day of her visit, she took him by the hand. "Come, lean on me. We're going to walk to the front windows and sit there for a while. It's warm out today. I've opened the windows a crack. The fresh air will do you good."

"Hrumph," was all Harry said. He walked slowly but steadily, giving her very little of his weight; Branwen thought this a good sign. She settled him in a comfortable chair and took one nearby. Harry winced at the light, but when Branwen moved to draw the curtains, he said, "Leave them. I can see, just enough to help me remember. I used to like the view from here."

"Yes, I believe you did."

After a while Harry said, "I fought so hard to live, but now I'm dying anyway." He laughed, a dry cackle. "That's funny, isn't it?"

"Only if you have a very warped sense of humor."

Harry gave another dry cackle. He turned his silver eyes on her. "I know what you've been thinking. My body is shot, but the rest of me works quite well. Better than ever. You've always been a determined woman, Branwen, determined to go your way. I've decided to tell you about the Cognoscenti and what happened to me. After I've told you, what will be will be."

"Yes!" Branwen scarcely dared to breathe. "Please go on."

"I believe I told you a little before, but I was still afraid then. I'm beyond that now, and so are you. Your determination precludes fear. Nevertheless I should warn you: It is a fantastically ugly story, much too bizarre for you to put on your television. No one would believe you. People would either laugh at you or think you are insane. Do you still want to hear?"

"I do."

"Very well. I have never seen the Cognoscenti assembled as a group so I do not know how many members there are. Not many, I should think. Probably twelve or thirteen, the traditional number. When I first heard of them, I believed they were simply very skilled contemporary magicians. I had heard them called Adepts, and they are. But they are also much more than that, which is why they are so dangerous." Bones creaking, Harry settled in his chair, prepared to talk more than he had in a long time. "Jason worked for the Cognoscenti, and it was they who killed him. I know this for a fact. My own Master, one of their number, told me in considerable detail. In a way, the Cognoscenti did you a favor, Branwen. Jason returned to this country for one purpose only, and that was to take revenge on you—he had a twisted idea that you deliberately murdered his child while it was still in your womb, and he intended to take your life in return. The Cognoscenti did not want Jason here. If he had simply come, killed you, and gone back to Europe, one-two-three, they might have let him live. But you eluded him, and he was trapped by his own vanity."

"He was also trapped by something else," said Branwen, "a malevolent spirit. I saw and felt it with him, or in him, a few days before he died. Was that their doing, too? Did the Cognoscenti assign that Entity to Jason?"

"Only indirectly. I'll get to that shortly. Mark well that the Cognoscenti know of you—they know that you were able to avoid Jason, and that is no small thing. What they do not know is that you are a spiritually powerful person in your own right, with a power diametrically opposed to theirs. Your power has grown, Branwen—I feel it in you."

She shrugged. "I don't know. I haven't used it in a long time. The reality of Jason's murder, and of the evil thing with him, got to me. I wanted no part of it. Now, though. . . . Go on with your story, Harry."

"All right. Initially I went to the Cognoscenti on an introduction from Jason. I met one man who more or less interviewed me and decided I was who I said I was, a relatively harmless professor who wanted to learn from true Adepts. I was only interested in the magical arts, and I thought that was their main interest, too. It isn't. Magic is only a means to an end for them, just as Jason was only their tool, their instrument. The Cognoscenti are literally a group of the most powerful men and women in the world. They build up and break down governments, influence the stock market worldwide, concoct events that shape history. They can even control the weather to a certain extent. I didn't know all that at first. The man who interviewed me, Orson, assigned me to a Master teacher—"

"Orson!"

"Yes. I see you know him. He is the only one of the Cognoscenti who openly acknowledges his psychic ability. The others are bankers, lawyers, politicians, entrepreneurs—professional people at the top of their fields. Orson is probably their greatest magician. Very possibly it was he who taught the others. Now we come to the heart of the matter. Through many lifetimes, Branwen, I myself have used the magical arts without regard to the concepts of Good and Evil. For me, the Power was power. I wanted only results. From the Cognoscenti I have learned the error of my ways. They deal exclusively with the Power of Darkness, and they are indeed Adepts at this. They are Users: of things, of people, of disembodied spirits. Each individual Adept Cognoscent has learned to summon and control an entity from out of Darkness. I was taught to do the same—unfortunately it's rather easy—by my Master who called it a Familiar Spirit. He should have called it a Demon. That is what happened to Jason—he somehow got the formula and used it, but he could not control the entity he summoned. It controlled him instead. God knows, I had enough trouble controlling mine! The Cognoscenti, Branwen, have literally opened the Gates of the Abyss. They are people after the mold of the Angel Lucifer in the legend—they want to be gods on the earth."

"In fact, that is what Orson teaches indiscriminately," Branwen said, "to any and all who listen. It's disgusting. People pay him millions to hear it. But tell me, Harry, what happened to you? I understand about Jason—they wanted to make an exam-

ple of him. And his body was laid out in a way that suggested
that after he was dead they wanted to control the evil spirit he
had summoned. Perhaps they wanted to send it back to the
Abyss—if so, I hope they succeeded. You couldn't have been
the threat to them that Jason was, and yet here you are, barely
alive!"

Harry laughed. "Oh, my dear, it turned out that I was a far
worse threat than Jason Faraday, but in an entirely different
way. You see, I did recover my powers. As weak as I am, I think
I will give you a little demonstration. Just watch."

Branwen looked at Harry, wondering what he could possibly
do when he was barely able to walk from one end of the room to
another. As she looked, the edges of his body began to blur. He
wavered, like a developing photograph in reverse. Soon there
was nothing but an opaque grayness in the chair where he had
sat. She checked her impulse to reach out and touch that
grayness—she would not have wanted to deal with the shock if
her hand had gone right through it. His seeming return to the
chair was less gradual: one moment he was not there, and the
next moment he was. And, oddly, he looked more substantial,
even a shade healthier than he had before.

"An illusion," said Branwen. "I admit I'm amazed."

"Ah! But was it illusion, or was I able to turn myself from
matter to energy and back again? Even the great Orson cannot
do what I just did. Orson and all the Cognoscenti rely on ritual,
spells, formulas. They are not harnessing their own power so
much as pulling from the power of the Other. Whereas I, my
dear, have in fact recovered my powers. As, you recall, I sought
to do. Shape-shifting, Branwen, that is what I had forgotten and
wanted most to be able to do again. Along the way I recovered
other skills as well. I need more practice on the shape-shifting
. . . if I live, that is. The Cognoscenti did not fail to observe that
I was quite good at the things of which they are so fond. Sum-
moning and commanding those horrid Demons was easy for
me—with one notable exception I'll tell you about. Making
storms. Likewise I do that beautifully. Moving objects without
touching them, disturbing magnetic fields, and so on. I was having a wonderful time until my ability became so remarkable that
my Master decided that *I* could be as valuable to them as my
money and property, which they coveted. He took me to a kind
of hideaway in upstate New York, and I had to give demonstrations to two or three of them at a time. I recognized some of

them in the evenings or the early mornings when I'd stroll about the grounds of this retreat. But when they were getting down to their occult business, they wore strange robes that hid their faces. They wanted me to use my ability for their causes—and their causes are destructive. When I, with some degree of arrogance no doubt, proclaimed that I have always been and always will be an independent, free wizard, I discovered my so-called Familiar Spirit was not so much under my control as theirs. The one Demon I had difficulty in commanding was my own. It, like them, was destructive. Of me."

"Oh, no," Branwen whispered.

"Oh, yes. After I had refused them I knew I was going to be in trouble. That was when I escaped, came down here to make some plans. They were already trying to control me with their Demon, even then."

"I saw that," said Branwen.

"I never should have gone back. I don't know even now why I thought I had to go back . . . but no matter. They would most likely have tracked me down anyway. I'm sure I would not be alive today if it were not for the fact that they were so sure they could turn me to their Dark Side. I pretended to go along, while I practiced and got better at the skills I'd recovered. But eventually Orson caught on to what I was doing. He swooped down on me and engaged me in a sort of duel that neither of us won. It ended in a stand-off but left me so weak that others of the Cognoscenti were able to take me captive. They made me a prisoner, Branwen. They imprisoned me physically with their Demon, my so-called Familiar. Their aim, of course, was for the Demon to possess me. Plain old-fashioned demonic possession of Harry Ravenscroft, fancy that! I fought the Thing. It nearly killed me, but finally I won. I sent their damn demon back to the Abyss, and escaped by taking the noncorporeal form you have seen me take here in this chair, and I came back to Raven Hill."

"No wonder you seemed more dead than alive when I first got here!" Branwen exclaimed. She was exhausted, drained herself just from having listened. Then she had an alarming thought. "Won't they come after you?"

"I don't think so. They believe, rightly, that I am—or was—as good as dead. You see, my dear, they don't know about *you*. You can help me regain my strength, and when I do, I'll simply leave here. I won't bother the Cognoscenti, and they won't find me. I'll go home."

"Home? Harry, you are home, you're at Raven Hill."

"No, no, my dear." He shook his head. "You know what I mean. *Home.*"

Branwen realized that she did know: *Home.*

For two weeks Branwen stayed at Raven Hill with Harry. He wanted no visitors, and she left the house only to walk on the grounds for exercise. She thought of calling Xavier, but decided against it because he had neither written nor called her since Will's return. Xavier must be moving on to other things, other people, maybe other places—she felt the rightness of that. As she approached forty years of age, Branwen saw that life has both patterns and events. The patterns weave in and out, disappearing only to resurface again; the events stand out in sharp relief, whole unto themselves, never repeating. The passionate priest was an event, a unique love she would always cherish. Jason had been an oft-repeated pattern, one whose threads she hoped were now permanently severed from the fabric of her life. Will: Will was a new pattern, deep and abiding for all his newness. She missed him terribly in spite of his nightly calls, and she would return to him soon. Harry? Harry was the oldest and most intricate of all the patterns in her life.

There was no longer any question that Harry would live. He grew stronger every day. They meditated together daily, and in their meditation Branwen shared her Light with him. The experience did not weaken her but instead strengthened them both. While Branwen fed his spirit, Mrs. Beecher fed his body. Mrs. Beecher crooned and made a fuss over Harry; she trimmed his hair and his beard and his nails and bathed him like a baby. He loved it. Except for the silvery hue of his almost-blind eyes, Harry began to look much like his old self.

"I want to show you something," Harry said to Branwen at the end of their meditation one day, "something you may need to know. You will call it a trick. I call it a useful demonstration."

"All right," Branwen said. In his recovery, Harry had grown gentle, and she no longer felt she had to avoid his tricks.

"I am going to show you how to dazzle nonbelievers." Harry closed his eyes and cupped his hands together. If Branwen had not been able to feel how he summoned his energy, feel how the air thrummed and thickened around him, she would have thought he made no effort, for no strain showed on his face or in his body. Soon he opened his eyes and his hands, and held his hands out to her. There, nestled in his palms, was a ball of blue light. He tossed the ball of light into the air, and as he did so, all the lamps in the room flashed on and then off. He laughed, and the ball vanished with an audible *Pop!*

Branwen laughed, too; it was a pretty trick.

"Go on, your turn. You can do it, too."

The palms of her hands tingled, but she said, "No, thank you."

"No? Well, I know better than to argue with you when you say you won't do something like this. But just remember, Branwen, that it can be done. And remember, too, that the way to fight the Cognoscenti and others of their kind is with light."

Branwen's airline reservations were made; she would be returning to California the next day. "Come, Branwen," said Harry, "let us go for a walk outside."

"That would be lovely," she agreed.

Mrs. Beecher, in a fit of loving kindness, had restored Harry's old loden-cloth cape that she so detested. Branwen had brought her own forest-green cape from California, and both hung on pegs by the kitchen door. Branwen and Harry threw them on, and together the two caped figures, both tall and thin, walked out into the cold November day. They made a striking pair. Gray clouds scudded overhead, driven by the wind. Branwen and Harry went down the hill and around its base, making a wide circle.

"You're going after the Cognoscenti, aren't you, Branwen?" Harry asked. "I know you have been thinking about them."

"Not exactly. I'm going after Orson. I'm going to expose him. I expect that will have some effect on all of them."

"How can you expose him? He's a real magician. He can do all he claims publicly, and more."

"He's evil, Harry. Even if I do no more than get people to question his 'You are God' bit, I will have accomplished something. But I'd like to do more than that. He has Jason's kind of arrogant pride—he must have broken the law—"

"You'll never get him that way. These people don't do criminal acts themselves. They get others to act for them. Like Jason."

"Orson has a weakness," Branwen insisted, "a young woman named Miriam. He used her for trance channeling, but I don't think she's a medium. I think she's mentally ill, maybe a multiple personality. Although," Branwen continued, thinking out loud as they walked, "she could be all of that. Disburbed herself, but psychically gifted, open to equally disturbed spirits— Oh, my God! *That's* where I saw her before! In one of those mental hospitals when I was doing that program years ago . . . she was so beautiful, she looked like an angel, but she was tormented. The nurse said she was schizophrenic. She saw and heard things that terrified her. Now Orson has her, and he's using her."

"Interesting," Harry mused. "Tragic. As I said, the Cognoscenti are Users."

"Yes. All I have to do is expose him as an exploiter of a mentally ill young woman, and his followers will be gone, fast. The trouble is, he's gone to ground and Miriam with him. I can't find him anywhere. He's supposed to be doing private retreats somewhere in northern California, but I can't find the place."

Harry stopped on the drive, smiling his old quirky sideways smile. "I can help you there. I know where it is. Not exactly, but generally speaking. Orson has two retreats. The one where they kept me was in upstate New York. The other is in the mountains in a place called Mendocino, California."

Branwen's blue-green eyes widened in disbelief. "Mendocino! I have a house in Mendocino. I can't believe this. Of course, he can't be in Mendocino itself, or I would know. In the mountains? There is all of Mendocino County, and there's a Mendocino National Forest—it's huge. Think, Harry. Do you know anything else, anything that might narrow it down?"

"No-o. I can only tell you that he will have chosen a place in deep woods, where he can own the land for miles on every side. You might ask around, ask about a place in the woods with a clearing where helicopters land. Many of the Cognoscenti travel by helicopter."

The next day, Branwen kissed Harry good-bye, then lingered on Raven Hill's porch. "One last thing, Harry."

"Yes, my dear?"

"What happened to our rune stones? Do you still have them?"

"Alas, no. I gave them back to the earth. I buried them in the woods near the retreat in New York, when I realized the Cognoscenti were going to lock me up. I was afraid Orson or one of the others might get hold of them and pervert the power of the bluestones."

Remembering the evil apparition that had tempted her with a bag of rune stones, Branwen asked, "Could they have found them?"

"No. After I buried them I sealed the place with a bindrune. I am sorry to have had to let them go, but the rune stones are quite safe."

"I'll tell you good-bye then." She kissed his cheek again. It felt like thinnest parchment, but smooth and warm. "I love you, Harry. I expect I will not see you again, not in this life. Be well."

"I love you also, dearest Branwen. Don't be too sure you won't see me. After all, I am going *home*."

5

Will was waiting. Branwen spied his tall, lanky form in the crowd long before she was able to detach herself from the line of disembarking passengers and hurl herself into his arms.

"Oh, I missed you," he said huskily, "how I missed you!"

"And I missed you."

He kissed her with a restrained hunger that promised more to come. "Being without you was like being without a part of myself. I felt incomplete."

"I know." With their arms around each other, they walked toward the baggage area. "It's amazing. I was alone for so many years, and I was never lonely. I preferred being independent, on my own. Now after living with you for a year, I'm ruined." Branwen lowered her voice. "There were times when I missed you so much that I actually ached for you, especially at night."

"Oh, Branwen." Will looked down at her, at the heart-shaped face, the soft mouth he loved to kiss, the incomparable eyes. He hurt with loving her. His insides trembled at the thought that he might ever lose her again, as he thought he once had. He longed to ask her to marry him. . . . But he knew how much marriage to Jason had traumatized her. She had said then that she would never marry again; and she had said only a year ago, "Marriage is not an option." He couldn't ask her to change that decision, not in order to assuage his own insecurity.

Branwen looked up at Will, at his kind, open, and now distinguished face. In his face she could easily see all the love and tenderness he felt for her. Surely his love was enough. Yet all through the long flight back to San Francisco she had entertained a fantasy of marriage to Will. A real marriage, a happy marriage of souls as well as bodies. She thought, not for the first time, that if Will would only ask her to marry him, her happiness would be complete . . . and she felt selfish for thinking it. She had no memory whatever of the words she had blurted out, "Marriage is not an option."

Will had driven Branwen's Camry wagon, still packed with her things, to the airport, and from there they went straight to the Mendocino cabin. He explained that his Cherokee was already there; he had paid one of the Nature Conservancy's student interns, who was always short of money, to drive it up for him. "I knew you'd want to come here," he explained, "and I didn't want us to have to take separate cars. I'll have to go back to the city Monday morning, but you'll want to stay on, I expect, since that was what you had planned before you went to be with Harry. Maybe I should have asked you. Your plans haven't changed, have they?"

"No. McClosky is what I want, what I need. I appreciate your thoughtfulness. I have a lot of writing to do, and now I'm two weeks behind where I thought I'd be."

Actually Branwen's plans *had* changed, but she couldn't tell Will that. Not yet. She had realized while she was still at Raven Hill that if Will knew that Orson's retreat was in the mountains above Mendocino, he would go charging in to rescue Miriam, and everything else be damned. They might get Miriam, but Branwen would lose her chance to learn more than she already knew about Orson, not to mention the Cognoscenti. Branwen had told Will almost nothing about the Cognoscenti, and he knew nothing of their connection with Orson.

She also had to consider her obligation to the television station. After so many months of research, during which she had done little else, she owed them a program on California psychics. She would write it, exactly as she would have done before she'd learned about Orson and the Cognoscenti from Harry. She would write the program, turn it over to her V.P., and he could assign someone else to produce it—because at the same time she intended to turn in her resignation. Branwen was going after Orson, and she had no idea how much Darkness that would bring her up against. She wanted no ties, no obligations, no deadlines. If everything went as she hoped it would, she would get her own program out of it, written and produced independently. If not . . . well, no one but herself would be the loser.

Branwen worked hard at the fastest pace of which she was capable. She turned in her program and her resignation just after the first of the year. She told Will she was tired and wanted to spend a quiet winter in Mendocino. She hated not telling him the whole truth, but she would rectify that as soon as she had located Orson's retreat, which she had heard called the Lodge.

Having cleared the way, Branwen felt a curious lethargy set in. She made excuses. The weather was daunting; the winter of 1984 was a harsh one. The wind blew in so hard and cold off the sea that she could not walk on the bluffs. And she *was* tired, she felt tired all the way into her soul. She wanted rest, not to be running around all over the county on some wild-goose chase in the cold. There would be snow in the mountains. In her cabin there were piles of books to read, books she had been waiting to get to when she had finished her project, and she wanted to read them. There was the new TV with VCR she'd bought for the cabin for Christmas, and a whole world of movies to be rented. There was McClosky, the cabin itself, like a comfortable old friend, warm and cozy with a driftwood fire burning in the fireplace while the wind howled outside and the sea rushed through the cliff tunnels wailing like a banshee. There was more time to cook than she'd had in years, time for gourmet meals to be prepared and frozen until Will was there to share them, time for frivolous, wonderful-smelling treats like fresh-baked chocolate chip cookies. On the weekend and sometimes during the week, Will would come and make love to her. Let someone else pursue Orson, she thought, let someone else struggle against the evil that most people preferred not to see, not to believe existed.

But then the dreams began, horrible dreams such as Branwen had not had in years. Dreams that belonged more to the Jason-times, and reminded her that though Jason was gone, the horrid things that had claimed him still roamed the world. When she woke from such dreams, she felt dirty, rotten, degraded; however, as the day wore on, she would forget the dreams. She lost herself in books, rented old movies, wished the bad things away.

Visions came. Branwen's Sight returned and was harder to fight than the dreams. At last a day came when she saw clearly a small, black, ugly Thing crouched in the corner of the cabin, her cabin, her beloved McClosky! This evil thing, she knew instantly, had been sapping her strength and her resolve.

"Go away!" Branwen cried. "Be gone, Dark Creature!" She summoned Light, blazing light; she filled her small house with blinding radiance and drove the Demon from her place. Then, exhausted, she sank down on her couch. She curled herself into a ball and thought of Harry and his silvery eyes, Harry who over a long period of time had done battle with a Demon far bigger than the little thing she had just chased away. No wonder that in his fight he had almost blinded himself. She felt chastened and knew she could delay no longer. The next morning Branwen set out in her Camry to look for Orson.

Every mile she drove she wanted to turn around and go back. She knew that Orson's Lodge could not be anywhere near the coast, where she knew her way around and the roads were reasonably good; if he'd been that close, she would have heard long since. She headed for the mountains.

The search for Orson was desperately hard work. Mendocino County was large and mostly undeveloped. Many of the mountain roads Branwen drove turned out to be not roads at all but abandoned logging trails that would lead her into deep woods and then simply stop, leaving her stranded. Without the four-wheel drive she would have been stuck dozens of times. Often she drove all day without seeing a living soul or any sign of civilization. She began to feel that Something was blocking her. She realized she would have felt much better if she'd had the sacred bluestones with her, but she did not.

In the sometimes scary solitude of her station wagon, Branwen Faraday gave up her methodical, rational, map-directed approach to finding Orson and relied on her intuition instead. It was a strange way to travel, as very often she had no idea where she was going and no idea how, at the end of the day, she found her way home again. But she always did, and she felt better. It might be self-delusion, but she didn't think so. She thought she was getting somewhere, getting close.

There was a truck stop about five miles east of 101 from Willets. At midday in early March, Branwen pulled in by the diner that had trucks out front, ignoring a better-looking restaurant across the road. She was wearing heavy corduroy slacks, a plaid flannel shirt with a turtleneck underneath, a sheepskin-lined leather jacket, and boots. Her hair was braided and her face bare of makeup. She didn't think she'd look or feel out of place. She went into the diner, sat down at the counter, ordered a hamburger and coffee, and started a conversation with the waitress. "I've been looking for a place that's supposed to be around here and I can't find it. Big house out in the woods on a lot of acres. Maybe has a clearing nearby where helicopters land. Do you know it?"

"Nah," the waitress said. "There's nothing like that around here. You came to the wrong spot, honey. You lookin' for work? We got an openin' for a waitress here nights, twelve to eight."

"I'm not looking for work," Branwen said. "I'm looking for a friend."

"Too bad." The waitress sighed. "I sure could use some more help in this place."

Branwen wasn't overly discouraged. When her hamburger came, she ate with enjoyment and lingered over a second cup of coffee. A big, burly man with the muscular arms and torso of a lumberjack climbed onto the stool next to her. "I heard what you said to the waitress. This friend of yours, what's she look like?"

Branwen's heartbeat accelerated. "She's small, blond, very pretty. Looks young for her age. Have you seen her?"

"Maybe." The man's eyes, under bushy eyebrows, scrutinized Branwen thoroughly but without insolence. "Why're you looking for her?"

"I think she may be in trouble."

"Okay, lady. I believe you. I seen a girl like that with a great big dark-haired fella wears a beard, taller'n me but maybe not as much muscle." He grinned and flexed his impressive biceps. Branwen obligingly grinned in return. He continued, "If she's in trouble, I'd bet it's him got her into it. He's one mean-looking s.o.b."

"*Where* did you see them?"

"Now listen, I didn't have no business there. I was just curious, you know? If you go there, you got to be real careful, like I was. They got guards would just as soon shoot you as take a leak, and they got the guns to do it with. It's a big place back up in the woods along the Eel River, about twenty miles from here. They call it the Lodge, no other name, just the Lodge. There's something fishy about that, you know. You'd think a place that big the fella that owns it would want to have his name on it. Somebody's Lodge. Makes me think somebody's trying to hide something. My brother-in-law drives a truck and delivers food up there once a week, that's how I know about it. Like you said, there's a helicopter landing place there, too, no more'n a little clearing in the woods. Strange-feelin' place, if you ask me. If'n I was you, I'd get my friend out of there."

"I intend to."

"You'll need some help. I'll help you, if'n you like." It was a sincere offer of help, by the serious expression on his blunt, pockmarked face. He seemed an honest man.

"No, thanks. I have some people who will help when the times comes. But first I have to find the place. Can you give me directions?"

"Yeah, sure, no problem. Here, I'll make you a map."

The Lodge was not difficult to locate once she had the directions. Off the state-maintained road you took a logging track marked by an unobtrusive wooden post. Four or five miles down the logging track a well-tended paved drive appeared. Branwen pulled the station wagon off the logging track into the trees, got out, and walked through the woods parallel to the paved drive. She was very careful, proceeding slowly, keeping watch for the guards with the guns, but she saw no one. She crept cautiously along through the trees on a carpet of evergreen needles that deadened sound. Finally she came in sight of the Lodge itself. It was large, long, and low, all one story though the main building had a peaked roof. An attractive building, in a rustic way—except that, oddly enough, the main building seemed to have no windows. A close inspection revealed that there were skylights in the peaked roof instead.

Where were the guards? Branwen wondered. If it were not for a thin wisp of smoke issuing from a chimney at one end of the peaked roof, she would have thought the Lodge deserted. She began to make a wide circle of the place and soon saw it had outbuildings—squat, squarish, windowless. They seemed to be storage sheds. One, bigger than the others, might be a kind of guest cottage—but it, too, had no windows, at least none that she could see. What was it, she wondered, that whoever had built this place had against windows?

Before Branwen had completed a quarter of her circle around the Lodge, an eerie feeling came over her like a warning. She called her Light, and the feeling faded, but one word appeared in her mind: late. Yes, it was getting late in the day. The cast of light through the high trees confirmed the dying afternoon. She could not do the thorough inspection she wanted and needed to do, not if she was to get back on a main road before darkness fell. Branwen did not like to drive the mountain roads at night; they were difficult enough in daylight.

So close to her goal, she was tempted to stay. She could sleep overnight at a motel in Willets. The warning came again, stronger this time. She wasn't sure, distracted as she was by staring at the Lodge, but Branwen thought she heard her old inner Voice say, *Go! Now!* Looking back over her shoulder almost wistfully, Branwen obeyed. She left.

Back at McClosky, Branwen made plans. The next day was Friday, and by seven P.M. Will would be there. She would leave early for the Lodge, do her scouting, figure out what if anything was going on in the place, and how she herself might gain admission. Or perhaps she could sneak in, hide herself, sneak back out again after a day of eavesdropping? She didn't know. She would just have to play it by ear . . . which made a day of observation all the more important. Will was going to want to be included somehow; she would tell him everything, and she would be sure to be back from the Lodge before he got to Mendocino Friday evening. Will wasn't going to like it, she was sure, when he found out that she had not only found the place, but scouted it without him. He'd like it even less if he knew what she was thinking: that the best way in the world to get what she needed for an exposé of Orson would be if she could go into the Lodge undercover, the way she had into the mental hospitals. How? Did they hire maids or cooks for the Lodge?

Branwen slept little as her chaotic thoughts kept her awake. No matter how she tried to keep it at bay, one idea kept returning: She could present herself to Orson the same way Harry had done, as a student seeking a teacher. It would be less dangerous if Will were on the outside, knowing where she was and able to come for her, to get her out at a prearranged time. Will wouldn't want her to do that. Maybe her day of observation would suggest something better; or maybe she would see something that would make further observation unnecessary. . . . Sleepy at last, Branwen dreamed that there were chittering, sightless Black Things locked in the sheds at the Lodge, things that preferred the Dark, which was why there were no windows.

She did not sleep long but she slept hard, and after some initial difficulty waking to the alarm, she felt both rested and charged with energy. Excited. She ate a big breakfast since she

doubted she would be in a position to have lunch; then she
dressed in dark clothes. Because she never wore black—black
being a color that to her represented Darkness—she chose navy:
navy corduroys, a navy sweatshirt with a hood, and a navy
down vest. Only her boots were brown. In the pockets of her
vest she stuffed necessary items, so that she wouldn't have to
take a purse. Her minicassette fit neatly into one vest pocket. Instead of braiding her hair, she pulled it back into a ponytail,
wrapped the ends around her head, and tucked it all under a
navy knit watch-cap. She hoped from a distance she might look
like a boy.

Just as the Camry began to climb foothills that would soon
turn to mountains, Branwen exclaimed aloud, "Oh, damn! I forgot the map!" In her mind's eye she could see a rough drawing
the man had made on the back of one of those paper placemats
that takes the place of a menu. The map was lying on the breakfast bar, where she'd been studying it just in case she lost it.
Well, she hoped she had studied hard enough because it was as
good as lost. She certainly wasn't going back for it now.

Even without the map Branwen found the Lodge again without difficulty. Will, however, did not find either Branwen or the
map when he got to McClosky at seven o'clock that evening. In
the gust of Mendocino's ever-blowing wind that preceded him
through the door, the map had fallen to the floor—menu side
up.

Will did not become truly alarmed until two hours later, past
the latest dinnertime he had ever known Branwen to plan. Feeling both foolish and desperate, he walked the streets of
Mendocino, looking for her car. When he still had not found it
an hour later, he went to the Mendocino police station. The policeman was a middle-aged, pleasant fellow, very polite as he
listened to Will's story of a missing "friend."

"You aren't taking me seriously," Will complained to the
smiling officer.

"In the first place," the officer said pleasantly, "nobody is
considered missing until they've been gone forty-eight hours,
so you've got a ways to go yet. In the second place, the lady
isn't even your wife. So she's not here when you come for the
weekend. She could have changed her plans. The way I see it,
she's a free agent, not a missing person."

The Highway Patrol at least gave Will the assurance that

there had been no accidents involving a Toyota Camry station wagon. Missing persons were not their thing. If the town police couldn't handle it, Will should call the Mendocino County Sheriff's Office. But not until tomorrow. You always had to wait at least forty-eight hours. And really, waiting three days was better. Most so-called missing persons came home of their own accord.

So Will went back to McClosky, frustrated, baffled, a little frightened, and a little humiliated that in the eyes of the law his relationship with Branwen was casual, since she was not legally his wife. He sat, staring blankly, drinking coffee at the breakfast bar through the night while the map, unheeded, lay under his feet on the cabin floor.

On another cabin floor lay Branwen, alone, in utter darkness. She was naked and unconscious, and her unconsciousness was a good thing—had she been alert, she would have recalled her dreams of horrors locked away in the Lodge's windowless cabins. The guards had felled her from behind with a stun gun as soon as she set foot on the Lodge's private property; then, per their routine instructions for dealing with intruders, they had administered a drug that would keep her out for twenty-four hours. Also per instructions, they had stripped her and taken all her clothes for Orson to examine. She was certainly the best-looking intruder they'd ever had, but that made no difference. Orson always wanted to question everyone to find out how they'd gotten there, but then the guards got them again for disposal. No one who chanced on the Lodge ever left alive. This one had been pressing her luck—they'd seen her yesterday and let her go because she was just a woman and so pretty. The bitch shouldn't have come back. Especially since they were all here today, for some sort of big deal meeting. The poor bitch would probably be questioned by the whole group.

6

No birds sang. No brightness broke through the gray, opaque sky. There was no wind to speak in the towering tops of the trees. Branwen stood in the unnatural silence and waited for the dark-timbered doors of the Lodge to open. Her bare feet were cold on the stone steps. They'd taken all her clothes and given her a long robe of some unbleached material to wear. She closed her eyes briefly and found in the center of herself the point of Light that was her only protection against the dangers on the other side of those dark double doors. One small, clear light against so much darkness.

The doors opened soundlessly. Branwen felt rather than heard the summons. She walked into the Greatroom, and the doors closed behind her, again without sound and without the aid of human hand. Step by step she advanced until she stood in the center of the floor, its polished boards slick and cool against the soles of her feet. In the center she stopped and folded her arms into the wide sleeves of her robe. In a protective reflex, her thick, dark eyelashes lowered to veil her eyes. Again Branwen waited, silent as the birds, still as the windless air outside. But inside herself, every sense was alert.

The room was large, rectangular, its walls the same dark wood as the doors. There were no windows; where windows might have been, the walls were fitted with iron sconces, each bearing a large clear glass bulb shaped like a flame. These were unlit. What little light there was fell through skylights in the crossbeamed ceiling high above. Twelve figures—it was impossible to tell if they were men or women—sat in high-backed, heavy, elaborately carved wooden chairs, arranged in a wide circle around the room's center like numerals on the face of a clock. They, too, wore robes; unlike Branwen's robe, theirs were hooded. The edges of their hoods extended two or three inches forward, so that it was impossible to see the features of a face within the hooded shadows. The fabric of their robes was dark gray with a metallic sheen that caught and reflected the thin, pale light from above. Not one of the twelve moved a muscle. All sat with arms on the arms of their chairs, hands concealed in flowing sleeves, feet invisible beneath the folds of their garments. The effect was eerie. Disturbing.

One spoke. "Who are you?"

She looked up, unsure which of the figures to address. "My name is Branwen," she said, her voice clear and bell-like in the strange assemblage.

Another said, "Your full name."

Her chin came up a notch. "Branwen is all the name I need here."

Silence. Branwen felt their disapproval of her withholding, felt their thoughts probing at her. She kindled the point of light in her center and brought it up into her head, to protect her mind. As she did this, the room seemed to grow darker. She could not take time to think what this might mean, for another voice spoke, and this one she recognized.

"Well, then, Branwen." It was Orson. "Why have you come here?"

She answered carefully. She must convince them to accept her into their group, yet she must speak only the truth. To lie to these people, even with the best of causes, would make her a deceiver like them. She said, "I believe you are people who have great power, together and separately. I want to learn from you."

A harsh, mirthless laugh came from one of the motionless figures. Branwen turned her head, seeking the laughter, but even as she turned, the sound rose and shattered on the rafters. It was disorienting, not knowing from which point on the circle each voice came. She was unable to identify even the smallest individual characteristic. Or the largest—Orson in any other setting was remarkable for his physical size, but here he was mysteriously indistinguishable from the rest.

Following on the shards of laughter came another voice,

cold, mocking. "We don't take in people off the street, you know. It's not that we have something you want—that goes without saying. *You* must have something *we* want."

Another took up the drill, and then another and another.

"Do you have money?"

"No," said Branwen.

"An influential position?"

"No."

"What, then, do you have that could possibly interest us?"

The timbre of Branwen's voice increased. "I have special abilities of a kind I'm sure do interest you."

"Name your abilities," Orson said.

"I have the Sight."

One, not Orson, asked, "Clairvoyance?"

"Yes," Branwen affirmed.

On the side of the circle behind her back, one muttered, "There's nothing very special about *that*."

Branwen turned. She was no longer disoriented. Their costumes and immobile postures seemed merely theatrical. She saw them now not only with her eyes, but with a surer, inner vision. She addressed the one who had made the disparaging remark. "I found you, didn't I? And your secret meeting place? I doubt many others have been able to do so."

A murmur of grudging acknowledgment moved around the circle. It was true. No petitioner had ever come before them uninvited, until this woman. No one had discovered this, their most private and remote place, until this Branwen.

A new voice, low and husky but unmistakably female, asked, "How did you get the Sight?"

"I was born with it."

The woman persisted. "Then why aren't you rich? Why haven't you used it to your advantage?"

Branwen hesitated. She was unprepared for the question. Her lack of concern for material wealth was so total that she had never even considered it. Haltingly she replied, "I lack practice in the use of my power. I've never had the support of a group such as yours. I've had no teacher, no Master." The words, though true, threw up dark shadows of temptations against the light that encircled her mind.

The energy that Branwen recognized as the physical expression of her Light pulsed a warning. These people were powerful. Right now they held their power in abeyance because of their curiosity. But if they were who she suspected them to be, they could seduce and corrupt. They could insinuate their self-ish, deceitful visions through the smallest crack in her spiritual facade. They could poison her soul. Conversely, if she held true to her purpose and they discovered that she wanted to join them only to learn their secrets in order to expose them, they would certainly kill her.

Orson moved. By the authority with which he raised his hand, and the fact that he was the first to break from the motion-less pose, Branwen felt sure that he was their leader. His tone was no longer neutral, but threatened and challenged. "Your clairvoyance is not sufficient for acceptance into this august group, even if you have managed to find your way among us. If you have any other claim to power, you must demonstrate. Not tell, but *show* us."

Suddenly Branwen understood that if she did not convince these people to accept her, they would kill her simply because she had penetrated their inner sanctum. One by one they moved, swayed, leaned forward in their thronelike seats. Eyes glinted avidly within their hoods.

"Show, show, show!" The word rippled around the circle and became a chant. "Show! Show! Show!"

Branwen closed her eyes. Visions of the thirty-eight years of her life reeled through her brain: times when she'd touched the energy that ran through earth and rock and all living things, times when an ancient knowledge of the power to use that energy had seemed present in her; she heard her old friend Harry's voice saying, as he had said more than twenty years ago, "The power to make and to change, to summon and to bind!" Her body rocked with the remembrance of the power.

"Show! Show! Show!"

Branwen raised her arms. She opened her eyes but no longer saw the Greatroom of Orson's Lodge. She saw only her own Light and felt its energy growing, coursing through her body. With the light came heat. The soles of her feet were hot, her pel-vic center burned, her arms and hands radiated, and her fore-head blazed. She hurled a silent plea into the universe with the force of a thunderbolt: *Help me!*"

The chanting stopped. The very air was charged. Something was happening here—without ritual, without symbols, without words. They could all feel it. Orson was contemptuous; two or three were afraid. Some, whose inner vision was more acute,

saw woven around the woman Branwen a fine glimmering
thread. Here, where only the Other had ever raised the wind, a
wind now swirled around Branwen. It whipped the folds of her
robe, streamed her long dark hair back from her glowing face.
From Branwen the wind flew like a gale into their circle, lifting
skirts, tearing off hoods, snatching away their breath.

Branwen felt the wind she had raised, and more. The vibrant
humming she knew of Old thrummed through her, body and
soul. She lifted her arms higher, closed her fingers into fists,
gathering the thrumming power into her hands.

"*Ortis an arach!*" she screamed out of ancient memory, and
flung her fingers wide.

The room crackled and flooded with light. Every filament in
every wall sconce glowed. Huge logs laid in the fireplace burst
into flame. Sparkling arcs of electricity danced among the
crossbeams and made dazzling reflections in the skylights.

In the center of this display, Branwen lowered her arms and
crossed them over her breasts, the palms of her hands at each
opposite shoulder. Her head drooped in exhaustion, and her hair
fell forward in a curtain around her face. As she prayed silent
words of thanks, the lights in the sconces went out, the arcing
sparks fell harmlessly to the floor, and the logs in the fireplace
sputtered and died.

"So!" Orson's voice tolled through the sudden stillness like a
deep bell.

Branwen lifted her head and with a little toss shook her hair
back over her shoulders. She looked at Orson. Like the others,
he had not bothered to replace his hood. Slowly she revolved,
gazing at faces. Ten men, two women. None much younger than
she, some considerably older; several well enough known that
they would have been recognized by at least half the country's
population.

Orson waited until she had completed the circle. When she
faced him again, he said, "You've proved that you do have
power. Of a particular kind. Now the question is, what are we
going to do with you?"

"Teach me more, make me your apprentice." Branwen tossed
her head again. She did it out of nervousness, unaware of the effect that unconsciously regal gesture had on others. Equally unaware of the effect she was having on Orson, who was
something of a connoisseur of women and who had grown tired
of his blond playmate, she fixed her blue-green eyes on him. "I

will do anything for you, Great Adept, if you will only teach me. Anything."

This woman's demonstration of remarkable untamed power had already excited Orson; power always excited him, and he had never before seen such power combined with physical beauty, which she certainly had. Now, with her promise that she would do anything for him to be her teacher, a hot spasm of lust seized him, beginning at his groin and heating his entire body. He would have her—this one would not be killed. But the others of the Cognoscenti must not know that his decision had already been made. He said, "We will consider making you our pupil. But first you must satisfy our need for secrecy. Did you come here alone?"

"Yes."

"Did anyone know where you were going?"

"No."

Satisfied, Orson addressed the circle. "She speaks the truth. We will consider her apprenticeship." He clapped his hands loudly, and two men in the uniform of security guards entered the room. "Take her to the guest house. Give her food and return her clothes, but lock her in." He looked at Branwen and made the total eye contact that so mesmerized his audiences. "I will come myself to tell you when we have made our decision. Do not be impatient. We have more important matters to discuss first, before we deal with anything so trivial as an apprenticeship. This much I can tell you now: You will be accepted or you will be killed. One or the other. No one, unless he is bound to us body and soul, may see our entire group assembled, and live."

Branwen raised her chin. She met his queer, colorless eyes with a gaze equally intense. "Of course," she said. She followed the guards from the Greatroom, walking with stately grace on bare feet and legs that felt like water.

"What do you think?" one guard asked the other after they had locked Branwen into the guest house.

"I think she must have been telling the truth when we let her out this morning and she insisted she'd come here to get Orson to take her on as his pupil. Otherwise he wouldn't be putting her in here. This is for the bigwigs, man."

"Yeah? Well, I'll tell you what *I* think. I think Orson knows a good thing when he sees it, and the only kind of teaching he's going to be doing with her is the kind that goes on in the sack, if you get my drift. And I think there's gonna be hell to pay when that Miriam finds out. Miriam's been acting real strange lately anyway. Did you notice? Maybe we ought to be keeping an eye on her."

"Naw. Miriam's just a kid, and she always acts strange. Nothing to worry about there. We'd better go get this new bitch some breakfast."

So, Branwen thought, *I have seen the Cognoscenti.* And she'd survived, at least so far. Now what?

The guest house was comfortable to the point of elegance, and it had windows—a blessed contrast to the dark place in which she had regained consciousness earlier. She'd been frightened then, not knowing where she was and unable to see so much as her hand in front of her face. But her captors seemed to know when she would wake up; they'd opened the door almost immediately. And in spite of the fact that the guards had stood there and watched her dress in the robe they gave her, they had not been unkind. She had told them immediately that she meant no harm, and seeing that she was caught anyway, had gone ahead with the half-formed plan of saying that she had come to the Lodge to gain acceptance as Orson's pupil. So far, so good.

Except that she had no idea how long she'd been at the Lodge, no idea how long she had been unconscious. She didn't even know how she had been so effectively rendered unconscious—she didn't feel drugged, and the only thing she remembered before waking up in the dark cabin was a sudden buzzing that produced a sharp pain, and she went out. Perhaps it hadn't been long; perhaps when Orson came to tell her she would be accepted as an apprentice she could persuade him to let her go home to get her clothes, and she would be there when Will came. Then everything could go on without a hitch. On the other hand, she could have lost a whole day, or days, and Will would be frantic. She wished they had returned her watch along with her clothes—but they hadn't, only the clothes. Not watch, or car keys, and certainly not the tape recorder.

Of course, there was the third possibility: They wouldn't accept her, and she would be killed. There was absolutely no point thinking about that.

She thought about it anyway—she couldn't help it—and as she did, she began to feel trapped for the first time. There had

been no opportunity to feel trapped before. She had either been
unconscious or mentally preparing herself for that incredible interview. Questioning, the guards had called it. Branwen felt she
had done well and knew she could not have done it if she had
not remembered lessons from two sources: Harry and Gracia.
Harry had said to use light against the Cognoscenti, and Gracia
had said to ask for help. She had asked, had gotten it, and was
very, very grateful. But what if that had not been enough? What
if the Cognoscenti still didn't accept her? Was there any way out
of here? Could she possibly escape?

Branwen went to the windows. She could see only trees, not
even a patch of sky. The windows faced the woods, but the
Lodge was in the opposite direction. If she could get out of
these windows, maybe no one would see her leave. . . . It did
not look promising. The windows were thick glass, and they
were sealed. She went into the bathroom—no window there.
There was a window in the bedroom, but it, too, was thick glass
and sealed. There was only the one door, a heavy slab of wood,
cross-timbered, like the door of the Lodge. It opened outward
on great metal hinges, and the guards had locked it from the outside. The guest house was like a little fortress, and she was
locked inside. Branwen didn't think she would ever get out until
someone let her out. Orson had said he would come but that it
would be a while. All she could do was wait. The thought that
the whole future of her life might depend on Orson made her almost physically ill.

I'll think of Will instead, she resolved, whereupon she began
to cry. She realized that she was exhausted, depleted by the light
show she had put on for the Cognoscenti, but that was no excuse
for getting hysterical. Crying would do no good—and yet she
could not seem to stop.

"No doubt the universe is unfolding as it should," Branwen
said aloud through gulping sobs. Again: "No doubt the universe
is unfolding as it should." An affirmation she had learned from
Will, who had learned it from his mother. Over and over she
said the words aloud until she stopped sobbing; then she continued to repeat them in her mind, over and over and over. She
sank down on the carpeted floor and folded her legs beneath
her. The affirmation had become a mantra; nothing else existed
for Branwen except those words. She sank deep, deep into meditation. She forgot where she was—she forgot who she was. She
was one with the universe, unfolding as it should.

Whap, whap, whap! Whap, whap, whap, whap, whap! The huge noise, only slightly muffled by the walls and roof around her, brought Branwen back into the room. *Whap, whap, whap*—a helicopter, of course. Her legs and feet had gone numb. They were all pins and needles as she tried to stand. She must have been meditating for quite some time. In the few moments before her legs would support her, Branwen heard other sounds: people yelling, a general commotion of running about, car doors slamming, tires squealing. One helicopter took off, its departure signaled by a change of pitch and speed in the sound of its rotors. Another one revved up. *Whap, whap, whap!* The Cognoscenti were leaving, and not in any planned, orderly fashion.

Branwen limped to the window, rubbing her legs. She would see only trees, of course, but still she had to look out—and she saw more than trees. Smoke! Thick, dense, black smoke in great rolling plumes poured past the guest house, mounting on the wind to the tops of the trees. Alarmed, Branwen turned. Sniffed. She couldn't smell the smoke—she could only see it through the windows. The Lodge must be on fire.

A second helicopter took off, leaving in its wake a devastating silence. Branwen's mind could not process all the bits and pieces of information at once. All she could think was: *Orson isn't coming. I'm trapped in here, and they've all gone off and left me!* Fear gripped her, and then panic. "I've got to get out of here!" she cried.

In a rush of adrenaline, Branwen picked up a heavy chair and hurled it at the window. The chair shattered; the window didn't even crack. She bent to seize another chair, but the adrenaline had been used up. Her back muscles spasmed, and Branwen cried out at the sudden, unexpected pain.

There was a furious pounding on her door, the sound of a voice muffled by the door's thickness. Branwen yelled a reply with all her might. "Here! Help!" She hurried to the door, oblivious to the pain in her back. She pounded on her side of the door. "I'm here, I'm here! Help me, please help me!"

The pounding on the other side stopped. "Branwen?"

Will's voice! Oh, God, Will's voice. "Will!" she called out. "I'm here, but the door is locked from the outside. Your side, Will." She heard him cough. The smoke, she thought. The fire must be terrible.

"Stand back," he called, and she did. Will flung himself at the door once, twice. "No good. Branwen, can you hear me?"

"Yes," she yelled, "just barely."

"I know where there's a gun. I'm going to have to shoot the lock off. There's no other way. This is the only door into that cottage."

"Okay. I know. Go ahead."

Minutes ticked by before Will returned. She heard him approach in spasms of coughing. "Get away from the door," he yelled.

Two shots blasted the lock to pieces, and Will kicked the door open. "No time for a reunion," he said, thrusting a wet washcloth at her face. "Breathe through that. Let's go. The roof of your cottage is on fire already. Run!"

It was like running through hell. The heat was unbelievable. The Lodge was a mass of flames, and most of the outbuildings had caught fire. Huge burning sparks were propelled by the updraft and touched the trees to flame. As Branwen ran after Will, she saw tree after tree ignite in a *whoosh!* from the top down, turning the trees to towering columns of fire.

They ran past the Jeep Cherokee. "Your car—" Branwen cried. Will pulled her on. "We're taking yours. I'll explain. Keep running. The fire is gaining on us."

Indeed it was. Tree after tree turned to fiery columns around them. Branwen's chest hurt, and her throat was raw—the washcloth didn't help. She threw it away. Then Will's jacket caught fire. Breaking stride, he flung Branwen ahead of him, then shrugged out of the jacket. Stumbling, coughing, he ran after her.

They reached Branwen's station wagon seconds ahead of the fire. The metal door handle was almost too hot to touch. Branwen snatched her hand away, remembering that she had locked the car doors. "They took my keys!" she wailed through the sound of crackling flames.

Not bothering to take time to speak, Will held up the extra set with one hand while he jerked the car door open with the other. Understanding, Branwen pulled open her door and scrambled in as Will started the motor. A tree right in front of them burst into flame. Will reversed, backed, turned. The Camry obeyed and carried them with blessed speed away from the raging fire. Both Branwen and Will coughed and coughed; tears streamed from their eyes. She turned on the air conditioner. "Good idea," said Will.

Only then did Branwen realize they were not alone in the car. She screamed but was so hoarse from smoke inhalation that she made only a croak.

"Is she still alive?" Will asked. "She was when I got her to the car. That's why I decided to use your wagon, so we could get her to the hospital."

"She?" Branwen had seen only a human shape on the back-seat in the rearview mirror, had been too terrified to tell who it was. She climbed on her knees, turned, and looked at Miriam who lay, propped in a half-sitting position, on the backseat. Her eyes were closed. She was wearing a blue dress, a sweet little dress with tiny tucks all over the bodice and a white collar trimmed in lace. She had the whitest skin Branwen had ever seen. And there was blood coming out of holes in her chest, running into all the tiny tucks in the bodice of the sweet blue dress, a maternity dress. . . . Miriam was pregnant, and to Branwen she looked very, very dead. But she wasn't. Even as Branwen looked, Miriam's eyelids fluttered. That was all, just fluttered. "She's alive," Branwen said, turning back around. Her stomach began to heave, and there was nothing she could do about it. "I think I'm going to be sick," she declared. Will made no comment when she vomited out of the car window.

"We've got to get her to a hospital and hope she lives to tell the authorities what happened. Otherwise I could be in a lot of trouble. I used the gun she shot herself and Orson with to shoot the lock off your door."

"She shot Orson?"

"Yep."

"Is he dead?"

"I thought so, but Miriam wasn't, so I brought her to the car. She didn't know who you were, much less where you were, and it took a hell of a long time to find you!"

"Did she start the fire, too, or is it just a forest fire?"

"*Just* a forest fire?" Will was very angry now that he had Branwen with him again, his emotions naturally volatile in the wake of crisis of terrible proportions. "There's no such thing as just a forest fire! But for your information, this is the wrong season for forest fires. Miriam set fire to the Lodge. I got there just as someone had discovered it, and with all those people running around, they didn't even notice me. I was looking for you, and I blundered in on a murder-suicide. Orson was already gone, and Miriam was babbling about burning down the Lodge and all the people in it. She'd shot herself once, and she did it again with me right there looking at her. God!" His voice rose, and he slapped the steering wheel with the palm of his hand. "What were you doing up there, Branwen? How could you do that to me? Why didn't you tell me? Are you crazy? Do you realize if I hadn't found that place mat on the floor, if the place mat hadn't had the name of the place on it, if I hadn't turned it over and seen the map, you could've, *we* could've—"

"Hush, Will, hush," she soothed. "Thank God you found me. Thank you for finding me. And take 101 South up here. I think there's a hospital in Ukiah."

Miriam died in the hospital. She regained consciousness long enough to say, "I killed Orson. He was a bad man. He would have been a bad father for the baby. All those people were bad, that's why I tried to burn them up. I'm not sorry."

The doctors tried to save the baby, but could not. It was a girl, and she died just after being delivered by cesarean of her deceased mother.

After being treated for smoke inhalation, Branwen and Will were released. There was still some tension between them. In the car on the way back to Mendocino, Will tried to explain his feelings. "Don't think I'm not so glad to have you back safe and sound that I could become a religious man over it. I prayed, Branwen. I didn't know what else to do, so I prayed. I think God helped me find that map—I'd been stepping on it all night without paying any attention. But at the same time I'm angry with you. I can't explain it, I just am."

Branwen decided that the best thing to do was to say nothing and to leave him alone. She was numb—that was her main reaction. Glad to be with Will, glad to be alive, but numb.

They sat together on the couch that night and watched the local news on television and were surprised to learn that the fire near the Eel River, *their* fire, had actually burned little of the forest. The Lodge and all its buildings had been completely destroyed. "You see," said Will with all the superiority of a professional environmentalist, "I told you it was the wrong time of year for forest fires. When the great heat generated by the wooden buildings was gone, the fire died. It's too damp to burn long."

"You could have fooled me," said Branwen, who would

never forget trees turning to columns of flame right before her eyes. She and Will were using the quartz heater that she usually kept in the bedroom because she had not been able to stand the thought of a fire in the fireplace.

The ice between them had been broken. Branwen said reluctantly, "I suppose you'd like to know what I was doing up there without telling you."

Will hugged her close to his side and kissed her temple. "You don't have to tell me. I can guess, now that I've calmed down enough to think straight. I don't know how, and it doesn't matter now, but you found Orson. You wanted a story and you were afraid I'd mess it up for you."

"Something like that—but I wasn't quite that hard on you. I was going to tell you, I was even going to ask you to help me, but first I was going to have one day—Friday—to do some scouting on my own. But I got caught. I was knocked out somehow. Will, I didn't even know what day it was until we got to the hospital. I would have told you, I really would!"

"Okay, I believe you, but please don't ever do anything like that again. No more investigative reporting unless I know what you're doing, where you're going. Not even the tiniest little bit, no scouting! Promise?"

"I promise."

"There's another thing you need to know," said Will, moving her out of his arms so that he could see her face. "When I tried to report you missing, the police wouldn't take me seriously because you aren't my wife. I don't ever again want to feel the way I felt when that policeman made it clear to me that I have no claim on you. There is nothing and no one in my life more important to me than you are. I do have a claim on you, I need you. Will you be my wife, Branwen, will you marry me?"

Joy broke over her face as she realized what he was saying, what he had asked. "Yes, oh, yes. I will be your wife, Will Tracy! I thought you'd never ask!"

EPILOGUE

Wales, Llanfaren on the Isle of Anglesey

"So, this is where it all started," Will said, his arm tight about his bride's waist. They were on a honeymoon delayed by three months. Wales in high summer was beautiful. They had survived breaking the news of their marriage to his father, and to her mother and father and brothers and sisters. She had shown him the old Abbey ruins. Now they were to see Llanfaren Castle, and then they could go home. To San Francisco, and to Mendocino. Will had bought a house in Mendocino, a small house but bigger than McClosky, as a wedding present for Branwen. California was home to him now, *their* home. But Branwen had a right to visit her roots. He tried not to be impatient although he longed to go back home. He tried to envision Branwen here, and how all this must have been for her when she was young.

"This is where I met Jason and Harry, right here." Branwen pointed to the long ramp that led up to the castle. "I was standing there, and they walked up. I first saw them when they were right about where you and I are now."

"I think I'd like to erase that memory and replace it with this one," said Will, kissing her.

Branwen looked up at Will and stroked his face. "I love you," she said. "I'm so glad we're married."

"Me, too. Now let's go see this pile of rocks!"

"You're so unromantic," Branwen kidded. It was not true at all, and they both knew it.

Llanfaren had not changed much in twenty years. Nor had its caretaker. John Kerr was still there. He greeted them at the door, looking only slightly older. Will paid, and Branwen waited, amused, to see if John would recognize her. He didn't, and suddenly Branwen realized why. She reached up, removed the clasp from her hair, and shook her head so that it fell over her shoulders and down her back. Of course the white streak was different, but that couldn't be helped.

"Hello, John," she said, and felt immediately as she always had, that she should have said Mr. Kerr.

"Bless my soul! It's Branwen!" He seized her hand, smiling. Age and years without being under Lucy's thumb had cured him of lechery. He turned immediately to Will. "And this must be your husband. Oh, how I hated to lose Branwen all those years ago."

"This is Will Tracy, my second husband. Will, this is John Kerr."

"Heh, heh." John laughed. "Well, I thought he looked different. You're still a lucky man, sir, and I'm glad to make your acquaintance."

Shaking the man's hand, Will said, "Thank you. I agree with you—I'm a lucky man to have Branwen for my wife. She's told me a lot about this place."

They walked into the Great Hall, which seemed cleaner, brighter. Branwen looked around, seeking the source of the subtle difference. Then she had it. "You have electricity, John. You finally got a generator. Lucy must be pleased."

"Er—uh, Lucy isn't here anymore, Branwen. I've been here alone for twenty years. Since shortly after you left, in fact."

"I'm sorry," said Branwen. Will moved slightly apart to give them a bit of privacy.

"No need to be sorry. It was the best thing that could have happened. I doubt you knew it, but Lucy wasn't entirely well. In her head. I mean, she was mentally unbalanced. She went totally 'round the bend that summer, and I didn't know what to do. I couldn't keep her here, so I took her home to her father. Wasn't long before he couldn't keep her either, so he put her in a nursing home. Very nice, private, he could afford it. I had some peace in my life, and she was well taken care of. Until her death a couple of years ago."

"I see. You do seem much more . . . content."

"That I am, that I am. And the generator is the apple of my eye. I expect you'd like to show your husband around yourself? We've opened a few new rooms, got some paintings and a rug in the Long Gallery, but otherwise it's still the same. Even the room where you stayed. I kept it as it was, no one has used it since."

Branwen found that rather touching, but she did not say so. She was still a little cautious with John, even after all these years. She asked, "Is it safe to go up on the wall-walk?"

"Oh, yes. That was a favorite place of yours, as I remember." John gestured to Will to include him. "You can go anywhere you like, as well as you know the place. I haven't been able to make many improvements, but at least I've kept it from falling apart. Oh, there's one exception. The cistern fell through in the Fifth Tower, about ten years ago. Don't go in there."

Branwen took Will's hand. "Let's start at the top and work down. I'll show you my favorite place. On a clear day you can see all the way to Ireland."

Llanfaren Village had a bed-and-breakfast now, and that was where Branwen and Will were staying the night. It was a house in the little row of houses all identical to the one Jason and Harry had rented for a summer. After a supper at the pub Will and Branwen walked up the street to their lodgings. But Branwen was restless. She needed to make her peace with Llanfaren, and to do that she needed to be alone. She told Will so, and he said he understood. She set out walking by herself.

The moon was full in the blue-black sky trailing wisps of high clouds. The tide was out. The beach, with little ripples of sand in the moonlight, shone like beaten silver. Out on its promontory, the Point Lynas light swept 'round, 'round. Branwen walked. She lifted her head and listened. The very silence was familiar. Familiar, too, the faint murmur of low tide in the cove. Farther around the beach, where it curled into a crescent against the cliff, the sea would heave itself hard against the cliff face below the ramparts of Llanfaren Castle—that sound, too, she knew though at the moment she did not hear it with her ears. She would not walk there tonight; that was not her goal.

Branwen turned inland. She felt a breeze on her face and heard it rustle in the grass. She walked up the rise, knowing the way by heart to the abbey ruins.

There stood the great open arch, and there the section of wall with its one high window. Under the arch stood a man: an old man wearing a long white robe belted in at the waist. He had flowing white hair and a flowing white beard, and he held a staff in one hand—a wizard's staff.

He must be an apparition, Branwen thought, but she was unafraid. She came closer. He looked very familiar. His eyes glinted silver in the moonlight.

"Harry," Branwen whispered, drawing near. "Harry Ravenscroft!"

"Yes, my dear, the very same." His lips curved a smile in a luminous face. "I told you that I would come home, and here I am. Here you are also. Shall we sit on these fallen stones and talk for a while, as we used to do?" He took her hand, and his was warm and firm, not the hand of an apparition. He seated her gallantly, and then himself next to her.

"The only thing I can think of to say," said Branwen, "is that you are amazing. What are you doing here?"

"Oh, I do a little of this and a little of that. I fly from place to place." He winked, a blink of silver. "I came here to Llanfaren because I wanted to see you. So you married young Will Tracy. I expect he makes you happy."

"Very."

"And Orson is dead, and little Miriam. Tell me, Branwen, do you ever worry that the Cognoscenti, who all except Orson escaped the fire, may wish you harm?"

"Yes." It was, in fact, Branwen's major unresolved problem and the only thing in her life that she did not share with Will. "I do worry about that."

"Then worry no more. One and all, they believe that you died in the fire. Keep your lovely face off of television and yourself out of the public eye, and you'll have no problem. You did well, Branwen. Orson was the strongest of the Cognoscenti, and their leader. Without him the others are not nearly so dangerous. They may even end up destroying each other."

"I did nothing. It was Miriam, poor mad Miriam, who killed Orson."

"Oh," he said and cocked his head to one side, "you have done more than you know. And when you write your book about Orson and Miriam and Melvin and Gracia, you must do it under a pseudonym. The book will do much good."

"How did you know I was thinking about writing a book about them? I haven't told *anyone*, not even Will!"

"I know everything." Harry winked again and stood up, holding his staff high. "But never fear, for after oh so many years, I have become a good wizard. As you see, observe the costume. White from head to foot!"

"Oh, Harry!" Branwen laughed.

"In my wisdom I perceive that unlike me you have not come home to stay."

Branwen said softly, feeling as she spoke all the restlessness in her heart resolve, "This is not my home anymore, Harry. My home is with Will, in a little house in Mendocino, California. It's not Wales, but it has cliffs and sea, and I think it's even more beautiful than Llanfaren. Best of all, it's where Mr. and Mrs. Will Tracy live. Mendocino is my new home."

"Alas for me. Then I shall not see you unless you come here again. My flying back and forth does not include flying across the sea—even I have not found a way to do that yet. But look, Branwen"—Harry gestured with his staff—"the bridegroom cometh!"

Branwen turned and saw Will coming through the grass. She jumped up and went to him. "Will, you'll never guess who's here—Harry Ravenscroft. I was just telling him about our house in Mendocino, our new home. . . ."

Will smiled down at Branwen, thrilled to his core by the sound of the word "home" on her lips. "Darling, I don't see anyone. You were sitting in this beautiful place all by yourself. Except for that impressive fellow up there." Will pointed, and Branwen's eyes followed his hand as his other arm went around her.

Perched on the peak of the ancient abbey arch was a large, white snowy owl. An owl with silver eyes.

"Perhaps I was dreaming," said Branwen, suddenly immensely happy. "Then again, perhaps I wasn't."

The owl hooted softly, blinked his silver eyes, spread his great feathered wings, and flew away.